Readers Love KIM FIELDING

Potential Energy
"This heartfelt sci-fi romance… will please fans of diverse space opera and queer romance alike."

—*Publishers Weekly*

Love Can't Conquer
"I thought this story was quite beautiful, even in it's dark moments."

—Just Love: Queer Romance Reviews

Love Is Heartless
"Full of tons of emotion, two memorable and extremely charismatic characters, and a story line that will pull you in right from the beginning, this book is a gem and truly not to be missed."

—Diverse Reader

Love Has No Direction
"This story is a great addition to this series. It keeps you invested in these flawed and beautiful men from the first page.."

—Paranormal Romance Guild

Blyd and Pearce
"I think I've forgotten how much I enjoy it when Kim Fielding decides to do fantasy stories. Which I really shouldn't, because all the ones I have read have turned out really well."

—Love Bytes Reviews

By KIM FIELDING

Alaska
Anyplace Else
Astounding!
Blyd and Pearce
The Border
Brute
Dear Ruth
Exit Through the Gift Shop
Get Lit
Grateful
A Great Miracle Happened There
Grown-up
Housekeeping
Motel. Pool.
Night Shift
Phoenix
Pilgrimage
Potential Energy
The Pillar
Rattlesnake
With Venona Keyes: Running Blind
Saint Martin's Day
Speechless
The Gig
The Taste of Desert Green
The Tin Box
Venetian Masks
Violet's Present

By KIM FIELDING (cont'd)

BONES
Good Bones
Buried Bones
Bone Dry
The Gig

DREAMSPUN BEYOND
Ante Up

DREAMSPUN DESIRES
A Full Plate
STARS FROM PERIL
The Spy's Love Song
Redesigning Landry Bishop
Drawing the Prince

LOVE CAN'T
Love Can't Conquer
Love Is Heartless
Love Has No Direction

Published by DSP Publications
ENNEK TRILOGY
Stasis
Flux
Equipoise

Published by DREAMSPINNER PRESS
www.dreamspinnerpress.com

THE TASTE OF DESERT GREEN

KIM FIELDING

Published by
DREAMSPINNER PRESS

5032 Capital Circle SW, Suite 2, PMB# 279, Tallahassee, FL 32305-7886 USA
www.dreamspinnerpress.com

This is a work of fiction. Names, characters, places, and incidents either are the product of author imagination or are used fictitiously, and any resemblance to actual persons, living or dead, business establishments, events, or locales is entirely coincidental.

The Taste of Desert Green
© 2022 Kim Fielding

Cover Art
© 2022 L.C. Chase
http://www.lcchase.com
Cover content is for illustrative purposes only and any person depicted on the cover is a model.

Trade Paperback ISBN: 978-1-64108-438-3
Digital ISBN: 978-1-64108-437-6
Published August 2022
v. 1.0

Printed in the United States of America
∞
This paper meets the requirements of
ANSI/NISO Z39.48-1992 (Permanence of Paper).

Author's Note

THIS BOOK percolated for several years, and I'd like to thank several people who helped me bring George and Zephyr's story to light.

A few years back, I was taking Amtrak from my house to Los Angeles, which requires a change from train to bus in Bakersfield. As the bus was rolling out of the station toward the highway, we passed several seedy-looking motels. And there, crossing the parking lot of one of them, was a person who'd stopped to adjust their stocking. I began to imagine who that person might be and what their story was… and Zephyr was born. I'm indebted to that person for giving me a tiny glimpse of themselves, which eventually evolved into a novel.

A smart author knows how much to appreciate an excellent editorial team, and I'm very grateful to mine. Special thanks to Karen Witzke, Brenda Chin, and Ginnifer Eastwick, all of whom were incredibly helpful as this book evolved.

Finally, while it may be unusual to acknowledge a geographic feature, I'd like to thank the Mojave Desert, which has proved paradoxically fruitful for my muse. Maybe that's because, like many of my characters, the desert's complexity and beauty isn't obvious until you take the time to look at it carefully.

PROLOGUE

Bakersfield, California
August 2019

ZEPHYR'S STOCKINGS had a run.

In the grand scale of things, maybe it wasn't such a big problem. And really, Bakersfield in late summer was too hot for nylon and lace anyway. But Zephyr's legs looked fucking good in them, long and lean and slick, and the damn things had cost twenty bucks.

Not that Zephyr had actually paid for them, but it was the principle.

So he twisted them a bit, aligning the run less visibly against his inner calf, and he adjusted his sunflower-yellow skirt to show exactly the right amount of bare skin beneath the hem. After checking his lipstick in the plastic hand mirror atop the dresser, he took a few deep breaths and stepped out into the parking lot.

The sun beat down on him immediately, its rays so bright that they drained everything of color, as if the world were nothing but a faded old photograph. The air smelled of tar and dust and diesel exhaust, and nearby, engines thrummed and tires rolled.

There was nothing natural about a place like this, but if Zephyr squinted just right, he could imagine hints of beauty in the faded signs of the nearby businesses. Alvarez Tires. Nieves Bail Bonds. Jorge's Tacos. PNG Equipment Rental. Despite being surrounded by a landscape of weathered plastic, peeling letters, and sagging vinyl and paper, Zephyr knew he looked good, ruined stockings notwithstanding.

He waved to Jasvir, who worked the late-afternoon shift at the Sleep-Tite Inn and who spent long hours staring over the check-in desk and out the front window, as if expecting someone to arrive at any moment and whisk him away. Unsmiling, Jasvir waved back.

Two blocks away from the Sleep-Tite, MaryLou's Café occupied a corner near the highway interchange. That location, plus a parking lot big enough for semis, made it a favorite spot for truckers who wanted strong coffee and cheap, greasy burgers. And *that* made it a favorite location for Zephyr too, at least on days like this when he owed the motel for another night, and when the barrier between what was and what loomed felt whisper-thin.

Zephyr slid into a booth, smoothing his skirt beneath his thighs, and tried not to shiver. The AC was cranked up so high that he almost expected to see his breath. He didn't bother looking at the cracked plastic menu. "Coke, please," he said to the waitress when she ambled over. "No ice."

The staff at MaryLou's tolerated him. Maybe they figured that he, like the oversized stretch of patched tarmac outside, was a lure to potential customers. Maybe they just didn't care as long as he paid his meager bill and didn't bother anyone. Which he never did.

Today he smiled at the waitress, a woman not much older than him but who looked washed out, as if the sun had beaten her too. He wondered what she went home to, footsore after a long shift. He wondered if she had dreamed of something better, back when she was a kid, and whether she'd resigned herself to settling permanently in this corner of purgatory.

"You want something to eat, honey?" she asked, a thread of kindness in her voice.

Zephyr, who hadn't eaten today, thought about the two crumpled dollar bills in his little heart-shaped purse and the handful of coins that jingled when he shook it. "No, thanks." The Coke would have to do. Refills were free.

She brought his drink right away, the plastic cup so full that he wondered how she'd carried it without spilling. She set it down, along with a paper-wrapped straw, and then remained standing by the table.

"Do you want me to pay now?"

"Nah." She tilted her head a little. "That's a real pretty blouse."

"Thanks." He liked it too. It was pale green with tiny yellow and red flowers, and it showed off his bare midriff and shoulders. The ruched fabric meant it fit well, despite his lack of cleavage.

She hesitated as if she wanted to say more but then gave him a tiny smile and walked away.

It was a slow afternoon at MaryLou's, and Zephyr was on his second refill before several men in a corner booth began giving him the eye. They wore old jeans and T-shirts, their heads topped with faded baseball caps advertising beer and sports teams. He couldn't hear what they were saying, but sometimes the ones facing away twisted around to look at him, and when they turned back to their companions, they all laughed.

He wanted to leave. But his stomach reminded him that sugar and caffeine weren't enough to keep him going. And if he returned to the Sleep-Tite without money for another night, Jasvir would frown at him and make Zephyr pack all his belongings into a couple of plastic trash bags, which Jasvir would lock in a closet behind his desk until Zephyr came back with twenty bucks or enough for another night's lodging. Storage fee, Jasvir called it. It felt more like ransom.

And dammit, Zephyr didn't want to try sleeping on a bench at the Amtrak or Greyhound station, all the while hoping that security wouldn't kick him out too quickly. He didn't want to wander the streets of Bakersfield through the hours of deep darkness, exhausted and hungry. Knowing he'd only end up at MaryLou's the next day anyway, but without even enough money for a Coke.

Ignoring the truckers in the corner, he slurped at his drink and was struck with an impulse to leave town. Temperatures would be cooler in the East Bay. Maybe he could find someone who'd let him crash on their couch for a little while. Or he could head up north. Portland? He hadn't been there in a long time.

A beefy man appeared, as if by magic, beside the table. Zephyr had noticed the guy sitting alone on the other side of the room, one paw holding a phone while the other shoved a burger and fries into his mouth. He was fortyish. Sweat stains darkened his gray T-shirt; pale brown hair hung listlessly down the nape of his neck. He stared hungrily at Zephyr.

"You look kinda lonely, missy."

Pasting on a coquettish smile, Zephyr twirled a tendril of his nearly waist-length dark hair around one finger. "Maybe."

"Want some company?"

There was a strange intensity in the man's watery blue eyes.

Zephyr looked down at the table. "What I really want is a ride out of this dump."

"'M heading to Phoenix."

Where it would be hot, maybe even hotter than here, but at least somewhere different. A place to make a fresh start, maybe.

"Pay for my Coke?" Zephyr asked.

The man laughed, dug out his wallet, and dropped a five onto the table. Then he hooked a thumb toward the door. "Ain't got all day."

The waitress didn't say anything, but she gave Zephyr a worried look as he followed the man across the scuffed linoleum.

The heat outside hit him like a blow, and the interior of the semi's cab wasn't any cooler. The seat was pretty comfortable, though, and the cab smelled of coffee and air freshener. Zephyr decided his possessions could stay with Jasvir for now. They weren't really worth dragging around.

He clicked his seat belt and watched through the side window as they merged onto the highway, heading east.

CHAPTER ONE

GEORGE

Conrad Junction, California
August 2019

GEORGE CHUCKLED quietly as he rearranged the display of plastic dinosaurs in his shop. They were cheap, the sort of thing a harried parent might buy to inexpensively placate a whining kid, and with their neon colors and skewed proportions, they bore little resemblance to real dinosaurs. What made him laugh, though, was that the triceratops's precise shade of hot pink tasted exactly like lima beans. If he'd been offered one of these toys when he was a boy, he would have flatly refused. He was aware that people with normal neural networks wouldn't taste hot pink—or any other colors, for that matter—but the phenomenon still entertained him. His own private joke.

Once the dinosaurs were neatly in order, George turned to look at Kayla, who was leaning against the checkout counter, staring at her phone. On the wall above her hung the museum logo: a dinosaur skeleton in the center of a celestial spiral, with *Wally Harlow's Fossil Galaxy* in neon-green lettering.

"Did you finish your trig homework?" he asked. He knew she dreaded math almost as much as he had when he was her age.

She rolled her eyes with an expression of amused fondness. "You're worse than my mother."

"You should listen to her. She wants what's best for you."

"I don't think trig is best for *anyone*. I think whoever invented it was just trying to torture people."

"Not true. You need math to get by in life."

She folded her arms. "Yeah? When's the last time *you* used trigonometry?"

They'd had this argument before, more than once, and he wasn't sure why he even bothered. Maybe because it helped pass the time.

He glanced at his watch and sighed. "Why don't you head home?"

"We don't close for another half hour."

He gestured at the gift shop, empty of customers. Nobody was browsing the exhibits, and the only cars in the parking lot were her old sedan and his even older van. "I think I can handle the crowds by myself. Don't worry—I'll pay you for the whole shift." One joy of being the sole owner was that he could make management-quality decisions like that.

"You sure?"

"Rock solid. You can go do your homework instead."

Kayla snorted and tucked her phone into her jeans pocket. After wiping down the glass counter with its display of semiprecious gems and small fossils for sale, she fetched her bag from the office, waved goodbye, and walked out the door, the bell jingling merrily as she went.

George spent a few minutes straightening postcards and T-shirts before taking up Kayla's post behind the counter. He was supposed to remove all of the money from the till and stash it in the little safe in his office, but there wasn't enough to bother. If someone was misguided enough to presume the shop was a good robbery target, they'd learn soon enough that they were better off exercising their criminal urges elsewhere. "They'd do much better at the gas station up at the intersection," George informed his companion—Tommy, the seven-foot-high T. rex statue in the corner.

Tommy had no comment.

George dutifully kept the door unlocked until the official six o'clock closing time, at which point he engaged the locks and alarm system and turned off the exterior lights and most of the interior ones. He smiled, thinking of the oversized burrito and the bottles of root beer waiting in his fridge. He'd relax tonight, maybe binge *The Good Place*. He was a whole season behind.

But years of habit kept him in their thrall. Instead of retreating through the door that led to his apartment, he swept the floor, did a quick inventory of paper bags, and then, groaning, sat down in the cramped office to work on the day's receipts.

This was the only kind of math he did regularly, proving Kayla right: no trig was involved. But the process was its own form of torture, with the totals seeming to shrink every day. And the bypass wasn't even finished yet. When that was complete, most traffic wouldn't bother to stop in Conrad Junction at all. And if people weren't stopped at the traffic light, they wouldn't notice his sign and drop in out of curiosity or a sense of childhood nostalgia. Oh, he'd probably still get *some* customers—people who'd avoided the bypass because they needed to get gas or use a bathroom or grab some food. Curiosity seekers who'd found him via his website or on an online guide to quirky roadside attractions of the Southwest.

But that wouldn't bring in enough to pay his few employees or cover the bills for utilities and insurance.

Well, no use worrying about that tonight. Not when a burrito waited.

The sun had set by the time he emerged from the office. The parking lot was dark, but bright lights from the adjacent Burger King provided some illumination. They bounced off the fast-food joint's blue roof, which tasted like spicy salami during the day but like watermelon at night, when the color was more subdued. That spot used to house the Orbit Restaurant, which had closed years earlier. Asteroid Burger's empty building still remained but, judging from its dilapidated state, not for much longer. Space themes had been a big deal in Conrad Junction's heyday, especially with Air Force base not too far away.

"At least we're still here," George informed Tommy.

Tommy grinned back.

George's last task for the night was hauling the trash out to the dumpster, located along one side of the parking lot. He could wait until morning, he supposed, but his dad and grandfather had always done that chore after the museum closed for the evening, and so George did too. It was nice to open up in the morning with a clean slate.

He gathered a few empty boxes, flattened them, and then grabbed the bag from the bin near the cash register. It was filled only with paper, so juggling everything took little effort.

The rear of his building faced the highway, a configuration that protected the parking lot from most of the road noise. When he stepped outside, he mostly heard crickets chirping. The temperature had begun to fall, although plenty of heat still wafted off the blacktop. The air smelled faintly of sage and Mormon tea plants, familiar scents that made him smile.

Something small scurried across the pavement. A rodent, perhaps, or a lizard on its way to shelter for the night. He couldn't see well enough to tell. Maybe instead of Netflix, he should drive out of town to Wayne Maas's place, away from the lights, and watch the stars wheel across the sky. He hadn't done that in a while. Or maybe he'd wait for the Perseids to reach their peak, two nights from now.

The dumpster sat a few feet away from a concrete wall, and sometimes paper and debris blew into the space between them. He was about to toss the trash bag into the dumpster when he heard a different noise, still furtive but louder, as if something had scuttled behind the bin to hide. Last year he'd discovered a stray cat hanging around, a skinny little thing that turned out to be very friendly once George set out food and water for it. He'd captured the creature and taken it to the vet in Boron, where the cat had been pronounced healthy aside from fleas, worms, and lack of food. A couple of hundred bucks later, the cat—which he'd named Orbit after his former neighbor—had gone home with Kayla. She said Orbit slept on her pillow every night.

Maybe this time he'd keep the cat for himself.

George set the cardboard down and threw the bag into the dumpster. As he began to sidle around to the back of the bin, there was another scrabbling sound, this one louder. Maybe not a cat, then, but rather something that had wandered in from the open desert. Might be a jackrabbit, which could make a lot of noise if it was rustling around in discarded paper. Or a coyote, although it would be odd for one to hide like this. Now, as he peeked around the corner, he saw nothing but darkness.

"Hello?" George took a hesitant step forward. "Um, if you're carnivorous, you'll have better luck with the garbage next door." He wondered for a moment whether there was any nutrition left in fossilized bones. Not that there were any right here.

The whatever-it-was made another rustling sound, followed by a soft groan—one that sounded decidedly human.

Shit.

George pulled his phone from his pocket and, after a bit of fumbling, turned on the flashlight and aimed it into the gap.

Someone was huddled on the ground.

Definitely a person, not a cat or coyote. Although their face was hidden, he saw bright yellow shorts and a bare back covered in red welts and scratches.

George's heart was trying to gallop out of his chest, and his hand shook so much that the light wavered. The rest of him was frozen, though, including his brain. When he tried to speak, only a squeak came out. The temperature seemed to have dropped thirty degrees.

Then the person shifted again, just a little, and a few of George's brain cells managed to fire. "I'll call 911." He hoped the San Bernardino sheriff had a patrol nearby. The nearest station was in Barstow, half an hour away. The city of Boron was much closer, but that was in Kern County, so there was no help there. He swallowed. "First responders will be here soon." Not really a lie—just an optimistic half-truth.

"No cops." The voice was tiny and ragged, but at least it meant the person was conscious and lucid.

"I think you're hurt. They'll—"

"Please."

God, what was he supposed to do? George took a few steadying breaths. "C-can you walk? We can go inside. It's better than staying here."

The person moaned but didn't answer.

"Please?" George said. "I can't just leave you here." What would he do if they refused or remained silent? But after a few seconds, the person began to slowly unwind, reaching up to both the concrete wall and the dumpster for support. George decided they likely needed assistance more than light, so he shoved the phone back into his pocket and reached into the darkness. "Let me help."

They moved slowly, leaning almost all their weight on George and whimpering with every footstep. Long hair cast their face into shadow. They were a few inches shorter than George—maybe five foot six—and very slender. To distract himself from the smell of blood and sweat, George concentrated on the yellow shorts. Or maybe it was a skirt. In either case, the color was bright and cheerful, like lemons on a tree, and it tasted like birthday cake.

Halfway to the building, George realized that the person's skin was unnaturally hot, but the light wasn't good enough for him to tell whether it was fever or sunburn. Not that he could do anything about either in the middle of the parking lot. One step at a time. Literally.

He pushed the door open, making the bell jingle, and immediately had to decide on their next destination. The gift shop didn't offer any place to sit, other than the floor, and the two chairs in the tiny office wouldn't be comfortable.

There was only one good alternative. "This way." He steered them slowly over to, and then through, the unobtrusive wooden door near the cash register.

His grandfather had built this place, and this part of the building had originally housed a little restaurant that served coffee, burgers, and homemade pies. It hadn't been much—just a grill, a display case, and a dozen booths—but neither the Orbit nor Asteroid Burger had been built yet, so there weren't many local dining options.

The café had remained until George was eight or nine, at which point his dad had shut it down and used the space to store a small collection of antique cars, hoping to one day restore them and put them on display. That had never happened, though. The cars had been sold by the time George graduated high school, and the area had remained empty and sad until Dad died and George took over. He'd called in some favors and taken out new loans to build a little apartment here.

After crossing the threshold, George hesitated and then sighed, turning toward the bedroom. "Better than the couch," he mumbled, mostly to himself. Closer to the bathroom too.

The person collapsed onto George's bedspread with a drawn-out sigh, and only then did George step away to turn on the light.

What he saw made him gasp. The person's eyes were so swollen that it must have been hard for them to see, and smears of dried blood marked cheeks and chin. Bruises mottled the skin, deep purple clashing with sun-scorched red. The bottoms of their bare feet were filthy and ravaged, embedded with pebbles and bits of desert plants.

Just looking at the devastation made George feel light-headed. But fainting certainly wouldn't help; if he bashed his head on the tile floor, then where would they be?

"I have no clue how to help you," he admitted. "I think I should call—"

"Water."

Of course. If this person had spent a chunk of time out in the desert, which appeared likely, they'd be terribly dehydrated. George ran to the sink. The cup was plastic and, like most of his drinkware, adorned with dinosaur images and the Fossil Galaxy logo. He always had to close his eyes when he used these cups, because the many colors clashed with one another and affected the taste of whatever he was drinking. Of course, his visitor wouldn't have that problem. And due to the facial swelling, they probably couldn't see well anyway.

He propped the person into a seated position with pillows and held the cup for them. "Just a few sips at first," he warned. One benefit of growing up in the Mojave Desert was knowing how to deal with dehydration.

While the person drank, George tried to devise a plan. He had a pretty well-equipped first aid kit in the office and a few others tucked into cabinets in various rooms of the museum. He might also have an ice pack in his freezer, and he definitely owned some tweezers that could help remove debris from those feet. Beyond that? Not a clue.

"Are you Wally?"

George blinked. "What?"

"Wally Harlow?" They pointed at the wording on the cup: *Wally Harlow's Fossil Galaxy.*

"That was my grandpa. I'm George. After Georges Cuvier, the founding father of paleontology, who—" He stopped with a snort. "Who's absolutely irrelevant to you."

"Zephyr."

"What?"

"My name. Zephyr. After the west wind." That may have been an attempt at a smile on their face, but it was hard to tell.

"Oh. Okay. And, uh, what pronouns do you use?"

Even with the swelling, Zephyr looked surprised. "Seriously?"

"Yes. I mean, I don't want to be rude, but… but I'm not sure." Zephyr wore a skirt, not shorts, and George saw what might have been the vestiges of smeared eye makeup. But the chest was completely flat. Not that any of that was definitive, which was why he had asked. "Sorry if I'm being offensive."

Zephyr shook their head. "You're not. I'm male."

"He/him?"

"Yeah."

Relieved, George nodded. "Me too."

This time Zephyr laughed a bit. "I figured."

"Look, I guess you don't want the cops involved, which… okay, fine. But let me drive you to a hospital. There's one in Mojave and one in Barstow, both about the same distance away, so you can take your pick."

"No insurance. No money." Zephyr tried to move and winced. "Can I just stay until morning? Then I'll get out of your hair, I promise." He suddenly looked so thoroughly drained that George almost expected him to crumble to dust, like the undead in *Buffy*.

George tried to look reassuring. "Of course. Do you want me to try to patch you up a little? No guarantees, but it might help."

Zephyr seemed to be trying to peer at him. "You'd do that?"

"If I can."

Several minutes later, as he dabbed carefully at Zephyr's face with a damp washcloth and antiseptic wipes, George at least had the consolation of not fainting at the sight of blood. Okay, yeah, it did make him slightly queasy, but he soldiered through. "Your lip is split," he said, frowning. "It might need stitches."

Zephyr peeled one eyelid open a crack. "Are *you* going to sew it up?"

"No!"

"Then it'll be fine." He closed his eye again. A scab had formed on the lip, so maybe he was right. After a bit of worrying, George decided to let it be and hope for the best.

He tackled Zephyr's feet next. It was sad to see his damaged soles in contrast to the delicate petal-pink toenail polish. That particular shade tasted of candied ginger, a flavor he very much enjoyed. But cactus spines had worked their way deep into the skin, and getting them out was an exercise in patience. At least Zephyr managed to keep still during the process; George doubted he would have managed as well.

"Did you walk barefoot through the desert?"

Zephyr sighed. "My heel broke. I liked those shoes. It's hard to find cute sandals in my size. I ruined my stockings too, and my blouse—" He turned his head to the side. There was nothing for Zephyr to see but a wall painted very light blue, a shade that George tasted as Nilla Wafers. It had taken him some time to find a color that was restful to all of his twisty senses.

George eased out a particularly nasty-looking spike and dropped it into the plastic cup he'd been using to collect the debris. He wasn't sure what to say, but remaining silent while sitting on a bed with someone— and touching his feet—felt awkward, so he cleared his throat twice. "Do you want something to eat?"

"God, yes."

Hunger was a good sign, George assumed. He rarely felt hungry himself since his weird neurology meant that he experienced a flood of flavors all the time, so he often had to remind himself to eat. He enjoyed the food once it was in front of him, although sometimes he had to eat with his eyes closed so the food's taste didn't clash with the taste of its colors.

Moving carefully so as not to jostle Zephyr too much, George got up and padded into the kitchen. A burrito waited in the fridge, one of the ridiculously big ones made by Arturo's Restaurant. Twice a month George drove to Barstow for groceries and other supplies, and once a month he went to Mojave, where he bought four burritos from Arturo's, one to have each week. They were his bit of self-indulgence and one of the few splurges he allowed himself.

While the burrito heated, George poured a glass of orange juice. He'd squeezed it himself from the fruit grown on trees his grandfather had planted in the Ancient Gardens exhibit. George had been forced to close that exhibit to the public several years ago, when it became clear he could no longer afford the upkeep. But the citrus trees still produced well in the courtyard garden, among the overgrown palms, scraggly Joshua trees, and decaying plaster dinosaurs.

George almost expected to find his bed empty when he returned to the bedroom, the entire episode some weird dream he'd had after falling asleep at his desk. But no, Zephyr was still there, his bruised chest and yellow skirt vivid against the white bedding.

George set the glass on the nightstand next to the water cup and handed Zephyr the plate. "These burritos have been my favorites since I was a kid. I've heard there's a Mexican place in Boron with decent stuff, and that's closer, but I've never tried them. Why mess with success, right? Um, you should probably eat slowly." He added that last part because Zephyr had crammed a huge bite into his mouth and was chewing greedily.

"Want me to save you some?"

"No, it's all for you." Tonight, after he was through playing doctor, George would have a sandwich and some canned corn instead.

He resumed working on Zephyr's injuries. He had to hand it to the guy; he was tough. Getting his feet tended to must have hurt like hell, but all he did was hiss now and then while steadily—but now more slowly—devouring his meal. He drank all the juice and then fell back against the pillow, wearing an unexpectedly satisfied expression, considering his condition.

George fetched him an ice pack to hold against his face, then peered closely at Zephyr's torso. The worst damage seemed to be the bruises. The scratches, while likely painful, just needed some cleaning up. The sunburn would need soothing as well.

Zephyr must have concluded the same thing, because he said, "Do you think I could take a bath?"

"I don't have one. Just a shower."

"Damn," Zephyr sighed.

"I could get you a container of warm water and some soap. A sponge bath, right?"

"That sounds…. Ugh. Sorry. Would it freak you out if I asked you to spot me in the shower? I think I can manage on my own, but in case I can't…."

"But your feet."

Zephyr gave a small shrug. "It'll be worth it to get clean. I need to scrub."

And that was how, against his better judgment, George ended up sitting on the closed toilet, ready to leap up the moment his naked guest showed signs of collapsing. Zephyr seemed to be doing all right, however, having lowered the water temperature to avoid further trauma to his skin. He didn't appear at all self-conscious. George, on the other hand, wasn't sure how to keep an eye out for signs of imminent danger without also seeming to ogle.

Zephyr glanced at him and laughed. "It's okay. I figure I owe you at least a little show. Not that I'm looking my best right now."

"You don't— I'm not—" George felt his face flush as red as Zephyr's sunburn. Redder, maybe, because while Zephyr's skin was somewhat olive-toned, George, as a strawberry blond, had the traditional corresponding milky complexion. When he blushed, his cheeks practically glowed. "You don't owe me anything," he managed to say.

With a skeptical expression, Zephyr rinsed away the last of the soap suds and turned off the water. He accepted a towel from George but used it only on his long hair, allowing the water on the rest of his body to drip onto the tile floor. Then, with a groan of relief, he took George's vacated spot on the toilet seat while George carefully smoothed aloe gel over his back and shoulders.

When was the last time George had experienced so much physical contact with another person? He couldn't remember.

"I can wash your clothing," he offered as he rinsed his hands. "And loan you some of mine. They're not, uh…."

"No skirts and panties in your dresser?" Zephyr chuckled. "It's fine. I can be butch too. But if you don't mind, I'd rather sleep au naturel."

"Sure. Probably better with your, um…."

"Fucked-up condition? Yeah."

George helped him back to the bed, but Zephyr didn't go to sleep right away. Instead, he asked to borrow a comb, and he sat on the edge of the mattress untangling his mahogany hair—a color that tasted tangy, like grapefruit.

"Zephyr? Were you in an accident?"

That produced a snort. "Nope."

"Then someone did this to you?"

Zephyr didn't even bother to answer, so George tried another tactic. "Why didn't you want me to call 911?"

"Because I didn't need all that, did I? Just a little patching up and some rest, and I'll be fine."

"But someone hurt you. The police—"

"Can mind their own fucking business." Zephyr set the comb on the nightstand and looked at him through puffy eyes. "I have found that members of the law enforcement community are not especially sympathetic to my problems. 'Fucking asked for it' was the immortal phrase, I believe. And I don't need them either. We're not talking about this anymore."

Moving gingerly, Zephyr managed to get between the sheets. George spread a warm blanket over him and then stood near the doorway, hovering uncertainly.

Zephyr picked up the plastic cup, took a sip of water, and squinted at the lettering. "Wally Harlow's Fossil Galaxy," he read. "What is this place?"

"Conrad Junction's most famous tourist attraction." Also its *only* tourist attraction, but George didn't mention that.

"What do you attract tourists with?"

Not much, nowadays. "We have exhibits on fossils, meteors, minerals, and dinosaurs." They weren't fancy interactive exhibits like you'd find in modern museums, just rocks and models set out for display, with signs explaining the nature and significance of each piece. "We have one of the largest meteorite fragments on the West Coast and a really nice collection of tektites. We also have a bear-dog footprint and a fossilized bison skull, both found right here in the Mojave. Those are the stars, but we have a bunch of other stuff too."

He realized that none of this sounded impressive. But he was proud of it all, including the anatomically inaccurate dinosaur models—with geographically inaccurate legends—that his grandfather had built. And even the hokey and ridiculous diorama of extraterrestrials emerging from a flying saucer, seemingly at high risk of wandering into a clump of jumping cholla, was something he loved. That one had been his father's masterpiece.

Zephyr didn't scoff, at least. In fact, he grinned as well as his battered face allowed. "Cool. And you live here too?"

"Makes for an easy commute."

"How come you...?" Zephyr paused for a jaw-cracking yawn. "Sorry. I'm kinda wiped."

"You've had a rough day. Get some sleep." George flipped the light switch.

"Hey, George? Thank you."

Smiling, George stepped out, shut the door, and went to make himself a sandwich.

Chapter Two

GEORGE SLEPT on the couch, which was reasonably comfortable. He kept waking up with the urge to check on Zephyr, but he resisted. He'd always been an early riser, but the next morning, he awoke even earlier than usual, when the sun was just beginning to brighten the sky through the window over the kitchen sink. The delicate colors tasted like meringue and cinnamon, which would have served as breakfast if he hadn't reminded himself that he needed actual food with real calories and nutrition.

"What if I could eat the sky?" he mused quietly to himself as he slipped into the gift shop. He always kept a dim light on in the office, and now he used that to poke around on the shop's shelves and racks, gathering a few things. "I'd save a lot on groceries, but would my bites make holes?" He imagined himself nibbling away until nothing remained overhead except a dark, star-studded space that didn't taste like anything.

When he was little, he used to let his mind wander in ridiculous ways like that. Flights of fancy that took him far from the desert—hell, sometimes far from Earth. Eventually, after repeated reminders from his father, he'd realized that he always needed to land again, and where he'd end up was back in Conrad Junction. So why bother wasting time on these imaginary voyages? Today he blamed his lack of sleep and the disruption to his routine.

He returned to the apartment to find the door to the bedroom still closed. At least his guest was getting a good rest. While a double batch of coffee brewed in the machine on the kitchen counter, George contemplated breakfast. Real food, not the tastes from his neurological anomaly. It was getting near the end of the two weeks and his supplies were running low, but he set some eggs to boil, poured OJ, and slid bread into the toaster, ready to go.

Just as he'd decided to wake Zephyr up, the bedroom door opened and Zephyr appeared with a towel wrapped around his waist. He was still walking gingerly and the bruises were more obvious, but the swelling on his face had subsided and none of his other wounds looked worse than they had the night before. His hair hung long and dark and straight, over his shoulders and down his back like an elegant cape. He was smiling.

"I smell coffee."

"How do you take it?"

"Lots of milk and sugar."

George waved him to the kitchen table and poured two mugs. It felt odd to have someone so frankly watching him as he assembled the coffee additions, activated the toaster, and set butter and jam and cutlery on the table. He wasn't used to having that kind of attention.

Zephyr didn't speak again until George was sitting across from him, peeling an egg. "You're a minimalist with your décor. I wouldn't have expected that from a man who owns a tourist attraction. I'd have guessed you'd have collections."

"I do. They're on display." George gestured in the direction of the exhibit rooms beyond the gift shop. He wasn't in the mood to explain that his minimalism was due to being born with oddly wired senses, making him taste colors that most people could only see. He didn't mind being different in that way—in fact, he tended to enjoy the gustatory enhancements—but he did have to make some accommodations to keep things from becoming too confusing and complicated. Thus, the pale blue walls of his bedroom and the unadorned white of the rest of the apartment. His floors were sealed concrete, and he'd painted all the wooden parts of his furniture an identical shade of dark gray. The 1980s pastel upholstery of the couch and armchair added the only real variety, and fortunately, those colors were bland and inoffensive.

Although Zephyr was progressing enthusiastically through his breakfast, his attention stayed on George. "Were you one of those kids who was obsessed with dinosaurs? The ones who can rattle off all the species before they can spell their own names?"

George knew those kids. Sometimes they dragged their parents into Fossil Galaxy. The kids would loudly criticize the inaccuracy of the models, but they usually enjoyed the real specimens, and they almost always posed for a photo with Tommy the T. rex.

"Not really," he answered. "I knew stuff about dinos, but it wasn't a huge thing for me."

"Then why run a place like this?"

"Family business."

For some reason, that made Zephyr laugh. He had a light voice, somewhat high-pitched for a man, but his laughter was deeper and fuller. The rest of him was complicated too: thin eyebrows and full lips; a strong forehead and delicate pointed chin; hazel eyes that shifted color depending on the angle of the light. Like his limbs, his fingers were long and slender, the ragged nails still showing flecks of pink polish.

George realized he was staring, but although he blushed, he didn't look away. Mainly because Zephyr had been staring back.

"You're not freaked out by a boy who wears a skirt and lacy panties?"

"I'm freaked out by finding someone who looks half-dead hiding behind my dumpster. What he's wearing isn't relevant."

"You asked me for my pronouns."

"I didn't want to presume. You were obviously dealing with enough problems already, without getting misgendered."

Zephyr quirked his lips. "Not what I'd expect around here."

"Just because I grew up in the desert doesn't mean I'm a troglodyte. Most of my neighbors aren't either."

In fact, a lot of the people who lived in the area were eccentric. Living relatively isolated, and in a challenging climate, didn't suit ordinary types. And because people around here tended to have their own quirks, they also accepted other people's. As Lyle Cohen—who created and sold yard sculptures made from recycled car parts—liked to say, "If I wanted boring, I would have stayed in Cleveland."

"Well, it's a nice surprise," Zephyr said. "And you slept on the couch. You're a gentleman, aren't you?"

George shook his head, stood, and started gathering dishes. "I have to get to work soon."

"Of course. I promised to get out of your hair early."

"You can stick around if you want. I only meant—"

"Nah. I gotta go."

George doubted that, but it wasn't any of his business. "I washed your clothes, but I think you might need...."

"I can go shopping."

"Not here you can't. The gas station mini-mart might have a hat or something, but that about exhausts your options." He didn't add the obvious: Zephyr was flat broke. No wallet, no nothing. "I found a few things in my gift shop that might work for you, though."

He fetched the pile he'd left on the couch and watched as Zephyr looked through the items. A T-shirt, hoodie, and baseball cap, all with the Fossil Galaxy logo. "Not very fashionable, I'm afraid."

Zephyr stroked the soft fabric of the hoodie. "You know I can't pay for any of this, right?"

"I should pay you. You'll be giving me free advertising wherever you go."

"I'll tell everyone that their life is not complete until they visit you. But I'm not sure about my skirt…."

"I have a pair of sweatpants I could give you. Boring and black, but—"

"I'd love that. Thanks."

George went to get them, and by the time he returned, Zephyr had dropped the towel and put on his panties and the new T-shirt. He took the sweats with a grin and pulled them on. After he tightened the drawstring, they fit well enough. This outfit was considerably more pedestrian than the one in which George had found him, yet Zephyr still didn't look ordinary. George doubted he'd *ever* look boring, no matter how run-of-the-mill his attire.

"I don't think my shoes will fit you," George said. "But maybe these will work?" He handed Zephyr a pair of slipper socks with non-slip tread. They were blue with neon green dinosaurs woven in.

Zephyr laughed and put them on. "Better than bare feet. Thanks."

"Do you have a way to get home? Someone you can call to pick you up, or—"

"I'll be fine."

George shifted uneasily. He didn't even know where home was for this man. Or if the person who'd hurt him might be waiting for him there. "Are you sure?"

"I'm a big boy. I can take care of myself. But if you could spot me a little cash, that would help a lot."

George ended up giving him most of the previous day's receipts, which wasn't much. He'd have to skimp on groceries this week, but he could handle packaged ramen for a while.

Zephyr tucked the bills into his hoodie pocket without counting them. He and George stood for a moment at the apartment's exterior door, leading to the parking lot.

"A gentleman," Zephyr said, repeating his earlier claim. "You guys are rarer than anything in that collection of yours. Thank you for your kindness."

"Be careful."

"You too." Zephyr gave George's cheek a quick stroke with his thumb, turned, and walked outside.

George waited until he'd disappeared around the corner, heading toward the intersection with the gas stations. He closed the door and locked it. Then he went to shower and get ready to open the shop.

CHAPTER THREE

Conrad Junction
January 2020

"SIXTEEN MILLION years ago, this region was a savannah instead of a desert, and it was teeming with mammals. Saber-toothed cats, camels, mastodons, and lots more. The fossil beds that were created during that time are so rich that they named an entire geological stage after this area. Barstovian, after Barstow."

The middle-aged tourist in the red baseball cap—which tasted like boiled cabbage—scrunched up his face. "*Cats.* I bet they weren't a match for a T. rex."

George was saved from responding when the guy's adolescent daughter sighed with exasperation. "Dad. Dinosaurs died out, like, millions of years before the mammals this dude's talking about. And when the dinos ruled, California was mostly under water."

Although George wanted to give her a high five, he had to be satisfied with a grin. It was unwise to antagonize a paying customer. The girl's mother had refused to enter the exhibits at all; she took a few steps into the gift shop, muttered something about everything being tacky, and announced she'd wait in the car.

The kid, though, was having a ball. She'd taken time to inspect every artifact and read every sign, ignoring how her father sulked along like a bored toddler. She asked questions too, even though George had the feeling she knew almost as much as he did. She was the one who'd insisted her parents avoid the bypass just so they could stop at Fossil Galaxy, which she'd read about somewhere online. And she didn't seem disappointed in the very old-fashioned and low-tech displays. She simply wanted to admire them.

Now the father crossed his arms. "Why was California under water?"

"Because sea levels were higher," she answered. "The climate was warmer. Then we had an ice age and the oceans receded."

"See? I told you that global warming shit is a hoax."

She shot George a long-suffering look. Poor kid. It must be hard growing up with a parent who was so resistant to facts. George's own father had been almost religious about the importance of science, even though his formal education had ended at high school. He used to drive George and his siblings to the public library and instruct them to check out nonfiction books on subjects like astronomy, chemistry, and yes, paleontology. Then he'd insist that they take turns presenting book reports to the family over dinner. George might have preferred to haunt the fiction section instead, but at least his dad didn't deny the truth.

The girl continued her tour of the displays, and George enjoyed chatting with her as she progressed. But the place wasn't that big, and soon enough, she and her father were back in the gift shop. She used her own money to buy a nice ammonite fossil; George threw in a little book about the Barstow Fossil Beds for free. It had been written by a professor—long since retired and possibly no longer alive—who used to serve as his grandfather's technical advisor.

"Thanks!" The girl beamed at George before following her disgruntled father into the parking lot.

"That's how you go broke," Judith Frank said as she wiped down the glass on the cooler where George kept bottled water and soft drinks for sale.

"I'm already broke."

"Broke-r, then."

"Lost cause. Anyway, I made that girl happy. Maybe she'll grow up to be a paleontologist despite her parents."

Judith's face expressed deep skepticism; she made that face a lot. She continued cleaning the surface of the cooler.

There were no other visitors in the building, and George could have found a task to keep him busy. There was always that pile of bills sitting in his office, waiting for his latest juggling act. Or he could do more online research about banks. If he could concoct a credible enough tale about how a little modernization would make him a roaring success, he might land a small-business loan. Or he could dig out some tools and tackle one or more of the never-ending repair jobs around here. He wasn't the world's greatest handyman, but out of necessity, he'd learned to do a fair range of work.

But none of those tasks appealed. George was in a weird mood, feeling numb and detached, as if someone had Novocained his soul.

"Judith, do you mind holding down the fort while I do some work in the gardens?"

"I think I can handle the hordes."

He was grateful to have her around—skepticism, sarcasm, and all. He'd been forced to lay off Kayla and his other two paid employees at the end of the previous year. Telling them had been incredibly hard, even though they'd all seen it coming. In fact, they'd ended up comforting him as he cried over it.

"I'm graduating soon anyway," Kayla had reminded him. "And hopefully I'll be headed to UCLA."

"But you're trying to stash away tuition money."

She'd shrugged. "Burger King's hiring."

He planned on running Fossil Galaxy solo, but Judith, a former middle-school teacher, was bored and a little lonely and had volunteered to work for free. "It's community service, really. Helping to keep this old place alive a little longer. I used to come here when I was a girl, and Conrad Junction wouldn't be the same without it."

So yeah, George could live with her slightly sour attitude.

He grabbed his old leather jacket from the hook inside the office and headed out a side door that led to what had once been labeled as the Ancient Gardens. It was actually a courtyard surrounded on three sides by the wings of the building and on the fourth by a tall wooden fence. When the café had been in operation, diners could sit at a window and look into a space as lush and green as the desert climate allowed.

The courtyard had been largely his mother's domain, although George's grandfather's citrus trees were there too, lush all year round, the flowers perfuming the air in early spring. She'd planted flowering sages, sculptural cactuses and yuccas, and anything else she could coax into flourishing. Bright bougainvillea had climbed over the fence, clumps of ornamental grass waved in the slightest breeze, and yarrows bloomed above their lacy leaves. Pathways had wound among the plants, with benches offering a place to sit and contemplate the insects and birds, as well as the dino statues peering out from among the flora. His mother had grown up on an almond ranch near Bakersfield, and sometimes she seemed to miss that life. The gardens were her way of reclaiming a bit of it.

When George was a boy, he'd sometimes escape to the gardens and sit on a bench, drinking in the colors as if he were gobbling down a feast. At least until his father noticed he was shirking his duties, and sent a sibling out to drag him back to work or his studies.

Visitors had never seemed to appreciate the gardens as much as George did, although they appeared to like the courtyard view while they ate. Eventually his dad had declared the water bills too high. Most of the gardens had been left to wither, and many of the statues were relocated elsewhere on the property. The benches and some of the cactuses and other native plants remained, and George had always kept the orange trees watered and otherwise maintained.

Now he went into the courtyard, walked to the bench nearest the trees, and sat down. He ignored the cold concrete under his ass and looked up at the glossy leaves and vibrant fruit. Oddly, the color orange tasted exactly like the fruit. The yellow of the lemons was the same shade—and same birthday-cake flavor—as the skirt Zephyr had left behind. George couldn't bring himself to get rid of it, so now it sat, neatly folded, atop his coffee table. As if Zephyr might walk through the door any moment and want it back.

George had given Zephyr a lot of thought over the past few months. Maybe because that was more pleasant than dwelling on his dire financial situation. Fossil Galaxy had been on a long, slow slide for… hell, for decades. But now with the bypass open, nobody stopped in Conrad Junction unless they needed to. They might fill up their gas tanks, grab a burger and fries, or use a bathroom, but then they were back on the highway, in a hurry to get to their destinations, wherever those might be. Almost nobody *intended* to visit Fossil Galaxy, and that long, slow slide had become a freefall.

I'm sorry, Dad.

George might have been able to prevent this if he'd acted earlier. He shouldn't have kept his head stuck in the fifties, as if he were channeling his grandfather, but should have instead explored modern ways to draw visitors in. Interactive exhibits. A 4-D movie experience, perhaps. Creative dining. Social media. What if he'd found a way to interest Instagram influencers? Maybe dino selfies would have become the latest trend.

If his dad were still alive, he would have thought of something. He always had ideas. And yeah, sure, they didn't all pan out, but at least he tried them. He worked hard and innovated as best he could.

George, in contrast, had stagnated. And soon, Fossil Galaxy would be as extinct as all of the creatures in his collection.

"Oh, stop," he growled. "Self-pity won't help." Besides, his butt was freezing.

Without glancing around at the ruins of the gardens, he made a pouch with the front of his T-shirt, plucked as many oranges as he could carry, and headed back inside. He might be bankrupt soon, but at least he wouldn't get scurvy.

Judith had given up on cleaning things that didn't need it and had the *New York Times* spread out on top of the glass case of the checkout counter. "I managed to keep up with the hordes," she said without looking up.

"Thanks. Want some oranges?"

"Nah, I have too many of my own. You know what you should do with that courtyard?"

"What?" he asked warily.

"Grow weed. You'd need some irrigation, but your mom amended the soil years ago, and I bet it's still not bad. And the courtyard is secure."

George wasn't sure whether she was serious. "I'm not going to grow marijuana."

"You sound like an old prude. It's natural, honey. Way better than any of that crap doctors are pushing, making the pharmacy CEOs rich. Weed's even legal nowadays. I think you need a license, that's all."

He walked to the office and put the fruit into a plastic bucket he kept for that very purpose. In addition to the Fossil Galaxy logo, the bucket was adorned with images of flying saucers hovering over a prehistoric swamp. He joined Judith behind the counter. "I'm not a prude. I don't care whether people enjoy some ganja. I just don't want to grow it."

She huffed. "Suit yourself." Then she settled her bifocals more comfortably on her nose. "Have you heard about that virus in China? They've quarantined an entire city."

"No, tell me about it." Better to hear about problems thousands of miles away than to worry about the ones right here at home.

CHAPTER FOUR

KAYLA PLOPPED a plastic grocery bag onto the sales counter. "Here."

"What's that?" The scent provided a clue.

"Tamales. My gran decided I didn't get enough practice making them at Christmastime, so she gave me more lessons. 'Someday I won't be here to make them for you, mija.'" Kayla did a credible impression of her grandmother, who'd been friends with George's mother. "And you know how it is with tamales: if you're gonna do them, you're gonna do a lot. These are for you."

George's stomach grumbled in appreciation. He'd given up on going to Arturo's; the extra gas and restaurant costs were no longer in his budget. He'd been getting by on whatever was cheap at the grocery store, relying on his quirky senses to keep him satisfied. The tamales would be a treat.

"Thank you. And thank your gran too. It was nice of you both to think of me."

"I have ulterior motives. I'm applying for a scholarship—it's a really good one, George. It'll pay most of my housing costs at UCLA. And I need letters of recommendation. I asked a couple teachers, but I was hoping you'd write one too. 'Cause you could talk about how wonderful I am outside the classroom." She flashed a wide grin.

"I'd love to." George's heart felt big and warm. He'd never written a letter like that, and he was proud that Kayla considered him important enough to ask. It meant he could play a tiny part in helping her succeed, even if he couldn't employ her any longer.

"Cool! Thanks. I'll text you the link so you can do the online thingie."

"I'll get right on it."

She nodded and looked around. "So… how are things?"

He tried not to wince. "Hanging in there." At the moment, a couple in their seventies was wandering through the exhibits. Maybe they wouldn't be disappointed in his low-tech offerings, but they also wouldn't likely be interested in buying T-shirts. Nowadays, his gift shop receipts were the only thing preventing him from a complete crash and burn. This couple was only the third set of visitors today, and he'd be closing in less than two hours.

"The bypass has made us a ghost town." She gnawed on a fingernail. "Um, I hear there's a company making offers to buy up property."

Scowling, George grabbed the bag of tamales, stomped to the office, and shoved the bag into the little fridge. By the time he returned to Kayla, he'd managed to control his temper enough for him to speak without growling—too much. "Vultures," he said.

Her eyebrows raised expectantly.

"They don't care about Conrad Junction, or its history, or any of the people living here. They just want to swoop in and take advantage of people during hard times."

"What do they want to do with the property?"

"Solar farms. Don't get me wrong—I'm all in favor of renewable energy. Hell, if I could afford it, I'd put panels on my roof myself. But do they have to be *here*? This is a community, not just a sunny spot in the desert. Why can't they—?" He stopped, chagrined. "Sorry. Didn't mean to rant."

"Did they make you an offer?"

He nodded. It had been ridiculously low, but even if had been much higher, he would have refused. The buyer would destroy the building—George's home as well as his livelihood. His grandfather's trees would be uprooted and his mother's garden trashed. Nothing would remain of his family legacy except for an empty lot covered in reflective panels.

No, his ship might be sinking, but George was determined to go down with it, rather than hand it over to privateers.

"George? What are you gonna do?" Kayla's voice was soft, her expression compassionate and far more mature than her years.

"I don't know. A collector from Denver emailed me last month. He said he'd pay top dollar for my bison skull. Maybe I'll consider that." Selling off his collection piece by piece wasn't a great option, but he was running out of alternatives. That skull could keep his doors open for a couple more months. By then, maybe he'd have thought of something else.

And that reminded him. "Hey, Kayla, want to give me some advice? You're young and hip."

She laughed. "I'm not hip."

"Well, you're better attuned than I am to the kids today."

"What are you, George? Eighty?"

It was the second time this month he'd been accused of sounding old, but he waved it away. Heck, every time he sat down to stare at Fossil Galaxy's accounts, he probably aged another year. He might have had only thirty trips around the sun, but it felt as if it had been one hundred.

"What would it take to make this place Instagrammable?"

Kayla blinked. "What?"

"You know what I'm talking about. Obviously we don't have a great view and I can't offer flashy luxury. But if there was something that looked amazing in selfies, people would tag us, right? And then other people would make a point of exiting the highway and paying us a visit. If we got big enough, maybe we could even lure people from LA or the Bay Area."

She pursed her lips and tapped her fingernails on the counter. "What kind of something?"

"Dunno. Maybe something with Tommy. He's kitschy and big. Or I could do something with the gardens, like adding exotic flora. Maybe stick a couple of café tables out there and serve fancy coffee drinks." He was stabbing blindly here, but maybe he'd inspire Kayla to come up with something.

She didn't look inspired. In fact, instead of thoughtful, she simply looked sad. "I don't think anyone's going to drive a hundred and twenty miles to take a photo with Tommy. Or to have coffee with pretty flowers, especially when it's, like, a hundred and ten degrees out."

George sighed.

Probably taking pity on him, Kayla tried a smile. "But I'll tell you what. I'll do some research, okay? Maybe I'll figure something out."

"Will you help me go viral?" he asked with a wan smile.

"Sure. Next thing you know, you'll have a million followers."

"Thanks, Kayla. And thanks for the tamales. Send me that recommendation-letter link, okay?"

She texted it only minutes later, probably while sitting in her car. He planned to write the letter immediately, but just then, the older couple finished touring the exhibits. They browsed the gift shop for a bit, and George even held out hope they'd choose a souvenir coffee mug or tea towel. But in the end, they just picked up two bottles of water from the cooler—George had priced them barely above cost—and regaled him with an incredibly long story about their teenage grandson who used to love dinosaurs but was now only interested in video games and girls.

"Well, you know how boys are," said the woman, who wore a Fresno State sweatshirt, the blue tasting like vinegar. "I bet you went through a girl-crazy stage too."

Instead of correcting her, he rang up the bottles of water, gave them their change, and encouraged them to tell their friends about Wally Harlow's Fossil Galaxy. He even offered them a free postcard, but they declined. "Nobody sends snail mail anymore," the woman said, seeming incredulous.

George was glad to see them go, even if it meant he was again without customers.

Maybe he should close early. After writing Kayla's letter, he could sit down with a tamale and notepad and really brainstorm social media ideas. Then he might get cozy with a tall glass of orange juice and some TV. He'd canceled all his paid streaming services, but he still had internet—which he needed for the business—and he could surely find something on YouTube.

Or maybe he'd email that collector in Denver.

He decided to keep the shop open and was two pages into Kayla's letter, going on at great length about her maturity, responsibility, and capacity for leadership, when a beautiful woman stepped into the building. No—George corrected himself almost at once: a beautiful *man*.

"Zephyr!"

Smiling broadly, Zephyr hurried over. "You remember me."

"You kind of made an impression."

"You don't find guys in skirts behind your dumpster every day?"

"Hardly ever." George's heart was beating rapidly, which was stupid. He took a deep breath and tried very hard to seem relaxed.

"Well, I'm glad you recognize me. I look a little better today."

"You look great," George said with complete honesty.

Zephyr smiled even wider and took a couple of steps back, apparently to better show off his ensemble. Like a model on a runway, he did a slow spin. He wore a skintight jumpsuit in neon orange, with mesh panels scattered on his legs and torso. His knee-high boots were a shiny black with platform heels. His white shaggy faux-fur coat hung nearly to his ankles and reminded George of a Hostess coconut snack. Zephyr's hair, thick and shiny, flowed far down his back, and when he moved his hands, several rings flashed.

George had never seen anyone so exotic. Quite likely no one in Conrad Junction had ever seen anyone so exotic.

"Suits you better than my sweatpants," he said.

"Maybe, but I was sure grateful for them at the time. That's why I'm here, in fact." Zephyr moved close to the counter again and leaned toward George. He smelled of a very masculine wood-and-spice cologne, but his outfit tasted ethereally light: marshmallow cotton candy, perhaps.

"You're here to tell me you appreciate my sweatpants?" Oh God, George was flirting, wasn't he? Or trying to. He was terrible at it.

"To appreciate *you*." Zephyr's expression turned serious. "I don't think you necessarily saved my life that night, but you sure made my situation less… dire. And you were kind and compassionate. Thank you."

"I… uh… I'm sure anyone in my position would've done the same."

Zephyr shook his head slowly. "No. They wouldn't. But you did. And without a hint of judginess." He shook himself slightly and his grin returned, although it now seemed more superficial. "And everything turned out fine, as you can see. I have a boyfriend now. He's loaded and generous. I don't have to— Well, I'm not hiding behind garbage bins anymore."

A small, irrational blade of jealousy pricked George's soul, but it was only bad enough to sting. After all, he and Zephyr weren't anything to each other. George had been a safe port in a storm and that was all.

But there was something else bothering him, a cold unease at the edge of his mind. He didn't understand it. Zephyr looked better fed than he'd been during his last appearance and in considerably better physical shape. His outfit was probably expensive, and those glittering jewels on his fingers looked real. Yet there was something brittle about him, a thin bright shell hiding a vulnerable softness.

Or maybe jealousy was clouding George's perception.

Realizing he'd been silent too long, George nodded. "I'm really happy to hear that."

"And I came to repay you." Zephyr reached into his coat pocket, pulled out a stack of money, and set it on the counter. George couldn't tell how much it was, but the topmost bill was a fifty.

"No need."

"There is a need. Look, George. I can tell you're not rolling in dough. But you gave me enough cash to get somewhere safe, not to mention a fabulous selection of attire from the Fossil Galaxy collection. You gave me your food and your fresh-squeezed OJ and even your bed. You gave me a… a sanctuary, where I could catch my breath and get a good night's sleep." Zephyr let out a long breath. "And don't give me any of that pay-it-forward crap. Life isn't a Starbucks drive-through. You helped *me*, not some hypothetical future person in need." He pushed the money a few inches closer to George.

Refusing might have been the more gallant approach, but George couldn't do it. His creditors were circling overhead and his cupboards were bare. Besides, Zephyr's jaw was firmly set, and it occurred to George that this might be a matter of pride, of Zephyr showing that he was more than a victim.

"Thank you," George said, and Zephyr visibly relaxed. "But this looks like way too much."

"It's not."

A couple hundred bucks could mean several more days on life support for the family business.

"Thanks," George repeated. "How about if I show you around? You're at least entitled to the grand deluxe guided tour."

Something flickered across Zephyr's face, too fast for George to decipher, before a plastic smile immediately replaced it. "I'd love to, but I can't stay."

"But you drove all the way here from…."

"LA. I'm on my way to Vegas, actually, but I made a little detour."

"We could grab something quick to eat, at least. I have tamales."

The smile turned warmer and more genuine, but Zephyr's eyes remained sad. "I can't. I'm running late already, and Brandon doesn't like it when I—" He looked away for a moment and then back. "I gotta go."

Anything more would be begging, and that was just pathetic. So George had to settle for a shoddy substitute. "Maybe you'll stop by when you have more time." Assuming, of course, he wasn't replaced by then with an array of solar panels.

"Sure. That'd be nice."

Zephyr walked quickly to the door, but when he reached it, he twisted around to look at George. "If things were different, I'd really want to get to know you better. It's not every day I meet a hero."

Before George could respond, Zephyr was gone.

The little pile of money turned out to be two thousand dollars—far, far more than the value of anything George had given him. And it was enough to keep the vultures away for at least a month.

George sat down in his office and cried.

CHAPTER FIVE

April 2020

"IT COULD be worse," George confided to Tommy the T. rex.

It was true. Due to the new plague, lots of people were confined to tiny apartments right now. But George had the entire square footage of Fossil Galaxy to roam, not to mention the private outdoor space afforded by the garden. And thanks to the business supplies he'd bought in bulk, he was in no danger of running out of toilet paper anytime soon.

But Fossil Galaxy was shuttered, along with all the other nonessential businesses, so the slow trickle of ticket purchases and gift shop receipts had dried up completely. Zephyr's money was dwindling, and it turned out that George wasn't eligible for unemployment benefits—he'd checked. He was perilously close to losing not just the business but his home. "Everything," he told Tommy sadly.

Even that collector in Denver wasn't interested now; apparently, he was worried about a shaky economy if the lockdown continued and had curbed all investments for the time being.

"But at least I won't starve." The previous day, George's friend Santiago had stopped by with an SUV full of grocery staples, and he'd insisted on leaving a large portion of them with George.

"You can't say no, man," Santiago had said as they stood six feet apart in the parking lot, masks on. "I drove to the Costco in Lancaster 'cause trying to get stuff in the Junction sucks right now. And you know how it is when you go to Costco—you gotta buy everything in bulk. You're doing me a favor by taking some of it off my hands."

George knew that was a polite fiction, but he'd pretended to believe it. So now his fridge and cupboards were full, at least.

Things could be worse.

This morning he'd called Carlsbad to see how things were going with his oldest brother. James was hanging in there, but he and his wife were attempting to work from home while also guiding their three grade-schoolers through Zoom lessons. He sounded frazzled and exhausted, and the background din had made George wince. So yeah, James had a job and income, but was potentially at risk of losing his patience, his marriage, and his sanity.

Poor Kayla was supposed to be enjoying all the fun activities of her senior year in high school, but instead of prom and the senior trip, she was stuck at home. Judith couldn't visit her grandkids in Chicago. Arturo's was closed, maybe for good. Takeout wasn't profitable enough for them, and they had no space for outdoor seating. George's friend Seth—a nurse in Riverside—was working incredibly long hours and staying in a hotel to avoid exposing his family to the new virus. George's neighbor Lyle Cohen had gotten sick, and although he was still experiencing extreme fatigue and other symptoms, at least he hadn't ended up in the ICU.

Things could be far worse.

"And yet things could be a whole lot better," George admitted to Tommy. And suddenly the weight of all his struggles felt so overwhelming and never-ending that he collapsed onto his ass on the gift shop floor. He sobbed so hard that his throat and chest hurt and he was blinded by tears. It was not cathartic. When he finally tapered off into whimpers and sniffles, he didn't feel any better.

But he stood, gave Tommy a friendly pat, and headed to his apartment.

WHAT HE needed, George decided the next day, was a project. He knew from his internet browsing that a lot of people were starting to bake, but he wasn't interested in that. He wasn't a great cook. Sometimes his synesthesia interfered in unexpected ways, so that whatever he made tasted weird both when he looked at it and when he didn't. He certainly didn't have the funds for home remodeling or renovating his exhibits or enrolling in online classes.

"I could start a new workout routine," he mused aloud over breakfast. He'd always envied people who carried some muscle on their frames, and maybe he could find a way to jury-rig some exercise equipment from stuff he had sitting around. Powerlifting meteorites, maybe?

Fine, but that would occupy only a small portion of each day. Besides, he preferred a project that wasn't so focused on himself. He'd had enough of his own company already and yearned for something more external.

He'd already been doing a lot of reading, thankful that he could access eBooks via the San Bernardino County Library. Mostly he read things related to his business, because although he didn't have a college degree, his dad had always advised him to pick up relevant knowledge via self-directed study. Sometimes George relaxed with fiction, but he often felt a bit guilty that—and he heard his dad's voice here—he wasn't using his time more wisely. He liked historical novels best but also strayed into science fiction and fantasy now and then. For him, the strange thing about reading stories was that there was no visual input aside from the printed page, so he didn't experience the flavors of everything as he did in real life. That made the imaginary people and places feel a little flat.

Reading didn't feel like a true project, however, and especially with fiction, he felt restless if he did it too long.

In search of inspiration, he poked around the cavernous workshop and storage area behind the exhibit space. This was where his grandfather and father had housed their workbenches, where bits and pieces of things ended up when broken or replaced, where infrequent new additions to the collections waited to be placed on view. Everything was dusty and cobwebby, with some items nibbled on by mice. He didn't have a clue what a lot of the things were.

"Maybe I'll stumble upon a cache of diamonds that Dad forgot to mention. Then I can pay all the bills."

He didn't find any diamonds, although he did uncover some interesting fossils, which he set aside to add to the exhibits. There were also several handwritten descriptions of items drafted by his grandfather and set in frames. Grandpa had tended more toward the sensational than the factually accurate, but they were fun to read. A case in point: *Vast herds of Oreodons once roamed North America, striking fear in other animals with their terrifying fangs. Some scientists suggest they look like a cross between a giant boar and Dracula.*

A battered old suitcase contained several old watches, a few pieces of jewelry, a typewriter, and six carefully wrapped figurines of old-fashioned ladies in fancy dresses. He'd have to research it all, but maybe some of that stuff would be worth money. Although the idea was comforting, it was also distressing. He strongly suspected the items in the suitcase had belonged to his grandmother, who'd died when his father was still a boy. It felt like betrayal to consider hawking her belongings. But they'd been sitting here for decades, and George was desperate.

Okay, dealing with his grandmother's things counted as a project. George hoisted the suitcase and was heading toward the exit when his gaze fell on something else: his mom's gardening tools. A shelf of flowerpots, trowels, and clippers, with a hoe and rake and other implements leaning alongside.

He could restore the Ancient Gardens. Not to his mom's level, since he lacked both the know-how and the cash to buy plants and supplies. But he could certainly clean everything up and run some drip irrigation to a small area. If he was lucky, he'd find enough desert-plant survivors in the courtyard to set up some nice xeriscaping. He could fix up some of the dinosaur statues while he was at it.

Waste of time, said a nasty voice in his head. *Nobody's ever going to see it.*

"*I'll* see it," he responded out loud.

He left the suitcase in the office before heading to his apartment, where he changed into grubby clothing and slathered on sunscreen. He might be a third-generation resident of the Mojave, but his pale complexion wasn't well adapted for the desert. He even grabbed a dorky souvenir pith helmet from the gift shop. Sure, he'd look dumb, but nobody was going to see him, and it would help protect him from the sun.

It wasn't until he was in the courtyard, spade and clippers in hand, that he realized the enormity of the project. Yes, most of his mother's plants had died from lack of water long ago, but some tangles remained near the citrus trees. The rest of the courtyard housed creosote bushes, burro bushes, yucca, and an assortment of other native species, along with a few exotic desert species his mom had brought in. Most of these plants were a shade of pale, dusty green that tasted bitter, like the tonic water his dad had mixed with gin.

"What should I do?" George asked a pterodactyl perched on a fake tree branch. He'd never named this particular statue, but it was still good for conversation. "Keep most of the space looking like the Mojave, in which case it's not really a garden at all but just… more desert? Uproot everything and start from scratch? Or separate the garden into zones?"

The pterodactyl proved as unhelpful as Tommy. Although it had originally been painted red, it had long ago faded to a very pale pink that tasted like gasoline. Maybe George ought to repaint it before tackling the plants. There were probably some old paint cans tucked away in storage, although he had no idea whether the contents would be usable.

Fine. He'd poke around again in the workshop, and after that, he'd take some measurements of the courtyard so he could draw up some schematics. A plan was better than him going off half-cocked.

Abandoning the garden tools on a bench, he headed through the gift shop on his way to the office for a bottle of water from the little fridge. But before getting there, he stopped in his tracks. Someone was sitting totally still on the other side of the front door, their hunched back leaning against the glass. They wore a puffy coat the color of concord grapes, tasting of vanilla, and a gray knitted cap with a pompom.

George had been thinking about installing security cameras for years. It was stupid that he didn't have them. But he'd never found room in his budget, which meant that potential intruders could sneak up on him undetected.

Except this person wasn't intruding. Maybe they'd come from far away to visit Fossil Galaxy and were now gravely disappointed that the place was closed. Unlikely. A person would have to be living under a rock to not know that all tourist attractions were shut down, from the magic of Disneyland to almost-defunct fossil exhibits.

Frowning, George stomped to the door and knocked loudly, intending to shoo the person away with hand signals and facial expressions. But as soon as the person began to turn around, George recognized him, mask and all.

Zephyr.

George didn't have the keys on him. He signed that Zephyr should wait, and then he sped to the office and plucked the heavy ring off the hook. Zephyr was standing when George returned.

"Hi," said George as soon as he got the door open.

"I was afraid you were gone. Except I guessed that's your van, so I hoped not." Zephyr had his coat zipped up even though it wasn't cold. He was without makeup, and his eyes looked tired and a little red, as if he'd been rubbing them. At least he wasn't visibly bruised.

"I'm here." Which was a stupid thing to say. "Do you want to come in?"

"Yes. But… hang on." Zephyr moved a few steps to the side and hoisted a sleek silver suitcase questioningly.

Intrigued, George pulled the door wider and moved aside.

Zephyr entered, the suitcase clutched in one hand, and stopped several feet away. They stared at each other. It was hard to read much with Zephyr's mask on, although George did register that he was wearing jeans and sparkly pink sneakers. "Do you want me to get a mask?" George asked, belatedly.

"Are you sick?"

"I don't think so. I haven't been near anyone for a while." Santiago had been careful to maintain at least a six-foot distance when he'd delivered the groceries, and afterward, George had sanitized all the packages as well as his hands.

"Okay. Um… I've been around people. But I don't have any symptoms or anything." Zephyr glanced around. "It's a big place. I can keep away from you."

"Are you planning to stay?" Ridiculous excitement tingled under George's skin.

"If you don't mind. For a little while."

George didn't know how long a little while was—five minutes or a month—but either would be fine. "You can take off your mask. I'm not high risk, and…." *And I want to see your mouth.* Yeah, not creepy at all. George didn't finish the sentence.

Zephyr removed his mask and stuffed it into a pocket. Then he simply stood there, still holding his suitcase. Although his jaw was firm, there was something slightly defeated in the angle of his shoulders. George wanted to draw him in for a hug, which was all kinds of no.

"Make yourself comfortable," he finally said. "Do you want to put your stuff in the apartment?"

That made Zephyr smile. "Thanks. You're awfully cool. I keep showing up unannounced and you never bat an eye."

"Last time you showed up, you gave me enough cash to keep me afloat for a good while. I'm hardly going to complain about that."

"I don't have wads of dough this time."

"That's all right."

George locked the door, stuffed the keys into his pocket, and led the way to the apartment. It probably looked the same as it had when Zephyr had been there last, yet while George hovered uncertainly, Zephyr prowled around and inspected the place.

"Are you cold?" George asked. "I don't have the heat on, but I can…." *Run up my utility bills even higher.*

"No. Thanks. Could I maybe just crash for a while? I'm short on sleep."

There was a story that George desperately wanted to know but wasn't rude enough to ask. "Of course. I was doing some work in the garden, so I'll leave you alone."

"Garden?"

"It's…." George waved vaguely. "I'll show you later, if you want. In fact, I'll give you the whole tour."

"I'd like that."

Again they stood there, Zephyr in his bright coat, George worrying his lip with his teeth. Then George gave a small sigh. "You know where the bed is. Or the couch is comfy, if you'd prefer. Help yourself to anything in the kitchen. I'll just…."

"I'll be fine. Thank you."

George nodded awkwardly and retreated from the apartment. As he'd originally intended, he went to the workshop and rooted around in search of paint, but his thoughts were firmly with Zephyr. Why was he here? How did he get here? The only vehicle in the parking lot was George's. What did he want besides a nap? How long would he stay?

But George wouldn't get his answers now. He didn't find any usable paint either, just a bunch of dried-up cans that he stacked in one corner. Maybe cleaning up the storage area would make another good lockdown project. It suddenly felt so futile, though, just as tackling the courtyard was futile, just as *everything* was—

No. Giving in to despair wouldn't help. And now he had a mysterious, beautiful guest, which was a lot more than he had an hour ago. He should be thankful.

Sighing, he started the search for a tape measure.

CHAPTER SIX

EXHAUSTED AND grubby and generally cranky, George almost forgot about Zephyr until, approaching his apartment, he caught a whiff of frying bacon. He opened the door cautiously, not exactly sure what he'd find inside. Zephyr stood at the stove, wearing nothing but tight blue jeans. He had his hair tied back in a long, loose ponytail, and held a pair of tongs that he clacked rhythmically.

"Hi," George said as he stepped inside.

Zephyr startled, dropping the tongs. But he recovered quickly, picked them up, and rinsed them at the sink. "I hope it's okay." He pointed at the frying pan.

"Of course. I said you could."

"I'm making enough for two."

When was the last time anyone had cooked for George? There had been those tamales from Kayla back in January, and before that, he couldn't remember. "Let me wash up."

It didn't take him long to clean his hands and face, after which he spent a good five minutes trying to decide what to wear. As if it mattered. He settled on a pair of loose gray shorts and a T-shirt with, of course, the Fossil Galaxy logo. All of his tees had that. He gave his hair a critical look. He wasn't much for fussing with it, and he'd never been happy with the color. And now he was now more than a month overdue for a haircut. He wondered how his barber, whom George had been seeing since he was a kid, was managing during the lockdown. George certainly wasn't the only business owner who was suffering.

In the kitchen, Zephyr had set two plates on the table, each with what appeared to be a toasted bacon-and-turkey sandwich. He'd also found some of the strawberries Santiago had brought, plus some off-brand potato chips from George's last shopping trip. He stood beside the table, hands on hips. "I should warn you—this is about the limit of what I can cook."

"It smells great."

That seemed to please Zephyr, who grinned and took a seat. George sat across from him. They both ate without talking, which was a little awkward but not as much as it could have been. Zephyr's eyes were brighter than when he'd arrived, but he still seemed distracted, his thoughts clearly troubled and far away.

"You just opened your door to me. Again," he said when the meal was almost over.

"Did you expect me to just leave you out there?"

Zephyr gave a small shrug.

"How did you get here?" George asked, hoping it wasn't a sensitive topic.

"Hitched. Had to sweet-talk the guy into taking the exit instead of the bypass. Man, that bypass must have fucked things up for you."

Now it was George's turn to shrug. "Hard to tell what's the fault of the bypass and what's… entropy. And now, of course, a virus. I kind of envy the dinosaurs—at least their extinction didn't linger." He'd intended that last part as a joke, but it didn't come out that way. He really shouldn't attempt comedy.

"Do you at least get an eviction moratorium?"

"I own the place outright, so rent's not the issue. But there's taxes. Utilities. Insurance." He lifted his plate slightly. "Food."

"And I'm adding to your expenses."

George waved that away. "Not much. And it hardly matters at this point. Besides, I'd be belly-up already if not for that cash you gave me."

"Why not just walk away?"

Gritting his teeth, George tried not to snap at him. He couldn't expect Zephyr to understand—nobody did. Not even his own siblings, who'd been saying the same thing to him for years.

"My grandfather came to California from Arkansas as a teenager during the Dust Bowl days. He had nothing but the clothes on his back. His parents and baby sister died of dysentery, and he kept himself alive by picking produce on other people's farms. Then he served in Europe during World War II, and when he came back, he got married, took out a loan through the GI Bill, and bought a tract of land here because it was cheap. He built a house. Worked two, sometimes three jobs. And when he had enough money saved up, he built Wally Harlow's Fossil Galaxy."

A speech. He sounded like he was giving a tour.

Zephyr was watching him closely. "Why?"

"He worked on a construction job not far from here and they found some fossils. We still have some of them in our collection. He got interested and read books on the topic. Then he decided this would be a good way to have his own business."

That was the explanation George had been given by his own father. It wasn't very satisfactory—it raised more questions than it answered—but Wally had died when George was too young to get a clearer picture, and his father refused to elaborate. Anyway, maybe more details weren't necessary. People got ideas all the time from God knew where, and although those ideas were often strange or unlikely, sometimes they became a reality. Occasionally they were even a success. George's dad used to liken Wally to Walt Disney, as if Fossil Galaxy was on the same level as the House of Mouse.

Now, having begun the spiel, George felt compelled to continue. "My dad was born here in the Junction. He took over the place after Wally died. He had all kinds of ideas for expansion and change, and maybe they didn't work out, but at least he kept it afloat, I guess partly because he worked so hard. He was here all day, seven days a week, until the day he died." He let out a long breath. "I grew up here too, along with my brothers and sister. Aside from three years when I was away at college, I've spent my whole life here."

Zephyr had kept his gaze fixed on George while chasing crumbs around his plate with one finger. Now he popped his finger into his mouth for a quick lick, an action that made George flush and catch his breath. But Zephyr didn't seem to notice the effect he had. "So, you have a college degree."

"No, I have three years of coursework at San Bernardino State, which I'm sure have expired by now."

"In paleontology?"

"No. Dad said—" George huffed. "I can learn about the stuff in our collections from books, just like my dad and grandfather did. A business degree was more practical for me." Although he wasn't convinced it would have done much to save Fossil Galaxy, it wouldn't have hurt.

"Did you want to study business?"

An almost physical pain lanced through George's mind. "It wasn't my first choice. I always liked biology. Plants. But that wasn't going to do me much good here. I needed to learn how to run a business. Marketing, accounting, management…."

"Why didn't you finish?"

"Dad died in a car wreck. Mom was sick, and… and I took over."

And that was more than enough of his boring life story. George narrowed his eyes. "Look, you're welcome to stay here, but can you at least tell me why?"

Zephyr's expression tightened. "Brandon and I have been…. I needed to get away for a little while. To give us some space."

"But why here?"

"I've got nowhere else to go."

Zephyr stood abruptly, gathered the plates, and walked to the sink. He stood there without turning on the water, his pale, narrow back looking vulnerable despite his straight posture. George wondered what Zephyr would do if George went over and gave that skin a few comforting strokes. But then he remembered what Zephyr had said the first time he was here, when he took a shower with George nearby in case he collapsed. *I owe you.* George didn't want to imply that Zephyr had to pay off a debt.

That tightness in George's belly was *want*, a drive he rarely felt. He willed it to go away.

He stood, mumbled something about needing to do some work, and escaped to the gift shop, where Tommy glared at him reproachfully.

IT WAS late when George returned to his apartment. He expected to discover Zephyr either asleep or gone but instead found him curled up on the couch, earbuds in place, a book cradled in his hands. He was wearing a fuzzy pink sweater—its particular shade thankfully not conjuring gasoline—and his hair, released from the ponytail, spilled over a cushion like a shining waterfall.

"Borrowed this," he said, pulling out one earbud and waving the novel. It was a well-worn copy of *Dune*.

"No problem." George went into the kitchen, poured some water from a pitcher in the fridge, and after a moment's indecision, sat in the armchair.

"How come you keep all of your books locked up? Afraid they'll escape and take over the world?" Zephyr gestured at the cabinet George used as a bookshelf.

"They're not locked. You just have to open the doors."

"But why not let them peek out?"

Okay. Time to have this conversation. "The covers and spines are lots of different colors. If I let them all show at once, it's overwhelming because I *taste* colors." He waited for the response.

What he got was that little tilt of the head that he'd already learned meant Zephyr was interested. "What do you mean?"

"It's called synesthesia—a person's senses get tangled up. And it comes in a variety of forms. Some people might see shapes while listening to music, for instance. Others might see letters as certain colors, or see colors when they hear sounds. I taste colors, which is a rare form, I guess. That shade of orange on the book cover tastes like french fries."

At this point, people generally started pointing at things and demanding to know what they tasted like, or else they were so confused or freaked out at the concept that they changed the subject entirely. Instead, Zephyr asked, "Is it an affliction or a gift?"

George let out his breath in a noisy whoosh. Nobody had ever asked *that*. They never seemed interested in how he felt about it; they just wanted him to perform like a circus freak or shut up about the subject.

"A gift, mostly. The world would seem flat without it. But it means I have to make some adjustments. When I'm home, I like to keep colors simple. It's like other people turning down the music so they can rest. A lot of synesthetes have been able to use it in their art or other work. David Hockney and Duke Ellington. Richard Feynman. Nikola Tesla. My kind of synesthesia isn't very useful, but I like it."

"It's like a secret code or a hidden universe."

"It is," George replied, smiling. "But it's also weird."

Zephyr shook his head and stroked the soft fabric of his sweater, which was slipping down over one shoulder. "It's unusual. The world would be a better place if more people realized that jewels aren't the only rare things that are beautiful."

Then he stuck the earbud back in and returned his attention to *Dune*.

CHAPTER SEVEN

ZEPHYR SLEPT on the couch that night. He said he didn't mind, that he'd slept on much worse, and that this way he could stay up late and watch TV. In fact, the couch *was* pretty comfortable, but George felt a little bad about it anyway. His bed was big enough for two. Of course, just thinking about Zephyr lying next to him raised George's temperature several degrees, so it was probably just as well they slept in separate rooms. Hell, even that sent George's imagination soaring to places it didn't belong.

The thing was, George wasn't sure how he felt about... desiring someone. It was a rare phenomenon, and he was comfortable with that. Given his work schedule and geographic isolation, he would have ended up incredibly frustrated had he been eager for a sexual relationship. As it was, he was perfectly content with his friends for companionship and his deft right hand for release. But with Zephyr, he was beginning to feel all kinds of stirrings, and that was good too—except Zephyr hadn't come here to be a sex object, and George considered him strictly off-limits. It would have been easier if George's libido had remained in its usual tepid state.

By the time George was awake and showered and dressed, Zephyr was still fast asleep. He'd changed to pajamas—shorts and a button-up top with a flamingo print—and had put his hair into a loose braid. With his eyes closed and his hands softly curled under his chin, he looked absurdly innocent. George knew very little about his guest but was fairly certain innocence wasn't one of Zephyr's foremost attributes.

Coffee would have been nice, but George didn't want to wake Zephyr by making noise in the kitchen. Breakfast could wait. He tiptoed into the gift shop and closed the door carefully behind him.

And there he was, surrounded by shelves and racks of carefully displayed souvenirs that, most likely, nobody would ever buy. That was a miserable thought. He used to ask visitors where they were from, and then he'd enjoy thinking about them wearing Fossil Galaxy T-shirts in

Topeka, Toronto, and Taipei. He'd never visited any of those places—he'd barely stepped foot outside California—but those shirt sales meant there was a bit of Harlow everywhere.

"Stop it," he muttered. Putting aside thoughts of Fossil Galaxy's death spiral, he stomped out to the garden to wrestle the creosote bushes.

"AREN'T YOU hungry?"

George had been crouching in front of a cholla, trying to decide what to do with it, when the unexpected voice made him twist around so fast, he lost his balance and landed on his ass.

Zephyr laughed, but not unkindly. "Sorry. Didn't mean to startle you."

George stood slowly and brushed sandy soil from the seat of his pants. "I see you've been shopping."

Zephyr wore a V-neck Fossil Galaxy T-shirt with the sleeves rolled up and the bottom hem knotted halfway up his midriff. He also had on cut-off shorts and his sparkly pink sneakers. "You don't mind, do you? You gave me a shirt once before, but I don't have it anymore."

"Take all the shirts you want." George didn't quite manage to suppress a sigh.

"You didn't come inside for lunch."

As if on cue, George's stomach grumbled. He glanced at his watch and was surprised to see it was past two. And dammit, when had he last applied sunscreen? His skin wasn't too pink yet, so maybe it hadn't been that long.

"I got caught up in work," he said.

"What are you doing? And what exactly is going on out here?" Zephyr waved his arms to indicate the scrubby bit of enclosed desert, the citrus trees, the remains of exotic plants, the faded dinosaurs, the dusty benches.

So George told him about the Ancient Gardens. How his mother had loved working out here and had made an empty courtyard with only a few citrus trees into something special. How, as a young kid, he'd stalk through the leafier vegetation, pretending to be a jungle explorer. How one summer when he was twelve, he'd created a spreadsheet to keep track of all the birds and insects that visited the gardens. He'd been delighted to find carpenter bees making their home in the wood that supported a rickety triceratops statue, but then his father had declared the bees a nuisance and filled in the holes.

Somehow this explanation of the gardens grew so long and involved that George and Zephyr ended up sitting on a bench in the shade, both of them sipping from bottles of Coke that Zephyr pilfered from the gift-shop cooler.

"You're really into this place." Zephyr swept a hand to indicate the entire courtyard. He seemed genuinely interested, not judgmental.

"Yeah. It's peaceful. Not that the rest of Conrad Junction is a hotbed of activity. But this place…. Also, desert ecosystems are really interesting. I always kind of thought that if I didn't have Fossil Galaxy to run…." He let that sentence wither, just like the half-baked idea behind it.

"You came back here to take care of your mom after your dad died," Zephyr said after George had been silent for a few moments.

"Yeah. She died too, about two years later."

He hated to admit it, even to himself, but her final passing had brought him some relief. He'd been running himself ragged, trying to operate the business and also tend to her. She hadn't had health insurance, and she refused assistance from anyone but George until the end, when she'd been diminished and in severe pain.

"I had to sell the house, the one my grandfather built, to help pay her medical expenses. They tore it down and built an ampm gas station, but now with the bypass, that's gone too. I like my apartment here, though."

"It's cozy. But haven't you been tempted to do something different, now that they're both gone?"

George tamped down a spike of irritation and decided to fish for a little information. "Where are your folks?"

Zephyr gave a negligent shrug and looked away. After a moment or two he sighed. "I never think about them. Ancient history—like your dinosaurs."

It couldn't be *that* ancient. George guessed that Zephyr was no more than twenty-five. But again, he didn't push. "I should probably eat something."

"I'll make you some lunch. I might as well be at least a little useful, right?" he said with more than a hint of bitterness.

They had peanut butter sandwiches with prickly pear jelly made by Santiago's wife, Jessica, along with orange juice and the last of the discount potato chips. George did most of the talking during the meal, and Zephyr coaxed him into discussing his imprecise plans for the garden.

"I can help," Zephyr offered. "I'm gonna warn you, the only plant-related thing I've ever done was harvesting weed, but I'm willing to try."

"You'll ruin your manicure."

Zephyr's hands rested on the table. At George's words, he curled his nails under his palms. "Does the way I dress bother you?"

"I think you have more sense of style in one pinky than I have in my whole body."

Laughing, Zephyr leaned toward him. "So what's your story, George? I have the impression you are not straight as an arrow."

"I'm queer as a three-dollar bill."

That brought more chuckles. "And you're out, here in Conrad Junction?"

"I was never in."

"How'd that go over?"

"Nobody much cared. Look, I taste colors and spend all my time hanging out with extinct animals. My weirdness was already pretty much off the scale, so the fact that I liked boys instead of girls was a fairly minor thing. I think I got teased more about my hair color than anything else. When I was younger, it was really red. It's mellowed with age."

"I like your hair." Zephyr flashed a quick smile. "But seriously, even your parents were cool with you being out?"

"Mom was. Dad said I'd outgrow it as soon as I matured and became serious about life." He thought for a moment. "I would've gotten way more pushback from everyone if I'd dressed like you. Not that I could have pulled it off as well as you do, though. And anyway I'm comfortable like this. But I bet it takes a lot of courage to wear what you want to instead of what people expect."

Although Zephyr waved that away, George thought he looked pleased. "Boyfriend?" Zephyr asked.

"God. Do you really want to hear about my love life?"

Zephyr crossed his arms. "Yes. I really do."

"Ugh. Okay. I was kinda serious about someone back in college. But then I had to return home, and for some reason he didn't find Conrad Junction enticing." George hadn't thought about Zak in a long time. They'd lost touch after they broke up, and George had no clue where he was now.

"Since then, I've been too busy. And I'm sort of… well, I have a lot going on, and I'm stuck out in the middle of nowhere. But mostly I'm too—"

"Busy. Got it."

George felt defensive. "I am. And now with the lockdown…."

"Uh-huh," Zephyr said, as if a worldwide pandemic wasn't a good enough reason to be flying solo. "How long since your last steady guy?"

"Steady guy? Have we time-warped to the fifties? It's been since college. Nine—no, ten years ago."

Zephyr whistled. "That's a long time."

"So it's better to end up with Brandon and have things go so swimmingly that you have to flee to a stranger in the desert?"

George regretted the words as soon as he said them. Zephyr had poked a little too hard, but that didn't mean George had to stab back, especially into what must be a sensitive spot.

Surprisingly, however, Zephyr smiled. "You remembered his name."

"I'm good with names."

"You're not a stranger, George. You're my hero, remember? Saint George."

Zephyr stood and walked off to the bathroom.

CHAPTER EIGHT

ZEPHYR MADE dinner that night—spaghetti and toast and frozen veggies—and although it was simple, it tasted better with company. George was a little achy due to his gardening, which made it especially nice to have someone else prepare the meal.

"I hardly ever get a chance to cook," Zephyr explained. "I wish I knew how to really make stuff instead of just heating things from packages."

"You can probably tell from my kitchen that I'm not exactly a gourmet chef either."

"I've always really liked the concept of home-cooked meals. It sounds so… I don't know. Safe? Snug, maybe. Like hand-knitted sweaters and homemade bread. Did you have those things as a kid?"

George thought about it. "Meals, sure. Mom cooked. But she didn't bake or knit or anything like that. No time, with four kids and the business. I'm the youngest, so I ended up with lots of hand-me-downs, clothing-wise. Do you have brothers or sisters?"

"I guess," said Zephyr, which wasn't really an answer.

After finishing the dishes, George made them some herbal tea and they settled in the living room. Zephyr had his earbuds and *Dune*; George had YouTube videos and a library book about improving your business's social media impact. For a few hours, he almost forgot about his life's impending disasters, and Zephyr seemed unusually relaxed too. The only uncomfortable part of the evening was when George forgot himself and stared at Zephyr, who caught him and chuckled at George's blush. At least Zephyr wasn't offended.

They slept in separate rooms again. George dreamed that he was feverishly knitting sweaters for dinosaurs in hopes he'd save them from extinction.

The next day was considerably warmer, a harbinger of the brutal summer soon to arrive. Well before noon, George gave up on the garden and was making his way to the shower when Zephyr waylaid him in the gift shop. "Can I have that tour now? You promised."

George, who'd concluded that Zephyr wasn't interested in seeing the exhibits, wondered if this was simple boredom or a tactic to prime George for more favors. But Zephyr seemed to pay close attention as George led him through the first room.

"My grandpa organized the collections. I'm not sure if experts would have done things the same way, but I think they make sense. This exhibit shows the minerals of the Mojave. Um, as the sign indicates." This room was free of dinosaur statuary, although the walls had faded murals depicting desert landscapes. Most visitors hurried through this exhibit.

Zephyr strolled slowly, peering at the cases full of rocks, each item labeled in Wally Harlow's neatest writing. George could recite the names from memory, each one rolling off his tongue like a poem. Rosasite. Conichalcite. Miargyrite. Tincalconite. Quartz. Obsidian. Stolzite. Colemanite. Thenardite. Ulexite. Borax. Malachite—with its rich green color that tasted so strongly of chocolate cake that George used to beg to lick it when he was very small.

"Where did you get all of these?" Zephyr asked.

"Grandpa collected them. Some he found himself, back when he did construction projects. But a lot of them he bought or were donated. He had friends who worked in the mines. Dad added to the collection too."

Zephyr glanced up at him. "Have you?"

"Just these." George walked him over to a small case containing a dozen agates. "Zak and I spent a few days up in San Francisco once, and I collected these on a beach near there. They're probably not very interesting, but I thought they were pretty."

After asking a few more questions, Zephyr wandered into the invertebrates exhibit. Mostly this meant seashells, both fossilized and not, although there were also beetles and butterflies pinned to cards. Those had always made George slightly uneasy. The room also contained chunks of coral, and shells from barnacles and crabs. Again, no dinosaurs, but there was a plaster nautilus almost as tall as George, along with a grasshopper the size of a Great Dane and a huge plastic clam that little kids liked to climb into. There used to be a giant orange octopus made of fabric stretched over a wire frame, but it had disintegrated years ago. George missed it.

"Tell me about these," Zephyr demanded.

So George did, with snippets about long-vanished seas and the life cycles of swallowtails and tarantulas. Nothing too complicated or deep, because he was no expert, but enough to briefly catch guests' interest and make them feel as if their admission fees had been well spent.

The meteorite held center stage in the next room, along with other bits of space debris, including a chunk of metal purportedly from a lunar module. George wasn't sure that was true. One wall displayed a large variety of fluorescent minerals, and a guest could press a button to see them glow under a black light. These rocks had no particular ties to outer space, but Wally thought they looked otherworldly enough to reside in this room. Other artifacts included a spacesuit of dubious provenance, several small models of spacecraft, a case with plastic replicas of astronaut food, and a metal UFO five feet in diameter, with painted aliens peeking merrily through the portholes. A model of the solar system hung suspended from the ceiling.

"The Galaxy part of Fossil Galaxy," Zephyr said, smiling.

"Yeah. It's pretty tacky, but space stuff was popular when Wally opened the place. And he did have this cool meteorite to show off."

"I think if I'd hung around here as a kid, this would have been my favorite room."

George smiled, imagining a small version of Zephyr. "Not the dinos? Vertebrates are the next exhibit. Sort of the grand finale."

"Nah. I was never into them. They were big and scary. But I would have enjoyed imagining myself escaping the Earth and exploring the universe."

"Yeah? How come—?"

Zephyr's pocket chimed, and he looked apprehensive as he pulled out his phone. His expression darkened as he read the screen. "Fuck."

"Everything okay?"

Busy typing with his thumbs, Zephyr didn't answer right away. But eventually he looked grimly at George. "Brandon's here."

George glanced around, as if Brandon might suddenly emerge from the UFO, but then realized what Zephyr must mean. "Here, outside?"

Zephyr was already striding rapidly toward the vertebrate room, which he must have correctly surmised was the quickest way to get to the gift shop and the main entrance. He moved really fast. Despite having longer legs, George almost had to jog to keep up. When they reached the gift shop, a scowling man stood outside the glass door, arms crossed.

"Unlock it, please," said Zephyr, his voice low. "Don't worry. We'll stay outside."

Until that warning, it hadn't occurred to George that he should worry, but of course, he did now. What did Zephyr expect from this guy?

"Look, if you don't want to talk to him—"

"It's okay."

Zephyr neither looked nor sounded confident, but he was an adult capable of making his own decisions. Brandon had dropped his arms to his sides and was possibly trying to make puppy dog eyes at Zephyr, although if so, he wasn't good at it. Glaring seemed more his style.

After hesitating a moment, George fetched the keys from his office. He'd barely gotten the door unlocked before Zephyr pushed past him, went outside, and pulled the door firmly closed. He shot George a quick glance along the way; it might have been an apology or maybe a plea, but for what, George didn't know.

Zephyr and Brandon immediately fell into a conversation that involved a lot of gesturing on Brandon's part, but they remained too quiet to hear through the glass. Not that George should be eavesdropping anyway. In fact, he should probably step away and give them complete privacy. But he couldn't force himself to do so; it felt too much like abandoning Zephyr. So he hovered awkwardly a few yards from the door, feeling like a voyeur.

At least he finally had the opportunity to get a good look at Brandon, who'd been looming in the corners of George's mind since Zephyr arrived. He wasn't impressive in any particular way—nothing that would have made George look twice under other circumstances. Well, except for the very expensive-looking yellow sports car parked crookedly in front of the building. George didn't know much about cars, but he believed that the prancing-horse emblem meant it was a Ferrari. The yellow tasted like liver. Zephyr had mentioned once, in passing, that Brandon drove like a maniac and had crashed two previous vehicles. "Imagine having that kind of money to throw around," George muttered.

Brandon himself was less flashy by far. White, fortyish, of middling height and weight, dark slacks and white shirt, and light brown hair slicked back from his forehead. No gold chains around his neck or diamonds on his fingers, but there was something subtle about him that spoke of wealth and power. Even without the car or Zephyr's previous comments about his boyfriend, George would have guessed this guy never needed to worry about how to pay the bills.

Brandon was doing most of the talking. Zephyr's face was expressionless, but he'd crossed his arms and tucked in his shoulders a bit, as though he were chilly despite the warm evening.

At one point in the discussion, Brandon's attention turned to George. There was no way for George to act nonchalant or as if he'd been doing anything but watching. He lifted his chin and pretended that Brandon was one of those solar panel entrepreneurs, here to exploit George's difficult position. That helped a little.

After what felt like a very long time, Zephyr nodded. Then Brandon took out a money clip and handed him some bills. Zephyr nodded again, turned, and reentered the building, leaving Brandon outside. Brandon looked pleased.

"Sorry about this," Zephyr said right away.

"What does he want?"

"Peace and reconciliation." Zephyr sighed. "I'm going back home with him."

George's heart plummeted. "You said you needed time away."

"I know. But… half the time I don't know what I want, and the other half, what I want is a bad idea. It's fine. We'll work things out."

"Do you *want* to work things out?"

Zephyr hesitated only a split second before saying, "Yeah."

Considering George's track record with relationships—or lack thereof—he was in no position to give advice. Even if the voice in his head was motivated more by jealousy than genuine concern, it was loudly insisting that Zephyr should stay put.

Out loud, George said, "You could stay here awhile longer and then go back."

"That's only delaying things. I'm too old to run away from my problems. It won't make them disappear."

"Is he a problem?"

"No." Zephyr gave a small smile. "I am. I'm hard to live with. I don't— My background isn't the same as his. I need to adjust better. I need to communicate better and be less self-centered."

Maybe all of those things were true, but it sounded as if the relationship issues were all his fault. George doubted the accuracy of that.

"Seriously, Zephyr, you can—"

"I'll be *fine*. I always am. And Brandon's place is huge. I'll have plenty of room there if I need my own space. God, you could hold a socially-distanced board meeting in my closet, if you wanted to. Huge."

No doubt Brandon's mansion or penthouse or whatever was a lot more luxe than George's bare-bones apartment attached to a funky store and dusty museum. The entertainment was probably a lot more interesting than a bunch of rocks and bones too. And the company—well, George was pretty sick of himself, so he could easily imagine Zephyr feeling the same about him.

"Here," Zephyr said, holding out the wad of money. "For my room and board."

"We ate sandwiches and you slept on the couch."

"And I got a personalized guided tour of Wally Harlow's Fossil Galaxy by the cutest, most charming guide in Southern California. Here." He pressed the money against George's hand until he took it.

George tucked it into his pocket without looking at it. "You never saw the vertebrates."

"Told you. I prefer outer space."

Ignoring the tightness in his throat, George pasted on a wan smile. "Can I give you my cell number? You can call or text anytime."

Zephyr shook his head. "Not a good idea. He gets jealous." He brightened. "Hey, I've been meaning to tell you something."

Hope rekindled. "Yeah?"

"I was doing a little research yesterday. I think you could apply for a small-business loan—one of those Covid relief things. It might even be forgivable. I wrote down a couple of websites—the paper's near your couch."

And there went hope, fizzled to ashes. But George nodded anyway. "That's great. Thanks. I'll look into it."

They stood there for a minute, until Brandon rapped impatiently on the door and pointed at his watch.

"Thanks again," Zephyr said. "You really are my hero."

"I haven't done anything—"

"My *hero*. Someone I can turn to in a time of need. I can't tell you how valuable that is, and how rare."

"Oh." George didn't feel remotely heroic. "You're welcome here anytime, you know. If you need to get away. Or if you just want a change of scenery."

Zephyr gave him a warm and genuine smile. Then he turned and started toward the door.

"Wait! Your stuff! Your suitcase."

"I don't need it. Won't fit in his stupid car anyway."

He looked back at George for just a moment before stepping outside. The door closed. Brandon put his arm around Zephyr's waist and drew him toward the Ferrari.

George watched the car screech out of the parking lot. And then he locked the door.

CHAPTER NINE

June 2021

GEORGE ADJUSTED his mask, which had a tendency to slide off his nose. He was regretting ordering this particular model, although the visitors seemed to like them. The fabric was imprinted with the Fossil Galaxy logo, of course, along with a cartoonish roaring *T. rex*. At fourteen bucks a pop, they were currently his best-selling souvenir. People also liked the hand sanitizer with the label that said Don't Go Extinct! That had been Judith's idea. He found it slightly inappropriate, but they sold really well.

"Thanks so much for coming in today, folks," he said to the young family as he handed the mom their bag of souvenirs. "I hope you enjoyed the tour."

"We stopped here when I was a girl. I'm glad to see you're still open. We could all use a little nostalgia and familiarity right now, you know?"

"Definitely."

After a few more pleasantries, the parents and their three little kids left, the two older ones clamoring for Burger King. Just as they pulled out of the parking lot, Kayla entered with a plastic sack in hand. "Been busy today?"

"I wouldn't call it busy, but we've had seven or eight groups through. Are those tamales?" he added hopefully.

"Nope. Something way better."

"Nothing's better than your gran's tamales."

"Ha! That's what you think!" She skipped across the room to Tommy, where she opened the bag, pulled out a wad of fabric, and dropped the bag to the floor. She had to stand on tiptoe for the next part, and it wasn't until she stepped back that George realized what she'd done.

"A mask?" It was potato-flavored neon green with the Fossil Galaxy logo, and she'd tied it over his snout and mouth.

"I figured Tommy needed one too."

"Tommy is a statue, of a dinosaur."

She laughed. "And an excellent opportunity to model safe practices. Anyway, I bet he'll be even more popular for selfies now. Tell people to tag you when they post."

How did such a young person manage to be so practical and yet fun at the same time? George shook his head with wonder. "Where on earth did you find a dino-sized mask?"

"Online."

Normally George would have lectured her on the importance of supporting local businesses, but he was positive that neither the convenience store nor Lyle Cohen's art shop carried anything like this. "Tommy looks very nice in it. Thank you."

Kayla handed him the discarded bag, which he tucked below the cash register for later reuse or recycling. Then she leaned her elbows on the glass countertop and grinned. "Mom and I are heading to Lancaster tomorrow to buy supplies for my dorm."

"You'll get to be on campus this fall?"

"Looks like it! Man, I'm so sick of Zoomville. I can't wait to do, like, normal college stuff. Anyway, do you need us to pick up anything while we're there?"

"No, but thanks."

Although she nodded, she didn't seem inclined to leave. "When was the last time you left the Junction, George?"

He shrugged. Without any employees, he'd have to close Fossil Galaxy if he left. His trickle of income was thin enough that he couldn't afford to miss any potential visitors. He'd been mail-ordering nonperishable food because the mini-mart's prices were too high and its selection too low. Santiago brought him perishables when he went shopping in Barstow. It sufficed.

"I have everything I need right here."

"Uh-huh." She fixed him with a narrow-eyed stare. "And when was the last time you had a date?"

When real T. rexes *walked the land*. Or at least it felt that way. "There's a pandemic going on, Kayla. In case you haven't noticed."

She rolled her eyes. "Yeah, yeah. Look, I'm taking a summer chemistry class, right? And there's this guy in my class, Tony. He and I are in a study group, and he's super smart. Really nice too, like he's totally cool about helping people understand things without making them feel dumb. And he's a babe. I can show you his pic."

George finally realized where this was going. "Kayla, I don't—"

"And he's sort of nerdy too, which I think might be your thing. And he's funny."

"Kayla, he's way too young for me." There. That was a reasonable argument.

"But he's totally not! He's old, like—" She clapped her hand over her masked mouth and snorted a laugh before continuing. "He was in the Army, and then he had some jobs and stuff, but now he's going to get a degree so he can teach high school. And he's gay *and* single."

George fixed her with a skeptical look. "And where does Mr. Perfect live?"

She deflated a bit. "Rancho Cucamonga."

"That's gotta be eighty miles from here."

"That's not so far. People have relationships from, like, opposite coasts."

"I don't." He smiled at her. "I appreciate the thought, I really do. But I'm not pining away from loneliness. I'm too busy."

She didn't buy it. But she dropped the subject, and they spent a little while talking about her plans for the fall. George told her about the time during his sophomore year when his roommate got drunk at a party, puked on the landing outside their dorm room, and by oversleeping the next morning, missed turning in an important assignment. He meant it as a cautionary tale, but Kayla seemed to find it hilarious.

After she left, the building felt far too quiet. Until a couple of years earlier, George had played music in the gift shop. Mostly he'd listen to classic rock because very few people objected to it and also because his brother James used to refer to it as dinosaur rock, which seemed appropriate. But one of the audio speakers had gone on the fritz, and replacing them hadn't been a priority. Most of the time, that was fine. Today, though, George wanted noise.

He was seriously considering serenading Tommy when he saw the mail truck park in front of the building. The mail carrier was an older woman named Debra who always apologized for bringing him bills. She loved her route because of the distances between deliveries. "I get paid to drive!" she'd crow.

Today, however, she looked especially cheerful as she entered the building with a stack of mail in her hands. "You got a package," she sang.

That was unusual. He wasn't expecting anything today, and most of his orders arrived via UPS. He ignored the little pile of sales circulars, catalogs, and invoices that she set on the counter and picked up the bulky manila envelope instead. It was heavier than he expected.

"No return address," Debra informed him. "But it's postmarked from New York City." She waited as if expecting him to open it in front of her.

But George suspected this might be a gag being played on him by one of his friends, and he didn't want to pull out a dildo or butt plug or something equally mortifying in front of Debra. "So how's Wayne Maas doing lately?" he asked in hopes of creating a distraction.

It worked. Wayne Maas was a crazy old codger who lived in a shack miles from everywhere, with a collection of rusted vehicles and mysterious industrial equipment parts scattered across his desert acreage. He was convinced that the government was out to get him. About half the time, he refused to let Debra onto his property because she was, of course, a federal employee and might therefore have evil intent. But the other half of the time he'd happily stand on his dilapidated front porch, bong or bottle in hand, lecturing her on ways to fool her bosses. Today had been a lecturing day, much to Debra's delight. Maas had told her that she should ditch the official mail truck at the beginning of each workday and do her route in a privately owned vehicle so that the feds would have a harder time tracking her.

After Debra sauntered back to her truck, George steeled himself and opened the envelope. No sex toys fell out. Instead there was a flat box encased in bubble wrap. He freed the box, cut the tape holding it closed, and pried open the lid. More bubble wrap and, beneath that, a thick layer of brown paper. If it hadn't been for the weight of the object, he would have thought there was nothing there but wrapping materials.

But it was finally revealed: a plate-shaped stone about six inches in diameter, inset with several detailed fossils of a five-armed sea creature. It was a lovely specimen in excellent condition, and probably worth a lot of money.

God, what if he'd ordered this while in a fugue state or something?

But no, there among the brown paper was a note written on a piece of stationery from the St. Regis Hotel. The scrawled note was hard to read.

These are Jimbacrinus bostocki, *according to the dude at the store. I thought they'd look cool in the invertebrates exhibit. Or they're weird enough to fit in with your aliens and stuff if you want.—Z*

RESEARCH REVEALED that the fossils likely came from Australia, and that this specimen was worth somewhere between two and three grand. But nothing online could tell George where the piece had been purchased. Even if he assumed it had been bought in New York City, there were a bunch of retailers that carried fossils and gems. Even more importantly, George couldn't tell *why* Zephyr had sent this to him. What he meant by it. Where he was now, and whether he was okay.

"He's shipping expensive rocks and writing on five-star-hotel stationery," George told himself. "He's fine." And the gift had probably just been an impulse. Zephyr had said Brandon was rich; maybe he had a whole driveway paved with precious stones and pricey artifacts.

According to the postmark, the package had left New York three days earlier. Maybe Zephyr was still there at the hotel. George could call, but who would he ask for? He didn't know Zephyr's last name—or if his real name even *was* Zephyr, which seemed somewhat doubtful. He didn't know Brandon's surname either.

And even if George did convince the hotel to connect him to the beautiful man who wore skirts and was probably accompanied by a controlling douche, then what? George had no idea what he'd say to Zephyr. *Thank you*, sure, but beyond that the conversation would fizzle. Zephyr had revealed only tiny glimpses of himself even when they were in the same room together for hours; he wasn't going to spill everything during a transcontinental phone call.

If Zephyr had wanted to speak to George, he would have sent his phone number. Hell, he could have called Fossil Galaxy's landline, which was clearly listed on the website.

"This isn't fair," George complained to Tommy, who, due to the mask, was even more impassive than usual. "It's been more than a year without a peep from him. I'd put him completely out of my head."

That was a bald-faced lie, and even a statue of a *T. rex* knew it. George had thought about Zephyr every damn day. When he looked at his couch, he could still see Zephyr curled up there with his book and earbuds, his hair loosely braided, his lips curved in a grin.

George still had Zephyr's suitcase, filled with his clothing, standing in a corner of the living room. It was reflective silver, which had no flavor at all.

Kayla was only nineteen, but maybe she was right. George should take off the monk's robe he'd wrapped so tightly around himself and reenter the dating pool. He didn't have to forge a relationship with some guy from Rancho Cucamonga, though. Surely he could find someone within a more reasonable driving radius. Someone might be interested in him if he tried. George wasn't bad-looking, he didn't have a criminal record or issues with addictions. And he wasn't dragging a lot of baggage.

Just Zephyr's suitcase.

"It doesn't even have to *be* a relationship. I could just get laid." But despite the fact that he hadn't had sex with another person in years, a casual hookup didn't appeal.

Several months before the pandemic, George had felt vaguely guilty about not making any effort at all to improve his sex life. Hooking up felt like something he should be doing, even if he wasn't into it. Maybe he'd discover, once he tried, that he actually did enjoy it. He'd used an app and ended up matching with a guy name Harbir, a truck driver who had a weekly route between Bakersfield and Oklahoma City. Harbir had been passing westbound through Conrad Junction that very afternoon, so at George's invitation he'd parked his rig in the Fossil Galaxy lot and joined George in his apartment.

Yes, George had been aware that he was taking a risk. But as it turned out, Harbir was a genuinely nice guy, sweet and a little shy. There was zero indication that he was a serial killer. He was also very handsome.

But although Harbir's blue shirt tasted like cream cheese frosting, and although he was a good kisser, George couldn't get into the spirit of things. It was embarrassing. Finally, Harbir had pulled back. "You're not into me, are you?"

"God, it's not— You're great. I'm sorry. Life's been kind of difficult lately, and my headspace…. I am *so* sorry." George had rubbed his forehead. "Maybe if we got to know each other a little bit first…."

Harbir had looked thoughtful. "Do you hook up often?"

George had barked a laugh. "No. Hardly ever. I just…. It doesn't seem…. Jesus. I'm sorry."

"It's fine," Harbir said, waving away the apology. "This is a personal question, but since we had been planning to get naked, maybe you'll give me a pass. Are you demisexual?"

"Um…." George had heard the term and knew it was one of the broad spectrum of orientations now recognized, but he wasn't sure of its meaning.

"Do you have to know someone fairly well before you're sexually attracted to them?"

George thought about this for a moment. He certainly appreciated seeing handsome men, even if he'd never met them before. Hell, he'd come to a realization that he was gay when he was twelve and found himself swooning over Legolas in *The Fellowship of the Ring*, and he hadn't been besties with Orlando Bloom. But admiring someone in the abstract was one thing; wanting to do the horizontal bop with them was something else.

"I don't know," he said to Harbir.

And instead of stomping out or calling him pathetic, Harbir had smiled warmly. "That's okay. Maybe you need some time to find yourself, yeah?"

And they'd eaten burritos from Arturo's and laughed at stories about each other's siblings and shared concerns over the upcoming election. Then Harbir climbed into his rig and rumbled off to Bakersfield.

Now, all this time later, George wasn't any closer to finding himself. Maybe he was demisexual, or maybe there was nothing to find—maybe his heart was as dried up and lifeless as the fossils on the counter in front of him. Except it didn't *feel* lifeless, not when he thought about Zephyr. Then his heart felt warm and heavy—alive, but a burden inside him.

George sighed and gently stroked the fossils. "Whattaya think, Tommy? Invertebrates or outer space?"

Tommy, inscrutable behind his mask, had no opinion on the matter.

CHAPTER TEN

August 2021

GEORGE FOUND high summer in the Mojave to be a strange, dreamy time, when air-conditioners struggled against the unrelenting heat and every movement felt labored. To compensate, he chugged gallons of water and iced tea. The few visitors who made it to Fossil Galaxy were red-faced and sweaty just from the short walk across the parking lot. They'd snag drinks from the cooler before they even considered paying the entrance fee and would exclaim over the day's high temperature, as if getting as hot as possible was some kind of contest.

George rarely ventured outdoors except to check on the gardens shortly after dawn or to take trash to the bin after dusk. He stood at the glass display case, waiting near the register for potential gift-shop purchases and feeling remarkably like a mammoth trapped in a tar pit.

Despite the small-business loans and the slight uptick in paying customers, George teetered on the edge of financial disaster. In fact, he suspected he'd already fallen but hadn't yet experienced impact. Sometimes a little voice inside his head urged him to close up shop and find a new path in life, but he rigorously ignored it. The only thing more terrifying than the wolves currently at his heels would be confronting the unknown that crouched somewhere ahead. Anyway, he'd face that unknown soon enough. Another couple of months, maybe.

The only bit of good news came from some online advice; he'd changed his status within the business so that now he was officially an employee. That meant that if there was another lockdown, he'd be eligible for unemployment. At least he hoped so. He wasn't sure of the technicalities.

This morning had been exciting because a summer camp from Lancaster had brought a busload of fourth graders. Despite the substantial discount George had given them on entrance fees, he'd done all right, perhaps because the kids had spent their allowance money on souvenir pens, snow globes, and plush dinosaurs. Plus, the group seemed to have had fun. Children that age weren't yet jaded and didn't notice how scruffy and timeworn the exhibits were. They'd found it fun to pose for pics in front of the dino statues, and they'd all thanked him as they left. Then they'd rushed off for their visit to the borax mine. He envied their energy and enthusiasm.

Now it was late afternoon, though, and George was alone in the building, considering his dinner options. He'd had ramen the past three nights, because the last time he went shopping, it had been on sale, four packages for a dollar. He really couldn't face it again tonight, though, not even with some frozen veggies mixed in for variety and nutrition.

He had some peanut butter. Eggs. Rice. Beans. He wasn't going to starve. But God, he'd have sold his soul for a restaurant dinner with a big steak, a buttery baked potato, a giant green salad with croutons, and for dessert—

Someone walked into the building, making the bell jingle merrily. George recognized him at once, despite his stiff and jerky movements and the fact that sunglasses, a mask, and a lowered head hid his face. And that he wore plain blue jeans and a gray T-shirt that said BTS in large letters.

"Zephyr!"

CHAPTER ELEVEN

ZEPHYR

ZEPHYR FELT encased in a concrete shell, numb to everything. Voices and other noises came to him from far away, little wisps of sound that usually blew away before he caught them. He felt neither the curious stares of the people around him nor the heat blanketing the earth.

But no, he wasn't encased. He was separated, watching his own body from afar, as if he were tethered to it like a balloon on a very long string.

He didn't remember making the decision to come here, and he could recall only snips and scraps of the journey. There had been a bus. Or a train. Or maybe both. Streets with sidewalks and roads with dusty, weedy shoulders. A few hours of uneasy sleep on a bench, or under trees, or in the passenger seat of a truck.

He didn't know when or what he'd eaten. He probably reeked from wearing the same clothes for days, but he couldn't smell anything. If he'd had any luggage at the beginning, he couldn't recall what had happened to it.

But this place drew him like a beacon, and even though he had no right to arrive and demand more, here he was. Once again. Walking through the door of Wally Harlow's Fossil Galaxy. A ghost of himself—yet he was still walking.

A familiar voice called his name, and then George was running to him. George didn't recoil when he saw Zephyr's condition, but then again, he hadn't turned away that time he'd found Zephyr behind the dumpster either.

George gripped Zephyr's biceps as if to keep him from floating away. "Stay here for a sec," he said urgently. "Just gonna lock up."

He was back a moment later, steering Zephyr out of the gift shop and into the bedroom in his apartment, where he pushed gently at Zephyr's shoulders. "Lie down. I'll bring you water and OJ."

"I'm dirty."

"Dirt washes away."

Not all of it. But Zephyr sat on the mattress, kicked off his flip-flops, and removed his sunglasses and mask. He lay back with his head on the pillow. The sheets were cool against his too-tight skin, the room's subdued décor soothing to his eyes. Or… eye. He was having trouble seeing anything through the left one, but his ragged mind couldn't work out why. Well, no matter. One was enough at the moment.

George returned with two filled glasses and a concerned frown at the condition of Zephyr's face. Zephyr sat up and drank from the water first—"Not too fast," George warned him—and then had a few sips of juice. "I can get you something to eat if you're up to it."

Zephyr shook his head. "Not now. Thanks."

"I should take you to the hospital."

"No."

"I knew you'd say that." George stood looking at him, hands on hips. It wasn't exactly the way Superman stood, but it was close enough, and that made Zephyr bark a crazy-sounding laugh.

"What?" asked George.

"My hero. Superhero."

"Do you have a head injury? Concussion?"

"No."

"You have a pretty epic shiner." George's mouth was scrunched up and his pale eyebrows made a deep V.

"Looks worse than it is. My head is fine." Zephyr wasn't entirely certain that either of those statements was accurate, but he wanted them to be. He sure as hell didn't want to be prodded by judgmental doctors and nurses, or to take time and attention away from people who were really sick. Weren't all the hospitals full anyway, due to the pandemic?

He felt George tenderly push a strand of hair away from Zephyr's face. Fuck, his hair must be a matted, greasy mop right now. George managed not to look disgusted, however. "Rest, Zephyr."

A thread of panic worked its way through the numbness. "Where will you be?"

"In the next room. Bellow as loud as you want if you need anything—nobody but me will hear. When you wake up, we can try some food."

"And a shower."

"And a shower," George agreed.

Zephyr didn't truly know this man very well, and George barely knew him at all. It was stupid to feel safe here or to trust anyone when Zephyr didn't trust himself. But he *did* feel safe, and he fell asleep almost immediately.

"I THINK," George said, "you're supposed to ice a black eye." He handed Zephyr, still sprawled on the bed, a towel-wrapped pack.

"It's too late for that. This happened...." When had it happened? He'd entirely lost track of time. "A while ago," he finished weakly.

"Well, this is basically the only treatment Dr. Google gave me, so we might as well go with it. I don't think it can hurt. From what I've read, it's a good sign that your other eye looks fine. That means you're less likely to have a skull fracture."

That was good news, Zephyr supposed, even if it was hard to feel excited about it. He placed the ice pack against the bruise, and although the contact hurt at first, the injury quickly started feeling better.

"Thanks for the bed and the juice. I'm doing okay. I can go if you want."

George rolled his eyes. "Right. It's past midnight and you look like you've gone twelve rounds with Sugar Ray Robinson. You think I'm just gonna throw you out?"

Zephyr hadn't realized it was so late. How long had he slept? "Can I have that shower now?"

"You really don't like feeling grubby, do you?"

Although George said it lightly, Zephyr had to suppress a wince. Someone like George could never understand what it felt like for dirt to work its way so deeply into your body that all the scrubbing in the world couldn't get it out. At least if you cleaned off the outside parts, the visible parts, you could pretend it wasn't there.

With an assist from George, Zephyr got to his feet. But after only two steps, dizziness hit him. He swayed and would have fallen if George hadn't caught him. "It's not a concussion," he said to George's worried face. "I just haven't eaten in a while."

"Sit down, then. More OJ first."

The demand was reasonable enough that Zephyr complied, and in fact he did feel a little stronger and more clear-headed by the time the glass was empty. George had grown these oranges from trees his grandfather had planted, and he'd squeezed the juice himself. It tasted better than anything the fanciest restaurant could serve.

"I can stand now." He demonstrated by remaining upright on his own to the count of ten. "But if you're still worried, you can supervise my shower."

He'd meant it as a sort of challenge, or maybe just a way to make George flush that charming shade of pink. But George simply nodded. "Fine. I guess that's my sideline."

There wasn't much space in the bathroom for two grown men, but that was okay. George lent a steadying hand as Zephyr took off his T-shirt and again when he peeled off jeans so stiff with sweat and dirt that they could have stood by themselves. "I'll wash them," George offered.

"Don't bother. Toss 'em." Then he remembered something. "There might be some money in the jeans pocket, so check for that first."

"Sure. I still have your suitcase full of clothes from last time you were here."

At first Zephyr smiled because George had held on to the thing for over a year. Maybe he'd hoped that Zephyr would return. But then Zephyr remembered what was in there: designer outfits composed of delicate fabric, bright colors, and occasional touches of whimsy. Among them, a kelly-green corset top with tulle sleeves, a tight black minidress with turquoise splotches and asymmetrical cutouts, and a floral smocked peasant blouse. Clothing he'd worn because it made him feel sexy and interesting and comfortable in his own skin. Right now, though, all the designer labels in the world wouldn't make him feel that way.

"Can I just borrow something from you?" Zephyr asked.

"Sure."

George watched over him as he showered. Zephyr had never minded an audience, but this one was interesting because George focused on his face rather than on his wet naked body. Both of which were bruised, but George didn't seem put off by that. Nor did he seem turned on. He was simply… vigilant.

Wrapped in a fluffy white towel, Zephyr returned to the bedroom, where George handed him clean boxers, lightweight gray shorts, and a plain white tee. Everything had the light, pleasant smell of laundry detergent.

"Sorry," George said. "Not quite your usual. It's sort of more…."

"Butch. I look like I'm ready to hit the gym."

"I can—"

"It's fine. Thank you." Zephyr thought for a moment. "Could I ask you another favor? Brush out my hair."

That made George blush, which would have been intriguing to investigate if only Zephyr had more energy. Instead, he sat on the edge of the mattress while George carefully worked a comb through the tangles. Sometimes he pulled at the scalp a bit, but the slight sting was far outweighed by the warm comfort of the slow, gentle contact. It took a long time, and George must have been tired due to the late hour, but he didn't hurry or complain. In fact, his gaze went soft and fuzzy, as if he were in a trance. He even startled a little when Zephyr touched the hand holding the comb.

"Time for some food, maybe?" Zephyr suggested.

Like every other meal he'd eaten here, it was simple. Peanut butter and prickly pear jam on bread George said had been baked by a friend, frozen mixed veggies, and a big bowl of instant ramen. George didn't eat anything, and he didn't press for information while Zephyr ate. He talked a little about the business—the loan he'd taken out, the masks and sanitizer he sold in the gift shop, the success of his gardening efforts. It was clear that his precarious financial situation hadn't much improved after the end of the lockdown, but he didn't mention that.

A shower and a late-night snack wasn't much activity, but Zephyr was sagging as he slurped the last of his soup. George stood. "I'm going to put on fresh bedding."

"I can sleep on the couch."

"Nope." The word had an air of finality.

The bed was big and inviting, and Zephyr was grateful to sink into it. "Wait," he said when George started for the door. "We can share." He'd take credit if George assumed the offer was for George's sake, but in fact, it was entirely selfish. Zephyr felt fragile, ready to disintegrate at the edges. Company would help.

"I don't know if that's such a great idea." But George was wavering; Zephyr could tell.

"C'mon. You're wiped, and I feel like I could sleep for a week." This was not a lie. "We're just friends. Didn't you ever have a sleepover when you were a kid?" Zephyr hadn't, but he was familiar with the concept.

"We're not kids."

"For fuck's sake, George. You're cute, but I can control myself around you. I bet you can do the same. In fact, I bet you're the *master* of controlling yourself."

George heaved a sigh that sounded as if it came from the depths of the earth. When he returned from the bathroom a few minutes later, smelling minty, he'd stripped down to his boxers.

He was thinner than when Zephyr had seen him last, ribs too prominent under his pearly skin. He had no tattoos, which didn't surprise Zephyr, but the amount of hair on his chest and belly did. Not that he expected George to go in for much manscaping. Probably not a lot of places to get waxed in Conrad Junction.

Ogling would have been fun if Zephyr had been in a very different mood, but he'd also promised to keep things platonic. So he made a little show of yawning, rolling toward the edge of the bed, and adjusting the pillow underneath his head. George doused the light and, moving carefully, climbed in beside him.

"Darkness is weird for me," George said after a few minutes.

"Why?"

"No colors. That means I lose flavors too. Everything feels a little flat. When I was a kid, I got a night-light so I'd have at least a bit of color in the room, even if it was muted. But my brothers complained. They said they couldn't sleep because it was too bright. Dad threw it away." He sounded wistful and far away.

"Nobody's stopping you from getting one now."

"I guess not. But it's stupid. I don't need one."

He fell silent after that, and pretty soon, his breaths became slow and deep.

CHAPTER TWELVE

GEORGE WAS gone when Zephyr woke up. The bedroom had no windows and no clock, so it was impossible to tell what time it was, and the air-conditioner kept the temperature pleasantly cool. Although Zephyr considered falling back asleep, his empty stomach complained. He got up and took a shower—despite having showered the night before—and dug around in the dresser for clean clothes, eventually choosing a pale blue tee and black fleecy shorts. He didn't think George would mind. Because dealing with his hair felt like too much bother, he braided it loosely and secured it with a rubber band he found in the kitchen.

He also found freshly squeezed OJ in the fridge and a note on the counter telling him to help himself to whatever he wanted for breakfast. George wrote in neat block letters, as if he was making an explanatory sign for one of his exhibits.

Zephyr made himself toast and eggs, although he felt a little guilty because the cupboards were noticeably bare. He'd assumed George was skinny because of the tasting colors thing, but maybe he just couldn't afford to eat much. "Been there, done that," Zephyr muttered. He ate because he needed to regain some strength and clarity. He'd find a way to repay George.

The living room window was set high in the wall and faced the parking lot. Zephyr had to stand on his toes to see outside, but there wasn't much of a view. The sun glared fiercely overhead, glinting off vehicles in the lot: an SUV, an old sedan, and George's van with the store logo on the sides. There too was the dumpster where George had first found him. The first time Zephyr had needed rescuing.

"I'm such a fuckup."

After hesitating a little, Zephyr made his way to the gift shop. He expected to find George behind the counter, but instead a short lady with wiry gray curls gave him the eye. "We're asking people to wear masks," she said, accusation in her voice.

"I, uh…." He was fairly certain he'd been wearing one when he arrived, but he couldn't remember where he'd put it.

She pointed a long, coral-painted fingernail at a display rack. "Take one of those."

He grabbed randomly, ending up with green aliens. The purple trim and ear straps matched the bruises around his eye. "Is George—"

"He's working. We have visitors."

"Oh, okay. I'm Zephyr."

"I know." She laced her hands together on top of the counter and stared, but Zephyr didn't know what he was supposed to do. After a few moments she relented a bit. "My name is Judith Frank. I'm a very old friend of George's and I volunteer here."

He tried to smile but lacked the stamina to be charming. "Nice to meet you." And then, because the silence grated on him, "Is there some work I can do to help out?"

"Do you know anything about minerology, paleontology, geology, or meteoritics?"

"I thought it was meteorology."

"Meteorologists study the weather. And I'll take that as a no."

He shifted his feet uncomfortably. "I can clean stuff. Or move stuff. Or… I helped George in his garden once. I could maybe do that again."

She softened a little, perhaps because she saw that he was sincerely trying. "There's always work in the garden. But it's very hot out already."

"I'll stay hydrated."

For some reason, that brought out her first smile. She came around the counter, revealing her lemon-hued Crocs, and walked to the shelves. She grabbed a souvenir water bottle and a woven straw hat with a pale pink ribbon around the crown. "It's a woman's hat. We don't have men's, just women and children."

Zephyr took it and slapped it on his head. "This will do fine." He wondered if George had told this woman that his houseguest liked to cross-dress. Until the hat, he'd been pretty butch.

After filling the bottle from the water cooler in George's office, he waved at Judith before walking through a narrow door into the courtyard. There were other ways to access the garden from elsewhere in the building, but during Zephyr's last visit, they'd been locked. George had said he wanted to reopen the garden to the public someday, but it hadn't been ready before the pandemic, and Zephyr didn't know if it met George's standards now.

Probably not, he concluded once he was out there. George had clearly done a lot of work. The scrubbier, untended portions had shrunk and signs with descriptive markers had been stuck in front of many plants in the more orderly sections. The citrus trees looked healthy, laden with unripe fruit. Nearby, the labels on some new shrubs identified them as pomegranates. Some of the dino statues were freshly repainted, and benches had been relocated to more favorable locations. But the pathways looked untended, and against one wall was a tangle of hoses, roughly stacked metal pieces, bits of weathered wood, and various gardening tools.

The building's mask mandate probably didn't extend to the vacant outdoor courtyard, so Zephyr took his off and set it on a bench along with the water bottle. Then he stood for a moment, trying to decide what to do. When he'd been in the garden before, George had been there to instruct him. On his own, Zephyr couldn't tell the difference between a desirable plant and a weed, especially in this climate where all the natives were as tough as thugs.

Well, maybe he could organize the supplies a little, making them easier to access. He tackled the hoses first, unsnarling them and then coiling them neatly. He was going to start in on the wood, but he got a splinter almost immediately, so he focused on the tools instead. A hoe, shovels—or maybe spades; he was vague about the difference—a couple of long-bladed clippers, a long metal pole with a blade at one end, a giant fork thing he thought might be some kind of rake, a—

Suddenly he felt light-headed, the sun too bright in his uninjured eye.

He started back toward the bench that held his water, but along the way someone pulled the ground out from under him like a magician with a tablecloth. He fell onto his hands and knees, stabbing his left hand on a bed of needles. When he tried to get up, the world swayed. Better to stay down, then. His leg muscles cramped, his heart raced, and it felt as if a herd of stegosauruses was stampeding through his skull. Sweat stung his eye. He—

"Dammit!" Strong arms seized his biceps. "Can you stand? You need to get out of the sun."

Zephyr allowed himself to be tugged to his feet and guided away. "My water," he said, trying to detour to the bench, but George ignored him and pulled him inside. A few moments later, Zephyr collapsed onto George's couch. The air-conditioning made him shiver.

"Wait here," George barked before rushing away. Less than a minute later he returned and thrust a plastic bottle at Zephyr. "Gatorade."

Although Zephyr wasn't a big fan of the stuff, he took the bottle and sipped at it under George's watchful glare. Surprisingly soon, his head began to clear and his tight muscles eased. "Thanks," he managed to say.

"You're supposed to be recovering from... yesterday. What the hell were you doing giving yourself heat exhaustion? What if I hadn't come outside? You could have died."

Although nothing was funny, Zephyr laughed. "I wanted to be helpful."

"Dying isn't helpful."

Zephyr laughed again and drank more Gatorade. After a moment, George sat beside him. He didn't say anything.

Until now, Zephyr had never noticed how loud the fan was. It wasn't an unpleasant sound, just steady. He often favored sounds like that: truck engines and the hum of tires on asphalt, radio static, running water. They could be a blanket or a camouflage.

"Don't you have to work?" he finally asked.

"Judith will let me know if she gets overwhelmed with visitors." George snorted. "And if pigs fly."

"I don't think she likes me."

"She doesn't like anyone at first. She's suspicious by nature. But she and my mom were good friends. And she has volunteered here for years and wouldn't accept pay, even when I could afford it."

Zephyr nodded. And then, because George still seemed upset, he said, "I'm sorry. I was just trying to organize your supplies a bit. You've made headway on the garden since I was last here."

"Not as much as I'd like. I mean, I'm glad we were allowed to reopen, but that means my only free hours are after dark. It's cooler then but a lot harder to see what I'm doing."

George sounded so defeated and exhausted that Zephyr reached to pat his knee with his free hand. But as soon as he made contact, he hissed.

"What is it?" George was immediately on alert.

"I think I landed on a cactus." Zephyr was trying to inspect his hand, but George grabbed his wrist so he could look instead. Whatever he saw made him sigh, release Zephyr, and stand up. Without explanation, he stomped to the bathroom. After some clattering, he returned with a comically large first aid box and a couple of folded washcloths.

"Exactly how many people are you planning to doctor?" Zephyr asked.

"Just you. Repeatedly, apparently." Which was a fair point. "I have to buy well-stocked kits for the business—you never know when a guest is going to have something catastrophic happen. It was cheaper to buy several of those and keep one in here."

George reclaimed his spot on the couch, spread a cloth on his thigh, and removed a pair of tweezers and magnifying glass from the kit. He gestured for Zephyr to give him his hand. Then he bent over the palm and began picking cactus spines out of the skin.

"You've done this before," Zephyr observed.

"I've spent almost my whole life in the desert. People get attacked by cactuses surprisingly often. Once my sister was chasing me through the gardens and she did a face-plant onto a spinystar. She's lucky she didn't take out an eye. Served her right for chasing me, though." He pulled out a particularly large spike, peered at it, and put it onto the other cloth, which he'd spread on the end table.

"What's your sister's name?"

"Mary, after Mary Anning. She was a paleontologist in the early nineteenth century. Um, the first Mary, not my sister. My Mary is a mammography tech or, as she likes to say, a professional boob squisher." Still squinting through the magnifying glass, George smiled fondly.

"Does she live around here?"

"Nope. She's in Wichita."

"You said you have a brother?"

George gave him a quick look. "Two. James is the oldest. He's an actuary in Carlsbad. Al is closest in age to me. He's in Oregon. He used to be a nurse, but the pandemic burned him out and he's going to start law school soon." George chuckled. "He's named after Alcide Dessalines d'Orbigny and, boy oh boy, does he hate it when anyone calls him Alcide. Which I used to do pretty regularly when we were kids, so it was usually him instead of Mary chasing me. That was good because he didn't hit as hard."

Zephyr wanted to ask why none of George's siblings seemed to be helping him with the business, but he held his tongue. A better question might be why George stuck to the place so stubbornly. It would have been a lot easier for him to give up long ago and to move someplace where he had more prospects—which would be pretty much anywhere.

"Your parents were pretty serious about the whole rocks-and-fossils theme."

"Says the guy named after a wind." George shot him a sly grin. "But yeah. I mean, Dad was. Our names were his idea. Mom said she was fine as long as none of us were juniors. Her father was, like, the fifth person in a row to carry his name, and she didn't like that at all."

It was interesting. When George spoke about his family, his tone was warm, as if even the memories of being beat up by his sister were happy ones. But there were some unexplored layers there, some frays around the edges—not that it was Zephyr's place to pick at loose threads. Maybe he just wanted confirmation that other people's childhoods had been miserable too.

The two of them remained quiet while George removed the rest of the needles. It seemed to take a long time, and staying still wasn't easy for Zephyr. But people had rarely taken such care over his well-being, and he liked the gentle way George touched him.

"Well, that's about as much as I can do." George set aside the tweezers and magnifier. "Time for phase two."

"Which is?"

With a flourish, like a magician pulling a rabbit from a hat, George held up a plastic bottle of Elmer's glue from the kit.

"Are you going to reattach all those needles to the cactus?" Zephyr asked, amused.

"Nope. Did you ever do that thing in school where you poured glue on your skin, let it dry, and then peeled it off? I don't know why, but that was always very satisfying."

Zephyr shrugged. His school memories were few and fragmented.

"Well, now's your chance." George squeezed a thick layer of the stuff over Zephyr's palm and fingers. "When you peel off the dried glue, it'll take the smaller barbs with it."

"Clever!"

George put the glue away and snapped the kit shut. "Wasn't my idea. Al got too cozy with a jumping cholla once, and Mom must've used a gallon of Elmer's that time. For weeks afterward, Mary and I pretended to get stuck to Al. He didn't much like that either."

Zephyr looked at the little pool of white, which was already going clear around the edges. His hand still rested on George's thigh. "You guys were close?"

George thought about that for a moment. "Yeah, I guess so. We didn't have much choice. The schools around here are pretty dinky, and whenever we weren't in school, we were all together here at the museum." He stood up suddenly and began collecting supplies with jerky movements. "When it's dry, just peel it off over a sink or trash can, then wash with the antibiotic soap in the kitchen. If you feel like you're having an allergic reaction, there's Benadryl in the bathroom."

"Okay."

"And please—stay inside and don't overexert yourself."

"Okay," Zephyr repeated. In fact, he thought a nap night be nice. Christ, how many hours of sleep did he need? But just thinking about it brought on a jaw-cracking yawn. Fine. He'd take advantage of a nice big bed while he had one available.

THERE EVIDENTLY had been money in Zephyr's jeans pocket. At least that memory had been correct. All that cash was now sitting there on the kitchen counter, held together by a bulldog clip that George must have provided. And it was a lot of cash: a couple thousand bucks in hundreds, which he'd snuck away from Brandon and hidden in case he needed it. Too bad that when he *did* need cash, he'd been too fucked-up to use it. He could have made the trip to Conrad Junction a lot more comfortably. But maybe that was a good thing now, because aside from a lot of instant ramen, the fridge and cabinets were damned near empty.

Yes, Zephyr had promised to stay inside. But this was... well, almost an emergency. Sort of. He drank the rest of the Gatorade and a glass of water to boot, found his sunglasses to hide his shiner, and peeled one of the bills off the stack. When he left the apartment and crossed the parking lot, he tried to stay out of sight of the gift shop doors. He didn't want George spying him.

As far as he could tell, the town's only grocery opportunity was the mini-mart attached to the big gas station. Although it was only about a block away, the sun was relentless, and he was dizzy by the time he stumbled into the air-conditioned oasis. The big guy behind the counter watched him suspiciously but didn't say anything.

The shelves predictably contained a lot of snack foods, but there were also a few staples like breakfast cereals and canned soup. Zephyr grabbed a plastic basket from near the door and filled it with anything that wasn't quite junk food: canned tuna, a quart of milk, sliced cheese and lunch meat, a loaf of bread, a half-carton of eggs, soup, chili with beans, crackers, noodles and tomato sauce, and potato chips. The final item was, strictly speaking, junk food, but that was okay. He also grabbed a couple pints of ice cream and a selection of candy bars. As the clerk rang everything up, Zephyr wondered what all the vivid packaging would taste like to George. He hoped that none of the colors were distasteful enough to put George off the food.

Zephyr managed to sneak back to the apartment without George noticing. It was nearly six o'clock by then, and he was fairly certain that was when Fossil Galaxy closed. He poked around the kitchen, feeling oddly domestic. He knew how to cook basic stuff—he'd been improvising meals, often under subpar conditions, since he was a toddler—but he wasn't exactly Jamie Oliver. He set a big pot of water on to boil, cut a couple of slices off what appeared to be a loaf of homemade sourdough, and poured a half bag of frozen mixed veggies into a bowl to nuke.

He was just setting the table when George entered the apartment and stopped in his tracks. "Dinner?" George said.

"I've heard it called that."

"You're supposed to be resting."

"I've slept about twenty hours today. I can manage."

George frowned at the empty jar of spaghetti sauce on the counter. "You went to the store."

"And got back, all in one piece." Zephyr would have been irritated at George's fussing, except he found it sweet that someone gave a crap. "C'mon, I'm hungry. Aren't you?"

Over dinner, George softened. Having a full stomach probably helped. He told a couple of funny stories about recent visitors and then mentioned Judith. "She made this bread," he said, waving his slice for emphasis. "She's one of those people who started baking during lockdown and then kept with it—at a faster rate than she and her husband can eat. Especially now that she's toying with eating low-carb. I reap the benefits."

"That's a good deal."

"Yeah. Sorry if she was kinda harsh to you today. She gets protective. She's known me my whole life."

Zephyr wondered what that would be like. He'd never stayed anywhere long enough to become that close to people. Or maybe his personality was to blame; he certainly wasn't kind and sweet like George. Zephyr looked out for himself.

George insisted on doing the dishes, then joined Zephyr on the couch, each with a book. It was as if no time had passed, as if Zephyr hadn't fled with Brandon. Even his bookmark was where he'd left it inside the pages of *Dune*.

At some point he glanced up from the book to see George staring ahead at nothing, his blue eyes troubled. "Are you okay?" Zephyr asked softly.

George startled slightly. "Yeah. Sorry. Just… thinking."

"About what?"

"All the problems I can't solve."

That made Zephyr laugh. "I never do that. What's the point? I just move on and let them solve themselves."

Shaking his head, George tapped his own left eye. It took Zephyr a moment to understand what he meant. "It's just a bruise. It'll be gone soon."

"Until he gives you another one. Or worse." George looked so distressed that Zephyr put down the book and moved closer to comfort him.

"Don't worry about it. I'm like a watch in those old Timex commercials—I can take a licking and keep on ticking. And anyway, I'm not going back to Brandon." Until the words left his mouth, he hadn't realized he'd reached that decision. It felt good.

George heaved a huge sigh. "Good. That bastard doesn't deserve you. He should be in prison."

"Oh, he should be in prison for a *lot* of things. Just his driving habits alone could get him locked up—he's hardly ever sober behind the wheel. But it's not gonna happen. He has connections. As for the deserving part… I'm still pretty, when my face isn't fucked-up. I still have that going for me. But that's about it. I'm not a great catch, George." Sometimes Brandon had called him used goods. That pretty much nailed it.

"Bull. But I'm not going to give you a hard time over it. Sometimes people decide something's the right thing to do, and by the time they realize their mistake, they're trapped. I'm really glad you were strong enough to get yourself free. That takes a lot of courage."

Nobody had ever called Zephyr strong or courageous. On his good days, he thought of himself as resourceful and resilient. He didn't know what the rest of the world thought of him—if they managed to think of him at all. But George was gazing earnestly at him, and even as Zephyr watched, that delicious blush colored George's cheeks.

Without pausing to second-guess himself, Zephyr leaned in and kissed him.

He'd been wanting to do that almost since they'd first met, and at times the impulse to see what reaction he could tease out of George had nearly overcome him. But George deserved better than to be toyed with, so Zephyr had resisted. Until now.

He expected George to be shocked, and in fact, George froze. But then instead of pulling away—or pushing Zephyr—he wrapped his arms around Zephyr's body and threw himself wholeheartedly into the kiss.

CHAPTER THIRTEEN

GEORGE WAS a good kisser. That surprised Zephyr, who'd thought he might be hesitant and a bit fumbling. However, he turned out to be tender—not ramming his tongue down Zephyr's throat or smooshing their lips together too hard—and thorough. He took his time, licking and nuzzling, exerting just enough pressure to keep things interesting, and opening his own mouth to Zephyr's tongue with a deep moan.

Zephyr was accustomed to feeling desirable, but most men went after him greedily, as if trying to get their dollars' worth at a buffet. George treated him instead like one of those fancy gourmet dishes served in tiny portions and savored slowly. And when Zephyr leaned in harder and took the lead, George didn't struggle to stay in charge as so many men did. In fact, George leaned back against the couch cushion and opened up his posture, allowing Zephyr to clamber onto his lap, press their torsos together, and intensify the making out.

Another nice thing: George didn't instantly start squeezing Zephyr's ass. He put one hand on Zephyr's waist and softly stroked his back with the other. And that turned out to be exactly the thing that drove Zephyr wild. He had to stop himself from grinding their groins together and tearing off his clothes. Which, if he'd thought about it, weren't even his.

That last thought made him go still. He owed this man so much. Panting, he leaned his forehead against George's. And although George was also breathing heavily, he didn't protest the break.

"Wow," Zephyr said after a moment, his voice a little shaky.

"Yeah."

"You're not going to tell me I should take it easy?" Zephyr ran teasing fingers through George's strawberry blond hair. He liked the color and, free of product, the soft texture. And the fact that, since the pandemic began, George had been having Judith cut his hair.

"I need to ask you something." George gave a small sigh. "The first time we met, when you were showering, you told me you owed me a little show. Do you remember that?"

"No, but it sounds like something I'd say."

"So… this." George gave Zephyr's arms a gentle squeeze. "Is it something you want to do or something you think you owe me?"

It was a fair question, and George clearly didn't intend it to be harsh, but it made Zephyr ache. He pulled back a little so he could look straight into George's eyes. "I want to."

This time George's sigh sounded relieved. "Me too. I mean… obviously."

Zephyr tried a little wiggle. "We could continue."

"Your face is still bruised from whatever that asshole did to you."

"I'm not fragile. I bounce back fast."

"I can tell," George said with a little smile. "But the thing is, I don't do… casual. I envy people who can, but I'm just not made for it."

That made perfect sense, given everything Zephyr knew about this man. And Jesus, George knew practically nothing about him, aside from the fact that he occasionally fucked up his life and needed a temporary refuge. But George's assumption hurt.

"How do you know I'm trying for casual?" Zephyr demanded. He dismounted from George's lap and scooted to the far end of the couch, then pulled up his legs and wrapped his arms around them.

"Because you are so much on the rebound that you haven't stopped bouncing. Besides, what are you going to do—move to the Junction?"

"You don't think I belong here?"

"Of course you don't!" Color had appeared on George's cheeks, and it wasn't from embarrassment. "You're beautiful and interesting and way too smart to let yourself get stuck in the middle of nowhere! The Junction is for misfits and weirdos and people with nowhere else to go. You have the whole world open to you—and you don't need goddamn Brandon for that either."

For a moment, Zephyr was too taken aback to respond. He was the boy who wore dresses, the kid who fucked for money or, when he was desperate enough, for a ride or a decent meal. People had been calling him strange since he was a child—when they weren't calling him something worse. Yet here was George, claiming Zephyr was too ordinary for Conrad Junction and possessed too much potential.

"So come with me," Zephyr suggested. He meant it.

George shot to his feet. "I can't!" His hands were balled at his sides, and now his fair skin had gone blotchy.

"Why not? It's like you're out in the middle of a lake, slowly drowning, and instead of trying to swim to shore, you just tread water. You're going to go under, George." Maybe it wasn't the best metaphor here in the desert, but Zephyr wasn't a wordsmith. "You've carried this burden long enough. You can walk away. Out there, away from this place, employers are desperate for good people. You'd find a job with no problem."

"No." It wasn't clear which part of Zephyr's assertions George was denying.

"Look at you! You work all the time and you're starving anyway. Seventy, eighty hours a week and all you get is cheap ramen." This was so frustrating. Why couldn't George *see*?

But George shook his head. "This is my home. Three generations of Harlows have lived here. And my grandfather's dreams, my dad's hopes… I'm supposed to just forget about them?"

"What about your hopes and dreams?" Zephyr stood up too, and moved right into George's space. "For God's sake, does Fossil Galaxy bring you joy? If it wasn't for the family legacy, would you even want to be here? This place isn't *your* dream—it's your nightmare. It's time to wake up!"

All the color drained from George's face, and for a split second, Zephyr was certain he was about to be hit. Again. But George only shook his head, took a step backward, and then turned and rushed out of the apartment and into the gift shop.

Zephyr sagged with regret. He'd opened his goddamn big mouth and ruined a good thing. The only *really* good thing he'd had in a long while. Because in addition to being his savior, George had been a friend, and Zephyr had always been woefully short of those.

He found his own clothes neatly folded atop the dryer and changed into them. He pocketed a few bills from the clipped stack, leaving the rest. For a few moments he contemplated his shiny suitcase. But he couldn't imagine wearing any of those outfits, not now, and the luggage would only weigh him down. He slipped into the pair of cheap flip-flops he didn't remember buying.

He started toward the exterior door.

"Don't go."

Zephyr whirled around to find George hurrying back into the apartment, his face tight with worry.

"I have to—"

"I'm sorry I yelled at you," said George.

That made Zephyr blink. "*You're* apologizing to *me*?"

"Yeah. But please don't go."

Zephyr took a few deep breaths in hopes of steadying himself. "I was just really nasty to you."

"You weren't. You were upset because my choices don't make any sense to you. I get that. I've had similar conversations with my own siblings, who really ought to understand."

"I *don't* understand," Zephyr said slowly. "But that doesn't give me the right…. You didn't hassle me about Brandon, even though I'm sure you don't get that whole mess any better than I get yours. I don't know when to shut my face sometimes." He laughed hollowly. "Now you can probably see why Brandon loses his cool with me."

George marched over and set a hand on Zephyr's shoulder. "You never deserve to get hit. You know that, right?"

Zephyr nodded, but only because he didn't want to argue. In fact, he was fairly certain that sometimes he *did* deserve it. He was good at pushing people's buttons—the most recent scene being a perfect example—and often got a perverse satisfaction out of pushing them. If he got walloped, he had nobody to blame but himself.

"I could go for some tea," George said. "I have some herbal stuff a friend makes for me. No caffeine. It's relaxing. Want some?"

THEY ENDED up back on the couch, tea mugs in hand and with a no-man's-land between them. "I'm not usually much of a tea guy, but this is nice," Zephyr said.

"Lavender, mint, calendula, and some other stuff. Debra, the mail carrier, makes it special for me because the yellow color tastes like honey."

"You have some good friends."

George beamed. "I do. They're great people, and they help me out a lot."

For once, Zephyr didn't just blurt out a question. He sat on it for a bit, trying to phrase it inoffensively. He didn't want to sound accusatory— he was genuinely curious. "You're the youngest Harlow, right?"

"Yep. Al's two years older than me."

"When your dad died and your mom needed help, how come you were the one to step up to the plate and not them?"

If George was upset, he didn't show it. "They had more going on. All I had to do was drop out and move seventy miles. They had careers, spouses. James had a kid already."

"You had a boyfriend. And a good chunk of a college degree."

"Yeah, but it wasn't the same. Anyway, none of them feel the way I do about this place. I think they'd all be perfectly happy if it went belly-up." He sounded sad and weary and maybe a little hurt. "They have no love for the Junction, that's for sure. They all escaped as soon as they could. They don't even come back for visits."

That was really shitty. With George chained here, it likely meant that he never saw any of them. But Zephyr couldn't truly blame the other Harlows. He just wished George could follow their example.

"Do you regret not finishing that degree?" Zephyr asked.

George's expression briefly tightened. "I guess," he said with an unconvincing shrug. "Maybe someday I'll get a chance to go back to school."

Suddenly, George brightened. "Hey! You haven't even looked at the fossil you sent me. Want to see it on display?"

They traversed the gift shop, which was subtly illuminated by the bright lights of the nearby Burger King. George clicked on the lights in the exhibit halls. The displays looked the same as when Zephyr last saw them: cared for, yet old-fashioned and lonely. Relics.

They stopped in the invertebrates room, where the crinoid was on prominent display atop a glass-covered column. A sign explained the fossil and had color drawings of what the creatures had looked like when alive. "You didn't put it in with the ET stuff?" Zephyr teased.

"I considered it. But Dad would be rolling in his grave. He really tried his best to achieve scientific accuracy. When he could, I mean."

"Well, it looks good here."

"It does. It's a nice addition. Thank you."

Zephyr smiled. He hadn't been sure that George could use it, but he'd spied the specimen in a shop window one afternoon after briefly slipping away from the hotel and Brandon, who was mired in some complex business deal. Zephyr had walked past the shop, but two blocks later, he'd turned on his heel and went back. The shopkeeper claimed it was museum-quality. Zephyr had enjoyed imagining George's expression when the surprise package arrived.

He was going to suggest that George finish the tour that Brandon had long ago interrupted. But then George yawned hugely, reminding

Zephyr that not everyone got to spend all day snoring in bed. He faked a yawn of his own. "I guess I could use more rest."

They walked back toward the apartment. At night, Fossil Galaxy was a little spooky. It wasn't so much the dead things on display, because they'd been gone for a really long time, and Zephyr wasn't too worried about being haunted by the ghosts of trilobites. But there were the dinosaur statues and the murals, and the signs hand-written by George's grandfather.

"What was Wally like?" Zephyr asked as they neared the gift shop.

George stopped, expression thoughtful. "I don't remember him very well. I was really young when he died. My brother James once told me that he never once saw grandpa being still—he was always moving, always working. I get the sense that after surviving the Depression and the war, he was driven to hang on to what he'd built."

And apparently the trait had been passed down through the generations, but Zephyr didn't point that out.

Things got awkward between them when they returned to the apartment and started getting ready for bed. George started carrying his pillow to the couch, but Zephyr stopped him. "We can still share."

"I don't think that's a good idea."

"I'm a grown man, and I can—despite what you may assume—control myself. I'm not going to throw myself at you."

George looked at him solemnly. "Wasn't you I was worried about." But he put the pillow back. He wore sweatpants and a T-shirt to bed, which was overkill, but Zephyr held his tongue. And really, George shouldn't have worried, because moments after he lay down, he was snoring softly.

Not surprisingly, however, Zephyr remained awake for a long time. Now he knew what George felt like, what he tasted like. How he reacted when he was angry. And while part of Zephyr wanted desperately to cling to this amiable, accepting man, another part of him clanged danger signals. George scared him. Not because of his temper—Zephyr was well accustomed to being on the receiving end of much more severe rage. In fact, the danger came from George's kindness, which threatened to trap Zephyr like the amber-encased beetle in George's collection. That bug had taken too many steps into something appealing and sweet, and it had never been able to escape.

Fuck. It was time to move on.

CHAPTER FOURTEEN

ZEPHYR AWOKE to the gentle clatter of dishes in the kitchen. It was one of the nicest sounds in the world—safe and comforting. Pushing down his unease from the night before, he listened for a while, until the smell of frying eggs hit him. Then he slipped into yesterday's borrowed shorts and padded into the kitchen.

"I would have made breakfast," he said.

George turned from the stove, spatula in hand. "I like cooking."

"What do eggs taste like?" Zephyr asked, coming closer. "I mean, the colors. Obviously, I know what they taste like on the tongue."

"White is flavorless. The yellow depends on the shade. These are cantaloupe. My friend Seth used to keep chickens, and his eggs had much brighter yolks. They tasted like birthday cake—just like your skirt the first time we met."

"You remember what I was wearing?"

"It was a memorable night."

Inexplicably pleased, Zephyr grabbed a pair of plates from the cupboard and brought them over. George transferred the eggs onto them, along with toasted sourdough, and they both sat down at the table. Orange juice and milk already awaited them.

"This is nice," George said. "I don't usually eat much breakfast, and never with company." Then he tilted his head a bit. "Can I ask you a personal question?"

Zephyr tensed. But Jesus, George had poured out most of his life history. The least Zephyr could do was listen. He could always avoid answering. "Sure."

"What's your last name? Or are you like Cher or Bono?"

A burst of relieved laughter escaped. "Steiber. I never use it, though. Zephyr Steiber sounds dumb. And yes, that is my legal birth name." A social worker had once urged him to change his name to something more conventional, claiming it would improve Zephyr's future job prospects. Zephyr told her exactly what she could do with her future job prospects. His first name and his pretty face had been the only good things his mother gave him.

George smiled and finished his breakfast.

"I'll clean up," Zephyr offered. "Is there anything else I can do to help today? And for fuck's sake, don't tell me to take it easy."

"Judith will be in. Ask her. I have to do a bunch of paperwork." He didn't look happy about that, but then, who was ever thrilled about paperwork?

"Um, can I borrow more clothes?"

"Sure. Help yourself to anything that fits."

Most of George's stuff would probably be a size or two too big, but Zephyr didn't mind. He liked wearing George's things—it was a little like wearing a costume, as if, for a little while, he could pretend to be a responsible person with a stable history and friends and family who loved him. But he also wanted to test the waters a little. "What if I wore my own clothes—the ones in the suitcase? Would that bother you?"

George looked genuinely puzzled. "Why would I be bothered by that?"

"Do you want your friends and customers to see a guy walking around in dresses and high heels?"

"My friends wouldn't care—well, some of them would probably admire your fashion sense. And if visitors are upset by it, they can leave."

"You need the business."

"Not that badly." George frowned. "Seriously, wear whatever you want. I don't exactly have a dress code, and it's not like I'm in any position to give people advice on clothing. I tend to choose things that taste pleasant. My shirt today is spearmint." He patted the pale blue fabric.

As far as Zephyr could tell, George was being entirely honest; he truly wasn't bothered by Zephyr's preferred attire. And that was unusual. Plenty of men thought Zephyr looked sexy in skirts and blouses, but if they were going to be seen with him in public, they wanted him to either wear men's clothes or try to pass as a woman. Being seen with a man in frilly things embarrassed them.

Zephyr found himself wanting to kiss George again, but that would be a mistake. "Go slay your paperwork, Saint George."

ZEPHYR WORE a pair of George's khaki shorts cinched tight with his own leopard-print belt and topped with a Fossil Galaxy tank top. He stuck to the flip-flops he'd been wearing when he journeyed here, and tied his hair into a neat ponytail. Nothing to be done about the bruising on his face, but oh well. He wasn't going to be walking the catwalk today.

Judith greeted him with less skepticism this time. "I've been told not to send you to the garden again. I warned you about staying hydrated."

"Yes, you did. Do you have any indoor chores for me?"

She set him to unpacking masks, shirts, and other souvenirs, and putting them on the shelves. When he experimentally rearranged shot glasses into what he thought was a more enticing display, she even nodded approvingly and gave him permission to move other things around as well. That turned out to be a surprisingly enjoyable activity. She also had him mop the floor, which quickly got dirty when guests tracked the desert in with them, and he washed the inside of the glass doors and display windows. Her job was to ring up purchases and supervise him, while George stayed in his office except when guests wanted a tour of the exhibits.

There weren't many guests.

When lunchtime rolled around, Judith produced a casserole— something involving green beans and hamburger—with plenty for all three of them. They ate gathered around the sales counter, with Judith and George trading stories about customers, like the man who'd wanted to know what kind of dinosaurs Noah took on his ark, or the teenage girl who was trying to convince her parents that a geology degree would be a good career plan.

Zephyr realized he was smiling and laughing a lot, and the knot of tension he usually carried in his shoulders loosened a bit. He felt as if he'd magically stepped into a TV sitcom in which he was an ordinary guy hanging out with his coworkers.

The afternoon went by quickly, and after closing, Zephyr finally got that tour of the vertebrate collection. There were a lot more dino statues in that gallery, plus a fun exhibit where visitors could compare their footprints to those of various extinct animals. George said that had been his father's idea. And there were bones, of course, plus a lot of teeth. Zephyr decided he preferred the outer-space room, but this one was good too.

Dinner was the rest of Judith's casserole and nuked potatoes with cheese, followed by dishwashing, laundry, and collapsing on the couch with books. Two feet of empty cushion stretched between them, but it was still really nice and comfortable and domestic.

Which was why all of the previous night's fears had descended on him again. Zephyr's heart began to race, as if he were being chased by one of George's dinosaurs.

George looked up from his book with a concerned expression. Could he hear Zephyr's panic? "What's wrong?" he asked.

"I need to go," Zephyr blurted as he jumped to his feet.

George stood too, allowing his book to drop. "Go where? What's happening?" He scanned the room, but of course there were no visible dangers.

"I just… I need to leave."

"Did I do something wrong?"

"No!" Zephyr almost sobbed. "It's not… I've leeched off you long enough. Again. You've got your own issues to deal with and you don't need… me."

George set a gentle hand on his arm. "You're contributing, not leeching. Also, I like having you here. You're good company. And dammit, Zephyr, I said I wasn't going to harp on this, but Brandon is trouble. Please don't go back to him."

"I won't." Zephyr meant that. Whatever pull Brandon had previously had on him was gone now. "I'm done with him for good."

"I'm glad to hear that. But where were you intending to go?"

Nothing came to Zephyr's mind. Nothing at all, which was stupid. He could head anywhere in the country by hitching a ride with a trucker or taking the stack of money and buying a bus or train ticket. He'd even have enough cash to survive for a while. *Say something!* he urged himself silently. *Phoenix. Pittsburgh. Dubuque. Tallahassee. Boise.* But for once, his mouth stubbornly refused to work. He shrugged instead.

With his hand still soft on Zephyr's arm, George's face hardened. "No destination, no plans. Maybe you're ready to eighty-six Brandon, but if you leave here now, you're going to end up with someone like him. Or like whoever beat the shit out of you the night you first came here."

Although Zephyr jerked his arm away, he didn't argue with George's assertion. "That's my own fault," he said quietly. "I won't expect you to rescue me again."

"That's not the point! It's not the rescuing that bothers me—it's the fact that you need rescuing. You're still mostly a great big mystery to me, Zephyr Steiber, but I care about you. I don't want you getting hurt."

Fuck. And there it was—Zephyr had already gone too far. He'd let someone care. "There are all sorts of things you don't know about me."

George barked a laugh. "That's a slight understatement."

"Well, let me tell you a few. I dropped out of school in eighth grade. I've been busted I don't know how many times. I don't have a driver's license, a Social Security card, or any of that shit. I've never had a for-real legit job. I've been turning tricks since… I don't know when. Forever. I turn tricks dressed like a girl because I'm more marketable that way. My thing with Brandon was more of the same on a larger scale—I was his full-time whore, not his damn boyfriend." He backed up a little and spread his arms. "*This* is what you've let into your home."

He didn't know how he was supposed to feel after that outburst. Relieved? Angry? Afraid? But he was none of those. When he reached deep inside, what he felt was far worse: a big, cold emptiness, a void that would someday consume him entirely.

As for George, he didn't step back. And thankfully he didn't look disgusted or awash in pity—either of which would have devastated Zephyr. "Those are things you've done, not who you are."

"What difference does that make?"

"All the difference." George chewed his lip for a moment. "Honestly, some of it I sort of guessed. And anyway, all of that only reinforces my opinion of you."

"Which is?" Zephyr spat, steeling himself.

"You're incredibly strong. I've never once heard you complain, not even when you've been in bad shape. You haven't given up, even when things looked grim—you dust yourself off and keep going. You're generous with your time and your money. You're unique, and I mean that in a good way. You're obviously smart and resourceful."

The first thing that struck Zephyr was that, although George had listed a lot of things, he'd never once mentioned Zephyr's looks. Those were the compliments he normally got: *You're gorgeous, babe*. Nobody had ever called him strong or resourceful, and they sure as hell had never called him smart.

"Eighth grade, remember? And I repeated seventh grade."

"I didn't say you were educated; I said you were smart."

"Fine. I'm fucking Einstein. That doesn't change what I've done."

George's jaw was set. "Do you think I'm some kind of princess who's spent her life locked in a tower? For God's sake, almost everyone here in the Junction would struggle to fit in anywhere else. That's why they landed here. Some are addicts and ex-cons, and some have mental health issues. Some of them are just plain old weird. None of those things make them any less valuable. They're my friends, Zephyr, the people I care about. They're the ones who keep me going."

Zephyr took a moment to think about that. "The ones who bring you bread and tamales."

"And run errands on my behalf. And volunteer at my business when I can't afford to pay them. Or they just stop by regularly to chat with me because they know I rarely get out."

Zephyr was wavering. He still felt an urgent need to run away before he caused any damage here, before he was too badly hurt. But he desperately wanted to believe in George. Wanted… a friend.

Maybe George sensed this. He moved another step closer. "Look, it's strange. I first met you almost two years ago, but we've spent very little time together. All I've known of your life are a few guesses and a couple of crumbs you've let slip. What has mattered to me are the parts of you I've seen—and I like those parts a lot." He blushed and chuckled, ducking his head. "And I didn't intend that to come out as a sex thing."

Zephyr laughed too, which felt good. "You have seen pretty much all of my parts." Then he sighed. "I can't hide out here forever. My money's not going to last long, and you definitely don't need another drain on your finances."

"You're a friend, not a drain. And you're not that expensive. Anyway, it doesn't have to be forever. You're going to get sick of me and this place soon enough, I'm sure. But stay until you have a plan. Until you have somewhere else to go."

Although Zephyr wasn't sure he'd *ever* have those things, he nodded and slowly returned to the couch. George went back to his spot too. They picked up their books—they'd both lost their places and had to flip pages to find them—and settled in.

ACCORDING TO George's weather app, it was 115 degrees Fahrenheit.

"But it's a dry heat," George said with a grin.

"So's an oven."

They stood in the gift shop and gazed out at the sun-beaten parking lot. Although the air-conditioners were keeping up, just looking outdoors was enough to make Zephyr feel droopy and enervated.

That morning had been his third time waking up in George's bed—during this visit, anyway. Again, George had made breakfast, as if it was already a routine. Then Zephyr had helped him open Fossil Galaxy, which didn't involve much more than turning on some lights, giving the gift shop floor a dry mop, and unlocking the door.

Judith had arrived soon after but announced she'd only stay for a short time. "My husband has a doctor's appointment in Lancaster," she explained.

George looked concerned. "Is everything all right?"

"Just a checkup. The oncologist sees him yearly to make sure we're still in the clear. We're making an excursion of it. You know, we haven't eaten in a restaurant in eighteen months."

"Is that safe?"

She waved his comment away. "Safe enough. We'll ask the doctor about it first."

Although George was still frowning, he changed the subject. "Can you show Zephyr how to run the shop before you go?"

That took Zephyr by surprise, but Judith seemed willing enough. She demonstrated how to work the cash register and the machine that read credit cards, and she gave him a few instructions on how to wrap fragile purchases. She also showed him where the extra bags were, in the unlikely event he ran out. Then she wished him luck and sailed out into the heat.

"You're trusting me here?" Zephyr asked as soon as she was gone.

"You have far more cash sitting in my kitchen than I have in my till. What else could you do? Haul away the dino-shaped paperweights to sell on the black market?"

Only a handful of visitors came that morning, and Zephyr enjoyed playing salesclerk.

Now it was afternoon, and the place felt as if it had been dead forever. He hadn't seen any signs of life outside either, not even a bird soaring by or a fly batting against the glass. Conrad Junction was feeling downright postapocalyptic.

"You don't have to hang out here if you don't want to," George offered. "Go take a nap or watch TV or something."

"Nope." A nap *would* be nice. But Zephyr was enjoying his temporary role as a bona fide employee, and people with real jobs didn't get to sack out in the middle of their workday. "*You* could do those things, though. I can come get you if someone needs a tour."

George shook his head. Then his expression brightened. "Do you want to see some old photos of this place?"

"Sure." It beat glaring at the sunshine and the empty parking lot.

George ducked into his office to fetch a photo album. It was thick and worn, the dark cover faded with age. He set it on the counter near the cash register.

"My grandmother started this—Wally's wife. She died before I was born. And then Dad took it over." He winced. "I haven't really kept it up very well, but the old stuff is pretty cool. At least, I think so. You don't have to be subjected to it if you don't want to."

Zephyr realized he *did* want to see, very much. Maybe these photos would help him understand George's stubborn dedication to the place.

All of the first photos were black-and-white. "These are a little weird for me," George mentioned. "No flavors." But he was smiling anyway.

The pages showed an empty patch of desert, then a foundation, and then walls and a roof. The building hadn't changed much since then, at least on the outside. In one picture, apparently taken after construction was completed, a man and woman stood outside the front door. They weren't touching each other and both looked serious. The woman wore a light-colored dress with short sleeves and a wide skirt, a narrow belt cinched at her waist. Her short hair, perhaps blond or light brown, was arranged in curls.

The man was unmistakably related to George. He had the same build, the same pale eyebrows, the same stubborn set to his mouth. His ears were just slightly pointed at the tips, exactly like George's, and his chin was a tiny bit knobby too. He wore dark trousers and a white shirt.

"Wally?" Zephyr asked.

"Yeah. And Grandma."

After a few pages, the photos were in color, although the hues had faded and some had changed over the decades. Still, it was easy to recognize the exhibits, which were very similar to those in the museum today. George showed him pictures of a diner and explained that it once occupied the space where his apartment was now.

"How come there aren't any images of your childhood house? Didn't you say Wally built that too?"

"Yeah, but I've never seen any pictures. It was all about Fossil Galaxy, you know?"

"Could I go see it?" He didn't know why, but he had the urge to see the place where little George had lived.

George shook his head. "It's gone. After Mom died, I had to sell it to keep this place afloat. It wasn't in good shape anyway. Nobody had been keeping it up. The buyer said he was going to fix it up and rent it out, but he never did. It burned down a few years ago. Squatters, probably. The owner built a gas station on the lot, but now that's closed too."

"I'm sorry."

"Mostly I only slept there. This building was my real home."

A couple of pages after that, a young boy began appearing in the photos. He had flaming red hair and familiar facial features. "Dad," said George unnecessarily. "He was an only child."

"What was his name?"

"Richard, but he went by Rick."

The resemblance became even more noticeable as Rick grew up and his hair paled to strawberry blond. He tended toward buzz cuts rather than George's slightly longer, floppier style, and once he got past his teens, he was built more heavily. But otherwise, they could almost have been twins.

Shortly after achieving adulthood, Rick occasionally appeared with a woman nearby. She was petite and pretty, but her dark eyes were sad and she rarely looked straight at the camera. Maybe she didn't like getting her picture taken.

"My mom's name was Lori. She worked really hard taking care of the four of us and keeping house and helping Dad here. I don't think—" George stopped abruptly and, chewing his lip, started to turn the page.

Zephyr caught his wrist gently, stopping him. "You don't think what?"

He realized suddenly how close they were standing, their bodies almost overlapping in space as they bent over the album. George was a few inches taller than him and, although too thin for his height, more broad-shouldered. He was also five years older but at the moment, seemed young and vulnerable. Zephyr had an impulse to hold him tightly, which was weird because Zephyr never consoled or comforted anyone.

"I have no idea why she married him," George said. "Okay, that's not true. He was handsome and, when he was in the right mood, incredibly charming. I don't remember them arguing much, but I also don't remember them... acting like they loved each other. They were more like coworkers. And I don't know what she wanted in life, but she wasn't happy here. Except in her gardens. She once told me that making things grow in the desert was like being a powerful wizard. It's one of the few times I remember her smiling."

Well, shit. Now Zephyr's heart ached for this woman he'd never met. And for her youngest son.

"Was she a good mother?" he asked.

"She loved us; I always knew that. She took good care of us. But I always felt as if there was sort of a distance between us. As if she wasn't a hundred percent there." He huffed. "Honestly, I'm fairly certain she had depression but was never diagnosed or treated. She hated seeing doctors. But she tried her best."

Now another emotion threaded through Zephyr: envy. He, himself, would have been able to forgive all of his mother's flaws if he'd thought she was at least making an effort to care for him.

George kept turning pages and his siblings began to appear. They weren't far apart in age, and they all had the Harlows' signature red hair, but other than that, the three oldest tended to favor their mother. George, on the other hand, resembled his father from the very start.

"You were a cute kid."

"I was a pain in the ass, or so I've been told. I bet you were adorable, though, with those big hazel eyes and long eyelashes."

Zephyr shrugged. If any photos had been taken of him as a child, he'd never seen them. There *had* been pictures taken by the cops and by social workers for various reasons, but those weren't exactly the types of snapshots anyone would save in a family album. Sometimes he told himself that his absolute lack of physical ties to his childhood meant he didn't have to be connected to it at all. Grown-up Zephyr was a blank slate and could be whomever he wanted. He didn't truly believe that, however.

To change the subject a bit, he pointed at a photo of a large space filled with old cars. "What's going on here?"

"Oh, that was Dad's—"

The bell on the door jingled, making them both look up. And Zephyr's heart nearly stopped as a familiar man entered.

CHAPTER FIFTEEN

"I SHOULD have known you'd run here." Brandon's voice was icy.

Zephyr noted Brandon's seven-hundred-dollar jeans and eight-hundred-dollar shirt. Despite the heat, his long sleeves weren't rolled up, and every hair was neatly in place. He had a bit of beard scruff, but it was the purposeful kind, maintained by his expensive barber. Zephyr's one satisfaction was that Brandon's face was tomato-red. Due to heat, or rage, or maybe both.

For a moment, Zephyr and George both froze, as if Brandon might be a mirage created by the Mojave sun. That gave him time to stomp over to the counter and glare. "Come on, Zephyr. Let's go."

"I'm not your bitch to call to heel."

Brandon's face darkened. "Stop being melodramatic. It's time to go home."

"It's not my home, and I'm not going. Get out of here."

And then a very interesting thing happened, something Zephyr didn't expect. George strode around the counter and right up into Brandon's face, placing himself between them and forcing Brandon back a couple of steps. "Leave, please. Now."

"Be happy to, as soon as Zephyr comes to his senses."

"Zephyr came to his senses when he left you."

Although Zephyr's heart raced and his chest felt tight, he grinned. Score one for George Harlow.

Brandon made a visible effort to get his temper under control. "Look. I don't know what he's told you, but Zephyr likes to play fast and loose with the truth, especially if lying gets him somewhere. If he's made you believe that he cares about you, don't fall for it. It's part of his act."

"Get out."

"He's nothing but a street rat in pretty clothes." Brandon sneered. "Ask him how he earns a living."

"I know how he earns a living. He's my employee of the month. This is *my* business and you're not welcome here."

Brandon allowed his gaze to theatrically sweep the room. "Business? What a joke. This is a dusty old shithole in the middle of nowhere. My dinner last night cost more than this place is worth. Look at those stupid fake dinosaurs. A three-year-old with a glob of Play-Doh could make something better." He waved in Tommy's direction.

Although those words must have been hurtful, George didn't flinch. "This is *my* shithole with the stupid fake dinosaurs, and I'm telling you to leave before I call the cops. Do you want to spend the night in the San Bernardino County jail?"

Brandon raised his chin. "They wouldn't arrest me."

"I wouldn't count on that. The captain is my uncle. And I bet he'd be very interested to hear how Zephyr got that nasty black eye."

"The fucking idiot got drunk and tripped over a chair," Brandon snarled.

George just crossed his arms. Zephyr had never seen anything so sexy.

Apparently deciding it was useless to argue with George, Brandon leaned to the side and looked around him at Zephyr. "Come on. You can't seriously want to stay here with this yokel in his dried-up tourist trap. Hop in the car and we'll head over to Robertson Boulevard and do some shopping," he cajoled. "I'll get us dinner reservations at that place you like." He smiled, showing his unnaturally straight, white teeth—an alligator trying to charm a toddler into its jaws.

"Fuck you," Zephyr said.

Brandon heaved a noisy sigh. "This is dumb, babe. Come talk to me. Whatever's bothering you, we'll work it out."

Zephyr clamped his lips shut. The crazy thing was, he almost wanted to listen to the son of a bitch. If he did as requested, Brandon would probably be sweet as honey to him for a little while. And if Zephyr was smart and didn't do the things he knew would upset Brandon, everything would be okay. For a while, anyway. Zephyr could comfortably play his familiar role.

As the silence hung heavily, George turned his head to look at Zephyr. "Your call. What do you want?"

Feeling unexpectedly powerful, Zephyr kept his voice clear and steady. "I want to never see his sorry face again."

"You heard him," George said, turning back to Brandon. "Leave and don't come back."

The color drained completely from Brandon's face. Zephyr seriously wondered whether he was going to drop dead. But his lips raised into a snarl. "Filthy little whore," he spat. "After everything I did for you. I dragged your skanky ass out of the fucking gutter. You'll pay for this." Little flecks of spittle flew as he spoke.

George reached into his pocket, pulled out his phone, and began to poke at it.

Growling like a beast, Brandon spun around and stomped toward the door. But along the way, he took a short detour and gave Tommy a vicious shove, toppling the statue with a resounding thud. George ran toward him, but Brandon sped outside.

To George's enormous credit, he didn't check on Tommy right away. He followed Brandon to the door and watched, narrow-eyed, until the sports car left the parking lot with screeching tires. Then George turned to look at Zephyr. "You okay?"

Zephyr wasn't sure how to answer. He felt shaky, as though he needed to sit down, but at the same time was so overcome with gratitude and admiration that he wanted to throw himself into George's arms. Instead of doing either, he walked slowly around the counter to get a better look at Tommy.

"Oh, George." The statue lay in pieces, surrounded by a thick spread of plaster dust. Tommy's head was partially crushed, his giant mask pathetically askew. The end of his tail and one tiny arm had broken off.

Obviously avoiding looking at the disaster, George grasped Zephyr's biceps. "That was incredibly brave."

A humorless laugh escaped, hurting Zephyr's throat. "Brave? I cowered behind the counter. You're the one who went all Rambo."

"You stood up to him, and you told him to go. That was brave."

Zephyr didn't believe that. He sure as hell didn't feel courageous. "Is the captain your mom's brother?"

"Huh?"

"The cop? You said your dad was an only child, so I figured…."

"My mom had only sisters." He looked genuinely amused. "As far as I know, I'm not related to anyone in law enforcement. Also, the nearest sheriff substation is in Barstow, and it'd probably take fifteen minutes or more before a patrol deputy could get out here. Plus, I don't know whether they'd have jurisdiction to arrest Brandon for assaulting you… wherever he did that."

"Seattle," Zephyr said a little absently.

"Probably not, then."

This time, Zephyr's laugh felt more natural. "That was some smooth bullshitting."

"One of my lesser-used talents."

And Zephyr couldn't help it—he *had* to kiss him. At that moment, it was as necessary as oxygen. More so, even, because Zephyr could hold his breath, which he did as he pressed his lips to George's and pulled him into a tight embrace.

George didn't fight it. He kissed back just as hungrily. His arms were around Zephyr, and none of the earth's Brandons mattered anymore. God, if they could only remain like this forever, the world would be a perfect place.

The bell rang again. Zephyr and George broke apart and spun to face the door, ready to resume the confrontation. But it was only a family of four, mouths agape.

SOMEWHAT SURPRISINGLY, the family didn't stomp off in a homophobic fit. In fact, they seemed mostly worried about the destroyed statue. The younger child, a boy of six or seven, started sobbing over poor Tommy.

The parents calmed the kid while George gave a brief explanation about an incident with an unhinged visitor. Which wasn't far from the truth. The adults seemed sympathetic while their daughter, who was somewhere in the preteen range, concluded that anyone who'd destroy a dino statue was, in her words, totally lame.

The family eagerly paid for their entry, and then George set off with them on a tour. But before he left, he came close to Zephyr and whispered, "If he comes back, shout. Sounds carry in here. I'll hear you. And here, take my phone." He pressed it into Zephyr's hand. "Dial 911 and the sheriffs will get here eventually."

Brandon didn't return. Zephyr did his best to clean up the smaller bits of Tommy, but the intact part of the statue was too big and heavy for him to right on his own. Besides, it would look pretty gruesome upright. He ended up drinking a bottle of Coke from the cooler and putting away the photo album. At least Brandon hadn't damaged that.

When George eventually reappeared with the family, they went on a spending spree, purchasing T-shirts for everyone, toys for the kids, an expensive hardcover book about the Mojave Desert, and enough postcards to send to everyone they'd ever met, apparently. They seemed happy when they left.

"I'm not too proud to take pity income," George said. "That was a good sale."

"I tried to clean up Tommy, but…."

"Yeah."

They both returned to the scene of the crime. "I am so sorry," said Zephyr.

"You're not the one who KO'd him."

"No. But if not for me, Brandon wouldn't have been here, and—"

"Forget the what-ifs and keep the blame where it belongs. On that shithead's shoulders."

Zephyr nodded. "Can you repair Tommy?"

George knelt, wincing when he got a better look at the head. "I don't think so. Poor old guy." He stroked it softly between the eyes, as if it were a favorite pet. "He's probably sixty years old. He's been patched several times already. I bet I could make an insurance claim, though."

"Tommy's insured?"

"The whole place is. My brother James works for an insurance company and gets me a good deal. So far I've been able to keep up with the premium payments. Dad used to lecture us on the importance of good insurance."

George stood up and wiped the dust from his hands. "I'm going to see if someone can help us move Tommy out of here. I've got a cart, so that'll help, but we'll have to get him onto it somehow."

His mouth quirked into a crooked grin. "Did I tell you that his car tastes like liver?"

That statement was so odd that it took Zephyr a moment to catch its meaning. But when he did, he snorted with laughter. And that felt almost as good as the kiss.

CHAPTER SIXTEEN

A COUPLE of George's friends showed up to help with Tommy. George didn't explain in detail what had happened, just that an enraged visitor had toppled the statue and fled.

"Man, everyone's batshit nowadays," Santiago said. "The other day an old lady had a screaming fit at Jessica's work because they asked her to wear a mask in the waiting room."

For Zephyr's benefit, George explained. "Jessica is Santiago's wife, and she's a receptionist at a dental office."

Santiago grinned, pulled out his phone, and brought up a photo to show to Zephyr. "That's her. Light of my life, dude."

She was a chubby woman with a dazzling smile. "She has warm eyes," Zephyr said with complete honesty.

"Yeah. Her heart's so huge. When we met, I was kind of a sad sack, going nowhere fast. But she says she always saw my potential."

"And we said she needed glasses," teased the other friend, Lucas.

A round of friendly banter continued while the four of them loaded Tommy and his broken pieces onto the cart. The three other men included Zephyr in the joking, making him feel like one of the gang very quickly. Neither Santiago nor Lucas had seemed at all taken aback when George had introduced Zephyr as a friend who was helping out at Fossil Galaxy. Of course, Zephyr wasn't wearing a dress today, but he knew he came across as femme no matter what he wore, and that bothered a lot of people. Apparently not these guys.

Together they managed to move Tommy into a large workshop and storage area, where they set him near what looked to be a couple of dino statues that had never been completed. George laughed along with everyone during the entire process, but Zephyr didn't miss the sad little pat he gave Tommy's back before they all left the room.

Back in the gift shop, they had a round of soft drinks from the cooler. Lucas disappeared into the parking lot for a few moments and returned with several plastic grocery bags, which he set on the sales counter with a grin.

"Yesterday I stopped at that fruit barn place near Bakersfield and I got sorta carried away. Will you help me out by taking some of this off my hands?"

His generosity was thinly disguised, but George responded gracefully. "I'd be happy to. Thanks."

Shortly after that, Santiago and Lucas left, and George and Zephyr inspected the produce haul. There were tomatoes still on the vine, along with peaches, grapes, nectarines, figs, and a melon. "Fruit salad for dinner," George said happily.

"That happens a lot, doesn't it? Your friends bring you stuff."

"Yeah, sure. And they do me favors, like helping move heavy things."

"Why?"

George looked puzzled. "Why wouldn't they? They're my friends."

"But what do they get out of it?"

"Oh." Now George just looked sad, although Zephyr didn't understand why. "I mean, sometimes I help them out too. Lucas's son had birthday parties at Fossil Galaxy three years running. I closed the place to the public for a couple of hours and dressed in this really embarrassing Jurassic Park costume. The kids loved it. And before Santiago met Jessica, he was going through a rough patch, and he camped out on my couch for a couple of weeks."

That made sense. "Reciprocal favors."

"I guess. But it's more than that. I didn't help them because I expected something in return, and I'm sure they feel the same way. It's just... friendship, you know? Doing what you can for someone because you care about them."

Something tightened in Zephyr's chest and he pretended great interest in a fig. He was grateful when, instead of pressing the matter, George turned to face the spot where Tommy had stood. "Man, that looks really empty now."

"Any ideas what you'll do with that space?"

George's shoulders slumped as if his burdens were suddenly too heavy to bear. "No."

"Would you let me do something with it?" Zephyr didn't have any idea what that might be, but surely he could come up with something. There seemed to be lots of interesting things sitting in that storage room.

"You want to do that? You don't have to, you know. But I'd love it if you would. You did a great job rearranging some of the things in here." George waved his arms to indicate the gift shop's wares.

Zephyr felt a little excited about the project, which was dumb, but he couldn't help it. "Any general ideas of what you want? Something more exciting than a rack of T-shirts, huh?"

"Tommy was our social-media star. People posted pictures on Instagram or whatever, and maybe that brought in a few customers." He shrugged. "I dunno."

"Got it. Quirky, unique, and Instagrammable." Zephyr realized he'd probably bitten off more than he could chew, but at least he could give it a shot. Then he had an idea. Well, the germ of one, anyway. "You spend a lot of time looking in that general direction—greeting visitors, checking the merch, keeping an eye on the parking lot. What colors would you most want to taste on a regular basis?"

George beamed. "Nobody's ever asked me that." He thought for a moment. "I liked your yellow skirt when we first met. And your pink toenail polish."

"Yeah?" A happy little glow warmed Zephyr's heart. "I can't guarantee I'll match those, but I'll try."

"Thanks, Zephyr."

Only then did Zephyr realize that, despite the earlier melodrama, he'd given barely any thought to Brandon in hours. That Brandon-shaped space in his brain—which had been there too long—was being filled in with much nicer things. Like George.

DINNER TURNED out to be a minor feast. George made salsa from some of the tomatoes and served it atop rice and black beans. There was the anticipated fruit salad and, for dessert, honey drizzled atop split figs. Zephyr was left feeling too full to do anything except help with the cleanup and then waddle over to collapse onto the couch. *His* spot on the couch, because now he had one, just like he had his side of George's bed.

He finished *Dune*, replaced it on the small bookshelf, and chose a replacement pretty much at random. "You're into spy stuff?" he asked, folding back into his seat.

George looked up from his book, which was something about rocks. "Not especially. They're okay."

Zephyr held up the paperback, a novel by Tom Clancy. "Then why this?"

"Judith. A couple times a year she goes to the library sale in Barstow. Paperbacks for fifty cents, hardcovers a buck. She looks for things related to the business, but she also ends up giving me a bunch of other stuff. I have no idea what her selection criteria are."

"I like books," said Zephyr. A bit defensively, as if George might scoff. But of course, George didn't, so he divulged more. "When I was little, sometimes I'd imagine I was Belle—you know, the Disney Belle?—dancing around in a library." It was a comforting fantasy, although the only real libraries he'd had the chance to visit were in schools, and those only rarely. He couldn't very well burst into song there.

"That's sweet. I can see you in that yellow ballgown she wears." George had set his rock book facedown on his lap and was leaning slightly in Zephyr's direction, as if he were genuinely fascinated by Zephyr's stupid childhood dreams.

"Oh, I pictured that too." He paused as a thought struck him. "In fact, that's the first time I remember imagining myself in girl clothes. It's just… I thought it would be nice to be pretty like that." He rarely explained this to anyone, and he'd never met anyone who truly understood. Although he'd implied to George earlier that cross-dressing was an economic decision for him, a way to attract more tricks, in truth that was only a side benefit. He'd worn girl stuff—when he could get away with it—even before he was in school. He liked the way he felt in it. More authentically himself. Which maybe didn't make a ton of sense, since he was also comfortable being male, but it wasn't a matter of logic.

George watched him, a soft smile on his face. Not judging or making fun. And also, it seemed, not fetishizing him.

"People like Brandon, they want me because I'm like one of those floofy dogs with the weird haircut dyed purple. I'm an exotic accessory they can show off to their friends. Only they can also take me home to fuck. But that's not really who I am." The last sentence came out almost as a plea.

George nodded solemnly. "You're so much more than a pretty boy in a dress."

Zephyr let out a long breath. "Have you ever heard of Barbette?"

"Um… no?"

"He's a little obscure. Maybe a lot obscure. But when I was, I don't know, maybe twelve? I was sitting in an office somewhere. Social worker, I think. I'm not sure. Anyway, I was bored and there was a magazine, so I picked it up. And it had an article about this circus performer a hundred years ago. Tightropes and trapezes and stuff like that. He performed in drag, as Barbette. And at the end of his performance, he'd take off his wig and show everyone he was a man. There were photos too. He was beautiful. Stockings, lace, feathers. But at the same time, he was a man."

Zephyr paused after this speech. So many words, and not necessarily clear in meaning. George didn't interrupt or hurry him, though. He just sat there, head a bit tilted, waiting for more.

"I ended up stealing the magazine," Zephyr said with a chuckle. "Read it I don't know how many times." Eventually he'd lost it, but he couldn't recall how or when. "And that's who I really wanted to be. Um, not the circus part. And not a girl in a ballgown. Not drag either, not really. Something else."

He'd never told this to anyone; Barbette had been a secret buried deep in his heart. But tonight, he wanted—no, *needed*—to tell George. And he needed George to understand, even if Zephyr couldn't explain it clearly.

"You wanted to be a man wearing what makes him feel his best. Authentically yourself," said George, very simply. He was absolutely correct, and Zephyr wanted to cry from relief.

Instead, he threw himself at George, assuming they were going to kiss. That was his intention, anyway, and certainly their previous kisses had created high expectations. But George surprised him by embracing him and holding him tight. And Jesus Christ, when was the last time he'd had human contact that had nothing to do with sex? It was almost too much, a sensory overload, but instead of pulling away, he burrowed in closer and pressed his face into the sweet, soft skin at the crook of George's neck. George held him and stroked his hair.

Unfortunately, with their torsos and legs angled awkwardly, it wasn't the most comfortable position long-term. When Zephyr repositioned himself, he somehow ended up on his back, down the length of the couch, with his head pillowed on George's lap. And that was nice too. George continued to play with Zephyr's hair, pushing the strands away from his face and smoothing them behind his ears. He was careful around the bruise.

"Maybe I am one of those floofy dogs," Zephyr said.

"Do you want me to stop?"

"Please don't." Zephyr sighed. "Although this is silly."

The corners of George's lips curled upward a little. "What's silly about it?"

"What are we? You. Me. Us."

"Friends."

"Do you pet Santiago? Or Lucas? Do you… cuddle with them?"

"Nope. Although we hug now and then. But I think different friends do different things. Like I wouldn't have asked Judith to help move Tommy."

Zephyr thought about the tiny woman attempting to haul large chunks of plaster-and-metal dinosaur, and he had to chuckle. "So I'm your petting friend."

"I guess."

They were quiet for a while after that. George's hand continued to move, slowly and gently, and Zephyr decided he felt more like a cat than a dog. He would have purred if he were capable of it. "How are you not married?" Zephyr asked after a while. "You're handsome, you're smart, you're kind and thoughtful…."

"I'm a sensory freak who is tied to a dying business in the middle of the desert."

Zephyr blinked up at him. "Do you really think of yourself as a freak?"

"No, not really. I think it's pretty cool, actually. But not everyone sees it that way."

"Who cares about 'everyone,'" Zephyr said dismissively. At this particular moment, he was satisfied that it was just the two of them; the rest of the world could take a flying leap. He closed his eyes and, in a pleasant stupor, lightly dozed. Until the buzz of George's phone on the end table jolted him fully awake.

"Sorry," George said. "If someone's texting me this late, it's probably important."

It wasn't really that late, at least by Zephyr's usual standards, but he didn't argue. He sat up so George wouldn't have to hold the phone awkwardly over Zephyr's face. As he was resettling himself, he almost missed George's reaction to his screen.

All the color had drained from George's face and his eyes widened.

"What's wrong?" Zephyr demanded, imagining a host of calamities befalling George's friends and family.

"It's nothing," George lied. He closed the screen and set the phone back down, then stared into space while biting his lip. His hands were clenched into fists.

"George?"

"I don't… I don't think you should see it."

Well then of course Zephyr *had* to see it. He reached across George and grabbed the phone—an older model, he noted, with the glass cracked in one corner—but of course he couldn't activate it. Grunting with annoyance, he pried George's right thumb loose and maneuvered the sensor against it. George passively allowed this, but his mouth was set into a thin line.

And then Zephyr read the text.

Tell that little shit that if he knows whats good for him hell crawl back and apologize. And you mind your own fucking business. You dont know who your dealing with fuckhead.

"Charming." Zephyr tried to come off as nonchalant, but all of his muscles had gone stiff. Why the hell hadn't he seen this coming? Because, as usual, he'd been too blind to see five minutes ahead of himself, that was why.

George's mouth was tight. "Brandon, I assume."

"I don't recognize the number, but yeah. Unless you have another little shit stashed around here somewhere."

"We can call the police. Get a restraining order."

"No cops. And he wouldn't pay attention to a restraining order."

He typed out a quick response with his thumbs.

Find another toy. We're done.

George snatched the phone away. "Responding is a bad idea. He'll just get angrier."

"It doesn't make any difference. Once he gets pissed off…." Zephyr snorted. "Anger management issues."

"I don't understand. Does he think this is how to treat someone he loves?"

No, George definitely didn't understand. "He doesn't love me. He owns me. You've taken away his plaything and now he's going to throw a tantrum. Except he's not a toddler—he's a spoiled, rich adult who always gets his way."

"You're a person, not a possession," George snapped.

It was lovely of him to get so upset on Zephyr's behalf. Zephyr gave George's knee a squeeze. "I knew exactly what I was getting myself into from the moment I met him, okay? So don't feel sorry for me."

"If you knew, why did you…?" George waved his hands around a little as if trying to grasp the right words.

"Let him get his paws on me? It seemed like the best alternative at the time."

George was frowning so heavily that it must have hurt, and his hands were back into fists. It was a marvel how clearly his pale skin showed his emotions; now instead of shocked and white, he had angry red blotches on his cheeks.

"The first night we met," George said. "Was he the one who did that to you?"

Zephyr had to think about that for a moment. "No. I hadn't even met him yet. That was just a random trucker who knew perfectly well that the person blowing him had a dick, but then got angry about it afterward." He shrugged. "It happens. Risk of the trade."

"But you shouldn't— You can't—" George shot clumsily to his feet and started pacing the room. It wasn't an especially big space, and the furniture took up a good chunk of it, but he briskly navigated without bumping into anything. And without looking at Zephyr, who blocked Brandon's number and put down the phone.

George had so easily grasped such important aspects of Zephyr's nature, but he couldn't seem to understand this. It was a shame.

"I'm not a victim," Zephyr continued quietly. "I made decisions. I—"

"You said he was your only alternative!"

"I said he was my *best* alternative. Look, I used him as much as he used me. Do you think I stuck with him for his charming company? It was the money. Lots and lots of it. And all the pretty things he could buy me."

"Bullshit!" George stopped his circling in front of the couch and glared down at Zephyr. "You've got a suitcase full of expensive clothing sitting right over there, and you haven't even touched it. You're not as materialistic as you claim. What did you really want from him?"

Now it was Zephyr's turn to jump up, almost knocking into George but then scuttling behind the couch and gripping the upholstery hard enough to make his fingers hurt. "Of course I wanted money! Clothes. Five-star hotels. Gourmet meals. First-class plane tickets. Top entertainment."

"You sound like a tourism ad." George shook his head. "Or maybe one for a platinum credit card."

And for no sane reason, that struck Zephyr as funny. All of the anger drained out of him and he began to laugh. George stared, clearly startled, but then his lips twitched and he joined in. When Zephyr came back around the couch a minute later, still chuckling, they moved straight into an embrace. It was as if they hugged all the time.

"Sorry," George said. "I shouldn't butt in. It's not my busin—"

"I've made it your business, though, haven't I?" Zephyr let himself sag against George, who held his weight easily. "I don't think Brandon's going to give up on me this easily."

"Too bad. He doesn't get to choose what you do."

"What if he comes back?"

"Then I tell him to fuck off. That was unexpectedly satisfying."

Zephyr pulled back far enough to look into his eyes. "He might be dangerous. He has money. Power. Um... I'm pretty sure he doesn't get that money through entirely legit means. I shouldn't have dragged you into this. I need to go."

"Do you *want* to go?" George held Zephyr's shoulders. Not to capture him—the grip wasn't tight—but to connect them. Zephyr understood that.

"No. I don't want to go."

"Good. Then stay."

Zephyr tried not to look relieved. "He might be dangerous," he repeated.

"Got that. Risk of the trade, right?"

"What trade is that? Tourist attraction owner?"

For a moment, George looked away. When he returned his gaze, his eyes looked a little watery. "I have a lot of friends. I'm really, really lucky that way. But I don't have... I don't fall for people easily. Or, well, hardly ever. There was Zak, but that was a decade ago. And when it comes to relationships, I don't do casual. I told you that. So there's been this absence in my life. But I've been okay with it; I have plenty else to do, and I feel complete without a partner. Then you came, and instead of an absence, I have a... a presence."

Zephyr felt a little light-headed, so he held George's arms to ground himself, lest he float up to the ceiling like that scene in the old Willy Wonka movie. "A presence?" he repeated carefully.

"I hope I'm not scaring you away."

"Still here." Zephyr gave a little squeeze to emphasize his point.

"Good. Because what I'm trying to say is... is... if you want it too... I want...." He made an incoherent growl before taking a deep breath and trying again. "If you're willing—and really *want* to do it—I'd like to go to bed with you."

"Non-platonically?" Zephyr felt his own smile spreading like warm honey.

"As much non-platonically as possible."

Zephyr tugged George's head down and finally got that kiss he'd been aiming for earlier. It was worth the wait. When they broke apart to catch their breath, Zephyr tapped George on the tip of his very cute nose. "It's time for bed."

CHAPTER SEVENTEEN

ZEPHYR WASN'T shy about sex, and he sure as hell wasn't shy about his body. Why should he be? Especially given his past. And in the current case, George had already seen him naked—the very first night they met, in fact—and they'd already shared a bed.

And yet, as they stood on opposite sides of the mattress, Zephyr found himself strangely bashful. What he was about to do wasn't for profit and wasn't just a quick poke-and-go. It was significant to George, and that meant it was significant to Zephyr too. And Jesus, how had he gotten himself into this situation? Not that he really wanted to get out of it.

George, on the other hand, started tearing off his own clothing with eager abandon. Which was a surprise. But then, the man was full of them, wasn't he? He was beautiful naked. He had wide shoulders and narrow hips and the kind of build that would be muscular if he ate and exercised more. His skin was tinged lightly pink, with a healthy growth of curly reddish hair on his chest, belly, and groin. Manscaping services were probably not available in the Junction, and even if they were and George had the time and money to use them, Zephyr was certain he wouldn't have bothered. There was no vanity to the man, no attempts to present himself as anything different from what he was. It made him even more attractive.

And he was also nicely hung, which was a bonus. His cock already stood at attention.

"Approval?" George asked, grinning widely.

"Much. You know, you come off as this sort of innocent nerd, but you have a heavy streak of confidence, don't you?"

"I don't know about innocent, but I'm definitely a nerd. And when I'm comfortable about something, yeah, I'm confident."

Comfortable. Well, Zephyr knew himself to be pretty and knew lots of men wanted to fuck him, so he should be comfortable about that. But he wasn't, at least not at the moment. Maybe because he didn't believe it was primarily his looks that had attracted George, who wanted *him*, the person, not the sexy thing in nice clothes. And that was even after Zephyr had spilled some of his secrets. And after George had seen him at his worst—hurt and lost and vulnerable.

Zephyr slowly took off his borrowed boxer briefs and stood motionless, the bed and a thousand bad decisions standing between him and George.

After a moment, George clambered over the mattress and took Zephyr into his arms.

This embrace was different from the previous one, and not just because they were both naked. This was a hug with *intent*. George was gentle and didn't aggressively grope Zephyr as if checking produce for ripeness. In fact, he didn't do anything but stroke his hair and press gentle lips just under his jawline.

And holy shit, did that set Zephyr's engines revving.

Maybe it was the contrast in textures: hard body and hard cock, soft hands and soft lips. Maybe it was the way George seemed so present, so in the moment, not trying to hurry things along. He was like a man on his way to an appointment, pausing to watch a gorgeous sunset.

"Stop and smell the flowers," Zephyr said.

"No flowers. Your hair tastes like grapefruit with sugar, and your skin… mmm… spice. Cloves. Maybe a little pepper too." He gave Zephyr's neck a little lick, making Zephyr shiver with need.

"I don't *really* taste like that. Not if you close your eyes." Zephyr didn't know why he was arguing at a time like this. Perhaps just to slow things down.

"But my eyes are open." And then, as if to stop any more debate, George kissed him. Thoroughly. Midway through, Zephyr realized he was wasting an opportunity, so he settled his palms on George's ass. Smooth warm skin, the slight flex of muscle. Perfection. Zephyr usually had to pretend a lot more enthusiasm than he actually felt, but not now. He could think of nowhere he'd rather be and nothing he'd rather be doing.

Well, almost nothing. Once he was totally breathless, he pushed at George and toppled him backward onto the bed. Zephyr went with him. That didn't prove to be especially comfortable, so with a bit of awkward disentanglement and some laughter, they reoriented themselves: George on his back with his legs stretched out and Zephyr kneeling astride him, which meant that they could pet each other's chests and bellies while keeping their groins pressed together.

"I don't have rubbers," George said suddenly, looking stricken.

Dammit, Zephyr hadn't even thought about that. It had been over a year since he'd had sex with anyone but Brandon—who, predictably, refused to use them. Brandon insisted that Zephyr get tested regularly, which was ironic because Brandon was the one who slept around. Zephyr had been using PrEP but hadn't taken the pills with him when he fled to George.

"I can make a run to the mini-mart," George offered.

"If you think I'm going to let you get out from under me and put on clothing, you are mistaken, George Harlow. We'll make do."

George raised one eyebrow. "Oh?"

So Zephyr proceeded to demonstrate. He began simply, by leaning forward and letting his hair form a curtain around George's face. That seemed to meet with approval: George sighed, flexed his pelvis up, and put his hands on Zephyr's hips.

"You're real," George whispered.

"You doubted it?"

"The way you appear and disappear... you're like a mirage."

"Can a mirage do this?" Zephyr bent lower and took one of George's hard nipples into his mouth. A few swipes of his tongue, a nibble that suggested sharp teeth but didn't cross over into pain, gentle suction. George hissed approvingly. He likely wasn't aware that his fingers were digging in firmly, and Zephyr wasn't about to say anything. It grounded him, and if he had bruises to show for it tomorrow, he'd be glad. They'd be like a temporary tattoo of George's desire.

Zephyr turned his attention to the other pink nipple before working his way down the torso, into the little divot of navel, to the clean musk where legs met body, over to—

It happened quickly: George flipping them over, caging Zephyr with his arms and legs. But it was a gilded cage, not at all confining, and George took care not to rest his greater weight atop Zephyr.

"I'm not fragile," Zephyr said. "Whatever you want to give me, I can take it."

Ah, but as it turned out, what George wanted to give was a slow torment of fingers and tongue. He watched carefully for reactions, and when something made Zephyr moan or gasp, he did it again, until Zephyr was nothing but a panting, writhing, sweating mess.

"I feel... like... those things.... Oh, God, do that again." He tried to recapture his thought. "In the fossil... I sent you."

"*Jimbacrinus bostocki.*"

Zephyr smiled up at him. "Say that again. It's sexy."

Chuckling, George did, and then he added in more Latin names for good measure. "You feel like a fossil?" he added. "Hard?" He licked the length of Zephyr's desperate cock.

It took a few seconds before Zephyr could answer. "No. Alive. All... squiggly fronds." Yeah, that didn't make sense, but his nervous system was occupied with other matters.

Then George slid his mouth over Zephyr's glans, and any remaining powers of coherent speech evaporated.

George's skills might not have been professional grade, but he more than made up for it in enthusiasm. Zephyr buried his fingers in that soft ginger hair and lost himself to pleasure, closing his eyes, arching his back, opening himself wide.

Far too soon—but almost too late—he managed a choked cry. "Going to—" George moved his head upward a bit, releasing Zephyr from his mouth and stroking the shaft firmly and efficiently with his big hand.

Zephyr, gloriously, came apart.

A few moments later, George snuggled close and sighed happily. Zephyr regained enough of himself to protest. "But you didn't—"

"I did. I can multitask."

A quick needle of disappointment stabbed Zephyr. He would have liked to bring George off, to see in his face the exact moment when Zephyr made him peak. But now George was making contented little humming sounds against him. And frankly, Zephyr felt too damned good to hold any regret for long.

Without bothering to clean up, they pulled the covers over themselves and, still pressed together, fell asleep.

IF WAKING up to kitchen sounds was nice, it was even better to wake up still warm from the body heat of the man currently making those noises. And when Zephyr padded naked into the kitchen and discovered George nude too, it was grounds for celebration.

"We skipping clothing now?" Zephyr asked as he watched George whisk some eggs.

"Breakfast au naturel. It's all the rage."

"You make a handsome bare chef."

"And I bet you'd make a handsome bare table-setter."

After arranging the place settings, Zephyr squeezed some juice, then plated up leftover fruit salad. George finished spreading jam onto slices of toast just as the coffeemaker gave its final sputter.

"You know," Zephyr said solemnly as he stirred sugar into his coffee, "I've had a lot of interesting experiences. But this is my very first naked breakfast for two."

"Ditto."

It was… silly. And fun. And an excellent way to start the day.

But as they were doing the dishes, Zephyr suddenly sobered. "This can't last."

Busily scrubbing at a bit of stubborn egg, George made an interrogative grunt.

"Us. You called me a mirage, but this… it's an oasis. Life-supporting, but you can't stay in an oasis forever."

"You're not a camel," George argued.

"No. But I am a guy who doesn't…. I'm temporary. You have three generations in Conrad Junction? I've rarely stayed three weeks anywhere. Even with Brandon. He has homes in LA and Hawaii. He has a fucking ranch in Wyoming. And we were always flying off to different cities, staying in different hotels."

"Jet-setting."

"I guess. But you see my point?"

George sighed. "You are a tumbleweed. And I'm a Joshua tree: deep roots, suited only for a very specific climate."

Zephyr bumped his hip against George. "I'd rather be a camel. But George—"

"I get it. I don't want you to leave, but I understand the limits of the Junction's appeal… and of mine. So I'm grateful for whatever time we have together."

Perversely, this kindness made Zephyr almost angry. "You're too understanding. Too forgiving. You should be pissed off at me. Hell, you should be pissed off at a *lot* of things."

George turned off the faucet and swiveled to face him. "You know how you said you took known risks? Well, I made decisions knowing all the circumstances. So I can't very well throw a tantrum over those circumstances, can I?" Then he stomped off to the bedroom.

JUDITH DIDN'T come in that day, so Zephyr manned the gift shop while George did the guided tours and various other tasks. There weren't many tours to guide; the morning was dead. Zephyr knew nothing about running a business, and he didn't know what George's expenses were, but the little trickle of entrance fees and souvenir purchases couldn't possibly be enough to keep this place going.

George didn't complain. After lunch, he turned to Zephyr thoughtfully. "Would you mind holding down the fort while I run some errands? I'm just heading into Mojave."

"What if visitors come? I can't do a tour." Zephyr felt slightly panicked at being responsible for… anything.

"The brochure has a self-guided one. That'll do fine. And I'll be back in a couple of hours."

With more than a little trepidation, Zephyr nodded.

George paused at the door. "If Fuckface shows up, head over to the mini-mart. I think Doug's working today and he's a big guy. Fuckface won't mess with him."

"Fuckface? You never swear."

"I do when it's justified."

The bell jangled merrily as he left.

Only two people visited while he was away, a pair of women in their midseventies who were quite clearly a couple. They even wore matching plaid masks. They were from Indiana, and midway through an epic road trip. The shorter one was a retired geology professor. She didn't need a guide, she said, or even the brochure. Her partner made a long-suffering face. "Yes, Helen. I'm sure you know everything already."

They were still wandering the exhibits when the Fossil Galaxy van returned to the parking lot. George waved when he got out, but after grabbing several bags, he went around to the apartment entrance instead of coming through the gift shop. It made perfect sense, but it also started Zephyr musing about George's living situation.

Perhaps it wasn't completely healthy to live and work in the same building. It meant that if—or more realistically *when*—George lost the business, he'd also lose his home. Zephyr had never really had a home, but George and his forebears had inhabited this spot for three generations. The concept of homelessness must terrify him.

And even if the business were a rousing success, George was too heavily cocooned here. He almost never left. Nearly everything he needed, including his social life, came to him at Fossil Galaxy. Convenient, sure, especially during a pandemic. But it meant he never had the chance to try anything new. "He doesn't even know if he'd be happier somewhere else," Zephyr murmured.

Further thoughts on the subject evaporated when George entered from the apartment, a sunny smile on his face. "Arturo's reopened. We'll have enormous burritos for dinner tonight."

"Is that a double entendre?"

As Zephyr had hoped, George blushed a little. Such a fascinating combination of assertive and bashful!

But before Zephyr could continue that pleasant line of inquiry, the guests finished their tour. The shorter one was still lecturing—something about extinct camels—and her partner smiled fondly and patiently.

"I hope you enjoyed," Zephyr said as they paused to examine the souvenirs. What was the appeal of snow globes, plastic pens, and magnets? He'd never understand, but he was grateful for George's sake.

The geologist sailed over while her partner considered the Christmas ornaments. "You have some interesting choices in your exhibits here," said the geologist. "I have questions."

"And I've got just the guy to answer them. Meet George Harlow, the owner." He waved his hand a little theatrically.

"Harlow? The same as on the sign?"

"Family owned for three generations," said George.

"Well, that's nice to know. You don't see that much nowadays. You know, you have some nice specimens in your collection, but the display…."

"Leaves much to be desired. I know. Sorry."

"Are you trying to maintain the retro vibe? Because honey, it's a bit much."

George laughed. "If someone wants to come along and dump a lot of money here, I'll happily go as modern as possible. But I don't think that's going to happen."

"A shame." She scrunched up her mouth thoughtfully. "Well, I'm glad you're here at all, then. It's nice that you highlight so many local specimens. It's such a fascinating region."

"Thank you. I think so too."

She asked more questions, most of them very specific, and although George fielded them admirably, Zephyr tuned them out. As had the other woman apparently, amassing a collection of items to purchase and bringing them over for Zephyr to ring up.

"Stuff for the grandkids," she explained. "We have three, and they're all crazy about dinosaurs. I wonder where they get that from."

"It's nice that it runs in the family."

"And far more interesting for the kids than my work. I'm a retired accountant." She glanced over to where her partner and George were still deep in conversation. "Sorry. She gets like this."

"Don't apologize. He's thrilled."

Zephyr and the accountant watched them for a few moments, until Zephyr realized he wore the same affectionate smile that she did. He returned to briskly manning the cash register.

She handed him her credit card. "That's the nice thing about a road trip. You can buy plenty of souvenirs without worrying too much whether you have room for them. We spent a few days in Taos and bought a lovely glass sculpture of a bear with a sort of petroglyph design. We both fell in love with it. It's big, though"—she held up her hands to demonstrate—"and fragile, of course. We never could have gotten it home safely on a plane."

"It sounds like you're having a great trip." He swiped the card and handed it back.

"We're lucky. We have the money, the time, and the health to travel." She leaned in closer and dropped her voice. "It keeps the excitement going, you know? Remember that when you two have been together for forty years." She winked.

Zephyr was going to protest that they weren't together at all, but that wasn't absolutely true. He did wonder how this woman could tell; it wasn't as if she had caught them in a make-out session. Just a lucky guess, maybe.

The women eventually left, after the shorter one gave George a business card.

"It was a good idea to keep her talking," Zephyr said. "Her wife spent a fortune."

"That wasn't why."

"I know. Dude, you know a *lot* about prehistoric stuff."

George gave him a puzzled look. "I own Fossil Galaxy."

"Yeah. But that lady was a professor, and you held your own, even though you never got to finish your degree. That's impressive."

"After three decades, I'm bound to have picked up a thing or two." He said it as if it was no big deal, as if he didn't see how impressive his knowledge was. Which he probably didn't. But Zephyr knew how hard it could be to learn things when they weren't handed to you wrapped in a nice educational bow. It meant having to work hard on your own behalf, to dig blindly, to struggle with no reward except a hoped-for satisfaction of success.

But maybe it was time to change the subject. "Errands a triumph? Burritos aside, I mean."

"Yep. I needed a few odds and ends that I can't get here in the Junction. I guess I could order them from Amazon, but the shop I go to in Mojave is independently owned. I like to support them." A hesitant expression settled on him. "Um, I sort of got you something."

"You can't afford to buy me gifts, and you don't need to."

"This was cheap, and I wanted to. Anyway, I don't know if you'll like it. You don't have to. I mean, you can say you hate it and it won't hurt my feelings. I'll only be out, like, five bucks. And maybe Kayla will want it. God, it's going to seem really stupid after all the stuff I bet Fuckface bought you, but I saw it and I thought—"

"George. If you don't tell me soon, I'll be dead of old age and then you'll never know whether I like it." Curiosity made him want to grab George and shake the information out of him.

Grinning, George reached into his pants pocket and set something on the counter between them.

Zephyr blinked. "Nail polish?"

"It's not whatever fancy brand you usually use, I'm sure. Maybe you don't want to wear any at all right now, and that's cool. No pressure. But I thought… maybe you did?"

Zephyr had to swallow a few times before he could speak, and even then, his voice came out tight. "What gave you that idea?"

"You were wearing some the night we met. Green on your fingers and pink on your toes. And the time you stopped by and dropped off money? Fingers sparkly red, like the ruby slippers in *The Wizard of Oz*. I don't know about your toes that day, though." He rubbed fingers through the back of his hair. "But you don't have any now, and *I* don't have any, and there's nowhere in the Junction to get a mani-pedi. So if you did want some, I figured you might be kind of stuck."

"Oh," Zephyr whispered.

"Where do you think they come up with all the crazy names for the colors?" George continued. "This one is Orchid Order. It's a nice pink. I'd call it Apple Pie, because that's what it tastes like. But that would probably confuse people. Anyway, I thought it would go nice with your skin tones."

Zephyr's eyes burned and he had to sniffle a few times. He didn't know why. George was right. Brandon had thought nothing of dropping a couple of grand on a necklace he liked or a pair of heels he thought would look sexy on Zephyr. When, on a whim, Zephyr had asked for four colors of Louboutin lipstick at a hundred bucks apiece, Brandon had nodded without even looking up from his phone. And if Zephyr had ever used drugstore nail polish and Brandon found out about it, he'd have been yelled at for being tawdry and crude.

But George had remembered every color he'd seen Zephyr wear. And he had bought this little bottle, which wasn't part of his very tight budget, because he thought it would make Zephyr happy.

Zephyr shook and opened the bottle, laid his hand on the counter, and began to apply the color.

AFTER ZEPHYR'S nails were thoroughly dry, and while George groaned over paperwork in his office, Zephyr began sketching ideas for something to replace poor Tommy. It needed to be appropriately themed, simple for him to construct, big enough not to look stupid in the space where Tommy had stood, and cool enough that people would want to take selfies in front of it. It had to be cheap or—better yet—free. And it should incorporate pink and yellow because those colors tasted good to George.

Zephyr wasn't much of an artist, so his drawings weren't that good. The process was more helpful than the results, really; his creative juices seemed to flow along with the ink. What if he could construct a stylized Joshua tree? They looked sort of otherworldly, and if he switched up the colors, it would seem like something from another planet. A friendly-looking ground sloth could be leaning against it. George said the creatures could grow to be nine feet long, and it was thought they'd been important in dispersing the trees. Maybe this guy could be juggling a couple of little planets? And there could be some big fake dino bones at its feet.

Okay, that was probably too ambitious for Zephyr's skills, but he was on the right track. He could probably ask George's friends for help. Maybe some of them were good at building or painting or whatever.

The best next step, Zephyr decided, was to do an inventory of all the stuff lying around in storage. That would give him lots of ideas.

He was about to tell George his plan when the landline rang, an old-fashioned corded phone that was probably older than George. The rare situation startled him, but George picked up right away. A few seconds later, he hung up. The phone immediately started ringing again, but this time he ignored it.

After at least the tenth ring, Zephyr asked, "Brandon?"

"I guess so. Someone was shrieking threats."

Fuck. "Do you want me to—"

"No." George picked up the receiver and listened, wincing, before disconnecting. He didn't put the receiver back in the cradle, however, but instead gave the phone a baleful glare and grumbled, "Fuckface."

"You can't just leave it off the hook forever."

"Why not? Who calls this number anyway? Just Fuckface and people wanting to renew my auto warranty."

Although George seemed only mildly annoyed, Zephyr's stomach lurched and his knees felt weak as a wave of despair hit him. Once again, he'd gotten himself entangled in trouble, and this time his escape wouldn't be so easy. And he'd *known* this, dammit. Almost from the first day he'd met Brandon, Zephyr was aware of what he was getting himself into. But he'd leapt into it anyway because—for then, anyway—it had felt like the best option. Just as he'd explained to George. And as usual, as long as he had what he needed at the moment, he didn't pay attention to what might happen in the future.

Now here was George, being perfectly perfect about the whole thing. Not blaming Zephyr for causing this mess. Not seeming to care that Zephyr's mess had fallen in George's lap. No, George was understanding and solicitous and willing to help.

George must have read something in Zephyr's face. He hopped out of his chair and hurried over to where Zephyr stood, rooted in the space between the sales counter and the office. "What is it?" He held out his hands as if he wanted to grasp Zephyr but was stopping himself.

"I'm not made of fucking glass!" Zephyr snapped, almost undone by George's concern. "You can stop hovering."

George didn't budge. "You look like you're going to be sick."

"Sick of all of you." The poison came pouring out of his mouth, and although he knew perfectly well that George wasn't like everyone else, Zephyr couldn't stop it. "It's all bullshit. Pretending to care. You even put that same fucking story into your movies, don't you? *Cinderella. Pretty* fucking *Woman.* As if the rich bastard won't get tired of the whore in a few weeks and dump her in the ditch where she belongs the second he finds a prettier toy." He was out of breath, and he didn't know if it was from yelling or from the effort to shut himself up. It was as if he were possessed by a demon. Maybe he was. It would certainly explain a hell of a lot.

Although those blotches of color had appeared on his cheeks, George kept his tone gentle. "I'm not Brandon."

"You are," Zephyr lied. "You all are."

And then he scurried to the door before he could blurt out something even worse.

"It's over a hundred degrees out there."

Zephyr grabbed the handle. "Don't fucking care. Need to go."

"Will you be back?"

Without answering, Zephyr hurried out into the glaring sun.

CHAPTER EIGHTEEN

AT FIRST, he stumbled along the road almost blindly, with no destination in mind, barely noticing the boarded-up houses and empty businesses, the naked cell towers and the power transformers behind chain-link fences. Soon he was out of the Junction altogether, racing along the dusty shoulder of the old highway, the heat beating down on him like a hammer. But he wasn't quite crazed enough to go wandering into the desert, and eventually he turned around.

As he plodded back into town, he noticed several empty lots where sand and scrub obscured the foundations of former buildings. One of those might have been the Harlow family home, a realization that made his guilt twice as deep. George didn't deserve to be treated this way. He was nothing like Brandon—a polar opposite, almost. And he'd never been anything but kind and thoughtful to Zephyr, even when they were having sex.

"Why couldn't he be a selfish asshole?"

Shit. Zephyr was about three minutes away from becoming a lunatic ranting to himself among the creosote bushes and cactuses. He needed to get out of the sun.

He skirted Fossil Galaxy, careful not to glance at the sign with the now-familiar logo, and ended up in the parking lot of the truck stop. It was new since the bypass, having gobbled up the space formerly occupied by a smaller gas station and, George had explained, a restaurant and a secondhand store. But the paint colors seemed to have faded already, the Mojave impatiently asserting its dominance over all life. The mini-mart was part of the truck stop, as were a sandwich shop, several rows of gas pumps, and a building that contained showers and other services for long-haul drivers.

Zephyr didn't have to go inside that building to know exactly what it would smell like: sweat, old cigarette smoke, fried food, cheap shampoo, and floral- or lemon-scented cleaning fluid. There would be televisions mounted up high in the lounge area and vending machines against the wall. Men and a few women would sit in chairs, eating and shooting the shit, some of them waiting for the light-up board to tell them it was their turn to use the showers. The air-conditioning would be cranked up high.

He didn't go inside but instead found a spot in the shade between two parked semis. Their engines idled, probably to power the AC in the cabs, and the diesel fumes made him light-headed. He considered knocking on some doors and begging a ride, maybe with an implied offer to pay his way with services rendered. But he couldn't make himself do it. He wasn't in a state to interact with anyone right now.

Then his gut clenched so hard that he almost collapsed to his knees. God, he wanted a nice bed with clean, crisp sheets and soft pillows. And he wanted a clean bathroom with big towels, and a full fridge and a comfortable place to sit, and maybe a little shelf stuffed with books. He wanted a refuge, an oasis. He wanted a home.

And God forgive him for his weakness, he wanted George.

Zephyr looked down at his fingernails with their flawless pink polish. Orchid Order, which tasted like apple pie.

He couldn't identify the emotion that roiled inside him then—relief? worry? regret?—but he took a few deep breaths and walked slowly back to Fossil Galaxy.

GEORGE MET him just inside the door with a bottle of cold water. Zephyr held it to his forehead and cheeks and let the condensed moisture seep into his parched skin. There wasn't a single word from George, of either reproach or welcome, and Zephyr didn't say anything either. No excuses, no apologies. George gave him a sad smile and a quick squeeze of the shoulder before returning to his office and the eternal pile of paperwork.

After lingering in place for several moments, Zephyr uncapped the water and took it into the apartment. He was sweaty. Dirty. A cool shower would feel amazing.

Later, he stood dripping onto the floor, staring at the stranger in the mirror. He'd spent a good portion of his life regarding his reflection—making sure his clothing was good, his hair perfect, his makeup flattering. But he wasn't sure he'd ever truly looked at himself, at the *person*. And now he didn't know what to make of that man gazing back.

Without consciously deciding to move, he padded naked into the kitchen, shivering a bit at the cold air on his wet skin. He opened a drawer and withdrew the scissors that George kept there, and he carried them back to the bathroom.

And then he hacked off his hair.

It took some time, and it hurt because the blades weren't especially sharp. When he finished, his hair stuck up in uneven spikes and clumps. He cleaned up the mess from the sink and floor—he wasn't a complete asshole—and put away the scissors. He used a towel to wipe stray strands from his body. And then he crawled naked between sheets that still smelled of him and George and sex, and he closed his eyes and shut out the world, at least for a little while.

Gentle pressure on his forehead woke him up. George was leaning over him, kissing him tenderly. "Do you want to get up and have some dinner?"

"Burritos," Zephyr said, remembering.

"If you want."

Zephyr slowly sat up, wincing at the ache in his head, and put on a pair of borrowed shorts. He didn't bother with the borrowed underwear or a borrowed shirt, but he took a few seconds to rub his hand over what remained of his hair. It felt alien, and not just because he'd cut it so badly. He hadn't worn it this short since he was a boy.

By the time he got into the kitchen, George had put plates of food and glasses of water on the table. "Do you want something else to drink?" he asked as Zephyr sat down. "I can grab something from the cooler." He didn't say a word about Zephyr's haircut, although he must have noticed it. Instead, he acted as if it was nothing new or unusual.

"Water's fine," Zephyr said. "How come you never have any beer or anything?"

"Want some? I can get some from the mini-mart."

"No."

George took the seat opposite him and spent a few seconds rearranging napkin and silverware. He wasn't looking at Zephyr, and his expression had closed in.

"Is it the cost?" Zephyr asked.

"No. I mean, not mostly." George traced a design on the tabletop with his fingertip, shot a quick glance at Zephyr, and looked down again. "My parents drank. Quietly, you know? Dad would wait until after he locked the doors in the evenings, and then he'd sit in his office with a bottle of Jack Daniels and a glass tumbler. Or maybe a gin and tonic when he was feeling optimistic about life. Mom, on the other hand, drank all day. Vodka and Diet Coke. James and Mary both picked up the habit in high school, although they've both been sober for a long time now. Al and I, we watched them and maybe learned a lesson. Neither of us touched the stuff."

"Did your parents abuse you?"

George looked up at him then, shocked. "No! I can't remember either of them even spanking me. Dad yelled, but he wasn't abusive—just demanding and stressed, I guess. Mom never even raised her voice."

Zephyr took a few bites of food. It seemed dry and tasteless, but that was almost certainly due to his own issues and not Arturo's lack of culinary skill. After he swallowed, he looked George straight in the eyes and replied. "I don't drink either. I don't use at all. It was an issue with Brandon, who enjoys his recreational pharmaceuticals and wanted me to join in."

"Why have you made that choice?"

"'Cause most people like me are junkies—is that what you're thinking?"

"I've never met anyone like you." George managed a tight smile.

Zephyr relented. "Same reason as you. Didn't want to repeat all of her mistakes." He didn't specify who he was referring to, but George looked as if he understood.

"It's hard," George said. "Sometimes I got angry with them. But Al took some psych classes—he was a psychiatric nurse for a while—and he and I talked about our parents a lot. We figure Mom was self-medicating for depression, and Dad…." He trailed off.

"Dad?" Zephyr prompted.

"Al and I don't agree about that." George got up, taking his plate with him. "Needs more nuking," he said.

The rest of the meal passed in a silence made heavy with unvoiced truths. But Zephyr was grateful for the company nonetheless and glad he wasn't lying in the bunk of a truck cab, feeling every bump in the road, trying hard not to wonder where he'd end up and what he'd do next.

He and George had a quiet evening on the couch with their books. George had his phone on silent, but it buzzed occasionally. He glanced at it the first couple of times and then ignored it. Brandon calling from different numbers, Zephyr assumed. He wondered whether the landline was still off the hook. Maybe George had simply unplugged it from the wall.

They got into bed without any of the previous night's passion or playfulness, although Zephyr was naked again and George wore nothing but a pair of boxer briefs that had a couple of holes below the elastic waistband. Yet as soon as they were both beneath the covers, they moved into each other's arms as smoothly as if they'd been doing it for years. Zephyr tucked his shorn head under George's chin and heaved a heavy sigh.

"Hinkley," George said.

"What?"

"You think the Junction is the most miserable little pocket of nowhere, but it's way better than Hinkley."

In fact, Zephyr hadn't been thinking negatively about Conrad Junction, even if it wasn't the most beautiful or exciting place he'd visited. "What's wrong with Hinkley?"

"Whole place is poisoned. Groundwater contamination that causes cancer. They made a movie about it, even. *Erin Brockovich*."

"More Julia Roberts." Zephyr winced at the memory of his earlier outburst.

"Yeah. It's about thirty miles from here. Whole place is basically a ghost town now. They don't even have a mini-mart."

"Or Fossil Galaxy."

George kissed the top of his head. "Nope. Anyway, my point is that there are places that suck even worse than this one. At least here, we can safely drink the water."

"I guess that's something." Zephyr felt George's heartbeat, solid and steady, and felt their body heat mingle. "Hey, George?"

"Hmm."

"Is there a barber in Conrad Junction?"

George chuckled softly. "Not exactly. But Judith's not bad with a pair of scissors."

"Think she'd fix mine?" He punctuated the question with a yawn.

"I bet she would."

CHAPTER NINETEEN

GEORGE

October 2021

GEORGE WATCHED as Zephyr passed through the gift shop with a wave and a secretive smile. He had paint on his clothes—an old pair of George's sweatpants and a Fossil Galaxy tee—and held a paper grocery sack in one hand. Zephyr was probably headed to the shower now, because that had been his routine these past few weeks, followed by making them lunch. Judith would arrive soon afterward, freeing George to work on projects for a while. Today he was going to spend some time in the garden. A light freeze was due tonight, and although the citrus trees were in a protected location, he wanted to water them as an extra safeguard. He wished he had the money to buy lights to string on them, as his mother used to do. She said that gave them a little warmth. It looked pretty too.

On the other hand, maybe he should just be thankful that he and the business were still here. When schools had started back in session, he'd had an unexpected rush of field trips. Even though he gave schools a deep discount, the reduced admissions were still better than nothing. Plus, many of the kids had spending money for cheap souvenirs. All those neon-hued pens and dino-shaped erasers added up eventually. So he'd managed to stay afloat a little longer, and although Zephyr kept offering the money he'd brought with him, George hadn't needed to touch it. Yet.

He got lost in memories of the previous night, when the two of them had been unusually gymnastic in bed. So much so, in fact, that he was still a little sore today but in such an absolutely pleasant way that he kept flexing the overtaxed muscles just to feel the remaining tightness. It had been a very good night. Lately, all his nights were good, whether or not he and Zephyr had sex. Because no matter what, they shared dinner and then had their quiet time together with books and TV and conversation. Although Zephyr sometimes still seemed on edge and he almost never discussed his past, his smiles came more easily than they used to. And when he'd ordered himself a few items of clothing online—he could only borrow George's meager wardrobe for so long—he'd included platform sandals and a few pairs of lacy panties in a hot pink that tasted like blueberry pie.

When Zephyr meandered back into the gift shop holding two plates of peanut-butter-and-jelly sandwiches and chips, he was wearing those sandals. He'd been keeping his hair even shorter than George's, which emphasized his cheekbones and slightly pointed chin. Now he'd used some kind of hair product to arrange it in little spikes that reminded George of some of the sauropod dinosaurs' spines, although he knew Zephyr's hair felt much softer.

"Are you ready to tell me your big secret?" George asked as Zephyr handed him his lunch.

"Which one? I'm nothing but secrets."

"I'd be happy to hear any of them, but I was referring specifically to the Project." That's how he thought of it, with a capital P. It was something Zephyr had been working on for weeks, sometimes with help from Santiago or Lucas and twice with an added mystery appearance by Lyle Cohen. So basically, all of the Junction knew what Zephyr was up to, but George was allowed to see only a large lumpy thing covered by tarps.

Zephyr swallowed a bite of sandwich. "It'll be ready soon."

"That's frustratingly vague." In truth, George didn't mind. Zephyr was clearly having fun with whatever it was, and George was enjoying the puzzle. It was a good distraction for them both.

"Hey, did you see what Maria brought me this morning? A really fantastic old leather biker jacket. It was her husband's."

Maria was Kayla's grandmother, and she'd taken an immediate liking to Zephyr, apparently seeing him as a good focus for her grandparenting now that Kayla was in LA. She stopped by weekly with tamales and other homemade treats, and she'd gifted him with some of her vintage costume jewelry. And now, it seemed, something to help fend off the nighttime cold.

"I bet you look good it in it," said George.

"Yeah. I'm thinking it'd go great with a short pleated skirt and maybe a strappy little camisole." He ran a finger across his chest as if to demonstrate. "If you wouldn't mind your employee dressing like that."

George shook his head, sad that Zephyr was still a little insecure about how George—and the public at large—would react to his clothing choices. "It doesn't violate the dress code."

Zephyr's eyes sparkled. "What *would* violate the dress code? 'Cause you haven't been at all clear about it, and I have yet to receive my copy of the employee handbook. What if I wore nothing but that jacket and, oh, maybe a red see-through thong?" He waggled his eyebrows for good measure.

"I think that might increase our business considerably. Just don't do it during a school field trip."

Zephyr opened his mouth as if to reply but closed it when the mail van stopped at the front door. Debra came inside the gift shop carrying a little stack of sales circulars and envelopes. "Shipping rates increased," she said by way of greeting. "All the way through Christmas. That's what those geniuses in Washington think is a good plan."

"Prices for everything are going up," said George gloomily.

"You oughta raise your entrance fees. Tack on another dollar."

"Maybe." He and Zephyr had been discussing just that but hadn't yet come to a decision. More income would be nice, but the increased cost might be enough to discourage people from coming. A marketing firm could probably figure out whether the increase was worth it, but if George could afford a marketing analysis, he wouldn't be sweating over an extra dollar per ticket.

"Gonna need your signature for this one." She held out her electronic pad, which George scribbled on with his fingertip, hoping he didn't look too panicked. As far as he was aware, none of his bills were overdue and all of his business paperwork was in order. But what if he'd missed something important? Or maybe some other financial disaster waited to spring from the unremarkable white envelope.

Debra headed out after a few moments of chitchat, leaving George to stare at the terrifying piece of mail. There was no indication of the source, other than an address in New York City.

Zephyr had paused his lunch to watch George. "Instead of stressing about it, you could just open the damn thing."

"I know."

"Maybe it's good news. A distant relative you've never heard of has died and left you a fortune. And a title. Now you're the Baron of, um...."

"Boron. The Baron of Boron. Sure. Or maybe the National Endowment for the Humanities has awarded Fossil Galaxy a million-dollar grant to modernize our galleries."

Zephyr nodded. "Or a famous producer wants to do a documentary on the Harlow family."

"Ugh. Nobody would watch that. Okay. Here goes." Wincing in anticipation, George slit open the envelope and pulled out a single sheet of paper. He glanced at the letterhead, which was from something called Sherburne Industries.

But before he could read the letter, Zephyr hissed.

"Oh fuck," he said, his jaw clenched.

"What's the matter?"

"That's Brandon's family company. He's Brandon Sherburne."

George had gone all this time without knowing—or wondering about—Fuckface's last name. He scowled. "What kind of business is it?"

"It's a…. They own lots of other companies. Insurance, real estate, restaurants, paper products… I don't know all of them."

"A conglomerate," said George, remembering his college business classes. He was somewhat relieved, actually. Zephyr's sparing descriptions of Brandon, together with the brief but nasty interactions George had experienced with the guy, had left the impression that Fuckface was into something nefarious. Drug dealing, organized crime… something like that. Now it looked as if he was more simply involved in exploiting workers and, most likely, contributing to climate change.

"Brandon's one of seven kids. His father's on wife number four or five, I forget. Brandon works for the company, but he and dear old Dad don't get along very well. I'm fairly sure that one of my main attractions, in Brandon's eyes, was that it would piss off the old man."

George didn't care how big an asshole the elder Sherburne was; he had no sympathy for Fuckface. "What does Sherburne the Younger do?"

Zephyr's laugh held little humor. "Dunno. He has a title—VP of something—and he does meetings." He looked as if he wanted to tear the letter out of George's hands, but instead he walked a few steps away and stood with his back to him. His posture was stiff, as if he were constructed from plywood, and George badly wanted to place a hand on his vulnerable nape. But George had learned already that there was a limit to how much comfort Zephyr would accept. Maybe, like Tommy, he'd shatter if pushed too hard.

So George kept his distance, even though it made his heart ache. He distracted himself by looking at the signature. The letter wasn't signed by Brandon but rather by someone identified as an associate general counsel. A lawyer. Lovely.

Predictably, the text was thick with legalese. George had to read it three times before it made any sense, and even then he was confused. "Fuckface's lawyer says that unless I immediately cease all contact with you, he's going to sue me for alienation of affections."

Zephyr spun around to stare at him. "What the fuck?"

"They'll be asking for one-point-four million dollars in damages. Plus attorneys' fees."

"That's fucking insane."

"Agreed."

"God." Zephyr pressed the heels of his hands against his forehead. "I fucked up so bad, and now he's after you, and—"

"Let him sue. What's he going to get out of me if he wins? I don't have any money for him to grab."

Unmollified, Zephyr shook his head. "You have assets. He could end up owning Fossil Galaxy."

"Lawsuits take years. By the time he gets this one to court, this place'll probably be a solar farm." George didn't have to feign calm; he wasn't the least bit worried about this threat. Maybe years of watching his business go slowly down the drain had desensitized him, and the general existential dread of recent years had done the rest. He just couldn't work up any concern over the letter.

Zephyr, on the other hand, was breathing hard. "You don't understand. He has a bottomless pit of money to draw from."

"And I'm what the legal profession would consider judgment-proof." He set the stupid paper on the counter. "Look, I'll call Al, okay? He's not a lawyer yet, but I bet he knows enough to tell us whether we need to worry."

After a long moment, Zephyr gave a shaky nod, although he still looked miserable. "If I go away, he'll leave you alone."

George had known from the beginning that whatever he and Zephyr had was incredibly fragile. There were dozens of reasons why their relationship was doomed, and eventually Zephyr would do as his name suggested and blow away. George also knew that when it happened, he'd be heartbroken. But he'd determined that whatever time he had with Zephyr was worth the inevitable pain and had promised himself he would accept Zephyr's departure with grace.

"Do you want to go?" George tried to keep his voice steady.

Zephyr walked closer and looked up at him. "No," he whispered.

George couldn't stop the huge relieved sigh. "Then stay. Forget about him."

"I've made so many bad decisions."

"Have any of your bad decisions ever harmed anyone else?"

Zephyr frowned thoughtfully. "Um… not that I can think of." He seemed taken aback, as if this thought had never occurred to him.

"All right, then." George wasn't precisely sure what point he was trying to make, but he felt that it was important to say these things anyway. "You're nothing like him, and you need to stop blaming yourself for his assholery."

"Assholery?" Zephyr almost smiled.

"That's the official name for it, yes."

They finished their lunch without mentioning the letter again, although Zephyr kept glancing over to where George had left it on the counter. Eventually George decided that he might as well move the elephant out of the room and set it on the messy desk in his office instead. When he came back out, he was smiling. "I just remembered something."

"Something important?"

"Nope, just funny. One of my dad's wild plans. He heard that a museum in Nebraska had one of the world's largest collections of fossil elephants and the biggest mammoth skeleton anywhere. So he decided we'd have the biggest collection of fossil camels and bear-dogs."

His father had gone on about these plans for months, drawing up sketches of a new exhibit hall and pondering whether he could start an annual Fossil Festival. "We'll have to build a hotel for all the tourists, of course," he'd said. "And more restaurants. Maybe we can get real, live camels and charge people for rides."

Even back then, when George had only been nine or ten, he'd realized that none of it would ever happen. His father couldn't begin to afford a collection like that, and even if he could, the general public would likely be less enthusiastic than he was. But Dad had been really excited about the idea for a while, which meant he drank less, so George had been supportive.

"Didn't work out, though, huh?" Zephyr asked gently.

"His plans never did. But at least he had them. Better to have pie-in-the-sky dreams than none at all."

"What are your dreams?"

"You know. Keeping this place alive as long as I can."

"Is that really your dream? Or your nightmare? What about finishing your college degree and doing something with plants?"

George didn't want to answer that. He collected the lunch dishes and carried them into the apartment, leaving them in the sink for later. While he was there, he called Al.

"Hey, Georgie, is everything all right?" There were voices in the background, along with a sound George suspected was an espresso machine.

"Yeah, I'm all good. Did I interrupt your studying?"

"I'm deep in the details of promissory estoppel, which means I'm happy to take a break to talk to my favorite younger brother. Is, um, that guy still there?"

George rolled his eyes. "Zephyr, and yes." He'd mentioned Zephyr to James a few weeks earlier, and apparently word had moved through the Harlow gossip circle. He hadn't shared many details, but James had been suspicious of Zephyr's character and morals on general principle alone.

"Is he treating you right?"

"Yes, Alcide. And I'm a grown man who can look out for himself, remember?"

There was a slight pause before Al replied. "I know. Sometimes I still picture you, like, twelve. All giraffe legs and dumb hair. And I worry about you, alone in that place."

"But I'm not alone. Zephyr's here." For the time being, anyway. "Look, I want to hear how law school is going, but I actually called for some advice. Can I be your first client?"

Al huffed a laugh. "I'll be happy to help with my vast six weeks of legal experience."

George told him about the letter. For context he had to disclose some aspects of Zephyr's situation, including the harassing phone calls they'd received. Al made a lot of unhappy noises over all of that, but he didn't even hint that any of it was Zephyr's fault, so that was good.

In the end, Al groaned. "What a mess."

"I hope not. I mean, what's the big deal if he does sue?"

"I don't know. Let me do a little research, okay? I'll get back to you."

They chatted for a few more minutes before Al needed to return to work. George ended the call, feeling thankful for family.

A RUSH of visitors arrived later that afternoon, with over a dozen groups stopping in. George had no idea why, but he wasn't about to look a gift tourist in the mouth. While he kept busy discussing the fossils, Zephyr must have been equally occupied in the gift shop. By the time the last of the horde left, the shelves looked a little bare and Zephyr was grinning delightedly.

"What was *that*?" he asked, watching George clear out the till.

"Sometimes the universe just sends us a gift."

Zephyr snorted. "The universe sends me coal in my stockings."

"That's Santa."

"Whatever." Zephyr moved in closer, pressing his sharp chin into George's shoulder. "The universe sent me you, though. So I guess it's not always shit."

George sighed; he'd thought about this part a lot. "What if I hadn't taken the trash out that night? Or what if you'd ended up at the Burger King dumpsters or the gas station instead?"

"You did and I didn't, and here we are."

Here we are, but where are we going? It wouldn't be fair for George to ask that out loud. Zephyr had never made any promises, never pretended there was more to them than there was. But it didn't mean that George couldn't yearn for more. He had the notion that after Zephyr blew out of town, his own heart would wither into a desiccated husk, never to be used again.

Maybe that wouldn't be such an awful thing. Plenty of people did just fine on their own, neither needing nor wanting a partner. And George had plenty of friends—the true kind, the kind he could count on, no matter what.

But God, it was going to hurt when he lost Zephyr.

"That's not the expression of a business owner unexpectedly flush with income," Zephyr said.

"It's not exactly a fortune."

"But it'll pay some bills."

George nodded. He didn't want to be a downer at the end of a good day—ignoring that stupid letter, of course—so he forced a smile. "Hey, *Dune* premieres today. Oscar Isaac, Timothée Chalamet, *and* Jason Momoa."

"On HBO. We don't have HBO."

Trying to ignore the delightful weight of that little pronoun, *we,* George gave an evil cackle. "Ah, but I know James's login and password."

Zephyr slapped a palm to his chest, feigning shock. "No! Is Saint George actually talking about breaking the *law*? Mercy me!"

"I doubt it'll put me on the FBI's Ten Most Wanted list. Anyway, James is my brother and he made me a profile and everything."

"Uh-huh. Next thing we know, you'll be knocking over liquor stores and robbing banks."

"We have neither of those in the Junction."

They continued the banter as they went through the comfortable routine of shutting down for the night. George had closed up shop by himself thousands of times, but it was so much nicer to do it with a companion.

Eventually, they moved into the apartment, where Zephyr set the table and chopped veggies for a salad as George reheated a potato-vegetable-ground beef casserole. Mary had sent him the recipe because it was cheap, easy, and filling. He wasn't too fond of the jumble of flavors the synesthesia gave him, but if he didn't look at his portion while he ate, it was tasty. Plus, the recipe made enough to last them for two or three meals.

They were halfway through dinner when George's phone buzzed. Zephyr froze, his fork halfway to his mouth. "If that's Brandon…."

George checked the screen and gave a little sigh of relief. He declined the call but sent a quick text saying he'd ring back after dinner. "It was Al. Fuckface hasn't called in a long time."

"He doesn't have to call. He can have his lawyers send letters instead."

"And I will shred those letters and add them to the compost bin, where they can do some good."

Zephyr snorted. "Don't. They're probably poisoned." He moved his hand as if intending to push away the long hair he didn't wear anymore. He did that often when he was upset. George found the gesture both endearing and a little sad. Not because he found Zephyr any less beautiful with short hair but because the movement seemed to speak to Zephyr's continuing uncertainty about who he was and who he wanted to be.

After they cleaned up, they played a little game Zephyr had invented a few weeks earlier, after he'd borrowed the van to collect supplies in Barstow for his mysterious project. The supplies must have come from a hardware store, because he'd returned with a thick stack of paint-chip cards. At first, he'd been hesitant to show them to George, until George realized what Zephyr was up to and joined in with enthusiasm. Now Zephyr would pull out a couple of cards each night and ask George what the colors tasted like.

"Bacon," George said tonight, pointing to a slightly greenish beige called Foggy Morning. "Ugh, Caribbean Sunset tastes like gasoline fumes. Coral Reef is… kiwi."

Zephyr made little notes on the back of each card, cataloging George's flavors. It was sweet of him—making George feel a bit like a scientific specimen worthy of study rather than a freak—but he didn't know why Zephyr bothered.

He wrinkled his nose at a chip labeled Jojoba. "Unsweetened chocolate."

"Really?"

"When this place was still a café, we used to serve hot chocolate in winter. Because the desert can get surprisingly cold, right? It was called Carnotaurus Cocoa because all the menu items were themed. Dad's idea. Each evening, one of us kids was allowed a mug of it as a special treat. Whoever had done the best on their chores or gotten a good grade— that kind of thing. Sort of a little contest." He smiled, remembering how proud he'd felt when his dad had praised him for a job well done. As the youngest child, George hadn't often been the winner, but it had sure felt good when he was.

"So one time, it had been a while since I'd earned the prize, and I was jonesing for the stuff pretty bad. When I thought nobody was looking, I grabbed the canister of cocoa from the shelf. It was… mmm… right over there." He pointed to the spot in the kitchen where staples such as that had once been stored. Of course, the space had looked entirely different then, with lots of stainless steel and a battered commercial stovetop.

"What did you do with it?" Zephyr's voice was soft.

"Well, I had no idea how to make it into a drink. But I figured, it's chocolate—it's gotta be good no matter what. I grabbed a spoon and dug in. Oh man."

"Not good?"

"Bitter and dry. Awful." He shuddered at the memory. "And then the cook saw me skulking in the corner, probably making gagging noises, and ratted me out to Dad. Who made me keep eating the stuff until I had to run off to the bathroom and puke."

Zephyr was frowning. "That's cruel."

"It was punishment. I knew better. Anyway, that's what sage green tastes like to me: unsweetened chocolate. Something that you'd expect to be delicious but it turns out to be really gross."

Although George chuckled, Zephyr's expression remained serious. He opened his mouth as if he was going to say something, then, after giving a little shake of his head, shut it again. He clapped George's shoulder and collected the day's paint cards into a little pile. "Didn't you say something about *Dune*?"

"Yeah. But I'd better call Al first."

"Do you want some privacy while you guys talk?" Zephyr jerked his head toward the door to the gift shop.

"No, of course not. This is your business too. Anyway, I don't have any secrets from you."

"But you do have some from yourself." Zephyr held up a hand, heading off George's objection. "Sorry. Let's just get this out of the way and settle in for some of *Dune*'s desert spice. As if we don't have plenty of desert already."

George sat on the couch to make the call, and Zephyr hovered nearby, seemingly ready to escape at any moment. Flashing what he hoped was a comforting smile, George turned his attention to the phone and dialed.

"Fine dining, little brother?"

"Sure. Prime rib and caviar. You?"

"I had contracts, with torts for dessert."

"Yum," George said.

"So, remember, I'm not exactly Clarence Darrow, but I did some research on that lawyer letter you got."

"And?" While George didn't feel especially worried, Zephyr was visibly thrumming with anxiety.

"And I dunno if that dude's a bona fide attorney, but he's certainly absolutely full of shit." Al had always had a strong streak of righteousness. When they were kids, he ratted out his siblings if they failed to follow the rules. He was teacher's pet many years running, mostly because he was smart and teachers could count on him to be the classroom narc. He'd become less obnoxious by high school, but now he was clearly enjoying catching a professional who was either a liar or a fool.

If there was a professional. "Maybe the lawyer doesn't even exist," George pointed out.

"Nah, I checked. The guy's a member of the New York bar and he works for Sherburne Industries. Of course, that doesn't mean he wrote it. Someone else could've slapped his name on it."

George wasn't sure which was worse: a fabricated lawyer letter or a nonsensical real one. "So the threatened lawsuit?"

Zephyr had slowly worked his way near the couch, close enough to hear Al's end of the conversation.

"Can't happen. Nowadays, alienation of affections is only a thing in six states, and New York and California aren't on the list."

"It does sound kind of… Victorian."

"It's older than that, but yeah. Plus, even where it's allowed, the plaintiff has to be legally married to the other person. Zephyr isn't, is he?"

That possibility had never crossed George's mind. Maybe not Zephyr's either, because he shook his head, wide-eyed.

"Nope," George reported.

"Cool. Not that it matters, but still good. Also, for an alienation claim to succeed, the plaintiff has to prove that the defendant lured the spouse away through malicious misconduct. I'm guessing that wasn't your game plan."

That brought a derisive snort. "Yeah, sure. I showcased my many attractions, such as my failing business in the middle of nowhere."

"Georgie, whoever wrote that letter is blowing it out their ass. Just trying to scare you. The potential lawsuit isn't a problem." He paused a moment and then spoke slowly, clearly choosing his words with care. "But how's everything else?"

"Fine."

Another pause, this one longer. "You know, my roommate's moving out in December, and this little house is pretty sweet. I've got a yard with an apple tree and blackberries, and plenty of stores and stuff in walking distance. Most of 'em are hiring. Salem's not exactly thrilling, but it beats the Junction, and Portland's not far."

Silence hung between them as George closed his eyes against the cold weight in his chest. He knew Al meant well by the offer, but it stung nonetheless.

"I'm staying here," George said finally.

"Zephyr's welcome too, of course. I'd love to meet him. You know, none of us have ever met anyone you were seeing."

George's eyes were still shut. "Then come here." He almost said *come home*, but he knew that was a lie.

"Sorry, Georgie. I can't." Al sounded thick with regret.

And dammit, George had no right to put him in that position, especially when Al was busy already and doing him a favor. "I get it. Thanks for helping us out today. I appreciate it."

"Any time. You take care, all right?"

As George set the phone aside, Zephyr startled him by plopping heavily onto the couch. Instead of looking relieved, he was frowning.

"See?" George said. "The letter is a nonissue."

"Al cares about you, doesn't he?"

Taken aback by what seemed to be a non sequitur, George blinked. "Of course. We're brothers."

Zephyr shook his head. The one time George had asked him about siblings, Zephyr had responded with something vague and noncommittal, his usual MO whenever his family history came up. George hadn't pushed since Zephyr seemed uncomfortable with the subject. Not everyone came from a loving family.

"If he cares about you, how come he won't visit?"

"Because he's nine hundred miles away in Oregon, and he's super busy with school. Before that, he was super busy with work. He's that type." All of that was absolutely true… but it wasn't an honest explanation. And Zephyr, judging from his expression, knew it.

"Okay, fine. Then what about your other sibs?"

"Mary's even farther away, in Kansas."

"James isn't. Didn't you say he lives in California?"

George looked away. "Carlsbad."

"So… what? Three hours' drive?"

"He's busy too. A wife, kids, a job, a—"

"Bullshit." Zephyr glared at him. "I don't care if he's running all of San Diego. He could plop his ass into a car and come up and visit you once in a while. George, when is the last time you saw any of them?"

George pretended to think, although he knew the answer perfectly well. He also knew that Zephyr wouldn't be placated by the fact that they'd all Zoomed a few times over the past eighteen months.

"Mom's funeral," he whispered.

"That was a long time ago."

"Nine years."

Zephyr moved nearer on the couch, so close that their thighs pressed together. When he spoke, he was uncharacteristically gentle. "How come?"

"Conrad Junction doesn't have many attractions. Except Fossil Galaxy, which they've seen."

"It has you. They know you can't really get away, and I don't think they want to avoid you. So they must be avoiding this place instead. Why?"

"How should I know? Ask them."

George lurched to his feet and stomped to the bathroom, where he slammed the door with unnecessary force. He didn't need the toilet, and he refused to look in the mirror. His face probably sported the ugly blotchy patches he got when he was upset. After a few steadying breaths, he splashed cold water on his cheeks.

He emerged a few minutes later to find Zephyr waiting exactly where he'd left him.

George sat down and grabbed the remote. "Ready for *Dune*?"

CHAPTER TWENTY

November 2021

THE FEW days before Thanksgiving were busy at Fossil Galaxy. A lot of families were road-tripping for the holiday, and college kids headed home with cars full of dirty laundry. Some of the travelers stopped in Conrad Junction, and a subset came to look at rocks and fossils. George gave tours while Judith put in extra volunteer time and Zephyr managed the gift shop.

It was great to have the hours pass so swiftly and even better to count the till and see extra zeroes at the end of the day's receipts. "The puzzles and toys were a good idea," George told Zephyr as they closed up on Wednesday. "They've been selling well."

Back around Halloween, Zephyr had suggested that they might temporarily decrease the orders for tank tops and other summer wear and instead bring in more toys—not just dino jigsaws but also plastic model kits and those excavation sets where kids could uncover fake fossils from a plaster matrix. George had been hesitant, but when Judith and Santiago took Zephyr's side, in the end he'd agreed.

"Selling really well," Zephyr agreed smugly. "I've been pushing 'em. Great Christmas gifts, right? A good chance to get a little ahead on holiday shopping."

"You win." George smiled at him.

Judith had gathered her coat, hat, and gloves, bundling up for the thirty-foot walk across the parking lot to her Prius. "You remember I won't be here next week, right?"

George nodded. "Spending Hanukkah with the grandkids. I remember."

"Chicago in late November and early December. I ought to have my head examined. Maybe next year I'll pay to take them on a cruise or off to Disney World, just so I won't have to deal with the weather."

"Is Benny going with you?" asked Zephyr. He'd never met Judith's husband and seemed to view him as a rather mythical character.

"Are you kidding? He says no family members living in subzero temperatures are worth holiday air travel during a pandemic. He'll be spending the week planted firmly in his Barcalounger, eyes glued to ESPN." She fluttered a hand dismissively before looking at them over the rim of her glasses. "Are you boys sure you don't want to join us for dinner tomorrow? We've got one of those all-natural, cage-free turkeys, and I made three kinds of pie."

She'd already tendered the invitation two or three times, pointing out that Fossil Galaxy would be closed. But Zephyr said he wasn't much for holiday gatherings, and George was looking forward to an entire day off with very little on his agenda. "Thanks," he said. "But we have a meal planned, and Zephyr needs the time to work on that secret project he's been dragging out for eons."

"I promised to have it ready by Christmas," Zephyr agreed.

"All right, then. But you won't get to try my famous candied yams, which I prepare without those horrible marshmallows, thank you very much." She dropped her voice and adopted a conspiratorial air. "My secret ingredient is dates."

After she left, George locked the door. There were still some chores to complete, but after a few moments, he looked over at Zephyr, who was restocking a shelf. "Let's knock off early tonight. We can catch up tomorrow."

Zephyr waggled his eyebrows. "You have a better activity in mind?"

"Mayyyyybe."

It was likely that George had enjoyed more sex during his short time with Zephyr than during his previous fifteen years. He'd never before suspected how wonderful it could be and that simply glancing at someone during the day—or even thinking about him—could set his skin tingling and blood rushing. It was all very heady. In the past, he'd assumed that the excitement would pall. That it would be like eating a five-course gourmet dinner at a Michelin-starred restaurant every night: lots of fun for a little while but then it would become too much, making you crave spartan toast and instant ramen. But that hadn't happened. In fact, if anything, his enjoyment had increased—so much that he seriously wondered if it was possible to die from too much pleasure.

Part of the attraction might be that this couldn't last forever. But it had already lasted far longer than he'd expected. Every moment with Zephyr was a cherished gift. He even liked it when they had a minor squabble over dumb things like what TV show to watch or whose turn it was to do the laundry.

Smiling at that thought, George set the security system while Zephyr stored the till in the office safe. There was now enough money to make a bank run worthwhile, which was cause for celebration. But there was no point in doing it until after the Thanksgiving travelers had all returned home. Maybe one evening next week, he and Zephyr could make a run to Boron to deposit the money and pick up groceries. Maybe they could even splurge a little by continuing on to Mojave for dinner at Arturo's. George hadn't eaten in a restaurant in over a year and a half.

"So," George said, dousing the lights and leading the way to the apartment door, "pasta for dinner? We have some—"

"There's someone there."

George spun around to find Zephyr staring out at the parking lot, posture stiff and eyes wide. The exterior motion-detector lights—which, together with the alarm, comprised the sum of Fossil Galaxy's security system—illuminated an empty parking lot. Which was odd. Any traveler who'd stopped by, unaware that the business was closed, would have come in a car.

"Who is it?" George asked.

"Dunno. I just saw a flicker of movement and then the lights came on."

George went to the glass doors and looked outside. He didn't see anything unusual, but his field of vision was limited and the security lights created deep shadows in corners.

"Could it have been an animal? Sometimes we get coyotes." He wasn't sure if they were big enough to trip the sensors, but maybe.

"I saw a person."

George didn't often worry about burglars. There wasn't much worth stealing here, certainly not enough to lure someone to the Junction. Would-be thieves could find much better pickings down the road in Boron.

He looked over at Zephyr, who'd remained rooted in place. "How about you do a quick survey of the interior? Double-check that all the doors are locked. I'll look outside."

"What if they're dangerous?"

George shrugged. "I guess I could find something to use as a weapon. Um…." He looked around quickly. Unless the potential intruder could be scared off with plastic dinosaurs inexpertly thrown at his head, there weren't many options.

"No," Zephyr said. "He could have a gun. You don't have one, do you?"

"Nope." And he'd never used one either. Also, his last physical fight had been with Mary when he was ten, and she'd won it quite easily. "I can call the cops."

"Who'll take forever to get here and be useless or worse once they arrive. Forget it." Zephyr set his jaw stubbornly. George knew that Zephyr distrusted the police; he had hinted about past abuse without offering details. While George had never had any negative experiences himself, he wanted to respect Zephyr's feelings. Besides, Zephyr was right—it would likely be at least fifteen or twenty minutes before a deputy arrived.

As they stood there, the exterior lights went off. Now there was almost complete darkness both outside and in, with just a little light creeping over from the Burger King lot.

"I'll tell you what. Santiago and Lucas can be here really fast, and they're both pretty big guys. Plus, Santiago has that ridiculously big truck. Jessica calls it his Overcompensationmobile. I'll ask them to swing by and take a look."

"Would they do that for you?"

"I don't see why not. Hang on."

He sent them both a quick text with the basics of his request, and within moments they'd both agreed. Judging from the emojis, Santiago was sort of excited over the prospect.

"I'll do a quick sweep of the inside while we wait." George was pleased with his choice of words. It made him feel bad-ass, which was a rare occasion in his life.

"I'll come with."

It didn't take them long. The building had only enough exterior doors to meet fire code: the main entrance, the apartment access, and two ancient doors that led into the courtyard garden from the storage area and from one of the exhibit rooms. There were no windows other than in the gift shop and the apartment. Creeping around the exhibits with nothing but the light from George's phone and the emergency exit signs was a little weird but not scary. George knew these spaces intimately and could have passed through them with his eyes closed. He deftly steered Zephyr away from obstacles along their route.

By the time they returned to the gift shop, the security lights were on again, but this time the cause was clear: Lucas stood in front of the glass doors, silhouetted by the glare of Santiago's headlights. George quickly fetched the keys and let him in.

"You guys okay?" Lucas asked, glancing around suspiciously.

"We're fine. Where's Santiago?"

Lucas jerked a thumb toward the parking lot. "Stomping around with a baseball bat. He's having a grand old time."

Apparently, George wasn't the only one who enjoyed feeling—temporarily, anyway—a little fierce. "Did you see anyone?"

"Nah. But they could've run off by now. You think someone was trying to rip you off?"

"It was Brandon."

That was almost the first thing Zephyr had said since discouraging George's call to the police. His voice was flat and his face expressionless, but George thought Zephyr's eyes looked hopeless.

"Did you see him?" asked George.

Zephyr shook his head. "But it was him. I know it."

"Is Brandon the dude who killed Tommy?" Lucas looked poised between confusion and anger.

"Yes." Zephyr winced as if he was remembering the bruises Brandon had inflicted on him. "My… ex. Sort of."

"Is he stalking you?"

George hadn't thought of it that way, which was stupid in retrospect. The threats, the phone calls, the fake lawyer letter… none of those were isolated events. Dammit, why had he been so oblivious?

Zephyr crossed his arms and hunched his shoulders, looking very young and small. "I guess," he whispered. Then he looked up at George, stricken. "Fuck, I'm so sorry. I shouldn't have—"

"It's not your fault." George put a gentle hand on Zephyr's arm, but his voice was firm as he repeated himself. "It's not your fault. Brandon is a horrible human being, and all the bad things he does are on him, not you."

Lucas nodded in agreement. "Yeah, man. An asshole is an asshole, pure and simple."

Zephyr didn't look convinced, so George was going to expound on the subject. But then Santiago rushed inside. He was dressed entirely in black—unless you counted the wooden bat he carried—and he was out of breath. "You're gonna want to come see this. Um, maybe turn on the parking lot lights first."

In retrospect, George should have done that at the start. But he was obviously a lot smarter in hindsight than in regular time. He ran to the office and flipped the switches, and then the four of them walked outside.

The cold bit into George immediately. He was wearing nothing but sneakers, jeans, and a flannel shirt, and the temperature was probably hovering right around freezing. Zephyr had even less protection in a lightweight Fossil Galaxy T-shirt. But none of that mattered when they saw why Santiago wanted them to come outside.

George's van had been attacked.

CHAPTER TWENTY-ONE

"MR. HARLOW, you really should have security cameras both outside and inside your premises."

"That would be great. Is the sheriff's department going to pay for them?"

Deputy Lee shook his head. "Sorry. Our budget doesn't allow it."

"Well, neither does mine." George crossed his arms, hoping he didn't look as exhausted as he felt. He just wanted to get this part over with, especially since it was becoming increasingly clear that the police weren't going to be any help.

Sure, Deputies Lee and Moore had dutifully taken photos of the van and notes for their report. And the report carefully listed all the damage: four slashed tires; several hoses and wires cut inside the engine compartment; back doors pried open and cargo area smeared with feces that might or might not be human; upholstery butchered; Fossil Galaxy logos on the sides sprayed over with Day-Glo orange paint that, to George, tasted like vomit. Deputy Lee had even recorded the precise wording of the graffiti, which was mostly variations on the word "fuck."

But there was no evidence that Brandon was the culprit. At least no obvious evidence, such as security camera footage. And the deputies didn't bother looking for fingerprints or other physical traces. Vehicle vandalism wasn't especially high in their crime-fighting priorities. Besides, Brandon was probably no longer in San Bernardino County, and they weren't about to start a national manhunt over this.

Deputy Lee was polite, but it was clear he didn't consider this worthy of his attention. Moore was worse. His expression had tightened as soon as he'd seen Zephyr's polished fingernails, and he'd glowered when George and Zephyr explained who Brandon was and what he'd already done. Of course, Zephyr noticed this immediately, and he kept shooting *I told you so* looks George's way.

George wondered what Santiago and Lucas would have made of the whole little melodrama, but after they gave their brief statements to the police, George sent them home. They had better ways to spend their time.

"He's going to come back," George told the cops. "What if he escalates things?"

"Call 911," Deputy Lee answered promptly.

"It took you half an hour to get here. He could do a lot of damage in that time."

"Sir, in terms of square miles, this is the largest county in the United States. There are nine states that are smaller than we are. We get to calls as fast as we can."

George bit back a sarcastic thanks for the geography lesson. "How are we supposed to stay safe?"

"As I said, cameras. You might consider hiring a private security firm. I'd recommend you consider filing for a restraining order, as well. Mr. Harlow, if you have evidence of, um, Brandon's involvement, you may be eligible for a civil harassment order. And Mr. Steiber, you could attempt a domestic violence order."

Very quietly—but not quietly enough—Deputy Moore snorted. Lee pretended not to hear, although Zephyr gave Moore a hostile glare.

"How do we do that?" George asked, trying to be patient.

"There's a how-to on the California Courts website. It involves paperwork and a court appearance."

Well, that wasn't going to happen. Especially now that George had no way to get to court, short of hitching a ride.

"You could call in for an EPO," Zephyr said to Deputy Lee. Catching George's look of surprise and confusion, he explained. "Emergency Protective Order. Cop calls a judge, judge issues an EPO. It goes into effect on the spot."

George, who didn't want to know how and why Zephyr knew this, looked at Lee expectantly. But Lee shook his head. "I don't have enough to go on. No concrete evidence of physical abuse or threats, nothing to tie your ex to the vandalism."

"We have the lawyer letter," George offered. He hadn't actually composed it, just in case he needed it for some reason. Like to show to the police.

"Sir, if EPOs were issued every time a lawyer made an empty threat, well, a whole lot more people would have EPOs."

They spoke for a few minutes longer, but Moore was already waiting by the door and Zephyr looked as if he was seriously considering lobbing souvenir snow globes at one or both deputies. George curtly thanked Lee—ignoring Moore—and locked the door behind them as soon as they left.

For a long time afterward, George and Zephyr were silent, not looking at each other. Then they both spoke at the same time, uttering the same word: "Sorry."

"Don't," said George, hands raised in a warding-off gesture. "I keep telling you. None of this is your fault."

"But I dragged you into my mess. If I hadn't come here—"

"Then I wouldn't have had you here all this time. God, Zephyr, if I had the choice between being forever free of Brandon's shit or spending another day with you, I'd choose you every time."

Zephyr's bleak expression didn't lighten. "He wrecked your van. You *need* that van, and we both know you can't afford to get it fixed."

George fought back the icy needles of panic that had first blossomed when he'd realized the scope of the damage. He wouldn't think about it right now. Worrying wouldn't help, and he needed to be strong to support Zephyr.

"I'm sorry I wasted our time calling the cops. And that Moore is a homophobe."

Zephyr smiled wryly. "If I'm not responsible for Brandon, you're sure as hell not responsible for Deputy Dolittle and his partner, Deputy Fragile Masculinity." He sighed. "Let's just go eat something. I'm hungry."

Although George was too jumpy to want food, he nodded, turned on the useless security system, and shut off the lights.

They had pancakes, bacon, and OJ, mostly because George hoped breakfast-for-dinner might help lift their mood. When he was too distracted to eat much, Zephyr scooted around to George's side of the table, grabbed a strip of bacon from the plate, and held it in front of George's mouth. "Open wide."

"I'm capable of feeding myself."

"Not as far as I can see. C'mon. The airplane is ready to fly into the hangar." Zephyr waggled the bacon a little. "Isn't that what parents say to get their kids to eat?"

"Mine never did."

"Mine either." But Zephyr kept the food right there until George gave in and took a bite. It was good. He liked bacon but didn't have it very often. Still chewing, he grabbed the rest of the piece from Zephyr's fingers and shoved it into his own mouth.

"Happy?" George demanded.

Smiling wickedly, Zephyr lifted George's right hand and gave the greasy fingers a long, slow lick. And as if that wasn't enough, he wrapped his lips around them and sucked lightly.

Instantly enthralled, George groaned softly and leaned closer, hoping to chase the flavors on Zephyr's damp lips. But Zephyr pulled back and let go of George's hand. "Preview of coming attractions. You have to finish your dinner before you get dessert."

"You're... blackmailing me." George was fairly certain that wasn't the right term, but he wasn't the Harlow who was going to law school, was he? He picked up his fork and stabbed his pancakes. Fine. He'd lick his plate clean if that was what it took to get Zephyr into bed. Or onto the couch. Or... hell. Even the floor wasn't looking too bad.

"How did you learn you had synesthesia?"

George stopped, food halfway to his mouth. "What?"

"I was just curious. When did you figure it out?"

"I've always tasted colors. I guess when I was really little, I assumed everyone did. Sometimes I'd take one look at a food and refuse to eat it because the color tasted yucky. Or I wouldn't want to wear a particular shirt or something. My parents just figured I was being difficult."

He didn't remember many of those episodes, but his siblings did. When he got older, they'd tell tales such as The Time George Pitched a Fit Because His Hand-me-down Pajamas Tasted Like Spoiled Lunchmeat. That one, in particular, was Mary's favorite.

"So how did they learn it was for real?"

"Mrs. Perez, my fourth-grade teacher, was really huge on science. All my siblings had her before me, and she'd bring the class to Fossil Galaxy a couple times a year and let whichever Harlow she had at the time play tour guide. Heady stuff for a nine-year-old. Anyway, I made some offhand comment to her one day about how the flavors of the school colors totally clashed, and she got all excited. Started giving me the third degree. I guess she'd read about synesthesia."

At the time, George had been surprised that an adult took him seriously. And he'd also been pleased with the attention. Sometimes he'd been a little hungry for that, probably because he was the youngest child.

"So Mrs. Perez figured you out."

"Yeah. She was going to talk about it at the next parent-teacher conference, but neither Mom nor Dad could make it. She ended up driving here on a Saturday instead. She told them I had a gift and should get evaluated by a psychologist. That wasn't going to happen—we couldn't afford it, and besides, neither of my parents were big fans of the mental health system. But Dad liked Mrs. Perez, so I guess he compromised and had Mom take me to a pediatrician instead. Voilà—official diagnosis. And that was pretty much that."

After that long burst of conversation, George started wolfing down the rest of his food. He was still focused on Zephyr's teasing promise.

But Zephyr seemed more interested in George's uneventful childhood. "What did your parents do about it?"

"Do?" George echoed, genuinely puzzled. "There wasn't anything they had to do. After that, if I complained about a color, Dad told me to close my eyes or look at something else. Mostly we didn't talk about it. It was just a weird genetic quirk, like how James can wiggle his ears and how all of us have red hair. At least Dad figured it wasn't as embarrassing as Al's stutter or expensive like Mary's asthma meds."

For some reason, that made Zephyr shake his head disapprovingly. But George had tolerated enough of the reminiscing. He swallowed the last of his dinner and washed it down with the remainder of his juice. "Satisfied? I certainly won't faint from lack of nourishment."

"Hmm." Moving slowly and deliberately, Zephyr stood and pulled George's chair away from the table with George still seated. Then he sat down, straddling George's lap and trapping him in place with his arms. "What do you want from me?" he purred.

George's answer came promptly. "Anything you'll give me."

"You're worth more than handouts and spare change, George Harlow. You're worth *everything*. But I can't give that to you." Zephyr's eyes glowed with intensity.

"I don't need everything. I'm not greedy." That was a lie. He was a glutton for Zephyr—but he was also a realist, and he'd never expect the impossible. Anyway, what he had now, warm and solid in his lap, was far more than he'd dreamed of.

Zephyr bent over and snuffled in George's hair before nibbling gently at the point of his ear. He could be so soft and gentle, so playful, so intense. Like the wind, he blew in all directions, but George enjoyed every facet of him. Every confounding contradiction.

As if to prove that point, Zephyr paused his nuzzling and leaned back to gaze into George's eyes. "Are you okay, really?" he asked.

"What do you mean?"

"Tonight was… eventful."

Nope. He'd ignore the panic spiders in his veins and they would just go away.

"It's fine. I'm fine. I mean, it's a mess, but I've handled messes before. You're the one being stalked. Are *you* okay?"

Zephyr laughed humorlessly. "We're both being stalked. A two-for-one deal. And I'm kinda used to… instability. Plus, I haven't lost a damn thing, and I've gained a place to stay, a job to keep me busy, and an amazing man to share my time."

George sighed and rested his head against Zephyr's chest. "Let's just not talk about it, okay?"

After a moment, Zephyr petted George's hair. "Okay. Let's leave the dishes for later too." He dismounted from George's lap, which was disappointing, but then he took George's hand and urged him to his feet. Slowly, fingers interlaced, they strolled to the bedroom, where they peeled off their clothing item by item.

George felt odd. Numb. Or maybe detached, as if he were observing himself in a movie. Sounds reached him from far away, and colors and tastes were muted. Moving was difficult, like striding in waist-high water. And yet deep inside himself, electricity popped and crackled. He didn't understand any of it and didn't know what to do about it, so he stood by the side of the bed, naked.

Zephyr walked over and folded him into a tight embrace. *That* George felt perfectly. The thin strong arms around him, the smooth warm skin against his. The heartbeats that seemed to match, pulse for pulse.

"You're a beautiful man," Zephyr murmured, and George laughed because it wasn't true, but it was nice to hear anyway. Zephyr stroked his back, all the way down to his ass, and then he grazed George's collarbones, his neck, his nipples, with his teeth. It wasn't really fair, because Zephyr was doing all the work while George simply stood there, feeling, but that was as much as he could manage at the moment.

"Tell me what you want," Zephyr demanded.

"Anything. Whatever you—"

"What *you* want."

The words came unbidden. "Hard. I want you in me, making me burn. Give me bruises."

Zephyr shuddered and groaned. "Jesus, George. Yes. I can do that."

And he did.

He pushed George back onto the bed, and he stroked and bit and sometimes even lightly slapped until George was writhing and begging, incoherent with need. It was as if his nervous system—twisty already—had knotted its pathways so that George couldn't distinguish sparks of pain from stabs of pleasure. He couldn't tell where he was, whether his eyes were open or closed, who was making those guttural moans, what parts of his body were currently being exquisitely tortured. The blending of senses became more complex, so that every scent was a symphony and every touch burst with flavor.

When Zephyr finally entered him and thrust, fast and deep, George fell apart completely. Lights flashed as bright as the Mojave sun and his nerves goddamn *sang*.

He floated back into himself eventually and curled up against Zephyr. They were both sweat-slick despite the chilly air. "You good?" George asked sleepily.

"Yeah. You just about did me in. That was…. That wasn't what people ever want from me."

"But you wanted to give it."

"Hell yes."

George smiled. "Okay, then." He gave a jaw-cracking yawn. "It's still pretty early."

"Take a nap if you want. We can get up later for a snack and TV. And we can sleep in tomorrow."

George couldn't remember the last time he'd stayed in bed late. Maybe during lockdown, when Fossil Galaxy had been closed, but maybe not even then.

Although worries about Brandon, the van, the business, and the possibility of Zephyr leaving all gnawed at the edges of his mind, he ignored them and burrowed in against Zephyr, allowing sleep to take him away.

CHAPTER TWENTY-TWO

ON THANKSGIVING morning, they woke up with an elephant in the room, and it wasn't a fossilized mastodon. In fact, it was an entire herd of elephants, each one bigger and heavier than the last. But by unspoken agreement, Zephyr and George tiptoed around the herd as they showered, brushed, and dressed. George did a load of laundry and a quick bathroom cleaning while Zephyr scrubbed up the remains of the previous night's dinner and squeezed some OJ.

Domestic. Simple. No worries in the world, right?

Over toast and eggs, they discussed the day's agenda. "Sorry I can't afford the whole Thanksgiving feast thing," George said.

"No worries. I've never really…. It's never been much of an event for me."

George played with his juice glass, watching the pulp swirl around like tiny undersea creatures. "We celebrated when I was a kid. Mom wasn't usually up to elaborate feast prepping, but Dad insisted we adhere to the traditions pretty strictly. He'd assign tasks to everyone. I got the easiest ones since I was the youngest. Setting the table, opening cans of cranberry sauce…." He shivered at that memory.

"You didn't like that?"

"I didn't mind the work. But cranberry sauce tastes like dirt—the color, I mean, not the sauce itself. One year I tried to open the cans with my eyes closed so I wouldn't taste it, but I ended up slicing my finger pretty deeply on the edge of a lid. See?" He held up his right index finger, where the silvery scar was still visible.

"Ow."

"Yeah. Dad was pissed off at me too. Bleeding everywhere. James ended up having to drive me to the hospital in Tehachapi—he was seventeen so he had his license—and we both missed dinner. We got leftovers, though." And James hadn't even been angry with him; he remembered that.

"Why didn't one of your parents take you?"

"Mom didn't drive, which was probably just as well. Dad was too busy dealing with Thanksgiving stuff." He'd most likely been drunk at that point as well, although George didn't know for sure. At that age, he'd been largely oblivious to the amount of booze his father consumed.

"Oh." Zephyr seemed slightly angry, his brow furrowed and mouth turned down.

"Anyway, I always enjoyed the food. Al learned to make these great rolls from scratch, and Mary's stuffing was the best. But man, it's been a long time."

He would have gone home for Thanksgiving when he was in college, but by then, his siblings had left and his father had abandoned the whole idea. After George returned to the Junction, it hadn't seemed worth the fuss when it was just him and his mother, who was too sick to eat much anyway. And then it was just him, alone. He always had invitations from friends, but joining other families would have felt awkward.

"Well, I never understood it," said Zephyr. "So much fuss over… a meal. Anyway, everyone knows the Pilgrims were disease-spreading assholes, and most of the time, I haven't felt real thankful, so…."

"What about today?"

Zephyr gave a small, fierce smile. "I have lots to be thankful for."

"Me too. I'll tell you what. I'm going to figure out how to make us a little feast for tonight. It won't be traditional, but it'll be…."

"Special?" Zephyr offered.

"Yeah."

WHILE ZEPHYR went off to finish the post-closing chores they'd abandoned the night before, George took a thorough inventory of the fridge and cabinets and then sat down with his phone to look up recipes. Growing frustrated with the small screen, he headed for the office computer instead.

Zephyr was just putting away the dust mop. "We're in pretty good shape here, I think. I'm going to the workshop."

"Mystery project?"

"Clock's a-tickin'."

George had tried not to look outside at the parking lot, but he couldn't resist once Zephyr was gone. His view of the ruined van was blocked, however, by Santiago's truck, idling near the door. Puzzled, George grabbed the keys and went to go out, but Santiago only waved and pulled away.

What the hell was that about? George sent the text, but since Santiago was driving, the response didn't arrive for ten minutes, at which point George was scrolling through appetizing recipe options.

Just checking in, Santiago wrote. *Is everything good?*

AOK. Happy TDay.

U 2.

Checking in. Had Santiago been looking for more evidence of Brandon, or making sure George hadn't had a meltdown? Either option was depressing, so George chose not to think about it. He had a menu to plan.

About twenty minutes later, though, he was at the front door, staring out at the van. It looked worse in the bright daylight, the spray paint even more vile. It squatted low on its ruined tires, reminding George of a prehistoric creature caught in a tar pit.

Shit. What was he going to do?

He was going to make dinner, that was what. But before he could return to the office, a car rolled into the lot. He recognized the silver Civic. Lucas stopped in the middle of the pavement but didn't park. He grinned and waved at George.

George sent a quick text. *What are you doing?*

Patrol.

What does that mean?

Keeping an eye out. Making sure there's no trouble. We have a schedule worked out.

George shook his head. *Who's we?*

Me, Santiago, Kayla & Maria, Lyle. Couple others. Don't worry. We won't bug you. We'll just roll through.

George's eyes prickled with tears, and he turned away so Lucas wouldn't see his face. *You don't have to. Should spend the day with family.*

Just takes a few mins. Having more than enough family time. When I left, Dad and BIL arguing over Bears-Lions game.

Thnx. To all of you.

Enjoy your day off, George.

George turned around and waved goodbye and then returned to meal planning.

He had a workable menu set by lunchtime. He felt pretty excited over it, actually. He never spent hours preparing food, so some quality kitchen time and more elaborate dishes than usual felt like fun. Yet he couldn't prevent a detour on his way from the office back to the apartment, and he stood again at the doors, gazing at the van.

It wasn't a great vehicle. When George was in college, he'd owned a cute little Mini Cooper. It had been his first car, and he'd gotten a great deal when he bought it used from another student who'd just graduated and was moving to Germany. He'd loved that thing. But it wasn't practical once he returned to the Junction and had to take his mother to medical appointments, transport groceries and supplies in bulk from other towns, and sometimes haul items for the business. There had been an official Fossil Galaxy vehicle, an older F-150 pickup with a camper shell. But the wreck that killed his father also destroyed the truck. So George had reluctantly traded in the Mini and taken out a loan for a used Chevy van with slightly scuffed white paint. A friend of a friend in Barstow had painted the Fossil Galaxy logo on both sides.

The van had already clocked fifty thousand miles by the time he'd bought it, and that was a decade ago. Although his lifestyle meant that he didn't drive often, the vehicle was old now. The radio had died long ago, the passenger window no longer rolled down, and the thing bumped and jostled along the highway while making ominous squeaks and rattles.

But he needed it, and he couldn't afford the repairs. He sure as hell couldn't replace it. Without an operational vehicle, he was stranded. He wouldn't be able to make his occasional shopping runs or bank deposits.

God, what was he going to do?

He spun on his heel and strode determinedly back to the kitchen.

THAT NIGHT they ate corn pudding, oven-fried chicken, and biscuits with prickly pear jam. Definitely not a traditional Thanksgiving meal, but it was a feast nonetheless, and their satiated groans as they rubbed their stomachs were genuine and satisfying. George hadn't prepared any dessert; it didn't really seem necessary after all those carbs. But while he and Zephyr still lolled at the table, Kayla texted him.

I'm outside your apt. It's me and not an evil ex. Open up.

He waddled to the door, and as soon as it swung open, Kayla thrust a covered pie tin at him. "Apple, pumpkin, cherry, cheesecake. Two slices of each."

"You didn't have to—"

"We had seven pies for six people, George. We're out of room to store leftovers. Take this."

As soon as he obeyed—he had little choice, really—she laughed and ran back toward the parking lot, where a car engine rumbled.

George closed and locked the door and returned to the kitchen. "Pie?"

"You have to be kidding."

"Isn't overindulgence mandatory?"

When Zephyr grinned like that, George could almost forget that they had any worries. Zephyr's eyes sparkled—not like diamonds, which were cold and dead, but like stars: warm and alive. "I'll take apple," he said.

George chose pumpkin for himself and rejoined Zephyr at the table. There was no room in his stomach for more food, but he ate anyway. And he enjoyed the feast of *looking* at his food, because it turned out that the burnt-orange hue of the pie tasted like salted caramel. The perfect foil for the pumpkin flavor, in fact.

"Kayla's uncle is a baker," George explained. "He co-owns a place somewhere near Burbank. It's where certain celebrities go on their cheat days."

"Don't blame 'em." Zephyr licked his fork before setting it on his empty dessert plate.

"It was nice of Kayla to stop by."

"All your friends have been stopping by all day."

George winced slightly. He hadn't been sure if Zephyr had noticed, and he hadn't wanted to mention the informal security because he didn't want to allude to Brandon in any way. "I have good friends. I'm really lucky."

"You've earned those friendships."

George blinked. "I don't think—"

"C'mon. I've seen with my own eyes, and I've heard stories too. Everyone knows you're broke—you've always been broke—but if someone you know needs something and it's in your power to give it, you do. Without even thinking twice. I called you a superhero, and you are. But you never even have to take off the glasses and put on Spandex and a cape to work your magic."

"I don't wear glasses." Actually, he was a little nearsighted, but he could see well enough to pass his driver's vision test without them, and so the expense had never seemed worthwhile. *Just sit closer to the front of the class*, his dad used to instruct him when George was a kid. That had worked well enough.

Zephyr shook his head, stood, and began to gather the dirty dishes.

AFTER PUTTING away the leftovers and washing up, Zephyr and George lay on the couch, too full and drowsy to do anything else. They watched TV using James's HBO account—*True Blood*, *Family Matters*, *Scooby-Doo*—and George lacked the mental energy to track what was happening in any of them. But that was fine. All that mattered at the moment was the man whose legs were tangled with his.

"What do you think about reincarnation?"

George blinked out of a semi-doze. "Huh?"

"Reincarnation. Your thoughts."

"I... don't know that I have any." He peered at the TV screen, where Shaggy and Scooby-Doo were running through a mansion being chased by a headless ghost. As far as he could tell, past lives weren't a theme of this episode.

But Zephyr wasn't watching TV. He was staring at a blank wall, his eyes unfocused. "One time, I got a ride from a trucker. White guy, fifties, with a big belly and a plaid shirt and a baseball cap. He didn't want sex—just someone to talk to, I guess. And it turned out that what he mostly wanted to talk about was what he might be in his next life."

"That's... not what I'd expect."

Zephyr shrugged. "Truckers have a lot of time to think. Turns some of 'em into philosophers. Anyway, this guy thought that we're supposed to solve... um, puzzles, sort of. In our lives. And if we're good enough at it, then after we die, we get to level up. Come back as someone or something better. But if we don't solve enough puzzles, we have to keep redoing the same level until we improve."

"Existence is a video game?"

"Why not?" Zephyr responded, unsmiling. "Makes as much sense as anything else."

George thought about it for a moment and concluded that Zephyr was right. "My family didn't do religion. Dad said it was too full of lies—he'd go on and on about it sometimes. I think my mom's parents were pretty into church and stuff, and so they didn't approve of him at all. He got into some fights with them early on, and then they all stopped talking to each other. I never met them." He frowned. "Sorry. Got sidetracked there."

"So, if that trucker guy was right, what do you see in your future? Me, I know I'm not moving on. Hell, I might even drop down a level or two. But what about you?"

"I don't think I have that many puzzles."

Zephyr gave him an incredulous look.

"No, it's true," George insisted. "I mean, fine, money. But so far, at least, I've always had a home. Always had family. I've never gone hungry. I've been healthy. I have good friends." *I have you, at least for now.* "I think I've already leveled up pretty far, in fact. Next time oughta be great."

"You don't see— Never mind."

George didn't want to know what Zephyr almost said, so he decided to turn the conversation around. "Anyway, I think you're doing pretty well. You got dealt a bad hand—and yes, I know I switched game metaphors—but you've survived. More than that, actually. You're smart and funny and sweet, and you have the courage to be yourself, even when it's hard. I think you've earned bonus points."

Zephyr looked at him for a very long time, then untangled himself and stood. He stretched luxuriously. "I'm ready to try more pie. You?"

CHAPTER TWENTY-THREE

THE CELL phone started ringing again the next day, well before Fossil Galaxy opened. After the second barrage of threats and obscenities, George had kept the landline disconnected. He blocked all the numbers that sent texts or left voicemails calling him and Zephyr every terrible name possible and promising to exact revenge. But Brandon kept using new numbers—perhaps from an endless supply of burner phones with which to harass people. It was one advantage of being rich, if not too bright.

He considered calling the sheriff's department and showing them some of the stuff Brandon had sent, but he decided it wasn't worth it. Zephyr would get upset if they stopped by, the police would be unwilling or unable to do anything, and George would end up angry. Not to mention that paying customers might be scared away when they saw cops parked outside.

So he kept his cell phone on silent and tried to pretend Brandon didn't exist. At least Zephyr was busy in the storage room and not there to witness the renewed harassment.

At exactly ten o'clock—opening time—Lucas showed up. "How was your Thanksgiving?" George asked as he let him in.

"Football. My sister's older kid sulked because she was making him spend the holiday with us instead of with his girlfriend."

"Isn't he, like, twelve?"

"Thirteen. Oh, and the oven broke before the turkey was quite done, so we had to use the neighbors', and that would've been okay except that I got put in charge of that task. Which meant I had to endure thirty minutes of listening to the neighbors talk politics." Despite the complaints, Lucas looked happy. He and his family were close and enjoyed one another's company.

"Sorry about the oven," George said.

"It's always something. Last year, Dad murdered the garbage disposal when he tried to stuff all the potato peels down there at once. Year before that, the furnace crapped out. I think we're cursed. But that's why I'm here, in fact."

"If you're looking for someone to break your curse, you're barking up the wrong tree."

Lucas laughed and patted George's shoulder. "No magical curse-lifting stones in stock, huh?"

"Not that I'm aware of." And if there were any on the premises, they weren't doing a great job.

"That's okay. I'm here to help out a little with your curse, actually." Lucas waved toward the parking lot. "Um, your van… doesn't look good. Your customers might, uh…."

"You think some of them might object to reading *die cocksucking bitches* in fluorescent paint?" George sighed. "I'm sure I have paint in storage, but it's not the right kind, and I don't know if it'll cover that or just make things worse."

"You know, my cousin has an auto shop in Apple Valley. If it's okay with you, he can truck the van down to his place and get you an estimate for repairs. He'll give you a good deal."

It was uncomfortable to feel gratitude and despair so tightly packaged. "That's really nice of you. But I can't afford anything. Even just the tires would be out of my budget. But thanks."

Lucas nodded as if he'd expected this. Which he probably had; George's financial woes weren't exactly a state secret. "He can take it anyway, though. Pay you something for it, even. Maybe he can fix it up and sell it, or at least use it for parts or scrap."

George considered for a moment. Apple Valley was fifty miles away. "He can have it for free. It'll probably cost him more to haul away than it's worth." At least that would get it out of the Fossil Galaxy lot, where it would haunt him and potentially scare away customers.

"Cool. I'll let him know." Lucas spent a moment texting and then looked up. "He'll be by to pick it up in an hour. Um, you know your pocket is buzzing, right?"

It was, like an angry wasp. He took out his phone, glanced at the screen, and put it away again.

"Bad news?" Lucas asked.

"Just… stupidity."

"Do you want everyone to continue the patrols?"

"You all have lives and jobs and family and you need to sleep. We'll be fine."

Lucas frowned. "Are you sure?"

"Completely."

That made Lucas sigh. "Fine. I'm heading home. We need to go oven shopping on Black Friday—lucky us. You guys be careful, though."

The day's first visitors arrived soon after Lucas departed, followed quickly by another family stopping in on their way back home. Before George became busy with the tours, he left the van keys with Zephyr, telling him to expect Lucas's cousin. By the time there was a lull in guests, the van was gone. It was a relief of sorts.

At some point, Judith had appeared. She'd apparently heard what had happened on Wednesday night, and she was both furious and concerned. "None of this is right. I thought we'd made good advances in how we dealt with stalkers and abusers, but I guess not."

Zephyr blew a raspberry. "Politicians don't really care. They pretend to, but it's all bullshit. Window dressing at best."

"I know," she said with a long sigh. "I marched for things when I was younger. Civil rights. Anti-war. AIDS research and prevention. Women's rights. We were so optimistic. But some days now, I feel like none of it did any good."

Although Zephyr looked as if he agreed, George shook his head. "But it has helped. Things are better—some of them, anyway. Women face way less discrimination than they did back in the seventies, right? All sorts of improvements have been made in HIV treatment. And heck, Zephyr and I could legally get married now if we wanted to. That's progress."

Zephyr had an odd expression. Slightly stunned, perhaps. Maybe George's offhand comment had terrified him. "Don't worry," George assured him. "I know that's not your thing. It was just an example."

Although honestly, now that the words were out of his mouth, he found the idea very attractive. Which was weird, because he'd never given marriage much thought. He'd been too young to even consider it back when he was dating Zak. And once he returned to the Junction, the chances of finding his soul mate and convincing the poor guy to stay with him had seemed extremely slim. Being hit by a meteor was more likely.

But now that he'd spent a few months living with Zephyr, he realized how much he liked it. Not just the sex, but the companionship. The partnership. The sense of being in his situation with someone else.

And this was a completely pointless train of thought.

"I'm going to do some work in the vertebrates exhibit," he announced. "Call me if you need anything."

BY TUESDAY, the holiday rush had ebbed away, leaving only the usual trickle of visitors. Brandon's calls and texts hadn't slowed—they came throughout the days and nights in fits and floods—but George had grown better at pretending they weren't happening. And anyway, he was too busy facing the ever-growing pile of bills.

How much longer could he hold on? December might bring another temporary increase in revenue, as people traveled for the holidays or simply took road trips during time off. If enough people came, he might be able to stay afloat through January or even February. But then what? Even if the pandemic was officially over by then, he didn't hold out much hope that guests would start flocking to Fossil Galaxy. And current news was reporting on another viral strain.

Sitting in his office shortly after the Tuesday closing, George put his head onto his folded arms atop the desk and tried not to cry.

"Hey."

The voice, although soft, made him startle slightly. It was Zephyr, of course, and he came into the office and settled a hand on George's shoulder. "How about some dinner?"

George answered without lifting his head. "I have work to do."

"It'll wait. C'mon. I want to show you something."

The two of them had spent the past several days working together, eating together, sitting on the couch together, sleeping together. Yet it felt as if there was a distance between them even when their bodies touched. George couldn't tell whether Zephyr was drawing away from him. Or perhaps his own numbness was to blame; he'd been feeling as if he were underwater again. And he didn't know what to do about it. Really, he didn't know what to do about *anything*.

Although George suspected the bills on his desk would multiply in his absence, he slowly stood, neatened the paper piles he had knocked askew, and turned off all the office lights but one. Thanks to Zephyr, the gift shop was already set for the morning, souvenirs waiting neatly for customers that would never come. George felt an unexpected pang when he glanced at the spot where Tommy used to be. He missed Tommy, as dumb as that was.

"I think tomorrow I'm going to call that guy in Denver," he said as he and Zephyr walked to the apartment.

"The one who wants the bison skull."

"Yeah. I haven't heard from him in a while, but I doubt he's found another one. Maybe he's still interested."

Zephyr led him to the table and pushed him gently into a chair, refusing George's halfhearted offer to help cook. "We're eating simply tonight. Ramen and tuna sandwiches. I could probably dig up some veggies if I tried."

George waved a dismissive hand. "Don't bother. I'm not hungry."

"You skipped breakfast today."

Great. So Zephyr had appointed himself Meal Monitor. Maybe George could redirect the discussion. "I spent a lot of time this morning looking at your hair and your sweater. Those tasted good enough to fill me up."

Zephyr had unearthed a few items from the silver suitcase, maybe because he was getting tired of wearing Fossil Galaxy shirts. The previous day, he'd worn a gauzy coral-colored blouse with a black camisole underneath, and today he had on a fuzzy sweater in saffron. The neckline tended to drop low, exposing one shoulder, which George found incredibly sexy despite his sense of detachment. And he liked the color as well; it tasted like butterscotch.

"My sweater doesn't give you calories or nutrition," Zephyr argued.

"But it does have fiber."

"Hah." Zephyr dropped a kiss on top of George's head and then sailed over to begin preparing dinner. It was diverting to watch him. He moved so smoothly and fluidly, almost making a dance out of putting water in a pot or opening a can. While he was waiting for the water to boil, he filled two glasses with juice from a pitcher in the fridge and brought them over.

"At least I won't develop scurvy," said George. "No shortage of vitamin C."

"Nope. Hey, you know what I was wondering today? You know how a lot of people who catch Covid lose their sense of smell and taste?"

"Have you lost yours?" George asked with alarm. They'd both been vaccinated long ago, and they were still being careful about masking and social distancing when there were guests in the building. But nothing was foolproof. Nobody was ever entirely safe.

"I'm fine, Georgie. But I was wondering—if *you* got Covid, would you still be able to taste colors?"

"I…." George frowned in thought. "I have no idea. I guess it would depend on which neural pathways are affected. Nobody is even sure how synesthesia works, exactly."

"It would be pretty cool if you weren't affected. Like you have special superpowers of immunity. As befits a hero."

"I'm not—"

"Hush." Grinning, Zephyr diced some onion and added it to the tuna. He liked his tuna salad with relish and George didn't, so they always split the batch into two. Santiago had brought a huge jar of relish from one of his Costco trips, and Zephyr still hadn't finished it off. The jar would probably still be there when Zephyr finally left, and then George would feel a weird obligation to eat it, even though he didn't like it very much. Like many shades of green, the color didn't taste good.

The ramen was good, however, and so was the tuna salad. Apparently, George hadn't realized how hungry he actually was.

After dinner and washing up, they relocated to the couch. George collapsed onto the cushions with a groan, as if today had included something more strenuous than staring at bills and walking through the occasional tour. Man, he was in bad physical shape. He knew that with his work schedule and the climate, he'd never have the chance for much in the way of outdoor exercise. And joining a gym was out of the question since it would involve both money and driving time. And a working vehicle. He used to fantasize about buying some home equipment—maybe a stationary bike and some weights—but he was never able to spare the cash.

"What did you want to show me?" he asked, remembering Zephyr's promise.

"Something I found in the storage room when I was rooting around for parts today. It was inside an old wooden cabinet."

"I don't have the energy to walk all the way over there."

Zephyr gave him a worried look. "That's okay. I brought it here. Hang on." He disappeared into the bedroom. When he returned, he carried a big cardboard box that looked ready to fall apart. He set it on the coffee table.

"What is it?" George leaned forward and saw that the box had no top. Inside was… a diorama.

"It's Fossil Galaxy, right?" Zephyr asked.

It was. The entire building in miniature but without the roof. His father's handwriting, in green felt-tip ink, labeled the gift shop and the various exhibit rooms, each of which had tiny clay and plastic models depicting some of the contents. A minuscule Tommy stood near the front door. Several matchbox cars were glued into the space that now housed the apartment.

"Parking garage?" Zephyr asked.

"No. An antique car collection. It was supposed to be another exhibit, but it fizzled out. The collection never grew big enough to make it worthwhile." He lightly tapped one of the cars, as if that might cause it to magically grow into something big enough to replace the van.

"Who made this diorama?"

"Must have been Dad. I've never seen it before, though. Didn't know it existed." But he could picture his father working on it for weeks, making sure all the dimensions were accurate and the details perfect. He could have done it simply to amuse himself, or maybe it was intended as a schematic to attract investors.

"What's going on here, in the gardens?" Zephyr asked.

The courtyard was properly located, but there were no little replica citrus trees. No plants at all, in fact. Instead, the space contained rows of cages, each with a teeny animal inside. Looking at it made George's chest feel tight. He'd forgotten about this.

"It's a… sort of a little zoo, I guess." His voice was barely above a whisper.

"Did you guys have one here?"

"No." He didn't want to explain, but Zephyr waited, his gaze sharp. George swallowed a few times and, for the first time ever, wished he had some booze. He halfheartedly considered running over to the mini-mart for some beer.

"It was another of Dad's ideas. He wanted to showcase animals native to the Mojave. Reptiles, rodents, some birds. Small creatures, because the courtyard doesn't really have much space. He said it would be a good tie-in with the vertebrates collection. We could have signage explaining how various creatures had evolved and how they compared to the extinct things we have fossils of."

Zephyr nodded. "That makes more sense to me than antique cars."

"I guess. He claimed it would be a big draw for tourists. There's a zoo down in Palm Desert called the Living Desert, and I think he envisioned us growing into something like that. But that place is huge—bigger than all of Conrad Junction, I'm sure."

His dad had been so excited about the concept, talking about it at every family meal for weeks. George had been ten or eleven at the time, and he'd loved the idea. He'd pictured himself feeding the animals, taming them, perhaps teaching them tricks, as if he were a nascent Dr. Dolittle or something. He'd even, at his father's request, done research on native animals, written up little reports, and made evening presentations to the family.

How had he forgotten all of this?

"The zoo didn't work out," Zephyr said. It wasn't a question, just a statement, because the truth of it was obvious.

"It wasn't practical. You need special licensing to exhibit live animals. And it's expensive. Fossilized creatures don't need food or vet care, but live ones do. Most of them have specialized diets too. Then there were the safety issues, since you can't have a complete collection of Mojave reptiles without a rattlesnake or two." In fact, the model included four of them, each with different patterns painstakingly painted on.

Zephyr seemed to be choosing his next words carefully. "I'd think your dad would be pretty discouraged by all that. It looks like his plans were pretty serious, though." He nodded toward the box.

"All his plans were serious, even when they were totally impossible. He never saw the flaws. Someone would point out a problem and he'd start yelling. 'You don't have any vision! Don't be so short-sighted!'" It was scary how much those words, coming out of George's mouth, sounded like his father. He could picture his dad as he'd said them, face red, balled hands waving.

"George—"

"You want to know what derailed the zoo? Mom. She hardly ever said anything when he was going on and on about his latest scheme. He'd just yell her down if she tried—he yelled everyone down—and I guess she figured he'd fail anyway, so why bother."

"George, maybe we should—"

George shook off Zephyr's hand from his shoulder. "This time, though, she spoke up. It was because he wanted to take over the gardens, and that was her thing. Her one thing. The only thing that ever made her happy in this damned place, because her husband didn't, and her kids didn't, and—" He broke off when he realized he was shouting, and he fell back onto the couch, breathing hard.

Zephyr stood watching him, wide-eyed.

"They fought about it for days," George said. "Weeks, maybe. They said some truly awful things to each other, like they were spitting poison, and when they weren't arguing, they were drinking. Both of them." He gave Zephyr a bleak look. "Dad was a drunk too. He just wasn't always as obvious about it as Mom."

Admitting that wasn't a relief. In fact, it made his throat feel closed-up and his skin too tight.

"It must have been hell on you," Zephyr said softly.

"I… I don't know. I don't remember. But I know it was hard on James. He took Mom's side, so Dad screamed at him too. Called him ungrateful and a traitor. Which he wasn't, okay? James just wanted…." A sob almost escaped, horrifying him. Something inside him was cracking, like stone under too much pressure. If he shut up now, he could stop it. He could rebuild his defenses and get on with everything. He could—

"James finally left." Now the words were coming out against his will. "Just threw his stuff in a suitcase and walked out the door. I think he got a ride to LA from a friend here in the Junction, and he stayed there, and he got a job and went to college and got married and had kids and…." Big whooping breath. "And he never came back. Except for Mom's funeral."

Zephyr sat beside him on the couch. But dammit, George didn't want comfort right now, and he didn't want to be too close to Zephyr in case the damage within him spread. He shot to his feet and paced to the opposite side of the room, which wasn't far in his tiny apartment.

"Dad finally gave up on the zoo. I dunno if it was because of Mom or something else. The fighting stopped; the drinking didn't. Mary started drinking and doing drugs right around then, and you'd think it would be hard to be a delinquent in a town this size, but she managed. Al was only a year younger than her, and he kept begging our parents to get her some help, but Mom did nothing and Dad just yelled. She ran away when she was fifteen, a year after James left. She never came back until the funeral either, although she eventually worked things out for herself. She's been doing well for a while now."

He started walking back and forth, because if he stayed still, he'd collapse. Everything inside him hurt, but at least his eyes were dry. At least he still had that. He couldn't look at Zephyr, so he didn't know his reaction.

"Mom withdrew more and more. She started neglecting the gardens, which should have been a sign of how bad things were getting, but nobody said anything. Al and I were afraid to even mention the gardens in case it resurrected the whole zoo thing. Business kept getting worse. Dad was selling off the cars, one by one. And he was working Al and me really hard, pretty much every minute we weren't in school. Al up and left the day after graduation and went to stay with James. He'd managed to land a good scholarship to nursing school, so that was good. Like the others, he stayed away too."

Back and forth, back and forth. Trapped between the walls of his own home. "Then it was just me and my parents."

"You went away to college." Zephyr's words almost startled George out of his rant. But not quite.

"You know why? Judith and her husband. They pulled some strings somewhere, and they leaned on Dad really hard, I think, although I never saw it firsthand. It was hard. Without me, what was going to happen to Fossil Galaxy? To the place my grandfather had built in the desert out of nothing? Anyway, I got a scholarship too, and I promised Dad I'd major in business, because that would help us the most. I promised I'd be back."

Zephyr got up and walked over, blocking George's path. He gripped George's shoulders. "You kept that promise, George. You did come back, and you've worked incredibly hard for over a decade. You've given this place your life's blood."

"Yes," George whispered.

"It's time to move on. Sell the place and come away. You can go anywhere, do anything." Zephyr's voice cracked with emotion. "Be who *you* want to be, instead of just Wally Harlow's grandson. I'll come with you, Georgie."

The image appeared in front of George like a mirage: he and Zephyr walking down a city street, laughing and holding hands, on their way out for the evening. Dinner somewhere nice and a movie, perhaps. And back at home—wherever that was—there'd be a framed college diploma hanging on the wall. And the next morning, a job to go to that involved making things grow instead of watching them die. It was a beautiful idea.

But that was replaced by another vision: Fossil Galaxy half in ruins, the remainder scarred by graffiti, the sign permanently dark.

"No!" He wrenched himself free from Zephyr's hold and lurched away until he was backed into a corner, hands held out at chest height. "I can't! Don't you understand?"

"I'm trying to. You feel an enormous obligation. You want to be loyal to your grandfather's legacy. And to your father's dream. But you don't owe him that. He was too caught up in his own shit to give you what you needed and deserved. You don't owe him anything." Tears spilled from Zephyr's eyes, and he impatiently wiped them away.

The cracks inside George widened. Everything began to crumble, as if it were made of sand.

"Do you see the ink Dad used in that model? Green. It tastes bitter, just like desert plants. Like the aspirin Mom used to swallow all the time—I snuck a handful of it when I was little and shoved it in my mouth, thinking it was candy. Like the peels of oranges on the trees that Dad wanted to kill to make room for his zoo. Like the crappy coffee I used to drink to stay awake in high school after I'd been up late the night before, working here. Like the stuff the dentist used to numb my mouth when she did all kinds of work on my teeth when I was in college—they were fucked up because my parents never took any of us to the dentist when we were kids. Like the tears I cried after Dad drove his car at ninety-three miles per hour over the edge of a fucking cliff!"

George rushed to the coffee table, picked up the box, and hurled it. The diorama fell out. He stomped all over it, crushing the clay models, tearing the cardboard walls, smashing the plastic and metal cars. Destroying the words written in bitter green ink.

And then he broke completely and collapsed to the floor. He was drowning—no, being buried alive in sand. He couldn't breathe.

George dimly registered Zephyr holding him tightly as he sobbed.

Chapter Twenty-Four

ZEPHYR AND GEORGE

IT WAS his fault.

Zephyr had witnessed a lot of painful things in his life. Often, he'd been more than a witness—he'd been the victim. But none of that hurt as much as watching George fall apart and knowing that Zephyr himself had caused it.

It was true that he wasn't responsible for George's bastard of a father, or for the mother too caught up in her own troubles to help. And Fossil Galaxy had been traveling down the slow road to ruin long before Zephyr had shown up. But Zephyr had pushed, hadn't he? Had prodded at the sore spots in George's psyche until they became open wounds. Not to mention that his presence had brought additional financial burdens and the affliction of that fucker Brandon as well.

And now George, strong George—Zephyr's hero—had cried so hard that he had to run to the bathroom and puke. And even after that, the tears continued. George's handsome face was puffy and blotchy, he'd gone through half a box of tissues, and although he remained on the couch in Zephyr's arms, George shook as if he were chilled.

Zephyr didn't offer false words of comfort. There was no way around it: George carried an enormous weight of grief, anger, and fear. Zephyr wasn't going to tell him everything was all right, because it hadn't been and probably wouldn't be.

But Zephyr could hold him and hand him fresh Kleenex. He could bring a glass of water and, later, some herbal tea with honey, which he hoped would soothe George's raw throat. And when, at very long last, the crying finally subsided and George started to apologize, Zephyr could tell him to knock it off.

"You didn't do anything wrong, Georgie."

George's answering laugh sounded more like a sob. "I… I melted down."

"You felt feelings. Legit ones. And you let them show."

"I shouldn't be complaining. I have—"

"Stop it. You've been hurt, and that's a fact. It's okay to acknowledge it. Healthy, even."

After a few deep breaths, George gave a tentative nod. "That sounds like good advice."

"I spent some time with shrinks when I was a kid. I don't know that anything they said helped me, but I can at least dish it back out."

With a wavery smile, George leaned his forehead against Zephyr's. "Thanks."

Guilt bubbled more harshly inside Zephyr. "It's not my place to… to tell you what you should do or feel."

"What is your place, then?" George sounded plaintive. "I don't even know what we are to each other. We haven't talked about it."

And Zephyr didn't want to. "We're friends. You know I can't promise more than that, but we're definitely friends. And that's… that's important." He swallowed. "I don't have any other friends."

George pulled back to gaze solemnly at him. "It is important. And even when you leave, we're still friends, okay? No matter what."

Well dammit, now Zephyr felt teary. He sniffled and then chuckled. "I believe that. If there's one thing I know about George Harlow, it's that he's loyal to those he cares about."

George kissed Zephyr's temple and then got up slowly, like an old man. He wandered into the kitchen and, after returning with the trash can, started cleaning up the used tissues and the mess from the Fossil Galaxy model.

Zephyr hopped up. "I'll help."

"I need to do this myself, I think." George picked up a piece of broken car and examined it in his palm for a moment before dropping it into the trash. Then he started talking again, not looking at Zephyr as he spoke. "I think my mom and dad tried to be good parents. I know they loved us. They just didn't have the right tools."

"I know. Humans are flawed—sometimes a lot. And sometimes the really fucked-up ones have kids. That doesn't make them horrible."

"No, it doesn't. Neither of them ever hit me or my sibs. Not once. I always… always felt safe. Always had enough food to eat and decent clothing and a comfortable bed to sleep in. They made sure we did well in school." Now he did look at Zephyr, his expression suggesting that he knew Zephyr couldn't make any of these statements about his own childhood.

Oh, George. Faithful to his family even now.

"I get it," said Zephyr. "They weren't monsters."

George continued picking up pieces and throwing them away. When he found the crushed remains of the miniature Tommy, he looked as if he might start crying again, but with visible effort, he pulled himself together and continued working.

He'd gotten most of it cleaned up when he stopped and frowned in Zephyr's direction. "You're blaming Mary and my brothers too."

"I'm not blaming anyone." Which wasn't quite true. They had known what conditions were like for their youngest brother, but they'd abandoned him here, leaving the entire burden on his shoulders while they went off and led their own lives.

George's frown deepened, as if he were reading Zephyr's mind. "They've all been telling me for years to get out of here. Begging me. Bribing me, even. And they've all offered me money, even if I stayed."

"You refused."

"This is *my* choice, not theirs."

"I get that they needed to avoid Conrad Junction. And your dad. But where were they when your mother was sick?"

"By then, they had other responsibilities elsewhere. They tried to talk Mom into leaving. They had a plan—she would move in with Al, who could care for her because he was a nurse, and James and Mary would pay her expenses. Mom absolutely refused. I don't even understand why she felt so tied to this place, but she insisted that she was going to die right here in the Junction. And she did." George shrugged.

"Stubbornness runs deep in your family, doesn't it?"

George's grin was a relief. "You've noticed?"

Once the debris was cleared away, Zephyr grabbed a bag of pretzels and they both snuggled on the couch with a blanket over their legs. George put something on the TV—a dumb movie with a forgettable title and bland actors—but neither of them really watched. Zephyr kept his mind as blank as he could, but George was clearly lost in thought.

"My mom refused to believe Dad killed himself," George said after a while. "There was plenty of evidence. For one thing, he had no reason to be on that highway that day. It was over near Tehachapi."

"On the way to Bakersfield."

"Where Mom was from, yeah. But he never went that way. Witnesses said they saw him driving too fast for a mile or two before he... before. Traffic was light. And when he came to a curve, he just steered straight and gunned it. Investigators said there were no skid marks and no signs of mechanical trouble. He didn't have any alcohol in his system. But he didn't leave a note or say anything beforehand, so nobody knows what he was thinking. Why did he make that decision that day?"

Since George genuinely seemed to want an answer, Zephyr gave him one. "Sometimes people do something they know is a really bad idea because all of the alternatives look worse."

"Yeah," George sighed. He readjusted the blanket, making sure Zephyr's legs were fully covered. For the first time, Zephyr consciously noticed that the blanket was pale gray, a color that George said carried no flavors for him.

"You know," George said, "we have a theory, my sibs and I. We've talked about it a little. At the time Dad died, the business was already struggling. With Mom sick and me gone, he was having to pay more employees to keep things running. Neither he nor Mom had health insurance, and her medical bills were starting to pile up. But Dad had life insurance. Not a huge policy, but enough to make sure Mom got the care she needed."

"I thought life insurance didn't pay if the death was suicide."

George shook his head. "Partial myth. The policy had been in place for more than a couple of years, so it was valid."

"You think he did it to solve your family's financial problems?"

"It's a theory."

Zephyr was skeptical, but he didn't say so. If George wanted to believe that his father's death had been a selfless sacrifice, well, that assumption wouldn't harm him. He shouldn't be expected to face the raw truth about his father all at once.

They went to bed early that night, and they made love. It felt a little sentimental to call it that, even in his head, yet it was apt. Everything they did that night was gentle and slow. Long caresses. Languid movements. Soft murmurs against skin. Zephyr enjoyed their sex when it was fast and a little rough, and when it was loud and playful, but this... this was special. But even as he reached a toe-curling climax, he ached with anticipatory loss.

GEORGE WAS subtly different on Wednesday. Although his eyes held new depths of pain, he also moved with a bit more looseness, as if a weight had been taken off his shoulders. A net gain, Zephyr thought.

Judith seemed to notice something too, because she kept casting shrewd glances in George's direction but didn't say anything. Zephyr remembered what George had told him about how Judith and her husband had helped him escape the Junction, albeit temporarily, so Zephyr was extra nice to her. She seemed suspicious about that too.

It was a slow day, with just a few visitors straggling through the exhibits. With George doing the tours and Judith staffing the gift shop, Zephyr spent a good chunk of the day in the storage room, working on George's surprise. He was nearly finished.

As he came back through the gift shop to refill his water bottle, Judith stopped him. "You're going to want to be here at four o'clock," she informed him.

He glanced at the clock on the wall, which pictured a different dinosaur in place of each number. It was a little over half past the stegosaurus—or just after three thirty. "How come?"

"Surprise. Just be here."

He tried wheedling more information out of her, but he got nothing. Giving up, he returned to his project.

When he came back to the gift shop just before four, Judith was hovering near a coffee mug display and failing to look nonchalant. George stood near the cash register, scowling at his phone. That almost certainly meant another barrage of texts. Brandon still did that several times a day, from several different numbers. George didn't like to show them, but sometimes Zephyr insisted on looking. The texts were becoming increasingly threatening and unhinged. There were certainly enough to get a restraining order, but Zephyr didn't want to deal with the cops again and didn't believe that a legal restriction would do any good. So George simply glowered at his phone and muttered under his breath.

Judith, apparently seeing something outside, perked up. "George, could you do me a favor? I have some Tic Tacs in the outer pocket of my purse. Could you bring them to me?"

"Sure." If George thought this was a strange request, he didn't show it. He entered the office, where Judith stowed her purse, and came out a moment later. "I can't find them. You're sure they're in the outer pocket?"

"Never mind that. Come here, George. You too, Zephyr."

They walked obediently to meet her at the door and peered outside. George's van was there.

It was parked right in front and parallel to the building, not huddled near the dumpster as usual, and the spray paint on the sides was gone. In fact, the faded old Fossil Galaxy logos were gone too, replaced by bright new ones, along with a scene of flying saucers hovering over a desert full of dinosaurs. The tires were no longer flat.

As George stood in front of the door, gaping, Lucas climbed out of the driver's seat, his smile so wide that it must have hurt. He left the door open and gestured impatiently at George.

"I can't afford…," George whispered.

Judith gave him a little push. "Go out there."

When George got emotional, his face went either bright red or ghostly white. This was one of the pale times—so pale that Zephyr worried about him. But George managed to get moving out the door and toward the van, and Zephyr followed hard at his heels.

"Don't start arguing," Lucas said by way of greeting.

"But—"

"My cousin owed me a favor 'cause I've helped him move three times now, and the last time there were stairs. He replaced all the ruined hoses and stuff. Did some other work while he was in there too. He explained it to me, but I'm not a car guy so I dunno what he was talking about. Upshot is the van's running way better than before that asshole damaged it."

"But—"

"My cousin also owns the building next door—a body shop—and the guy was a little behind on rent payments, so my cousin had him do the painting. Which I think looks really damn cool. I think the paint guy had fun. They got someone to fix the upholstery too." Looking pleased with himself, Lucas crossed his arms. "The tires are an early Christmas present from… well, everyone. Practically all of Junction chipped in."

George licked his lips a few times. "Lucas," he finally managed to say. "Why?"

"Because we're friends. And man, you deserve it." Lucas focused his gaze on Zephyr. "Do you know what this guy has done? I was a freshman in high school when my family moved to the Junction, and let me tell you, it sucked. But my very first day at school, when I didn't know a soul, this nerdy redheaded kid walked right up to me at lunchtime and dragged me over to his table. Introduced me to his friends, his brother Al, Al's friends…. Pretty soon I knew everyone."

This didn't surprise Zephyr one bit. He could picture it so clearly, in fact, that he couldn't help grinning.

"It wasn't that big a deal," George said, his paleness replaced by a blush.

"It was a huge fucking deal, and you know it. And don't forget how you helped me out with my English homework all the time, and you also took me to the school counselor and insisted they test me for dyslexia, which was the first time I realized I wasn't just stupid."

"You were never stupid."

"Nope, I never was." Lucas addressed Zephyr again. "And it wasn't just me. Santiago and Jessica got married here 'cause they were too broke to afford a reception hall or anything. It was nice—George strung little colored lights in the minerals room so it looked really pretty. He gave Kayla her first job and convinced her she should apply to college and not just set her sights on community college. For a couple of years he let Isaac and Alexis Thomas come over every day after school and do their homework in his apartment because their family was crammed into a noisy trailer and didn't have internet. They both ended up going to college too. And you know how hard he works and how little spare time he has, but he's helped almost everyone out. Before the pandemic, a couple of times a year he drove Lyle Cohen to some wrecking yard in Victorville to pick up parts for his sculptures."

"He's a hero," Zephyr said, nodding.

"Exactly. And now he's a hero with a nice set of wheels."

Although Zephyr had already known what a good man George was, hearing it from Lucas made his heart feel almost too big, like an overinflated balloon. That night two years ago, when the trucker had beat him up, then dumped him, Zephyr could have ended up anywhere. He could have wandered into the desert and died, or less catastrophically, landed outside the Burger King or the truck stop or Lyle's store. Someone would have called the cops. At the least, he would have been subjected to humiliation.

But instead, George had found him cowering among the garbage and had treated him with care and respect from the very beginning. He'd asked for Zephyr's pronouns. Doctored him and helped clean him up without making him feel ashamed. Given him clothes and money.

After that, George had twice more provided refuge to Zephyr. And had stood up to Brandon. And treated Zephyr as a partner. As a lover. As a man who wasn't an object to be admired for its beauty but instead a human being with value beyond a pretty face.

Zephyr was in love with George.

Oh no.

CHAPTER TWENTY-FIVE

A LOT of locals showed up to admire the van before Fossil Galaxy closed that day, and most of them took photos. "We'll tag you on Insta," said Kayla's grandmother, Maria. A teenage girl who was somehow related to Jessica recorded a TikTok video in which she told a very abbreviated version of the vandalism and restoration. Everyone agreed that the new paint job was wonderful.

People brought food, George handed out drinks from the gift-shop cooler, and although it was cold out, the parking lot turned into an impromptu party. Someone blasted music from their oversize car speakers, at which point George revealed that he could dance surprisingly well. Zephyr danced with him, almost forgetting all of life's cares.

Almost, but not quite. Every few minutes, he was hit anew by the same awareness he'd had the night before: he loved George. And that meant Zephyr had to go.

It was almost ten by the time the festivities died down and everyone went home. George looked exhausted as he locked the front doors, but it was a happy tiredness. "Not enough cash in the till to worry about," he announced. "And we can deal with everything else in the morning. Come to bed with me, Zephyr?"

How could Zephyr possibly refuse?

That night, he took the lead in their lovemaking and devoured George as if he were a feast—not just his body, but his scent, his taste, the sounds he made, the feel of his hot skin and wiry hairs. If Zephyr had been a wizard, he would have gobbled George up and locked him away in his heart.

But Zephyr was no wizard. And George was already in his heart.

The next morning Zephyr woke up first, which was unusual. In truth, he'd slept very little, spending the deep hours of the night listening to George's slow breathing. Now he simply sat on the edge of the mattress, waiting for George to open his eyes.

As soon as he did, George's expression turned grave. "You're leaving, aren't you?" He sat up.

George hadn't had a haircut in a while, and the red-blond strands stuck up in unruly tufts. His morning stubble, lighter than his hair, was barely visible, but Zephyr knew what it would feel like if he touched it.

"Yes."

"Thank you for not just disappearing without saying anything."

"Do you think I'd do that to you?"

"No…. Yes. Maybe."

Zephyr nodded and smoothed the comforter. It was plain white. No flavor.

"Is it because of Brandon?" George asked. "Because I don't—"

"It has nothing to do with Brandon."

The silence between them was heavy, and it took all of Zephyr's will to break it and speak again. "It's because of you."

George's exhale sounded almost like a groan. "I did something awful. I'm sorry. Was it my tantrum with that stupid model? Did I say something to—?"

"I'm afraid of you."

The color drained from George's face so quickly that it looked like an optical illusion. His eyes appeared shocked. "Oh God. I'm so sorry, Zephyr. I know I yelled at you the other day and I destroyed the diorama. But I'm not Brandon, okay? I'd never hurt you, I promise."

Zephyr reached over and stroked his cheek. "I know. That's not what I meant." Fuck. He wasn't expressing himself at all well.

He needed to give some context. "I have no idea who my father was. I doubt my mother knew either. And I never met her family. I heard about them from a social worker once—Mom's parents were both in prison, her grandmother who'd mostly raised her was an addict. She had me when she was fifteen. I don't even know why she kept me, because she sure as hell didn't want me. I was little when the cops took me away from her. After that… foster homes. Group homes. Juvie when I got older. I saw her now and then, usually at court hearings. She always looked really pretty, I remember that. I heard she had other kids after me, but I never met them. I don't know if she kept them."

This wasn't a good story; he knew that. It was predictable and full of clichés. It tended to evoke pity, which he didn't want. But the facts were important.

George looked serious but not appalled. "You turned out so well, though. Strong. Smart. You're a good person, Zeph."

A nickname. George was choosing *now* to give him a nickname, dammit. It was a cruel weapon, even if George didn't intend it that way.

"I survived," Zephyr said. "And I did it by learning to rely on myself. To take advantage of anything I could. Like my looks. Fuck knows what would have become of me if I hadn't been pretty."

"Do you think I judge you for that? Because I don't. An organism has three choices when faced with change: adapt to the environment, move on to a better environment, or go extinct. You've done a really good job at the first two options, and I'm glad of it."

Despite everything, Zephyr smiled a bit. "I don't think you judge me at all. The opposite, in fact. Once you decide you're on someone's side, you're all in, no matter what. Almost blind to their faults. But"— he held up a hand to stop George from interrupting—"that's not the problem."

"Then what is?" Now George simply looked bewildered.

"I've relied on other people when I've needed to. For money. For transportation or shelter. Sometimes I've loaned them my body in exchange. But I've never given them… me. Myself. I've never *needed* them here." He thumped his chest.

This next part was the hardest.

"Last night I realized something. I need you, George. Not for protection or shelter or even for sex." Now he let his palm rest over his heart. "I need you because I love you."

George inhaled sharply. "You love me."

"I have never loved anyone. Not a soul. And it scares the ever-living crap out of me. Because… because if I can't stand entirely on my own, what if that means I can't stand at all?"

Although his voice broke and his eyes welled with tears, he wouldn't really call it crying. He ignored the tears as he waited for a response.

"You know I love you too, right?" George finally said.

"I was kind of getting that impression."

"But I never expected this… us… to work. Over the long term, I mean. Because what do I have to offer you?"

"Everything you have. And that's the problem. Your apartment, your tourist trap, your self—they're worth so much more than Brandon's millions. You've seen that I can do without money and fancy clothing. But I can't let myself get into a position where I can't do without you."

"So you can't afford to be vulnerable."

That was an oversimplification, but it was close enough, and Zephyr nodded. "All I have is my self-reliance. I can't lose that. I just can't."

George was silent, his brows furrowed and eyes troubled, but it was clear he was trying hard to understand. Which only made Zephyr love him more. At the very least Zephyr owed him an explanation that made sense, even if Zephyr himself wasn't entirely clear about his own motives. He spent a moment staring at the pale blue wall, as if that might help clear his mind.

"There are so many things that make you *you*, George. You think your identity is entirely tied up in this place, and sure, that's part of you. But if you abandoned Fossil Galaxy today, you'd still be George Harlow, and your... your core would be the same. You're not just the guy who runs the museum, right? You're also a beloved little brother. A loyal friend. You're a smart, kind, accepting human being, and you'll carry that with you even if you relocate to Mars. But me...."

Comprehension seemed to dawn, and George countered, "You're beautiful, but beauty fades. You have great fashion sense, but that's just the decoration, not the core."

Grateful for George's willingness to *see*, Zephyr nodded and gave George's cheek another stroke. "The only thing that's always been at my center—my eternal truth—was that I don't need anyone else."

"There's a lot more inside you than that."

"Maybe. But I can't see it. I need...." Zephyr worried his lip for a moment. "If I let go of that now, there's nothing left of me. I love you, but that's not enough to keep me from being destroyed. I don't want to leave you. But I can't give myself to you if I don't know what that self is."

He couldn't explain it any better than that, which was a shame. He hoped George realized that Zephyr wasn't choosing to pick up and leave. He simply couldn't remain here right now, even though he knew he was breaking both their hearts.

George closed his eyes for a moment. When he opened them, it was clear he'd reached a decision. "Does being self-reliant mean you can't accept any help at all?"

"I can't stay here, George. It'll—"

"I understand that, and it's not what I mean. I just— Hang on." George left the bed and, naked, padded out of the room. When he returned a few moments later, he held a piece of paper with the Fossil Galaxy logo: a sheet from the pad that he kept in the kitchen for shopping lists and other reminders. George handed it over.

Zephyr glanced down. "Your brother's phone number and address?"

"Yeah. Al has some extra space in his house right now, and he says there are plenty of jobs up that way. Being independent doesn't mean you have to start from scratch, does it?"

"I don't know." Zephyr's emotions were a mess at the moment, so he wasn't sure how he felt about it.

"Well, keep the paper anyway. Just in case."

Yeah, Zephyr could do that much at least.

While George dressed, Zephyr went into the bathroom and spent a long time staring at his reflection, trying to read something in his own gaze. But the face staring back at him was a stranger's, his thoughts inscrutable. Without making a conscious decision to do so, Zephyr picked up the razor and shaved off what remained of his hair.

IT DIDN'T take him long to get ready. Black sneakers, jeans, a Fossil Galaxy tee, and the biker jacket Maria had given him. He dumped everything out of the silvery suitcase George had retained so faithfully, and he filled it with his meager new possessions, many of which carried a familiar logo.

"You can throw this away," he said, waving at the designer dresses, skirts, and blouses. "Or donate it. You could even try selling it online if you want. You could probably make some money off it."

George nodded distractedly, his attention clearly on other matters. "We don't have much cash on hand. I can go to the ATM at the mini-mart."

"Keep your money, Georgie."

"You came here with a pretty thick wad of bills."

"Which we spent on food I ate and clothing I wear." Zephyr had been trying to avoid going too close to George, as if he were afraid of getting locked into George's orbit. But now he moved in to stroke George's cheek. "I'll be fine. I won't do anything too risky, okay? No more picking up tricks or finding sugar daddies."

"I'm not judging you. I'm just worried."

Fair enough, considering the condition in which Zephyr had arrived. More than once. And it was surprisingly nice to know that George would worry—that somewhere on the planet, there was someone who cared.

There were a lot of things Zephyr wanted to say, but he couldn't find the right words. Besides, George had work to do. It was almost time for him to open for the day. So Zephyr walked to the exit, George following behind.

Zephyr paused at the open door and ran his free hand over his bald scalp. It felt strange. "Do you still think I'm pretty?"

"You will always be beautiful. No matter what you look like." George said it as if he was truly sincere.

"I want…." Zephyr let himself trail off, uncertain how to finish the sentence.

"Yeah, I want too. I wish to hell you weren't leaving. But I guess sometimes what we want isn't what we need."

Succinctly put. "If Brandon comes back—"

"Forget about him."

Well, of course that wasn't going to happen; Zephyr was concerned. But maybe once he was gone, Brandon would leave George alone. Or maybe not. But staying here certainly wouldn't keep George safer.

"It's not fair," Zephyr said softly. "It should be a good thing, learning that I'm capable of falling in love—not a disaster. That asshole Brandon can't take me away from us, but my stupid heart can."

"It isn't fair. And your heart's not stupid."

Just as Zephyr turned to leave, George reached out and stopped him. "Will you do something for me, please? It's selfish of me, but…. Will you check in every now and then, just to let me know you're doing okay? Nothing major. Just drop me a postcard. Send a quick text. Something."

"I will. But Georgie, you need to find someone who deserves you."

George shook his head. "If I spend the rest of my life single, I'm all right with that." He gave a small chuckle. "I don't need anyone else. I love you because you're *you*, not because I need to love someone."

That might have been the most amazing thing anyone had ever said to Zephyr.

So, before he could weaken, he walked out of the apartment.

CHAPTER TWENTY-SIX

ZEPHYR HAD heard that the country was experiencing some supply chain problems, but it wasn't evident at the Conrad Junction truck stop, where semis filled the lot. He took his time checking out the drivers, gleaning as much information as he could. Eventually he saw a tall man in a blue turban and a puffy black coat stretching and yawning as he waited for his rig to fuel. Zephyr knew that black—like white and gray—had no flavor for George, but he wondered what the blue tasted like, not to mention the lime green of the cab. Not knowing felt like a loss.

"Hey," Zephyr said as he approached the man. "I'm hoping for a ride. Where you heading?"

The man scrutinized him carefully, then hesitated before admitting, "Washington state. Walla Walla." It seemed promising that he was willing to provide the information. "But I won't get there until tomorrow. Too far for one day. I'll be stopping in Nevada first. Winnemucca."

"Can I tag along? I'll keep my mouth shut if you want quiet."

After a long pause, the trucker gave a little laugh. "I wouldn't mind some conversation, I suppose. Um, assuming you're not going to give me Covid. I can't afford to be sick."

"Fully vaxxed, no symptoms."

The man nodded. "Ekamjit Singh. You can call me Kam."

"I'm Zephyr Steiber, and I really appreciate this."

"Climb on in."

KAM TURNED out to be good company. He was Sikh and lived in Austin, in a house shared with his wife, young daughter, and several other relatives; and he'd been driving professionally for eight years.

"I like it. The pay's good, I get to see a lot of the country, and I have a lot of time to think. But I miss my family. We FaceTime, but it's not the same."

"Has it been harder to make a living with the pandemic?"

"It was for a while, yes. But now it's busy, busy. Sometimes, though, there are delays. Yesterday I had a delivery of machinery to make in San Diego, but the crew there was shorthanded, so it took much longer to get unloaded. That delayed me in picking up a load of sports apparel down there, and so by the time I reached Conrad Junction, I had to stop." He sighed. "And that's why I won't make it to Walla Walla until tomorrow."

"Everything's connected," Zephyr said thoughtfully.

"Precisely."

The scenery wasn't especially interesting—mile after mile of desert—but because Kam introduced Zephyr to songs by his favorite Punjabi musicians and they talked politics and movies and books, the miles rolled by reasonably quickly.

Zephyr thought about George only every two minutes or so. The wound of their separation felt raw, made worse by the fact that Zephyr had never before cared about being apart from someone. He'd never missed anyone before.

It sucked.

Somewhere in Nevada, Zephyr started talking about Fossil Galaxy. "It's really old-school," he explained. "But there's some interesting stuff in the collections. And it's… earnest, I guess. Genuine. Not corporate-slick."

"I know what you mean. When I can, I skip fast food and eat instead at little family-run restaurants. They're more interesting. And the people who run them truly care about their place."

"Yeah. Some of them care a lot."

And not just because it was their source of income, but also because it was part of their identity. It was a tie to parts of their past that they held dear—even if it was also a burden caused by parts of their past they'd rather forget.

"Did you work at Fossil Galaxy very long?" Kam asked.

"Just a couple of months."

"Why are you leaving—if you don't mind me asking."

That was an excellent question, and one without an easy answer. "I need to get my head together, and I can't do it there."

"And you can in Walla Walla?"

"Don't know. I've never been there."

Kam grinned and quoted, "The city so nice, they named it twice."

It was early evening when they arrived in Winnemucca. With three big truck stops, it was a good place to pause for the night. Kam pulled the rig into a parking spot, turned off the engine, and looked at Zephyr. "I'm taking us out to dinner."

"You don't have to do that."

"When I'm on the road, I don't often have company for my meals. So this will be a treat for me. I know a good place."

It was only a couple of blocks away, so they walked. Dark had already fallen, but bright signs lit the sky, and the air was scented with creosote bush and diesel fumes. Zephyr wondered whether there had been many visitors at Fossil Galaxy today and if George had remembered to eat lunch. And when he sat down at a table across from Kam, Zephyr thought about how long it must have been since George ate at a restaurant. What kind of food would George choose if he didn't have to worry about time and money? Would the décor—or at least the colors of the décor—matter to him as much as the menu? Even after spending so much time together over these past months, there were so many things Zephyr didn't know about him. They felt important.

Kam was right: the restaurant was very good. It served Basque food, which meant lots of meat and vast quantities of everything.

"We eat vegetarian at home," Kam said with a grin as he cut into his lamb. "I always feel like I'm cheating a little when I have dishes like this. But they're so good! And I keep the Panj Kakar—the Five Ks— which is far more important to my faith anyway."

"That's... not shaving or cutting your hair?"

"That's part of it, yes. Don't worry, I won't start preaching at you."

"I'm not worried. But do you mind if I ask questions? I don't know anything about Sikhism."

Kam looked delighted. "Of course not! I'm not necessarily the biggest expert, but I know some things."

It was an interesting mealtime conversation. Zephyr had never had patience for religion, but he liked the principles that Kam said formed the bedrock of Sikhism. And he wondered what George would think about them, especially since his father had been so opposed to religion of any kind.

After dinner, they returned to the truck stop, where Kam announced his intention to go inside and call his wife, then shower and maybe watch some TV. "I sleep in the bed here," he said, pointing at the back of the cab. "I can pay for a room for you at a nearby motel."

"If it's okay, I can just curl up in your passenger seat." It was roomy and Zephyr was small.

Kam paused a moment. "Is there someone you'd like to speak to first? You can borrow my phone."

"I…. No, thanks." Not yet.

IT WAS chilly and raining in Walla Walla, and Zephyr was in a bitchy mood. He ached from sleeping in the truck, and he still had no destination in mind. Not to mention, Walla Walla wasn't exactly the center of civilization. He knew that he'd allowed himself to get spoiled and should be thankful for what he did have.

He at least managed to be civil to Kam, who was a genuinely good human being. Zephyr owed him a great deal.

"Want to come while I unload? Or I could drop you off somewhere first. I was planning to spend the night in the Walmart lot, which might be a good place for you to pick up a ride."

"The Walla Walla Walmart?" Zephyr grinned despite his tetchy mood.

"Sadly, no. College Place. It's basically the suburbs. Walmarts are generally pretty cool about letting us use their lots overnight."

"I'll wait until after you unload, if you don't mind." If nothing else, it would postpone having to make a decision about his next step. Maybe he could try to catch a ride from the Walmart back down to I-84, which he and Kam had passed about forty miles back. From there, he could hitch either east or west and go… anywhere.

For a guy who insisted on being self-reliant, he was doing a really bad job at managing his life.

Kam pulled into a parking lot at a featureless building, backed up to one of the many loading bays, and hurried inside. He came out a few minutes later, however, looking angry. "They're shorthanded too. Everyone's quitting, the boss says. Maybe he ought to try paying a decent wage."

"Nobody to unload?"

"Nope. As if I don't have better things to do than sit here. Time is money in my profession." Then Kam brightened. "Hey. What about if I tell the guy the two of us will do it for a hundred bucks each? I bet he'll pay."

"I'm, uh, not exactly made of muscle." Zephyr flexed his arm to demonstrate.

"Can you lift a thirty-pound box? Hand trucks will do the rest of the work."

Thirty pounds. Some of the boxes of souvenirs at the Fossil Galaxy gift shop weighed more than that, and he'd managed. He'd moved some heavy pieces for George's surprise too. Shit. George's surprise—now it would never be finished. Regret made Zephyr's gut twist.

"Yeah, sure. I can do that."

As it turned out, the boss was willing to pay. He even threw in some decent hot coffee and donuts from the break room. And the exercise helped work out some of the kinks in Zephyr's muscles. Not a bad thing after two days of sitting in a truck.

On top of it all, he gained some useful information: a bus service ran from the Walmart, across the state line into Oregon, and to the town of Pendleton, which was right on I-84. Kam called the bus service and made an afternoon reservation for Zephyr. "Eight bucks," he said.

"I can afford that."

"Where to from there?"

Zephyr faked a smile. "Wherever the wind takes me."

CHAPTER TWENTY-SEVEN

December 2021
Conrad Junction

AFTER ZEPHYR left, George got through the day pretty well. He'd known Zephyr would leave sooner or later, and in fact, they'd had much more time together than he'd anticipated. Besides, George was used to being… well, *alone* wasn't quite the right word. He was lucky to have good friends.

Judith came in midmorning and at first didn't comment on Zephyr's absence. Maybe she thought he was in the workshop. But when lunchtime rolled around and George politely refused to share the giant dish of mac and cheese she'd brought and reheated, she quirked her lips unhappily. "He broke your heart, didn't he?"

"It's not like that. He needed… I'm not what he needs."

"You young people make things more complicated than they should be. And you don't understand priorities."

He raised his eyebrows. "Is this where you're going to accuse me of wasting my money on avocado toast?"

"No. Although you know what? That sounds good. We have some nice ripe avocados at home—I'll bring some tomorrow. I only mean that time goes by much faster than you think, and we ought to spend as much of it as we can in ways that make us and the people we care about happy."

"I don't know how to make Zephyr happy."

She shrugged. "Maybe you should concern yourself with your own happiness first."

"You want to see me ecstatic? Wave a magic wand so retro museums become the newest rage and we get so many visitors that we have to build a parking garage to handle them all."

"Do you really think that Fossil Galaxy's miraculous success would bring you joy?"

"Of course it would!"

He was almost glad when his cell phone suddenly blew up with a flood of barely coherent texts from Brandon's newest burner phone. At least it gave him an excuse to drop the discussion.

THE FOLLOWING afternoon, a careless guest bumped a plaster replica of a cave bear jaw. Luckily the piece wasn't too badly damaged, although one of the teeth was knocked loose. After that group of visitors left, George headed to the workshop in search of glue for repairs. He found it easily enough, but while he was in there, he couldn't help but notice the large tarp-covered lump—the project Zephyr had been working on so secretively.

George slowly approached it and stood staring. It was taller than he was and about six feet in diameter, but the shape was irregular and he couldn't guess what it was. He could look at it now. Why not? It wasn't as if Zephyr was going to finish it and do some sort of grand reveal. In fact, George should probably just get rid of it.

He reached out, but before his fingers brushed the canvas, he withdrew his hand. Then, clutching the bottle of glue, he marched out of the room. That jaw wasn't going to fix itself.

The days after that… flowed. One into another, with nothing much to distinguish them. Guests trickled in; George gave them tours. He kept Fossil Galaxy clean and as well repaired as possible. After closing, or during the slowest parts of the day, he did paperwork and numbly watched his debts accumulate. Then he'd fix himself a sandwich and soup, or reheat whatever his friends had dropped off, and go to sleep.

He didn't hear from Zephyr. And Al didn't call, which he undoubtedly would have if Zephyr showed up. Al had said as much when George warned him of the possibility.

The van ran well.

Brandon called and texted.

Kayla came home from winter break and announced her intention to set up a Go Fund Me for Fossil Galaxy right after Christmas. George seriously doubted she'd raise enough to keep him afloat for long. But he appreciated her efforts, so he didn't say anything to discourage her.

And once, just once, George took out the Fossil Galaxy photo album and flipped through the pages, trying to decipher hidden secrets in the family snapshots. How had his father placed a spell on George, rendering him unable to turn away from the Junction as his siblings had? Or maybe the problem lay inside George, a specific weakness not inherited by his brothers and sister.

He didn't find any answers in the old pictures, and he ended up locking the album away in the safe.

And then, a week after Zephyr left, Brandon showed up.

The morning had been busy due to a bus full of senior citizens from Fresno stopping by on the way to Vegas. They'd created a bit of a traffic jam in the restrooms, but then they seemed to enjoy the tour George gave them, and afterward they spent a lot of money in the gift shop. It was a nice little windfall.

Things had been pretty slow after that, so George sat in the office and dealt with tax paperwork while Judith and Kayla chatted near the cash register. George caught snatches of their conversation and smiled; it sounded as if Kayla was loving UCLA. She had straight As and had recently become involved in student government.

Then the bell on the front door jingled, and when George automatically glanced over, he saw Brandon Sherburne standing just inside the entrance.

He wore jeans, a long-sleeved shirt, and an orangey-brown quilted vest jacket that tasted like spoiled shrimp. His hair was carefully slicked back and he looked tanned, as if he'd just returned from a tropical island. His expression was oddly calm. He wasn't, of course, wearing a mask.

George rushed over, no doubt startling Judith and Kayla, who had no idea who this man was.

"Get out," George said firmly.

"I just want to speak with Zephyr for a few minutes. That's all."

So he didn't know that Zephyr had left. That was good, and George wasn't about to tell him.

"He doesn't want to talk to you."

"How do you know? Are you his spokesman now? If he refuses, fine. But I want to hear it in his own voice, not yours." Brandon said the last part with a sneer, as if George was too lowly to be considered.

George struggled to keep his voice calm. "You're not wanted here. You're trespassing. Go away and don't come back."

"Trespassing? As if this pile of shit is worth anything. I want to talk to Zephyr!"

Brandon took a step forward, but George was right there to block him. Brandon wasn't a big man, although he somehow managed to take up a lot of space, but George was taller. They were close enough that George smelled his cologne, which was probably expensive but had an irritating, cloying scent that clashed horribly with the bad shrimp taste.

"It may be a piece of shit, but it's mine. And I'm warning you to leave."

"You! Warning me! You little worm, do you know who I am? I could buy your entire fucking town and not even notice the dent in my bank accounts."

God, this man was insufferable. George had assumed that his own meltdown over his father's diorama had drained all of the anger from him, but now rage flowed through him like magma. "You can't buy my business, and you sure as hell can't buy Zephyr."

Brandon made a low growling noise. "Nobody can buy that little bitch. You can only rent him. But that's okay because he comes cheap, doesn't he? Get him a few pretty dresses and he bends over so sweetly. You can—" He stopped suddenly and worked his jaw a few times, clearly trying to get himself under control. When he spoke again, his tone was slightly wheedling.

"Look. You've had some fun with him, but I'm sure he's tired of this place by now. Someone like Zephyr doesn't belong here. I know I've made some poor decisions. He… he does that to me sometimes. Pushes me where I don't want to go, because I'm not that kind of person at all. I'm really not. I'm a good guy. At least let me apologize to him, okay?"

George wondered if this asshole believed what he was saying. Maybe. It was possible that he genuinely saw himself as an innocent victim of Zephyr's evil wiles. As George had recently realized, self-deception was an easy trap to fall into. But that didn't excuse the way Brandon had treated Zephyr.

"I don't care what you want," George said. And then he did something incredibly stupid—he put his hands on Brandon's chest and pushed.

It wasn't a hard shove, but it took Brandon by surprise and he stumbled back a little. His face tightened into a mask of hatred and he pushed back. Much more forcefully. It hurt. Yet George stood his ground.

So Brandon did it again. Somewhere behind George, women's voices were raised, but he didn't register what they were saying. This…

this *fuckface* had taken so much from him over the past months: Tommy, the van, his peace and quiet. Even more importantly, Brandon had damaged Zephyr both physically and mentally. He'd bruised his body and made Zephyr feel as if he deserved it. He'd treated Zephyr as though he were property.

Years of repressed anger erupted, setting George's mind on fire. He punched Brandon hard in the face. The crack of Brandon's nose beneath his fist was satisfying, but it didn't tamp his fury. If anything, he became less rational, more feral. Brandon squawked and swung back but missed, and this time George's fist connected with his jaw.

Brandon fell back a little, but instead of leaving, he roared like a beast and threw himself at George, taking both of them to the ground. He got his hands on George's neck and tried to squeeze, yet at the same time George was kicking and scratching for all he was worth, trying to roll them over so he'd have the upper hand.

This wasn't two men fighting—it was a pair of animals. Dimly, in the back of his mind, George saw the mural his grandfather had painted on one wall of the vertebrates room: two T. rexes locked in combat, jaws gaping, fangs bloody. The small bit of sense that remained intact in George's brain reminded him that while those dinosaurs may have been fierce, they were also extinct.

He reached up and boxed Brandon's ear with all his might, resulting in a spurt of blood. Despite it, Brandon kept trying to strangle him.

Then suddenly Brandon was moving up and away, which mystified George until his head cleared enough to register that Brandon was being *pulled* away by two large men—Santiago and his brother. Brandon kicked and swore, but he couldn't get free. When George rose to his feet with the intention of continuing his attack, strong arms held him back too.

"George! George, chill out, dude!"

That was Lucas. Doug from the mini-mart was there too, and a couple of men George didn't recognize. Judith stood with a baseball bat in her hands, looking ready to take someone's head off.

The fight left George all at once. He relaxed in his captors' grip. "It's okay," he said quietly. "I'm done."

With some reluctance, they set him free. He used the back of his arm to wipe blood from his face. He was pretty sure it wasn't his.

"He hit me first!" Brandon screeched. "He threw the first punch! I'm pressing charges. I'm gonna sue your fucking ass into oblivion. I'm gonna—"

"Shut up!" George roared. Surprisingly, Brandon did. So George continued. "You want to press charges? Fine. We can also explain to the cops what you did to my van. I'll show 'em all the threats you've texted me too. I bet you spend more time in jail than I do."

"Besides," said Kayla, appearing from the background. "George was clearly defending himself. You hit first, asshole. I saw it clearly. Right, Judith?"

Judith's smile was downright evil. "Absolutely."

There were murmurs of agreement from the assembled crowd even though none of them had been there when the fight began.

"I'll ruin you," snarled Brandon.

"I'm not scared of you. I have nothing to lose." And that was the truth of it. His dismal financial and personal circumstances were oddly freeing.

Smiling, Lucas took the bat from Judith and loomed in front of Brandon. "You're going to get the fuck out of Conrad Junction and never come back. No contact at all."

Brandon didn't resist when Santiago and his brother dragged him outside. George couldn't see what was happening, but a few moments after some raised voices, an engine revved and tires screeched. Santiago and his brother returned, looking smug.

At that point, everyone turned to look at George, who was almost overcome with embarrassment. He was bloody and disheveled. His hands were beginning to throb. "I'm sorry," he announced with a sigh.

"Zephyr's ex?" Lucas asked.

"Yeah."

"What did he want?"

"Zephyr."

Then everyone seemed to talk at once.

George wasn't just messy and humiliated and sore; now he was exhausted as well. He wanted to retreat to his apartment and crawl into bed, where Zephyr's scent might still linger on the pillows and George could shut away the entire world for a while.

"All right, everyone!" Judith sounded authoritative. "Thank you for coming to our rescue. Now go somewhere else to gossip about it—we have a business to run."

They obeyed. Most of them stopped to clap George on the shoulder and tell him they were available anytime, but soon everyone was gone except Judith and Kayla.

"Where did the bat come from?" George asked, as if that mattered.

Judith grinned. "My car. Benny used to play in the minor leagues, you know. Round about when your dinosaurs were roaming the earth. He insists I keep one of his old bats in my car. For self-defense, he says. We have a joke about it—an old bat for an old bat." She patted it fondly before turning her attention back to George. "Now go clean yourself up and let me take a look at you. Do you need to go to urgent care?"

"No," he said firmly.

Inside his apartment, he stripped and left the clothes in a careless pile on the floor. He took a quick shower and then, for good measure, scrubbed his face and hands at the sink. He refused to look at his reflection; he didn't think he'd like the man who looked back. Then he put on clean clothing and returned to the gift shop, where Kayla and Judith were deep in conversation. They stopped as soon as he entered.

"I'm so sorry I subjected you to that," he said.

Kayla shook her head. "That wasn't your fault."

"It's not my fault he came here, but I could have… I should've handled it better."

"Maybe socking the guy wasn't a great idea, but man, he sure deserved it. What a tool." She brightened. "I bet you broke his nose."

George discovered he didn't feel any remorse about that.

As promised—or threatened—Judith checked out his injuries and pronounced him likely to survive. "You'll want to ice your hand, though."

He did so, wincing a little at the knuckle he'd split, feeling stupid and useless… but also maybe the teeniest, tiniest bit proud. He'd stood up to Brandon and hadn't revealed that Zephyr was gone. And once again, his friends had proven how steadfast they were. He was a lucky man.

Kayla was straightening up a rack of postcards that had been knocked over during the scuffle. No damage, just a mess. George sighed as he pictured Zephyr carefully arranging those postcards in a way he claimed would tempt guests to buy them all.

"Thanks for calling in reinforcements," he said to Judith.

"My pleasure. You were brave, George."

He shrugged that away. "He's not going to give up."

"No."

He looked at her, his expression bleak. "I don't know how to stop him. It's not safe for you or Kayla to be around here."

"If you think I'm going leave you high and dry, you don't know me very well."

He considered arguing but lacked the stamina. Besides, she was stubborn, and if this afternoon's ugly fracas hadn't scared her away, it was unlikely that George's persuasive words would do the trick. Kayla looked perfectly happy, humming to herself as she sorted postcards.

George gave Judith a wry grin. "Well, if nothing else, I've been responsible for more thrills and excitement than the Junction has seen in years."

"You certainly have. And if that creep comes back, this old bat has her bat."

CHAPTER TWENTY-EIGHT

IT HAD been a long couple of days, and Zephyr couldn't remember making many conscious decisions. He'd just sort of gone wherever the road took him. He'd thanked Kam several times before boarding a bus to Pendleton. He'd arrived around dinnertime and wandered into the nearest fast-food joint, where he ordered the first item on the menu. Then he splurged on a room at Motel 6: fifty bucks plus tax. That still left money in his pocket, since Kam insisted that he take the entire two hundred they'd earned unloading boxes.

The bed was more comfortable than a truck seat, and it was nice to have a private bathroom. But Zephyr hugged his pillow tightly and dreamed fitfully about the desert.

He woke up much later than he'd intended and barely made checkout. Somehow, he found his way to the Greyhound station, where he learned there was a single daily bus to Portland, leaving in half an hour. The ticket set him back twenty-five dollars. He sat on a bench with his suitcase at his feet, thinking about nothing.

The bus arrived in Portland six hours later. He stayed for a few days, crashing in cheap motels and aimlessly wandering the streets, not caring about the rain or the boarded-up downtown businesses or his empty stomach. When he was almost broke, he caught another bus. Eleven dollars more, gone.

And now here he was in Salem, where it was raining, and his biker jacket wasn't warm enough, and he was pretty sure he hadn't eaten anything all day, and he didn't know what the fuck he was doing or why. His mind was as gray as the sky, and even walking felt pointless. So he sat on a bench for a while, knowing that eventually some security guy would chase him away.

Finally, as if his hand had made the choice without his brain's help, he reached into a pocket and pulled out the piece of paper with the Fossil Galaxy logo.

AS FAR as Zephyr could tell by the streetlamp's illumination, it was a cute little cottage with a dormer window over the front door. He couldn't tell whether the house was painted gray or light blue. Gray wouldn't taste like anything to George, but light blue likely had a flavor. He didn't know anything about architecture, but he was pretty sure this little place had been constructed sometime early in the twentieth century. The small front yard was mostly gravel with a few bushes, and the flowerpots on the tiny front porch looked empty, but maybe back in the summer, there had been blooms.

With a sense of mixed relief and surrender, he walked up the three brick steps and rang the bell.

The man who answered looked like a pudgier version of George, his ginger hair shorn close. He wore gray sweats and a lumpy brown cardigan, and he held a pencil in one hand. He spent a moment at the open door, staring.

Zephyr cleared his throat. "Um, hi. I'm—"

"Zephyr."

"How did you—?"

"George told me you might show up. Come on in." And it was as easy as that, as if his brother's erstwhile lovers showed up unannounced all the time.

The small room was cramped with mismatched but comfortable-looking furniture: a leather couch, two recliners, and an oval dining table with four wooden chairs. Fleece blankets and coffee cups were scattered everywhere, and a cat with long orange fur watched with mild interest from atop a carpeted cat tree.

"You want coffee?"

"If it's not too much trouble."

Al laughed. "I'm mainlining the stuff. Always have a pot going."

Zephyr left his suitcase near the door and trailed Al into the kitchen, which was also cluttered in a friendly sort of way. Al waved him to a small Formica-topped table, where a laptop perched among legal pads, textbooks, pencils, and more coffee cups. "Sorry," Al said. "Getting ready for finals."

"I'm disturbing you. Sorry. I'll just—"

"It's fine. My brain is about as full of res judicata as it's gonna get for now, and I need a break." Al waited for Zephyr to sit, then laid down his pencil and grabbed a clean cup from the cupboard. "Sugar? Milk?"

"Both, please."

When Al set down the cup, Zephyr recognized the logo with the familiar dinosaur skeleton and spiral galaxy. It made him smile, although he was surprised to see it, considering that Al refused to go anywhere near Conrad Junction.

Al refilled a cup for himself but didn't take a seat. "You have good timing. Pizza should be here any second. I thought you were the delivery guy."

"Sorry."

"One of the sucky things about the Junction is that you can't get decent pizza. There are lots of other sucky things too, as I'm sure you noticed, but that's definitely on my list."

Before Zephyr could answer, the doorbell rang. He wasn't sure what he would have said anyway. He didn't really know why he was here or what, if anything, he was going to ask of Al. He felt as if the decision to come hadn't really been his, although logically speaking, it wasn't anyone else's either.

Al returned a few moments later with a large pizza box. The scent hit Zephyr immediately, making him feel a little faint. When Al handed him a plate containing two slices, Zephyr tried not to fall on it like a starving wolf.

"It's good," he managed to say after several bites.

"Yeah. I get it a couple times a week. The other nights I rotate between Chinese, Mexican, and fried chicken, and yes, I realize I am eating my way into heart disease and God knows what else, but I'm spending all my time with school and work, and unhealthy food is currently my one joy in life." He took in a deep breath and let it out with a grin. "Except for Smiley."

"Smiley?"

"My cat. His full name is *Smilodon californicus*, which was the saber-toothed cat that is California's official state fossil. Anyway, help yourself to as much pizza as you want. And there's stuff in the fridge too. When we're done eating, I'll show you your room. It's pretty comfy and you have your own bathroom. Washer and dryer are in the basement. Remotes for the TV in the living room are… somewhere. I haven't watched in a while. Everything else you can probably find on your own—it's not a big house. All I ask is that you keep the noise down when I'm sleeping or studying, which is pretty much always when I'm home. Oh, and don't let Smiley out, no matter what he says, 'cause he's an indoor cat. No people food either. He has IBS and he'll just end up puking."

My room? Zephyr had intended to question that, seeing as he hadn't decided to stay, but Al had zoomed right on past. Getting a word in edgewise wasn't easy.

"I, uh, I'm broke. I can't—"

"Don't worry about it. I own this house outright—no mortgage payments for me. If you get a job, you can chip in for food and utilities. But there's no hurry. Oregon is one of the best-paying states for nurses, so I'm doing all right."

Zephyr blinked. "I thought you were a law student."

"I am. I go to school part-time and work about three-quarter time. Which leaves me hardly any time for sleep and zilch for a social life, but I knew that going in, and it's not like I'm stuck doing this forever. Just three and a half more years. I can tough that out."

How much caffeine had Al consumed this evening? Zephyr finished one piece of pizza and started in on the other, but paused after a couple of bites. "It's still a lot to ask of you. Putting up a stranger."

"You're not a stranger. You're someone my brother cares about."

Two simple statements, and yet their implications floored Zephyr. He was so accustomed to being alone in the world, but his time with George had… connected him. Like an astronaut with a line fastened to the spaceship. Maybe he wasn't connected to zillions of people, but even a single tether was a lot safer than floating free.

When Zephyr spoke, his voice was husky. "You already helped. With the info on that alienation-of-affections thing."

"And I'll keep on helping, as much as I can and as much as you need. George has welded himself to that goddamn museum and won't budge an inch, no matter how stupid it gets for him to stay. And he won't let any of us contribute toward his bills. He won't even shut the place down for a week so he can take a vacation for the first time in a decade. Maybe meet his nieces in person or go anywhere there's more to walk on than blacktop and sand. You know how Boron has all the Twenty Mule Team stuff? Well, my little brother is more stubborn than all twenty mules put together. But finally I can lend him a hand by helping you, so I'm sure as hell going to grab the chance while I've got it."

Zephyr decided he liked this man.

AFTER ZEPHYR finished making up the double bed with fresh linens, he sat on the edge of the mattress and looked around. He had the entire upstairs to himself: a room with a bed, dresser, closet, and a somewhat threadbare loveseat, plus a tiny bathroom that included a shower. The ceiling was sloped, so he had to stoop a little near the edges of the space, and windows looked out in all four directions. There was an eclectic collection of throw rugs, maybe to muffle the sound of footsteps on the wood floor. The walls and ceiling were painted sky blue. It was a comfortable space. Smiley must have thought so too, because a fair amount of orange fur adorned the furniture and lurked in the corners.

When Zephyr took a shower, he remembered the first night he'd met George—how filthy he'd felt, inside and out, after the encounter with the trucker who'd beaten and dumped him. He'd needed to get clean but hadn't been in good enough shape to do it on his own. George had treated him with respect, patiently waiting in the bathroom with him, not ogling, not acting disgusted or put out. It was possible that Zephyr had begun to fall in love with him that very evening.

Zephyr fell asleep in Al's upstairs bedroom, a cat purring against him and raindrops pattering on the roof.

Al was gone when Zephyr came downstairs in the morning, but there was a note attached to the fridge with a Fossil Galaxy magnet.

I'll be home @4:30. Eat anything you want. House key's hanging near front door if you want to go somewhere. You can use my old laptop if you want internet. It's in the living room. Password is Wally1952. Smiley is a liar—I already fed him.

Again, Zephyr felt a little stunned. Al had just met him, yet was trusting him with everything he owned. Maybe that shouldn't be surprising, considering he was George's brother, but it still made Zephyr shake his head in wonder.

After breakfast, he decided he ought to search for a job, so he found the computer, logged in, and… froze. He'd never job-hunted before and had only a vague notion of how to go about it. Out of desperation he tried typing "jobs Salem Oregon," which brought promising results. There were a lot of listings, just as Al had promised, and some of them required only Zephyr's limited skills. He could work retail, he figured, since he'd been doing basically that at Fossil Galaxy. And his brief experience with Kam suggested that he'd be able to load and unload things, maybe in a warehouse or distribution center.

His cautious optimism soon faded. His first problem was that he didn't have any transportation, and most of the employers were too far away to walk. He might be able to get to some of them by bus, but the routes were limited. The other problem was even worse, and it became evident as he stared at the first application. He had no high school diploma. No driver's license. No work history apart from his time in the gift shop. No professional references. No phone number where people could contact him.

"I wouldn't hire me," he told Smiley, who seemed indifferent to his plight.

Discouraged, Zephyr shut down the laptop and seriously considered crawling back into bed. It was another damp, gray day. The sort that called for down comforters and mugs of hot soup.

Ah—mugs. There was something useful he could do.

He reconnoitered the living room and kitchen, collecting dirty cups, glasses, plates, and silverware as he went. He suspected there might be more in Al's bedroom, but the door was closed and it would be far too intrusive to enter without permission. He washed and dried everything, then stored it in the cupboards, marveling at the size of Al's drinkware collection.

More tidying felt like a natural extension from that point. Zephyr found a broom, a mop, and other supplies in a closet and put them to use. Floors cleaned. Lap blankets folded. TV remotes found and set on the coffee table. Furniture dusted. Kitchen surfaces scrubbed. Microwave and refrigerator shelves wiped. Inedible leftovers discarded. Garbage to the gray bin beside the house. He wasn't sure what went into the empty bins—green, blue, and red—so left the recyclables alone. He even cleaned the insides of the windows, which Smiley found fascinating.

He hoped that Al would be pleased rather than offended or annoyed by his efforts. It wasn't that Zephyr minded staying in an untidy house; he simply wanted to contribute. And keep himself busy.

The second goal was only partially met, in that he ran out of tasks well before Al got home. There was nothing of interest on TV, and after a few months without a phone, Zephyr had gotten out of the habit of spending time online. He ended up perusing the knickknacks and books instead. Al apparently enjoyed reading thrillers and mysteries, and of course he owned books on nursing and law as well. He had a few school photos of redheaded children who were probably James's kids, some framed certificates of appreciation from his nursing job, three assembled Lego models of Star Wars ships, and a video-game console with a broken controller and a few games.

Here and there, Al had Fossil Galaxy souvenirs on display: a cluster of plastic dinosaurs, a baseball cap, and some small semiprecious stones and fossilized shark teeth affixed to explanatory cards. It had been a decade since Al last visited Conrad Junction, yet all of this stuff looked fairly new. Zephyr realized that George must have sent these things, and Al had chosen to not only keep them but to put them where he'd see them often.

And that wasn't all. A large framed photo hung on the wall behind the dining room table: a landscape of the desert at night, with a single Joshua tree reaching up to a star-flecked sky.

WHEN AL walked in the front door, Zephyr was slumped in an armchair, reading a spy novel with Smiley in his lap. Although Al looked exhausted as he took off his shoes and hung his jacket on a hook near the door, he brightened immensely as soon as he got a good look at the living room.

"Holy cow!"

"I hope you don't mind. I was—"

"Mind? It's amazing. This place hasn't looked this good since I started law school. My last roommate was pretty good about doing chores, actually, but then he started working an extra job, and after that he found a girlfriend, and there went all of his free time." Al walked toward the kitchen and peered through the doorway. "In here too! Thanks, man. I'll order us a celebratory dinner. What're you in the mood for? Thai? Indian? Ooh, how about Middle Eastern? I could go for some baba ganoush."

"That sounds great."

After consulting with Zephyr about specific items, Al placed their order. Then, after a quick explanation, he disappeared to shower and change out of his scrubs, the cat meowing mournfully outside the bathroom door. Al emerged later, sporting wet hair, sweats, and that same cardigan. "No class tonight," he explained. "Just studying."

"I'll get out of your way."

"Let's eat first. I'll even set the table like a genuine adult!"

Over dinner, Al chatted pretty much nonstop about work and school, which was fine with Zephyr. They were interesting topics, and he much preferred hearing about them to dealing with his own issues.

It wasn't until they were eating baklava and drinking coffee that Al leaned back in his chair and laughed. "Oh my God. I am *so* sorry."

"For?"

"Verbal diarrhea. I think it's the consequence of being the third child of semi-neglectful parents. If I never shut up, people might pay some attention to me."

"I guess that makes sense." Zephyr poked a bit of walnut across his plate with a fork tine. "Except George is the fourth kid and he's not, uh...."

"A chatterbox. Yeah, I know. His shtick was different. While I was busy getting in trouble all the time for talking in class, Pie was gonna impress Dad by being practically perfect in every way. Working harder than any of us to help keep that dump going."

That comported perfectly with Zephyr's impressions, but he backed up the conversation just a bit. "Pie?"

"As in 'Georgie Porgie pudding and.' When he was little, Mary and I could drive him up a wall calling him that. James was too old and dignified to participate. And then, oh, I think around seventh or eighth grade, a couple of kids at school started to sing the rhyme too, only they changed it to 'kissed the *boys* and made them cry.' Mary and I beat them up, 'cause nobody except us was allowed to dis our baby brother. And somehow that whole incident ended with George telling us he's gay, so there was that. We still called him Pie, though."

Zephyr had seen photos of George at that age—a little pudgy, unruly carroty hair, smile just a little tight around the edges, as if he were fighting off worries. Which he probably was. Screwed-up parents. Sibling drama. Coming out of the closet.

Al was watching him closely. "Did he tell you about our mom?"

"Some things, yeah. She wasn't very emotionally involved."

That made Al snort. "Understatement. I think when it was just James, it wasn't so bad. But she kept having kids, and by the time George came along she was just... used up. She worked really hard, don't get me wrong. But I can't remember her ever playing with us. Or talking to us about anything except chores and school." He shrugged. "Not her fault. Depression."

"That's what George said."

"Yeah. He could always see *her* pretty clearly."

Al's emphasis implied that there was someone else Zephyr couldn't see clearly. His father, of course.

Zephyr considered his words for a moment and then cleared his throat. "Your dad was—"

"Bipolar. Undiagnosed, of course. Self-medicated with booze." Al huffed. "I spent a few years as a psychiatric nurse. The symptoms of bipolar disorder can be so rough on people, especially when they don't get treatment. Rough on families too. But George won't admit this about Dad, who was his hero. I wish he would—it'd help him work through some things better, I think."

Zephyr thought about the night when he'd brought George the diorama. It seemed that George had seen pretty clearly then, although Zephyr didn't know whether it had helped him at all. In general, Zephyr believed that brutal self-honesty was important, especially in a world where you couldn't trust anyone else. But maybe it was sometimes self-protective to allow a little fuzzing around the edges of the truth. He wasn't sure. He didn't seem to be sure about anything anymore.

No, that wasn't accurate. He was sure of a few things. "George is the best person I've ever met. I've… I don't know what he told you about me. I'm rough, and I don't just mean the whole shitfest with my ex, Brandon. My entire past… isn't easy. But George likes me anyway. And not because he sees me as a project. He never tried to improve me. He just accepted me as I am."

He couldn't help heaving a substantial sigh after that, and Al gave him a small smile. "Yeah, that's our Pie. Look, he didn't say much about why you left the Junction, and it's really none of my damn business. But will you do me one favor?"

Although Zephyr didn't believe Al would ask anything unpleasant of him, he automatically tensed. In his experience, men wanted one particular brand of favors from him. But Al simply set his phone on the table in front of Zephyr. "Call or text him, will you? It can just be a word or two. Let him know you're okay."

"You didn't tell him?"

"I haven't told him you're here."

Zephyr almost gaped. "Why not?"

"You might not have noticed, but I'm categorically single, and it's not just because I have zero spare time. It's not lack of interest either—I'd love to find a woman who can put up with me. It's because I *suck* at relationships. Big-time. Always have. I find someone, we seem to get along, and then I manage to screw things up. So the very last thing I'm gonna do is put myself in the middle of someone else's thing. Whatever you guys have going—or don't have going—is up to you. I just want you to let him know you're safe so he doesn't worry himself sick."

"Okay." Zephyr picked up the phone and stared at the blank screen for a moment. "You know, your parents must have done *something* right, because you and George turned out to be wonderful people."

Al grinned widely. "Can I use you as a character reference next time I ask someone on a date?" Chortling, he grabbed the phone, unlocked the screen, and handed it back.

Zephyr found the text conversation with George. He stared at the blinking cursor as if it had all the answers, but when it remained inscrutable, he started to type.

I'm at Al's. He's great. Another Harlow Hero. I'm fine. I still love you, dammit. Z

Then, without waiting for a reply, he set the phone down, stood, and began gathering dirty dishes.

MAYBE GEORGE texted back, but Zephyr didn't ask and Al didn't tell. Zephyr went to bed early that night, accompanied by Smiley and the spy book, and spent a long time staring blankly at the page while he petted the cat.

When he came downstairs in the morning, Al was scurrying around the kitchen. "No work today. Classes. Cramming the last chunks of knowledge into our brains before finals. You okay for the day? We have leftovers for lunch. Think about what you want for dinner—I'll be home by then."

Without waiting for an answer, Al grabbed his backpack and ran out the front door.

The house was really quiet without him. Zephyr reminded himself that he was supposed to be self-reliant, and that meant he had to stop mooching off Al. He sat down with the laptop again, and this time he made a better effort to find a job. It was too bad he hadn't squirreled away a lot more money during his time with Brandon. George sure could've used it.

Zephyr wondered if he should hold off for a while on employment and instead get a GED. When he was a kid, life had been far too chaotic to succeed in school, but now he wished he was better educated, and not just because it would look good on a job application. Maybe with some additional schooling, he'd have some hope of… of being someone. Of a future.

His mother had dropped out of school in junior high. According to one of Zephyr's social workers, his mom's parents hadn't made it any further than that, nor had their parents before them. He could become the first one in his family to get a high school diploma. None of them would know, and they wouldn't have cared. But he suddenly realized that he did. He cared a lot.

Now he just had to find a way to make it happen.

He spent the day exploring his options, daydreaming about George, and entertaining Smiley. It was late afternoon when he found himself staring at his suitcase, then putting it on the bed, opening it, and taking out the clothes.

He didn't have much. Mostly a selection of Fossil Galaxy T-shirts. But there at the bottom, underneath a hoodie also emblazoned with that familiar logo, was an outfit he could have sworn he'd left behind. He'd bought it during one of the New York shopping sprees funded by Brandon's credit card. Now he smoothed his hand over the fabrics. There was a black leather miniskirt, a hot-pink cashmere sweater with a deep V-neck, and a pair of fishnet thigh-high stockings with a lacy pattern up the back. Panties too—hot pink with black lace edging. And a pair of black Jimmy Choos with four-inch stiletto heels.

A stupid outfit. Unsuited to his current circumstances and a total waste of money.

But he looked good in it. Felt good too. Powerful and attractive and strong.

Zephyr stripped out of the boring jeans, briefs, and tee he'd been wearing and slowly, almost lovingly, put on the clothes from New York. When he was done, he fetched the little Fossil Galaxy tote bag that held his toiletries and fished out the bottle of nail polish that George had given him. Orchid Order—the color tasting, to George, like apple pie. Zephyr brushed on two coats.

When he was finished, he took a long, critical look at himself in the full-length mirror that hung on the door. Maybe he looked dumb—a man dressed in pink cashmere and a short skirt, his head covered in stubble. But he didn't feel dumb. He felt like... like himself.

And he felt as if he was on the cusp of an important decision.

Zephyr Steiber: a person in control of himself and his destiny.

CHAPTER TWENTY-NINE

"I THOUGHT you weren't interested in selling."

George winced, glad the guy in Denver couldn't see him. "I wasn't. I'm still not… except, you know, the pandemic. Things are tight."

The Denver guy's name was Leo Abbott, but he preferred to be called by his nickname, Lion. He also used a signature roar whenever answering his phone or saying goodbye, which was almost as obnoxious as the fact that his fossil collection was kept locked away from public view. George pictured him gloating about the bison skull to his rich buddies.

"Yeah, yeah," said Lion. "Tough times for sure. But now you're willing to hand it over, huh?"

"I may be willing to sell it. For the right price." George reminded himself that if he could punch Brandon in the face, he could certainly stand up to this pompous jerk. And if he had to part with the skull, at least he'd get a decent amount of money for it.

God, his dad had been so proud of that specimen. On tours, he would spend the longest time telling visitors about its age and quality, about its significant contribution to the study of fossil mammals of the southwestern United States. "Professors from the best universities have come here to study it," he'd boast. George had never seen anyone from academia show an interest in the skull—or anything else at Fossil Galaxy—but maybe his dad hadn't been lying. Maybe all of that had happened before George was born.

"I can give you seven grand for it," said Lion carelessly, as if he was doing George a favor.

That would keep the doors open for another three, maybe four months. Enough to get through the postholiday dry spell. "It's worth a lot more than that."

"You said it yourself, George. Things are tight."

"But I think you can afford more, and a global emergency is no excuse to steal. Twenty-five thousand."

George was pulling that number out of a hat. It was difficult to figure comparable worth on a one-of-a-kind artifact, and although the skull was insured—as was most of the collection—it had been years since anything had been reevaluated.

Lion didn't hang up right away, which was something. After a long silence, he grunted. "I'm not gonna fork over that kinda dough for your dead cow, George."

"Well, that's too bad. I'm sure I'll find someone who will. I heard that Rita Tanaka is looking for some fresh acquisitions."

That was only partially a lie. George had read a magazine article about her a couple of months earlier. Evidently, she had one of the largest private fossil collections on the East Coast. There was a quote about how she used to travel the globe in search of new specimens, but the pandemic had slowed that activity way down. So, technically, she was looking. George had no idea whether she'd be remotely interested in his bison skull, but maybe it was worth a bluff.

"Tanaka!" Lion growled—like an angry human, not a pissed-off giant cat. "She has no taste, no discernment. She picks up any old rocks without any real appreciation for quality."

"Still, I hear she pays well."

Lion harrumphed. George, who had no idea what the man actually looked like, pictured a portly guy in a smoking jacket, holding a cigar and brandy snifter, sitting in a huge vaulted room with hunting trophies hanging on the walls.

After a moment, Lion spoke again. "Tell you what. I wanna support you and your little… exhibit. So I'll split the difference. Sixteen."

George would have been willing to accept that much, but he said, "Eighteen." A two-thousand-dollar charge for being patronizing seemed fair.

A heavy sigh came over the speaker. "Fine, fine. Eighteen."

"And you pay for shipping."

Lion chuckled.

They remained on the call for a few more minutes, finalizing arrangements. After George hung up, he spent a long time staring at his office wall, trying to sort out his emotions. There was relief at knowing he could stay above water a little longer. He also felt slightly giddy over his success at dickering. He doubted he'd have been brave enough to try it a few months ago. But at the same time, a part of him felt hollow and raw, like a pumpkin scooped out to make a jack-o'-lantern. That bison skull had been his father's pride, and his grandfather's before that. And now it would be gone.

Judith gave George a long look when he came out of the office. "You look like you need to sit down."

"I just was."

"Then maybe you should lie down instead." She frowned. "More threats from Zephyr's ex?"

Actually, yes, but George was just ignoring those now. There wasn't anything he could do about them anyway. "I'm going to sell the bison."

She didn't look upset or surprised. "Did you get a decent price for it?"

"I hope so."

"Honey, you know…." She stopped herself. "Never mind. You didn't ask for my advice or input."

George gave her a sincere smile. "It means a lot to me that you care. Thank you."

He was considering spending some time in the garden when the bell over the door rang and two men sauntered in. They looked as if they'd just finished shooting a music video or album cover. One was white, tall and reed-thin, with shoulder-length sandy hair. He wore all black—boots, low-slung skinny jeans, shirt unbuttoned halfway—and sported tattoos over much of his exposed skin. The other was Asian American, and he'd bleached his hair platinum. He also wore black skinny jeans, but his T-shirt was bright red and shiny and tasted like ranch dressing.

"Hey," said the one in the red shirt. "You guys open?"

"Until six tonight," George replied.

"Cool."

After they paid Judith for their entry, George said, "Would you like a guided tour or would you prefer to explore on your own?" He wasn't in a sociable mood but felt obligated to offer.

The man in black gave his companion a little punch to the arm and smiled at George. "We'll handle it, thanks."

As soon as they wandered into the minerals room, Judith gently elbowed George. "The platinum blond was flirting with you."

"He said, like, three words."

"I know flirting when I see it."

"Well, that's great, but I'm not interested." And then, to ward off any further discussion, he held up his hands. "I'm going to go dig up some packing materials for that skull."

He found what he was looking for in the workshop—a sturdy box, thick sheets of rubber foam, and a bunch of packing peanuts—and set everything on a table for later. He could get the package ready tonight and Debra could pick it up tomorrow. She was always willing to help him out on the rare occasions when he needed to ship something.

Zephyr's mystery project was still there, still covered. George pretended not to see it.

He returned to the gift shop just as his hip visitors finished their tour. They didn't show any interest in souvenirs, but the guy with the red shirt hovered near George for a few moments. "We're on our way to Vegas," he finally said.

George decided on a neutral response. "That sounds fun."

"Yeah. I have a little show going on in a gallery there. Some 3D-printed sculptures inspired by street art and current events. See?" He pulled a bright postcard out of his back pocket and handed it to George.

"Thanks." George examined the images: plastic statues of grinning virus molecules, a cargo ship jammed in a canal, protest marches. They looked interesting, although some of the colors didn't taste good. "And congratulations. That's great."

"We're from Oakland, and we've been looking for opportunities outside the Bay Area. Spreading our wings, right? I'm sort of almost a big deal, if that doesn't sound too pompous. Vegas is fantastic, but it's kind of a long haul, and LA… well, that's kinda cliché. So I was thinking… what if I had a show here?"

"Um… at Fossil Galaxy?"

"Right! I could set up in that room with all the rocks—it'd be perfect. Invite people from the Bay Area *and* LA. It could be sort of campy and fun. I'd get some friends to bring in some music, and I'd spring for some munchies too. You give me the space for free, but I pay you a commission on anything I sell. And my stuff's been selling really well. What do you think?"

"I… I don't know."

"Well, hang on." The man took back his postcard, grabbed a pen off the counter, and scrawled a name and number in a blank spot. "Think about it and let me know. We'll head back this way in a week and we can hammer out details then. Or, y'know, you could just give me a call." He waggled his eyebrows to make his meaning clear.

George managed to stammer out something akin to agreement, and then the guests left. Judith looked at him over the rim of her glasses. "That could be exciting."

"I never thought of this as a potentially hip event space."

"Imagine how thrilled us locals would be. A genuine happening, right here in the Junction."

"Huh." The money would be nice, if it materialized, and maybe other artists would follow this guy's lead. But he couldn't imagine hip, well-heeled art patrons making the trip to Conrad Junction or being very impressed by his run-down little museum.

She tilted her head at him. "I told you he was flirting."

"I guess."

"He's very handsome."

That was true. Objectively, the artist had everything: perfect face, nice body, charming manner. But subjectively, he did nothing for George. Didn't get his heart racing or blood rushing. "I'm not interested," George said again.

"I know. Can I share something your mother once said about you? You must have been about seven or eight at the time."

That took George by surprise, mostly because he wasn't aware his mother had spoken about him at all. When he was a kid, he sometimes wondered whether she remembered he existed. "What?" he asked cautiously.

"She said, and I quote, 'When George connects with someone, he hands his heart and soul over forever, no questions asked, and he'll defend his friends to the death. Such astonishing generosity. I hope the world doesn't rob him of this.'"

For a moment, George was speechless. Then he swallowed. "Mom said that?"

"She saw your strengths, Georgie, even if she wasn't good at telling you. You've handed Zephyr your heart, haven't you?"

He nodded. "He texted last night. He's at Al's. He told me he loves me. But I don't think it will work for us."

"I have a feeling that boy doesn't claim love easily. Maybe the two of you will find a way to make it work."

Unwilling to argue, George just shook his head. He didn't believe in fairy tales.

DEBRA FROWNED at him. "Oh, sweetie, you don't want to ship this through the USPS."

"Why not?"

She patted the box gently. "Because we won't insure past five grand. How much is it worth?"

"He's paying eighteen."

"Eighteen." She looked thoughtful. "Here's what you need to do. Take it to the hardware store in Boron. They're a UPS shipper, and UPS insures up to fifty grand."

"Yeah, okay. Thanks, Debra."

"Sure thing. I know this baby's important to you."

"It's just an old bone." He knew he wasn't fooling her, and he certainly wasn't fooling himself. But if he admitted how much this hurt, he would probably break down in big, ugly sobs. At least this way, he could pretend to retain his dignity.

Debra gave the box another pat before digging through her mailbag. "Hey, got a registered letter for you today."

And just like that, the sorrow he'd been feeling over the bison skull turned into sour fear. Only one person would send him registered mail. He considered refusing it, but he wasn't sure that was an option, and anyway, he doubted it would do any good. Besides, he didn't want to cause problems for Debra. So he took the envelope, signed her electronic register, and even managed a few more minutes of polite chatter until Debra waved and headed back to her truck.

The envelope sat on the sales counter like a rattlesnake waiting to strike. He could just throw it away. But in this case, ignorance was not bliss. He needed to know what that fuckface was up to. Maybe this time he'd found a valid reason to sue.

"Courage, Georgie." He picked up the envelope.

The letter was addressed to Mr. George Harlow. The return address was in LA, but there was no name or business name; just the street, city, and zip. George didn't know LA well enough to have any idea where the street was. It could have been a house or an office building. It might even be fictional, for all he knew.

Well, staring at it wouldn't do him any good. Might as well get it over with so he could get on with his day. He slit the envelope with a Fossil Galaxy souvenir letter opener. The gift shop hadn't sold those in years, and this one was probably older than he was. He wondered how many times his father had held it. And his grandfather before that. Had they ever dreaded what it would reveal, the way he felt now?

There was nothing inside except a single sheet of plain white paper with a message computer-printed in black ink.

I don't know how you turned him against me. It doesn't make any sense. You have nothing, and I can show him the world.

I think maybe he's testing me, the little tease. Trying to see if I'm serious about him.

I'm dead serious.

But you don't need to make this any harder on yourself. I'm a reasonable man.

Tell me where he's gone to and I won't take any actions against you. All I want is to talk to him. I'm sure he'll see reason.

Where is he?

It wasn't signed, but it didn't need to be.

George stared at the little squiggles of black ink and tried to calm himself. He could show this to the cops. And he could also imagine their dismissive response. Not only couldn't he prove that Brandon sent the damn thing, but the letter itself contained no overt threats. It didn't even sound too crazy, if you didn't know the context.

"George, what's wrong?"

He startled violently before realizing it was Judith who addressed him. God, he hadn't even heard her enter the store. "Brandon knows that Zephyr's not here."

Although Judith frowned, she didn't say anything right away. Instead, she tucked her hat, scarf, coat, and purse in the office, then returned to stand behind the counter with George. "How does he know?"

"No idea." Spies? Hidden cameras? Psychics? A lucky guess?

Judith gently took the letter from him. She always wore her reading glasses on a chain around her neck, and now she perched them on her nose to peruse the contents. She sighed a little when she was done. "He doesn't seem to have any clue where Zephyr is. That's a good thing."

George had been so distressed over the message that he hadn't noticed the silver lining. But he also wasn't ready to relax. "I bet he can find out, if he tries hard enough. You throw enough money at a mystery and you're bound to get an answer eventually."

She set the paper down and smoothed it, clearly taking time to choose her words carefully. "How afraid are you of this man?"

"I'm not—for me. But for Zephyr…." George remembered dark bruises blooming on Zephyr's face.

"And you still don't want to get a restraining order?"

"Wouldn't do any good. Brandon's not rational about Zephyr."

Judith clicked her tongue and shook her head. "It's terrible."

"Zephyr told me that Brandon had a pretty sucky family life, growing up. His mom died when he was young, his dad gave him a string of ever-younger stepmothers. The dad himself is a coldhearted, narcissistic bastard who hates that Brandon's gay." George frowned. "But dammit, that's no excuse. Zephyr didn't give me many details about his own upbringing, but I think it was pretty damn awful. No father and a too-young mother with addictions and a ton of baggage. But Zephyr's not going around threatening people or damaging their property. And my parents—"

He stopped himself so suddenly that he almost bit his tongue.

"Your parents loved you," Judith said quietly. "But that wasn't enough. They hurt you so deeply."

George growled and kicked the plastic wastebasket, sending it and its contents flying across the floor. If Brandon had showed up just then, George would have done a lot more than punch him in the nose. He would have taken that baseball bat and— It was a good thing Brandon was nowhere in sight.

If Judith was disturbed by George's outburst, she didn't show it. She simply folded the letter and tucked it into the envelope, which she carried into the office. By the time she returned a few minutes later, without the letter but with a cup of coffee, George was calmer. "Can you handle things here for a bit?" he asked. "I need to take that package to Boron."

"Of course. Take your time."

"What if Fuckface shows up?"

"Ivy's on duty at the gas station. I can call her if there's trouble."

"I thought she quit and got a job tending bar in California City."

Judith nodded. "But she's back here two days a week."

That eased George's fears a little. Ivy was almost as tall as he was and considerably heavier. She'd faced robbers and drunks without flinching and had struck fear into the heart of more than one arrogant motorist who treated her rudely. She'd probably be happy to face Brandon down, and she could be at Fossil Galaxy within a minute or two of being called.

George put on his coat, grabbed his keys and the package, and walked out to the van. It looked beautiful in the bright sunlight, the art brighter and of better quality than the original. But staring at it too long brought a confusion of flavors, so after settling the package onto the passenger seat, he quickly slid behind the wheel.

Before starting up the engine, he texted Al.

Fuckface knows Zephyr's not here but doesn't know where he is. Yet. Warn Z please.

The response came immediately.

Zephyr's gone. Left this morning.

CHAPTER THIRTY

WHEN AL came home from school and saw Zephyr in a skirt and hot-pink sweater, he hadn't looked shocked or even mildly surprised. He'd dumped his backpack on the table with a relieved grunt. "I think I finally get the difference between substantive and procedural due process. And it's not even hard. Dunno why I had such a block against it in the first place. It would help if my con-law prof wasn't as dry as the Mojave. That guy could market himself as a sleep aid."

They ate pasta and then Al studied while Zephyr channel-flipped. There was nothing he wanted to watch. He and George had spent a lot of quiet evenings together, doing nothing much—reading, chores, TV—and that hadn't felt like time wasted. It was peaceful. Restful. Comfortable.

Fuck. Was that what *home* felt like?

"Zephyr? Are you all right?"

Zephyr realized he'd scrunched himself into the corner of the couch, arms locked around his bent legs, and that he was shivering as if he had a fever. "I… I can't do this."

Al stood up from the table and, abandoning his books, came over to crouch in front of Zephyr. "Are you in withdrawal? Tell me what from and I can get you some help."

That made Zephyr emit a sound that couldn't decide whether it was a laugh or a sob. "George."

"You're…."

"In withdrawal from George." He took a few deep breaths and tried to sound sane. "I'm not an addict. Really. Believe it or not, I'm as sober as a Latter-day Saint."

Al looked doubtful. "Are you sure? It's nothing to be ashamed of. Maybe George told you that both our parents were alcoholics. James and Mary too."

"My mother was a junkie. I may not have made a lot of smart choices, but at least I knew better than to go there."

"Yeah, okay, I hear you. That's what it was like for me and George too. I've literally never once had booze or anything stronger than prescription ibuprofen. I think the same may be true for him." Al stood, wincing a little and rubbing his knees, and then collapsed onto the couch beside Zephyr. "So you're missing him, huh?"

"I've never missed anyone before."

"Sucks, doesn't it?"

Zephyr squeezed his legs tighter. "I don't *need* people. I just don't. Never have. I get what I want from them and move on. That's why I left George."

"Because you got from him what you wanted?"

"Because I...." Shit. This was hard to admit. "Because what I wanted was him. And I'm supposed to be self-reliant, right? But I wasn't doing that there. I'm still not." He waved one arm around a little, indicating Al's house, where Zephyr paid no rent and had done very little to earn his keep.

"You can get a job."

Zephyr made an impatient sound. "I don't know how, not really. And I don't have any of the things they want—diploma, references, work history."

"I can help—"

"I know! God. Sorry. I don't mean to yell."

They were both quiet for a few minutes, which was probably difficult for Al, given his tendency to talk. But he remained at Zephyr's side instead of returning to his studies, even though his exams were almost here. He was so giving of himself, just like his brother.

"I need to stand on my own two feet," Zephyr finally said.

"I get that. But there's nothing weak about getting help now and then, you know. God knows I've done it plenty of times. And look at George. He might refuse to let me, James, or Mary do anything for him, but how long do you think he'd have lasted without his friends? Do you think there's something wrong with him because he relies on them to do some of his errands and volunteer in his stupid fucking museum and bring him food and... and all the other things they do?"

"Of course not."

Al waited, eyebrows raised, as if the conclusion was obvious. And maybe it was. But Zephyr wasn't George, not by a long shot.

"I need to go" was what Zephyr said.

"Go where?"

"Dunno." Somewhere away from Harlows and their friendly, generous ways. Somewhere he could get his head on straight. He sighed. "I'm sorry. I like your house and your cat. I like you. But I have to leave."

Zephyr unwound himself and stood, but Al looked up at him sadly. "Can you at least wait for morning?"

Rain was pelting the windows. Zephyr thought about walking in the dark, shivering on a bench somewhere with the kind of cold that crept deep inside your body and hung on like invading frost spiders. About the way sounds would buffet him and shadows would lurk in corners, everything a potential threat.

"Morning," he agreed.

ZEPHYR AND Al stood just inside the front door, Zephyr holding his suitcase. Al was in scrubs with Smiley tucked into his arms. Zephyr wore jeans, a turquoise sweater, and his biker jacket.

"Don't tell George I'm gone. Unless he asks, I mean. Please. Is that okay?"

"Whatever you want, but why?"

"He has other things to worry about. I'll send him a message when I land somewhere." Assuming he *did* land somewhere.

Al looked deeply unhappy but didn't argue. Instead, he juggled the cat slightly as he reached into a pocket and pulled out a wad of bills. "Take 'em," he said, holding them out.

"I can't—"

"It's not much, and anyway, it's a loan. You'll pay me back someday."

That seemed unlikely, but Zephyr took the money. He didn't count it before tucking it into one of his zippered jacket pockets. Then he reached over to scratch Smiley's ears. "Thank you, Al."

"You're welcome here anytime. You got that?"

Zephyr nodded mutely, opened the door, and walked outside.

It wasn't quite raining, although the mist clung to him and made him wish he still had a lot of hair—or at least a hat. Gloves might be nice too. And so might a chauffeured limousine and a private jet, but at least he had a warm sweater and a decent jacket.

He walked several blocks before stopping to decide on a... well, not a destination. But a direction at least. His mind was absolutely blank, however, as if he'd never before ventured outside. He had absolutely no idea where to go. But he couldn't just stand here, where people driving by stared suspiciously. Finally, he just started walking forward.

His feet were sore and he was considering ditching the suitcase when he finally reached a busy gas station. He went inside and bought a cup of coffee, mainly so he could loiter for a little while without anyone yelling at him. Cars arrived, the gas station attendants filled them with gas, and they trundled away. All of those drivers with somewhere to go.

When the attendants started glaring at him, Zephyr tossed the empty paper cup, took a breath, and approached a man wearing jeans and a University of Oregon hoodie who was exiting the mini-mart with a bottle of Pepsi and a package of mini powdered donuts. He was in his late thirties, Zephyr estimated, and he'd given Zephyr a polite smile before entering the store.

"Hey." Zephyr tried to sound as un-serial-killer-like as possible. "Do you know if there's a truck stop anywhere around here? I'm trying to hitch a ride."

The man gave him a careful look. "There's one about twenty, twenty-five miles north of here. I'm heading that way if you want me to drop you off."

The man's name was Blake, he drove a newer Prius, and he did tech support for a software company south of Portland. He didn't say why he'd been in Salem that morning and didn't ask Zephyr any questions. Mostly they listened to a podcast about cryptocurrency as they rolled past harvested fields and tree nurseries and vineyards. Blake ate his donuts along the way, scattering powdered sugar. He offered some to Zephyr, who declined.

Less than half an hour later, Blake exited the freeway and pulled into a Flying J Travel Center, where Zephyr was pleased to see plenty of trucks. Blake wished him luck before speeding away.

A diner with weathered siding perched at the edge of the parking lot, its signs promising Indian food and hamburgers. Although Zephyr wasn't hungry, he trudged over, entered, and sat in a small booth near a window with a view toward a tire shop and an RV storage center. When a bored-looking waitress came by, Zephyr ordered a cup of chicken noodle soup and a Coke. She brought them right away, along with a small windfall of plastic-wrapped saltines.

Zephyr ate slowly as he surveyed the other customers. A middle-aged man and woman sat at one table, loudly bickering over what he should do about his back problems. At another table, three men in green John Deere polo shirts were talking politics. And elsewhere, men sat in ones and twos, drinking coffee and staring at their phones. None of them paid him any attention. Except... over there. A lean man in his forties, his mouse-brown hair tied back in a ponytail, a little stubble on his cheeks. He wore a down vest over a plain flannel shirt, and when he caught Zephyr's eye, the man smiled.

Zephyr could see the next steps as if they'd already happened. The man would pay and leave the diner, and a few minutes later, so would Zephyr, who would find the guy lingering outside the cab of his truck. The two of them would talk for a few minutes, negotiating terms. Zephyr would climb up into the passenger seat. The cab would smell of cigarette smoke, fast food, and sweat. They would pull out onto the access road, then the on-ramp, then the freeway, and at some point—maybe after dark—they'd park at a rest stop. If Zephyr was lucky, the man wouldn't be the type who hated himself for being attracted to Zephyr.

And then after that—

No.

Something settled inside of Zephyr with all the weight and bulk of a *T. rex*. It didn't have claws and fangs, however—it had roots. And those roots reached almost frantically for a place to hold fast.

Look at George. Sweet, kind George, who valued all the love he received, even when that love was imperfect. Who never felt himself diminished by receiving or giving aid. Who embraced his own flaws and those of others. George's roots were, in fact, far too deep, gripping with ferocious tenacity even as the sands shifted on the surface around him.

A few years earlier, Zephyr had found himself temporarily stranded at a state park near Highway 101 in far northern California, and on a whim, he'd taken a short walk through the redwoods. He'd seen two of the mighty trees that had grown together, their trunks grafted near the base and remaining close as they soared toward the sky. They remained two discrete specimens but were permanently entangled. Both trees looked as healthy—as mighty—as the others in the forest.

George and Zephyr could be those trees. Zephyr wouldn't lose himself at George's side—in fact, he would grow even better.

Ignoring the truck driver's disappointed expression, Zephyr leapt to his feet and slapped thirty dollars onto the table—far more than what he owed. Clutching his suitcase tightly, he hurried across the blacktop to the diesel pumps.

"Hey," Zephyr said to an older man who had just finished filling his tank. "I need a ride to a bus station. I can pay."

The man made a grunting sound and gestured with his head toward the cab.

THE DRIVER took him to Portland, where Zephyr ended up on a train instead of a bus. It was a little more expensive, but he could afford it. He had two seats to himself, which was nice; he wasn't feeling sociable. He leaned his seat back and let the gentle rocking lull him into a doze.

In the darkness, they climbed mountains and crossed into California, and shortly after dawn they stopped in Sacramento. Zephyr had a short time to freshen up in the bathroom and grab some potato chips from a vending machine. Then he boarded a bus that took him down the freeway to Stockton, and after another brief wait, he was on a train again, this time bound for Bakersfield.

A little over two years ago, he'd been in Bakersfield. The memories came to him as he watched winter-bare orchards and vineyards roll by. It was gray here in the Central Valley too, with fog rather than rain, but the last time he'd been in Bakersfield had been in late summer, with the sun relentless and the heat rising up from sidewalks and streets. He'd been staying at the Sleep-Tite Inn, on and off. When he could afford it. Roaches. Plumbing that groaned before grudgingly giving a trickle of water. Yelling and sirens in the parking lot.

He wondered if Jasvir stilled worked there. Maybe he still had Zephyr's plastic bag of belongings locked away somewhere in hopes that eventually Zephyr would return and pay the twenty-dollar ransom.

It was weird. That wasn't so long ago, but the Zephyr who'd walked to MaryLou's Café in stockings with a run in them felt like a stranger. Like... someone he'd met only once, long ago.

If that was true, who was this Zephyr now?

He had a distant memory of a man talking to him. A social worker or a probation officer probably, or maybe a teacher. Zephyr couldn't recall the specifics. The guy had been tall and skinny, very dark-skinned, with the type of forehead that seemed perpetually set into a scowl. His eyes had been warm, however.

"You can't do anything about your parents or grandparents," he'd said to Zephyr as they sat in a small windowless office that smelled of coffee. There had been a lot of papers, books, and brochures lying around. "You can't change the past. And you shouldn't change whoever you truly are, deep inside." The man had held a palm to his own chest. "But you can find the best parts of that real you, and you can use them to make choices about what to do with yourself in the future. That's your power, Zephyr."

At the time Zephyr hadn't paid much attention to the man. It was just another lecture by yet another adult, and in the end, Zephyr would be left to take care of himself.

But now, as the train chugged southward, he turned over the man's words in his head. The best parts of himself—what were they? Well, he *could* take care of himself pretty well. He'd been wise enough to stay away from drugs, even when the temptation had been strong. He could be satisfied and comfortable with very little in the way of possessions. He'd never harmed anyone, not even when they hurt him first. He'd eventually walked away from Brandon. He was brave enough to dress the way he wanted, in a way that felt authentic and made him feel like he looked good, even though he knew it would open him up to stares, ridicule, and sometimes even violence.

These were real strengths.

And there was another one, which he hadn't realized until recently. He was capable of loving someone. And of being loved.

Maybe, taken separately, these characteristics weren't much. But what if he put them together? It was like the surprise he'd been making for George, constructed of bits of this and pieces of that. Zephyr had been taking all of those parts and building them into something new. Maybe even something *good*.

He just needed to do the same with himself.

THE TRAIN reached Bakersfield midafternoon. The fog had cleared by then, but the sky still looked a little thin, as if the haze would resettle soon. Zephyr felt a sense of urgency he hadn't experienced in a long time. He had a destination in mind, and he wanted to get there right away.

It was over a mile and a half to MaryLou's Café, and despite the weight of his suitcase, he covered the distance quickly. Relieved to find the parking lot full of trucks, he hurried inside the restaurant. A few people glanced up at him, but most were busy with their food or phones.

Zephyr cleared his throat. "I need a ride to Conrad Junction. It's past Boron, on the way to Barstow. I can chip in for fuel. Is anyone heading that way?"

For a long moment, nobody said anything. Then some people returned their attention to other things, while the rest stared as if he were a strange exhibit in a museum. Zephyr thought about what else he could say, because surely *someone* was going his way. The highway was practically right outside the door.

But then a fiftyish man in a booth near a window spoke up. "I'm on my way to Santa Fe. I can take you."

Zephyr gave him a wide, relieved smile.

As it turned out, Jesús was navigating a box truck with a load of produce from his brother's ranch in Visalia. He spent every autumn at the ranch, helping to harvest almonds and persimmons, and then drove some of the yield to New Mexico, where a cousin ran a gourmet food store. "It's all organic," Jesús explained. "Top quality." From there, he would hit the road again for the long drive to a Mexican seaside town near Mazatlán where his wife and grown daughter would be waiting for him. He'd stay with them until it was time to return to Visalia in September.

"It's a long time to be away from home," he said as he steered the truck down the highway through Tehachapi. "But I make more money this way, and we appreciate each other more when I am there. Another few years, maybe I can retire."

"You seem pretty happy."

"I am. It's a good life. Maybe not for everyone, but for me, it's very good. Where are you going today? Also home?"

Zephyr thought about this for a moment. "Yeah. I think so."

By then they'd risen above the haze. And it was funny, because as the hillsides became drier and the first Joshua trees appeared, a tingle of anticipation began in Zephyr's chest. He felt that he was heading to the place he belonged.

When Jesús stopped his truck in the Fossil Galaxy parking lot, Zephyr's heart was racing as if he'd just run all the way from Bakersfield. Jesús wouldn't let him pay for gas because, he said, he was coming this way anyway. And he insisted on giving Zephyr a box of persimmons too. "They're hachiyas. Wait until they're very soft or they won't taste good."

"Thank you. Travel safely. Enjoy your family."

Jesús clapped him on the shoulder. "Enjoy being home."

The bell over the door jingled when Zephyr entered the building. George, standing behind the sales counter, looked up from a stack of papers. His immediate reaction was to gape—and then his face lit up with a smile so bright that it was almost blinding.

Zephyr set his suitcase and box on the floor and waited, unsure his legs could carry him any farther.

But then they didn't have to, because George zoomed over and engulfed him in an embrace so fierce that Zephyr could barely breathe. "Zeph. Oh God, Zeph, it's so good to see you."

A solidness settled inside of Zephyr, as if some loose part of himself had, at long last, clicked into place. He buried his face in George's shoulder and let himself bask in the familiar sensations of holding George Harlow.

"Hi, honey," Zephyr said when he could manage a few words. "I'm home."

Chapter Thirty-One

GEORGE CLOSED Fossil Galaxy early and didn't bother with the usual evening ritual of emptying the till and cleaning up. It could wait. Everything could wait except the most important thing in the world, which was the man beaming at him.

"Your shirt tastes like birthday cake," George said, knowing it was inane yet somehow important. They hadn't even left the gift shop yet, but he was afraid to stop touching Zephyr in case he disappeared like a mirage.

Zephyr smoothed a hand over his bright yellow blouse. "I didn't even realize this morning that I was going to come here, but I chose to wear this today—one of your favorite colors."

"I'm so glad you're here."

Zephyr smiled. "Me too. I think we need to talk."

Those words would have usually struck fear in George's heart. But discussing anything with Zephyr was better than not being able to talk at all—wondering where he was, how he was doing, whether George would ever see him again.

"Let's go sit down," George said. "Maybe some dinner? Kayla brought tamales."

Although Zephyr hadn't been gone long, he took a brief tour of the apartment, as if checking to see whether anything had changed. He picked up a few items—a book, the remote control, a Fossil Galaxy Christmas ornament—and put them down again.

George put the tamales into the microwave and then gestured at the full produce box. "What's with the persimmons?"

"Jesús gave them to me. The guy who drove me here from Bakersfield. He says they're organic, and we shouldn't eat them until they're gooey."

"Can we share them with some other people? There's a lot."

"Sure."

"Kayla's mom makes persimmon jam. I bet we could work out a deal with her."

For some reason, that made Zephyr smile widely.

They didn't discuss anything important over their meal. Mainly a little gossip about Al. Zephyr was clearly a fan. "Are all of you Harlows so nice? He took in a complete stranger and was totally there for me, no questions asked."

George snorted. "No questions asked because he can't shut up long enough to listen to answers."

"Yeah, your brother can talk."

"It used to get him in trouble at school all the time. But Dad put him to good use and trained him to lead the tours. Al loved that, even when he was young."

George noted that Zephyr's hair had grown out a little while he was gone and was now a soft brown stubble that George longed to caress. But as he watched, Zephyr's expression turned pensive. He used his fork to poke at a bit of masa still on his plate.

"Al refuses to come back to the Junction, right? And he has some stuff to say about it that, uh, isn't very flattering," Zephyr said.

"I bet," George had heard plenty of that invective straight from Al himself—and from James and Mary—and nothing they complained about was a lie. They'd seen the truth of their father long before George had.

"But he's got… stuff. Fossil Galaxy souvenirs. A big photo of the desert. He named his cat after a saber-toothed tiger."

"To be honest, I sent those souvenirs." George hadn't known until just now whether Al had kept them. It made him happy to learn that he had.

"But… I'd think he'd want to distance himself from all of that."

"He's nine hundred miles away—that's a pretty good distance." George held up a hand to forestall Zephyr's arguments. "Yeah, yeah, I know what you mean. I guess you'd have to ask Al why. I'm sure he'd be happy to tell you. At great length."

Zephyr grunted but still seemed deep in thought. He remained silent while they cleaned up, although sometimes he intentionally bumped against George in the small space of the kitchen. Maybe it was the way his bright clothing contrasted with the apartment's monochromatic décor, but the place seemed more like a home with Zephyr in it.

They settled on the couch eventually, squishing together in the middle instead sitting at opposite ends as they usually did. "Have you ever considered getting a pet?" Zephyr asked. "I've never had one, but Al's cat is nice."

"Maybe." When George was a kid, none of them had spent enough time at the house to have a pet there, and George's dad had insisted that having one at Fossil Galaxy would damage the exhibits.

Anyway, animals were clearly just a digression for Zephyr, who leaned against George, tracing patterns with a fingertip on George's leg. Little curves and swirls cut by occasional angles and lines.

"Al knows a lot about psychology," Zephyr finally said.

"He was a psychiatric nurse for a while."

"I think he realizes he can't ever separate himself entirely from the Junction. Doesn't matter how far you run—you're going to take your past with you. Maybe he figures he might as well acknowledge the good parts."

George nodded slowly; it made perfect sense. A species could evolve, but it would continue to carry vestiges of its earlier forms, like humans with their goose bumps and tailbones. A person could change without abandoning everything from his past.

"I have good parts," Zephyr said quietly.

"You have *great* parts. Spectacular."

"I don't mean the way I look."

"Neither do I."

Zephyr sat up straight and twisted a little, looking steadily into George's eyes. "My childhood was fucked up. But my mother must have given me *something*—even if just good genes. And maybe I should thank my father for those too, whoever the hell he was. Anyway, here I am. Not a complete disaster. I realized that just recently."

George had a lot of tight iron bands inside his chest, but those words loosened one of them a great deal. He had so badly wanted Zephyr to see his own self-worth. "I've known all along," George said.

"I think it's like your synesthesia. You see a color but taste a flavor nobody else does. You see a fucking mess of a human being and feel… like maybe he's worth something."

"He's worth everything."

Of course, they embraced after that, and they kissed, and George noted that Zephyr's lips were slightly chapped and his mouth tasted like tamales and orange juice and he was most definitely right *here* in their apartment and not a figment of George's imagination. Then they pulled slightly apart, both of them breathing hard.

"I want to stay," said Zephyr. "With you. Permanently." He was very solemn with this announcement.

George was trying not to hyperventilate. "Yes. God, yes. Please."

"I can't guarantee it'll work. I've never tried it before."

"We'll give it our best efforts."

They leaned their foreheads together, sealing the pact.

And then Zephyr sighed. "But we need to do something about Brandon, or he's just going to keep at us."

"Mafia hit men?"

"Do you know any?"

George gave a small smile. "I'm afraid they're in short supply in the Junction."

"Has he been bothering you?"

George seriously considered lying, or at least changing the subject, but that would be dishonest and unfair and a poor way to begin a serious relationship. "Phone calls, mostly. And I punched him. There was a letter too, and he knew you were gone, which is—"

"Wait wait wait! You *punched* him?"

"Several times. I think I broke his nose." That came out more cheerfully than George had intended, but he still held no regrets about the fight.

"What happened?" Zephyr asked incredulously.

"He showed up demanding to see you—he hadn't figured out yet that you'd left. And he was just... insufferable. So it got physical, but then Judith called in reinforcements and they separated us. That's the last time I saw him."

"I wish I'd seen it."

"I wish I'd hit him harder. Anyway, he sent me a letter after that. Threats. But by then, he knew you were gone, which is kind of freaking me out. Does he have this place under surveillance?"

Zephyr gave George's cheek a gentle stroke. "We can deal with that later. Tonight, it's just us. And tomorrow I'm finally going to finish your surprise."

George caught his hand and kissed it. "I didn't peek."

"Saint George."

"He slew dragons. I'd befriend them and keep them around. Great additions to the exhibits. They're sort of like dinosaurs." An idea suddenly popped into George's head. It felt important. "You work on that tomorrow. I'll see if Judith and Kayla can cover for us the next day. I want to take you somewhere and show you something."

"Sounds mysterious," Zephyr said with a grin.

"Very. And now, I know it's really early but—"

"Bedtime." Zephyr stood very fast, grabbed George's hand, and tugged him to his feet. They raced to the bedroom.

Just like the rest of the apartment, the bedroom felt homier with Zephyr in it. But this time, it wasn't due to his colorful clothing, because when he tore it off impatiently and stood naked and smiling, the sensations of comfort and belonging and *rightness* only increased. It was as if George had yearned for Zephyr his entire life without knowing it, as if Zephyr was an astounding discovery.

"What are you laughing about?' Zephyr asked, his expression fond. "I hope it's not me nude."

"You nude is no laughing matter. I was thinking about my grandfather."

Zephyr's good humor didn't lessen. "Do you always think about Wally before jumping into bed with some guy?"

"You're not 'some guy,' and I rarely jump, and no. Wally was working on a construction job somewhere in the desert, and when he made a hole in the ground, he discovered fossils. That changed his life forever. Changed the Harlow family destiny. And me, one night I took the cardboard out to the bin and discovered the most wonderful man I've ever met. That changed me forever too."

Zephyr came near, close enough that George felt his body heat but not quite close enough for their skin to touch. "You never know what surprises the desert has in store."

George gathered him close, just for the sheer joy of feeling Zephyr's body against his. Then he gave in to the urge to stroke the bristles on Zephyr's scalp. "Soft."

"Are you missing my long hair?"

"You looked good with it. You look good without it. You *are* good, no matter what you look like." Then, almost against his will, the words slipped out. "I love you."

"Oh." Zephyr went very still.

"You don't have to say it back. You don't owe me anything. I just needed you to—"

"I love you too."

Zephyr seemed almost as stunned by his own declaration as George was. Slowly, however, his mouth widened into a smile and his eyes lit with fire. "I do. I love you. Jesus Christ, George." He paused and then shouted, "I love you!" followed by a whoop of pure joy. At that moment, he was the most beautiful person to have ever walked the Earth.

Their lovemaking that night was part reunion and part celebration. It lasted for a long time, the journey worth even more than the destination, both of them determined to stretch out their combined pleasure for as long as possible. Zephyr marveled over George's body as if he'd never seen it before. And though George had never believed himself anything special to look at, under Zephyr's litany of compliments and accompanying caresses, he felt as gorgeous as a stunning work of art.

He explored Zephyr's body anew, loving how Zephyr could feel delicate and strong at the same time, adoring the little gasps and moans he drew from Zephyr's throat. And when he was finally inside him, moving deeply but with infinite slowness, George knew a type of wholeness that was almost transcendent. Their joining was a new religion that, instead of honoring deities, celebrated the perfection that could be found between two very human souls.

Afterward, there was cuddling, with Zephyr's head on George's shoulder, their legs twined, and the comforter pulled up to their chins. If George concentrated very hard, he could hear the faint sound of trucks and cars rumbling by on the highway. Tonight, he didn't even mind that the bypass had stolen so much of his business.

Zephyr yawned loudly. "I think you're a lucky charm."

"I don't feel all that lucky—except for finding you, of course."

"Mmm, maybe luck's not the right word. Before we met, though, it was like everyone I met wanted to use me or hurt me. The best I could hope for was… indifference. But you were kind to me, and ever since then, other people have been kind too. Your friends. Your brother. Random truck drivers I hit up for rides. It's like I got transported to a parallel universe where people are nice."

George had to think about this for a bit, maybe because he'd always lived in that universe. Of course, he'd faced struggles of his own, but even his parents had done the best they could with their limited emotional resources.

"I think the difference is that you've gotten better at finding good people."

"Maybe." Zephyr sighed luxuriantly and snuggled a little closer. "Because you've helped me feel like I deserve them."

CHAPTER THIRTY-TWO

JUDITH SEEMED happy to see Zephyr. "George missed you," she confided while George led a tour. "He wasn't eating right."

"He gets caught up with his colors and forgets he hasn't had real food. I remind him. I hear you swing a mean baseball bat."

"I think I like being scary," she replied with a grin.

"Did George really punch my ex?"

"George beat the crap out of him. I honestly think he might have killed that man if his friends hadn't pulled him away." She shook her head. "I've never seen George like that. He was like that cartoon character, the muscular green one?"

"The Hulk?"

Judith nodded eagerly. "Yes, him. Normally nerdy and mild-mannered, but when he got angry…."

It was sort of an appealing image, but it also made Zephyr a little sad. "I'm sorry I did that to him."

She patted his arm. "That wasn't you, honey. I think he's had a lot of anger bottled up for a very long time. Maybe it's a good thing he released some of it on someone as deserving as your ex."

Zephyr remembered the night George destroyed his father's diorama. "Is it anger or bitterness?"

"I don't know if there's much of a difference."

Although Zephyr wandered off to rearrange the postcard display and fold T-shirts, his thoughts weren't on the gift shop but on what Judith had said. For the first time in forever, Zephyr examined his own feelings about his mother. It was like poking his tongue at a sore tooth, and it made him want to wince and avoid the subject. But he prodded anyway.

And what he found, surprisingly, was mostly sorrow.

His mother hadn't been equipped to be a parent. Her own parents had screwed her up royally, and she'd been so very young when Zephyr was born. He'd heard from social workers that she'd had a couple more kids after him, although Zephyr had never met them. Hopefully, they ended up with better fates than his. She'd kept trying, though, didn't she? She'd even shown up for a few of his court hearings, back before they'd permanently terminated her rights. For all of these years, Zephyr had assumed she'd wanted him because she'd get bigger aid payments from the state, and maybe that *was* part of it. But perhaps she was also lonely and desperate to find love.

It had been well over a decade since Zephyr last saw her. He didn't know whether she was still alive, and he felt no urge to seek her out, or his half-siblings. But now something shifted inside of him, easing a pain he hadn't realized he was carrying.

"I forgive you," he whispered.

ZEPHYR SPENT the rest of the day in the workshop, finishing his masterpiece. He laughed at himself when he thought of it that way, but it didn't look bad. He was kind of proud of it, in fact. He put on the final touches just before closing time and then covered it again with the large canvas tarp and went in search of George.

"Good day?" he asked as George counted out the till.

"Not bad. Don't worry about money, though. We're okay for a while."

"Did you rob a bank?"

"There are no banks to rob in the Junction. I sold the bison skull." He said it almost cheerfully.

"Oh, Georgie, I'm sorry."

George patted Zephyr's shoulder as if he was the one needing comforting. "Don't be. I'm okay with it. I got a good price. And there's still plenty of items in the collection."

Although Zephyr knew perfectly well it hadn't been as easy as George tried to make it seem, there was no point in making a big deal out of it. "So... does this mean we can have a real Christmas celebration? Roast beast, etcetera? I've, uh, never really done that."

One thing Zephyr loved was that George didn't pity him. Now George smiled warmly. "Sure! We can plan a fancy menu. Most years we have decorations—lights and stuff—and we used to put a giant Santa hat on Tommy's head. I've been having trouble getting in the spirit this year, but now that you're back.... Yeah. Let's do it."

Zephyr actually felt a little excited. "I bet we can improvise some appropriate décor. I noticed tumbleweeds during the drive yesterday. What if we stacked some up and stuck on some tinsel and stuff? Sort of a Mojave Christmas tree?"

George clapped his hands. "Yes! They're an invasive species, you know. So we can make a silk purse out of a sow's ear. We can look for some tomorrow."

"On our mystery outing?"

"Yep."

It felt wonderful to be looking forward to something, even if it was such a small thing as putting up holiday decorations.

Zephyr helped George with the nighttime duties, but when George began to head for the apartment, Zephyr blocked his way. "You get your present early."

George's face lit up as if *he* were a Christmas tree. "You finished it?"

"Yes. I was going to wait to give it to you, but I'm too impatient. C'mon." Zephyr grabbed George's hand and tugged.

Giggling like a pair of kids, they ran hand-in-hand to the workshop. Truth be told, Zephyr usually found the exhibits a little spooky at night, the rooms illuminated by only the emergency exit signs, the display items making weird shapes as they loomed on pedestals and in cases. He didn't feel that way tonight, however. Not with George at his side.

The big fluorescent lamps in the workshop seemed exceptionally bright, and the scents of paint, plaster, wood, old metal, and dust seemed stronger than usual. Zephyr wondered how many hours Rick Harlow had spent in this room, and Wally before him, and whether they'd been happy while they were there. Did either of them think about what the future of Fossil Galaxy might be once they were gone?

George screeched to a halt in front of his surprise, then bounced on his feet like an eager little kid. "What is it, what is it?"

Laughing, Zephyr gave him a one-armed hug and a kiss on the cheek. "You're adorable."

"My sibs send me presents for my birthday and Christmas. Practical things, because they know I'm poor. You know—money for grocery and gas, Amazon gift cards, clothes without a Fossil Galaxy logo. Which I really appreciate. But…. Oh my God, Zephyr, let me see it before I die."

Now Zephyr felt nervous. What if George hated it? Oh, he'd be polite, of course; he was George, after all. But Zephyr wanted him to love it almost as much as he'd loved Tommy the *T. rex*. Zephyr had never in his entire life put so much time and effort into a project. It was the first thing he had every truly accomplished.

He bit his lip, took a few deep breaths, and then, with as much showmanship as he could muster, he tugged the canvas away from his masterpiece, a rather unique Mojave scene.

For a terrifying moment, George simply stared, wide-eyed, his mouth hanging open a little. Then he turned to Zephyr, grabbed him in a crushing embrace, and swung him around in a complete circle. "Oh my God!"

Zephyr waited until George set him down again so he could speak. "It's… okay?"

"Jesus, Zephyr, it's the most amazing thing I've ever seen. It's— You made this?"

"With a little help from your friends," Zephyr replied with a grin. "I had to learn how to use tools."

George stepped closer to the sculpture and spent several minutes closely inspecting it. Sometimes he'd touch a piece very gingerly, but mostly he just looked. "What's the Joshua tree made from?" he asked after a while.

"The trunk and branches have a wire armature covered with plaster. I stuck some of those old frond things from a real Joshua tree on there for texture. The leaves are toilet brushes painted green. Santiago gave me those from his work, and don't worry—we sanitized them first."

"Clever!"

And with the praise, Zephyr actually felt clever, which was nice. "Notice that I chose a shade of green way darker than sage. I think that makes sense for this tree, but also, I'm hoping it doesn't taste bad."

"Forest green. Tastes like an oatmeal raisin cookie. Which I like very much."

That made Zephyr beam. "I wanted to make a sloth, but that's outside my skill set. So I used a bunch of bits and pieces you had lying around to make the alien. We can name him Tommy, if you want. I salvaged and reused Tommy's teeth and eyes."

George hooted. "Tommy lives!"

"Notice that I painted him colors you like? Birthday-cake yellow with apple-pie pink spots. Those plaster dinosaur bones? I found those in here too and used them pretty much as is. I hope that's okay."

"It's great."

Whew. Zephyr had been a little worried that George had some special plan for the bones or that, like the diorama, they carried uncomfortable emotional baggage. "And the rest…. Well, obviously the alien is a fan of Fossil Galaxy souvenirs. You can see that he's been playing with a bunch of the plastic dinosaurs. Some are even up in the Joshua tree."

"And he has a T-shirt and hat peeking out of his shopping bag."

"He has to take something back home to Planet Xyjvok for his family."

"I especially like that he's taking a selfie—nice touch."

Zephyr smiled. "A plastic fake iPhone. The scene isn't, uh, exactly scientifically accurate."

George tugged him close again and kissed his head. "But it's funny and sort of kitschy. It'll make me smile every time I look at it. And guests will love it. Thank you, Zephyr. It's the best thing anyone has ever given me."

"My technical skills are a pretty ba—"

"Zephyr." George grabbed Zephyr's shoulders and stared earnestly into his eyes. "It really does look fantastic. Better than most of the Harlow attempts at the visual arts. And you also made it special for me, even down to the colors, and that's—" He stopped and pressed his lips together. Then he gave a little sniffle. "Dammit, I'm not gonna cry."

"My big, tough Saint George, who beats up nasty exes and rescues strays from the trash and would probably help little old ladies across the street if that was a thing in Conrad Junction—he gets to cry whenever he wants to."

And so George did, but it was a sweet little shedding of tears mixed with smiles, and damned if Zephyr didn't find himself joining in the fun. They were laughing, sniffling, hugging, snotty balls of emotions, which ultimately ended with both of them naked atop the pile of musty canvas, writhing and howling like a pair of coyotes.

"We're a mess," George said as they panted on the floor afterward.

"Yep." Zephyr picked a bit of construction debris out of George's hair. "Do you think your friends could come in tomorrow and help me move this thing to the gift shop? Assuming you want it there, I mean."

"Of course I do, and now they're your friends too. And yeah, probably, but after our excursion."

"Right," Zephyr said, remembering. "You have a surprise for me too."

"It's not as good as this one."

Zephyr rolled over onto his belly and blew a raspberry on George's stomach. Then he leapt to his feet and reached a hand down to help George. "I'm starving. Let's go find some dinner."

George allowed himself to be pulled up, although he groaned theatrically, and then he ineffectually brushed dust and the residue of workshop projects off the front of his torso. Zephyr helped by brushing off George's backside. Well, *groping* George's backside, because that was more fun.

They both realized they were cold at about the same time, so they laughed as they shivered and threw on their clothing. Just as they reached the door to the workshop, George grasped Zephyr's arm and brought him to a stop. "Thank you, Zeph. Really."

"You're welcome." Despite the chilly air, Zephyr felt an inner warmth. "You know something? You and me—we're going to make this work. Our life together is going to be a real thing. Maybe even a forever thing."

George's eyes shone. "Yeah?"

"Yeah. We'll have some challenges, but… I have a feeling."

Love. Hope. Optimism. Confidence. It was amazing how well things could grow in a desert climate, given the proper nurturing.

CHAPTER THIRTY-THREE

"WOW," KAYLA said. "This rocks."

She was apparently referring to the entire gift shop area, and George had to agree. He'd been so excited over Zephyr's sculpture that he'd texted Santiago and Lucas the previous night after dinner, and they'd appeared early this morning to help load the sculpture onto George's cart and set everything up near the gift shop's front window. Exactly where Tommy had once stood. Zephyr's work looked even better there than Tommy had.

George had gotten into the spirit of things and dragged the Christmas boxes from storage, unveiling Christmas lights, synthetic wreaths and garlands, tree ornaments, and other seasonal decorations. Judith had magically shown up with home-baked cinnamon rolls, George made hot chocolate, and they'd all held an impromptu decorating party.

Now, as Kayla pointed out, everything looked great: bright and cheery and festive. Zephyr had hung some ornaments on his faux Joshua tree, and Kayla had stuck cloves into oranges to make pomanders, scenting the air with citrus and spice.

Everyone took pictures and promised to bring their family members by to see the results.

But despite the fun, George didn't forget the activity he'd planned for the afternoon. After hurrying into the apartment, he packed sandwiches, chips, apples, and water bottles into a bag, which he tucked into the back of the van along with a few other items. Then he returned to the gift shop, where a family with three young kids had just arrived. Kayla was taking photos of them in front of the new sculpture.

"We've got places to go, things to see," George informed Zephyr.

"What should I wear?"

"Whatever makes you feel good."

Judging from Zephyr's expression, that was the right answer. When he emerged from their apartment fifteen minutes later, he was stunning in a long-sleeved catsuit with a black-and-white geometric print, a tangerine-hued belt, and matching platform sandals. He'd put on a little lipstick and even polished his nails.

"Wow." It was the most George could manage.

"Too much?"

"No. You're… wow." Not for the first time, George wondered how Zephyr had developed his sense of style. He vowed to ask about it later. Maybe he'd even glean a few precious tidbits of information about Zephyr's childhood—some that weren't too painful.

Lucas and Santiago had left by then, and Kayla was leading a tour, but Judith looked impressed. "Even when I was young and svelte, I'd never have been brave enough to wear something like that. George is right—wow."

Zephyr grinned and struck a pose, as if he were on a runway. Then he and George said goodbye to Judith, grabbed their jackets, and headed out to the van.

"We have never been anywhere together," Zephyr said as George pulled out of the parking lot.

"So this is our first date?"

"I guess so."

"Don't expect anything as glamorous as your outfit."

Zephyr patted George's knee. "Not Vegas, huh?"

"You know, I've only been there once. In college. Zak and I went to celebrate my twenty-first birthday." They'd driven in Zak's car, and even though they went right through Conrad Junction and paused at the traffic light almost directly in front of Fossil Galaxy, they hadn't stopped. George hadn't even told his parents he'd be passing through, because if his dad had known he had a few days off from school, he'd have expected George to come in and work.

"Did you enjoy it?" asked Zephyr.

"Not really. I don't drink, and it turned out I didn't like gambling. Not that I had money to squander anyway. And the crowds. The colors! I had a headache *and* a stomachache the whole time. Vegas tastes awful."

Zephyr threw his head back and laughed. "That doesn't surprise me one bit. And don't worry. I had enough glitz when I was with Brandon. I'd rather be with you in Conrad Junction."

George believed that Zephyr made any place glamorous just by being there, no matter what he looked like, but he didn't say so. He didn't want him to think he was laying it on too thick. It was true, though.

Instead of going east or west, as George usually did, he headed north. Ridgecrest was about an hour away, with some tiny communities in between, but he wasn't going to any of those places. Instead, after about fifteen minutes, he turned left onto a road that had once been paved but was now mainly ruts, sand, and chunks of asphalt. It had been a long time since he'd been out this way, and he nearly missed the turnoff. There were no real landmarks, just low scrub and power lines, with a few rock outcroppings here and there. The van bumped and jostled along, even at low speed.

"If this was anyone but you, Saint George, I'd start to worry I was about to be murdered and dumped in the desert." Zephyr sounded cheerful despite his words.

But George remembered what Zephyr had looked like that night by the dumpster. "That's not funny."

"It is, because I know I'm safe with you. Anyway, maybe dying in the Mojave's not such a bad thing. A couple million years from now, maybe a distant Harlow descendant would dig me up and stick my bones in a museum."

That made George laugh despite himself.

The road dipped into a shallow valley where few plants grew, then rose back up and skirted a rock formation that George had always thought resembled giant witches having a meeting.

"Why are there even roads here?" Zephyr asked.

"All sorts of reasons. Mining operations. Old military stuff. Some lead to hiking or dirt biking areas. And a few people live out here."

"The ones who want to avoid the hustle and bustle of Conrad Junction."

George flashed him a grin. "Exactly."

A moment later, he turned onto a road that was nothing more than a narrow sand trail. He drove for another minute or so before coming to a stop and turning off the engine. Then he unbuckled his seat belt, opened the door, and hopped out. "C'mon," he urged.

Although Zephyr looked bewildered, he obeyed, then stood beside the van, looking around as if he expected something to appear. Walking would probably be a pain in those shoes, but that was okay because they were staying put. George walked around and opened the back of the van. "Come sit here with me?"

Zephyr held the side of the van for balance and then hopped up next to George, both of them dangling their legs out the back. There was no wind, and at this time of day, the temperature was almost sixty, so they were comfortable enough in Zephyr's jacket and George's thick hoodie.

"A guy named Wayne Maas owns this land," George said. "He bought it not long after Wally opened Fossil Galaxy. Back then, Wayne was a young man, but he'd fought in the Korean War and came back... well, pretty much done with humanity, I guess. He'd inherited some money, so he made a mining claim, bought a lot of acreage, and built himself a house. He still lives here."

"I don't see a house."

"It's a little farther down the road, in a valley. I think he put it there because it would be sort of hidden. Wayne doesn't trust people. But at some point, he found some fossils while he was digging on his property, and he brought them to Wally, and they became friends. Wally and Wayne—both eccentric even by local standards. My mom used to call them the Woo-woo Wa-Was when she was several vodka-and-Diet-Cokes into her day." The name had made George's dad angry enough to stomp away, slamming doors as he went.

"Is some weird old guy going to appear and scream at us for trespassing?" Zephyr seemed more amused than worried.

"Nope. Wayne gave my grandfather permission to come here and look for fossils, and later he let Dad come too, and then us kids. When James was a teenager, he had an old quad bike, and Wayne allowed us to ride it around on his property." It was one of the very few family excursions the Harlows had been allowed to have, and it only happened on holidays—when Fossil Galaxy was closed—or when their father was in an unusually good mood.

"So he's okay with us here now?"

"Yep. I haven't seen him in a few years—I don't think he goes much of anywhere nowadays—but he's told Debra to let me know I'm still welcome. As long as I don't decide to work for the government." George grinned. "And I have to agree to turn off all cell phones and any similar devices, which I've done."

"Cool."

"I'd like to check on him later, if you don't mind. I brought some of your persimmons to give him, and a bunch of oranges and a loaf of Judith's bread." He knew from Debra's reports that Wayne was doing all right. He had a connection in Boron who brought him weekly deliveries of food, weed, and beer, and although he was even less enthusiastic about doctors than George's parents had been, he seemed to be healthy for a man pushing ninety. And as Debra liked to point out, pandemic lockdowns and social distancing hadn't posed any problem for him.

Zephyr and George sat and silently stared out at the desert. A couple of ravens circled in the sky at a distance, but the only other living things visible were plants. The sky was pale blue, as if permanently faded by the sun, and it was streaked with fading jet contrails. There were almost no sounds apart from two men breathing and the small rustlings of their bodies.

After a while George asked quietly, "Are you ready for a picnic?"

That earned him a bright smile. "Yeah. I'd love that."

Since walking in the sand was a challenge for Zephyr, George did all the work. Not that there was much to do. He laid out a canvas tarp on a plant-free area of the road and then spread an old blanket over it. He helped Zephyr take the few steps over, and when they were both seated face-to-face, George unpacked the bag of food. "Not the most gourmet picnic," he commented as he handed over a sandwich.

"And here I was, expecting caviar and champagne. Except neither of us drinks and I'm not a fan of fish eggs. I prefer lunchmeat on Judith's sourdough."

"I've never had caviar."

"You're not missing anything. I think it's one of those things people pretend to like just because it's expensive."

Anyway, the sandwiches were good, and the chips were name-brand, thick-cut, and kettle-cooked, instead of a cheap discount type. The crunchy apples were faultlessly tart. It was all just so perfect, George thought: sitting with the man he loved, their cares temporarily ignored, the world around them seeming vast and full of promise.

George put their trash into the bag and set it in the van, then rejoined Zephyr side by side on the blanket. "It's been a while since you've tried to convince me to give up on Fossil Galaxy."

"You won't listen anyway, and it hurt you when I tried." As if in apology, Zephyr squeezed George's thigh.

"I appreciate that you're not pushing. But I still… I really want you to understand why I'm being so stubborn about it. Look out at the Mojave, Zeph. It's an incredibly harsh place, and you know what the green tastes like. But isn't it beautiful too? Special? There's so much more complexity when you take the time to *notice*. Even now in December, look—the sagebrush is flowering. If we get some decent rains this winter, there will be carpets of color."

"I can see why you love the desert," Zephyr said carefully. "But there are other things you could do aside from running a...."

"A failing tourist trap. Yeah, I know."

"What would you do if you were free to choose anything, George? What's your wildest dream?"

George swallowed hard. He didn't intend to answer—didn't even know what to say—and yet somehow the words came anyway. And every one of them was true. "I'd get a degree. Not in business—in something to do with plants. Horticulture, maybe. I want to know about different ecosystems and how they can be preserved or restored. I'd get a job where I could use that degree. I'd buy a modest house somewhere near here and make enough money to support us and help out my friends when they needed it. And I'd give you whatever help you needed to be your very best self. We'd be happy together."

"You make me happy."

That was perhaps the very best response Zephyr could have given.

"You're the most loyal person I've ever met," he continued. "It's one of your biggest strengths, and as personality traits go, it's incredibly valuable. But I've recently come to see that even positive traits need to have limits." Zephyr gave a wry little smile. "Self-reliance is great, but maybe sometimes it's a good idea to ask for help."

George gave him a one-armed hug. "Forgive the dumb analogy, but you are a desert plant. Tough. Able to thrive despite formidable conditions. But even desert plants need a little water. They need insects to pollinate them and animals or the wind to spread their seed. And don't snicker over the *spreading your seed* part—I'm being serious." He bumped his shoulder against Zephyr's. "But you know, out of all that hardship, with a little assistance, desert plants can be stunningly gorgeous."

"Yeah. I get that now. But what about you, George?" Zephyr asked it kindly and patiently, in a tone clearly not meant to goad.

"I know how to ask for help."

Zephyr poked him in the side, which George totally deserved since they both knew he'd deliberately misunderstood Zephyr's question. Then George swigged some water as he tried to find words for what was in his heart.

"We don't know much about dinosaur brains," he said at last.

Zephyr, bless him, didn't scoff at the non sequitur. He simply realigned his body a bit, at a better angle to see George's face. And he waited, expression open and attentive.

It gave George the courage to continue. "We find the stuff that gets fossilized. Bones, footprints, eggs, even the impression of their feathers. But all the soft tissue is long gone. We have to guess what colors they were. I'll probably never know what a T. rex would have tasted like to me. And of course, we can't directly study their brains."

"Braaaaiiiins." Zephyr indulged in a zombie impression before gesturing him to continue.

"But we've got plenty of human brains, right? I mean, we all have one. And we even have machines that can sort of watch them work while the owners are using them, which is pretty cool. But there's still so many things we don't understand about them. Even though I think we totally should. Take me, for instance."

"I'll take you," said Zephyr without any irony.

"I'm yours. But my brain…. Nobody knows why I taste colors. Or how most people can get turned on just by looking at someone else— someone in a picture or video, even—but some of us don't feel that way until we get to know another person." He'd thought about this a lot during lockdown, before Zephyr reappeared in his life. He still wasn't sure if the demisexual label fit him perfectly, although he figured it was close enough.

"There's nothing wrong with either of those. Not any more than there's anything wrong with the way I like to dress."

"I know. I'm perfectly satisfied with my own quirks, and I love your fashion sense. Still, it's all a mystery, right? And you know what else is a mystery? How a brain—*my* brain—can know something, yet at the same time, completely pretend to itself that it *doesn't* know."

Feeling a little agitated, George suddenly stood and began pacing the road, sending up little clouds of dust with every footstep. If *those* footsteps became fossilized, some future paleontologist would really wonder what the hell the human had been doing.

Zephyr waited a few moments before a gentle prod. "What's your brain fooling itself over?"

"It isn't, anymore. But it was for… for most of my life. I *saw* my father, Zephyr. I knew how he treated us and Mom. I knew his plans were… pipe dreams. But he was my dad. I did what he wanted because it felt like the right thing to do. And…. Jesus. I never wanted to run that stupid goddamn museum. It's been like a huge boulder on my back, but one I shouldered willingly. And I keep telling myself it doesn't weigh anything at all. But it does. It's so fucking heavy."

George's voice broke, and he stopped pacing, faced away from Zephyr at the edge of the road, and stared out at bitter plants and distant mountains.

Swearing under his breath, Zephyr teetered over and set a hand on George's shoulder. "You can drop that boulder, Georgie. Any time."

"I can't," George rasped.

"Then I'll help you carry it."

Such a simple statement, yet it made George's heart soar.

And it was the strangest thing, but knowing that someone was willing to share his burden somehow made the setting down a real possibility. Even when George had been away at college, he'd never imagined a future aside from the one his father had created for him. The long-impending demise of Fossil Galaxy hadn't done the trick either; George hadn't seen any other possibilities for himself. There was no point in reaching for the stars—his father's failures had taught him that.

It was as if he'd always lived in a sort of reverse mirage. Instead of seeing things that weren't there, he hadn't seen things that were.

But now he stood with Zephyr at his side, gazing out at the landscape, and it didn't seem barren. It was huge. Open. Given the right support, a person could proceed in any direction at all. Could escape the prison he'd built. All George had to do was take that first step.

He cleared his throat and gave Zephyr a wide and genuine smile. "Let's pack up our stuff, and I'll take you to meet Wayne Maas."

CHAPTER THIRTY-FOUR

'TWAS THE night before Christmas.

No, in fact, 'twas the night before Christmas Eve, and George was exhausted. It seemed that everyone in California was on the move, and while many might have gone over the river and through the woods, a fair number had come through the desert instead. And they'd stopped at Fossil Galaxy out of curiosity, maybe after seeing the sign from the bypass. Some just used the bathrooms. Others simply bought a bottle of water or Pepsi. But a steady stream of them shelled out a few bucks to tour the exhibits and, when they were finished, browsed the gift shop. Nearly all of them took photos in front of Zephyr's sculpture.

Judith had brought in candy canes and wrapped pieces of peppermint fudge and peppermint bark, which she distributed on the principle that everyone would at least have good breath. She also kept a slow cooker of mulled cider warm in the office, refilling her mug as well as Kayla's, Zephyr's, and George's. When Zephyr pointed out that Judith didn't celebrate Christmas, she said that she was a firm believer in enjoying everyone's holiday treats.

The bell over the door chimed regularly—evidently lots of angels were getting their wings—while carols wafted from Kayla's portable speaker. Zephyr looked all kinds of adorable in a sparkly silver blouse and a Santa hat he'd acquired from God knew where. It was a festive day, made even more so by George's decision to close early the next day. Yes, he'd miss some visitors, but the afternoon of Christmas Eve was usually very slow, and he wanted to attempt some baking projects with Zephyr. And enjoy some corny Christmas movies and enthusiastic snuggling. That would leave Christmas Day for a holiday feast. Zephyr had suggested maybe eating early and then doing some easy hikes at a state park northwest of Boron. After that, they could return home for leftovers, a nap, and cuddling. An excellent plan, George thought. And maybe a good opportunity to make more plans—plans that would take shape away from Conrad Junction.

But first, he had to get through tonight and tomorrow morning.

After the final visitors left and Judith and Kayla went home, Zephyr swept the floors, tidied the gift shop displays, and cleaned the bathrooms while George locked the door, cleared out the till, and went over the day's receipts. They'd taken in what felt like a lot of money, but George knew it wouldn't last long. Now, though, that prospect didn't worry him.

"There's trash and cardboard to go out," Zephyr said. "Want me to do it?"

"Nah. It can wait until morning."

"Are you afraid I'll discover a pretty man near the dumpster?" Zephyr teased.

"Stray cat is more likely."

"Hmm. Hey, would you consider maybe adopting one? A cat, not a pretty man. I kinda liked Smiley."

George looked up from his calculator with a grin. "Sure. And that reminds me, we should call Al when we're done here tonight. I think he works tomorrow and Christmas."

"Okay." Zephyr set the trash and recycling near the front door, where it would be easy to grab in the morning. "He doesn't get the holiday off, huh?"

"I don't think he minds. He's putting in lots of hours during his school's winter break, and I think they pay extra on Christmas."

Yule celebrations had never been a Harlow family tradition, thanks to their parents' aversion to anything religious. Even now, his sister Mary and her husband generally took a staycation and did home improvement projects. James and his family hung out at a timeshare in Mammoth Lakes, where the kids and James's wife snowboarded while he binge-watched movies with lots of explosions and car chases. Gift-giving had never been much of a thing for any of them, but George and his siblings always called one another on or around Christmas. That was a nice tradition.

Now Zephyr waited patiently for George, as he did at the end of every workday. He could have hung out in their apartment while George finished up, but he never did. It was unbelievably nice to have each other's company while doing the mundane final chores of the evening.

George put the till into the safe. He thought about taking out the photo album that he stored in there but decided against it. Maybe tomorrow night or on Christmas Day, he'd be in the mood to reminisce about family and consider his future, but tonight he'd prefer to focus on the present—and on Zephyr.

"All set," he said as he emerged from the office.

They'd both been snacking on Judith's treats all day, so they opted for a light dinner of tuna salad and nuked frozen veggies. As soon as they were settled on the couch, George turned on the phone volume, which he'd silenced due to the continuing calls and texts from Brandon. Then he called Al on speakerphone.

"How's it going, Alcide?"

"Ugh. Holidays seem to bring out the crazy in everyone. Had a guy come in last night who got mad because his neighbor's Christmas light show was better than his. So our hero runs out to Target, buys more decorations, and then proceeds to install them on his roof. At ten at night, when after a daylong drizzle, the temps had dropped into the upper twenties."

"Uh-oh."

"Yeah. He goes skidding off the roof—spectacularly. I know this because his wife caught it on video and shared it with everyone in the ER. He falls two stories, and probably the only thing that saved him was landing on a large inflatable penguin. He still ended up with a pelvic fracture and a dislocated shoulder. And I understand the penguin did not survive the ordeal. But you want to know the best part? While we're trying to work on him, he keeps yelling at everyone to make sure to document everything carefully for evidence in his lawsuits. He's a lawyer, of course."

Zephyr was snickering loudly, his eyes dancing with humor. "Who's he gonna sue?" he asked.

"Who the hell knows. Target? The neighbor? The inflatable penguin manufacturer? Santa Claus? And by the way, what the fuck's the deal with penguins as Christmas décor? They're from the South Pole, not the North."

"Maybe," George said, "you should offer to help him out with the lawsuits in exchange for a cut."

"No, but the whole time he was in there, I was going over scenarios in my mind, trying to think how he could have a cause of action. Law school has rotted my brain."

"Wasn't that great a brain to begin with," George teased.

"Right back at ya, Pie."

The three of them chatted for another half hour or so. George loved seeing how well Al and Zephyr got along; it was clear each was fond of the other. Not that he'd expected them to hate each other or anything, but he'd never been in a situation where a lover had interacted with his family. Zak had never met any of the other Harlows—George's decision, not Zak's—and the entire concept was a little nerve-racking. What if his brother and his lover hated each other? But they didn't, and that made George feel warm and cozy.

After the call was over, Zephyr smiled at him. "I used to be mad at Al. And James and Mary."

"Why?"

"For abandoning you here."

"They didn't—"

"I know." Zephyr squeezed George's shoulder. "I get that now. But families are a mystery to me. Give me some time to figure them out."

George snorted. "Nobody figures out families, especially their own. And we're all yours now."

At first Zephyr looked surprised at this, and then an expression of wonder spread across his face. "I have family now?"

"Yep. I mean, if you want us. You don't— Oof!" Zephyr had launched himself at George so hard that the couch almost toppled backward. And then George couldn't say anything at all because they were fiercely kissing. Apparently, Zephyr didn't mind that he'd gotten himself tethered to a bunch of eccentrics who carried a big collective load of emotional baggage.

"That is the best gift anyone's ever given me," Zephyr finally said breathlessly. Then he froze—still straddling George—an odd light in his eyes. Zephyr bit his lip and looked away, a slight blush on his cheeks, and George realized he was being shy about something. Which was odd, considering what they'd done together and all the confidences they'd shared.

"What?" George stroked Zephyr's back to encourage him.

"Do you think…. Not now, but maybe someday…. And you can say no…." Zephyr muttered something that sounded like a curse and then straightened his shoulders. "Steiber never meant anything to me— it's just a name on my birth certificate. I never felt like a part of the Steiber family, such as it was, and I didn't want to be. Do you think someday I could be a Harlow?"

George nearly choked on his tongue. But he didn't want Zephyr to mistake his silence for disapproval, so he quickly got control of himself. "Is that a marriage proposal?"

"I… It could be. Yes." Zephyr gave a firm nod.

"Yes."

"I don't have a ring to give you. Wait!" Zephyr launched himself off George and raced to the bedroom, returning a few seconds later. "Ta-da!" He took George's hand and dropped something into the palm.

It was a necklace—the letter Z on a simple chain.

"It's just gold-plated," Zephyr said. "Ten bucks at a drugstore. But it's not that common to find stuff with my initial, so I bought it. Brandon hated it because it was so cheap, so I hid it away in my suitcase and almost forgot about it. Is it too girly for you?"

"It's perfect."

Zephyr clasped it around George's neck, where it felt more solid than its weight implied. It was a comforting sensation.

They kissed some more, and then they spent some time happily discussing potential wedding plans. Something simple, of course. Zephyr suggested the museum, but George rejected that because he didn't know if his siblings would attend—or if they did, whether they'd be uncomfortable in a place that held so many negative associations for all of them. Besides, a new beginning ought to start somewhere not so heavily tied to a troubled past.

"How about outdoors? There's an area of Wayne Mass's property that gets a gorgeous bloom in the spring. I bet he'd let us use it if we promised no government surveillance."

"Perfect. Can I wear a fancy dress even if the wedding is simple?"

"Zeph, you can wear anything you want. You'll be beautiful no matter what."

Zephyr gave a happy little wiggle. "We'll have to feed our guests, I suppose, but something easy. Little sandwiches on Judith's bread?"

With a full heart, George nodded. But then he remembered something. "Judith. I promised to give her some nopales tomorrow."

Zephyr made a shooing motion. "Go collect your cactus bits. I have a party to plan: an engagement celebration for two." He waggled his eyebrows suggestively.

After another irresistible kiss, and after slipping into a hoodie and boots, George left the apartment through the gift shop and out the back door into the courtyard garden. Even though night had fallen, several nearby lights provided enough illumination for his work. All color had washed away, however, depriving him of his usual flavors. How strange it must be for most people, who could only *see* colors! Didn't they feel cheated?

He went to the corner shed and selected thick gloves, a canvas bag, and a sharp blade he kept for this specific purpose. Suitably armed, he headed for the little stand of prickly pears.

He had to work carefully—those spines were dangerous!—but once he'd cut enough pads, he decided to harvest some of the fruit too. He could make it into a syrup for Christmas morning pancakes or send it to Jessica for her jam.

Although he was very much looking forward to that celebration with Zephyr, he lingered. The garden was the one place where he felt close to his mother, and this seemed like a good time to spend a few minutes remembering her. The ghosts of his and his siblings' younger selves seemed to haunt the courtyard too, in a friendly sort of way. He could almost hear the laughter, the shouts when somebody found a lizard, the noisy teasing that inevitably ended in someone being chased. He didn't envy those children, but it was good to recall that they'd all had some happy times in this place.

George took a critical look around, as much as the limited lighting allowed. He hadn't had much time to work on the garden lately, but it was better than what it had been. He wandered over to the orange tree and picked several pieces of fruit to squeeze in the morning. He held one to his nose and inhaled the bright, almost floral fragrance. Soon the trees would begin to bloom, filling the entire garden with their intoxicating scent.

He puttered around a little, admiring the shadows cast by fronds and spikes, listening to the crunch of the pea gravel pathway under his feet. He loved this place, despite everything. And no matter where he went, he'd carry with him the memories of the garden, echoes of the flavors and scents and even the sharp pricks of cactus spines. The garden would always grow inside his heart.

"You're sort of an idiot, George," he mumbled. And then he laughed.

He was tucking the gloves back into the shed when he heard the crash.

The noise startled him so badly that he froze like a frightened animal, unable for a moment to identify what he'd heard. Belatedly, his brain solved the puzzle: that had been the din of shattering glass.

Everything became blurry, like in a terrible dream. He dropped the oranges and ran as fast as he could toward the back door of the gift shop, jumping over plants and small statuary along the way, but he still seemed to be moving with terrible slowness, as if the Earth were exerting ten times its normal gravitational pull.

As soon as he opened the door, he began to choke and cough. The gift shop's front window was broken and the entire front of the room was a wall of flame. Even as he watched, fire bloomed on Zephyr's Joshua tree sculpture, and for a wild moment, George almost ran over to try to rescue it.

But of course, it wasn't the statue that mattered.

Alarms began to blare, deafening him. The overhead sprinkler system kicked in, but he doubted it would do much good against the growing danger. Access from the front of the building was now completely blocked off.

"Zephyr!" he screamed, but he could barely hear himself over the din, and then he was coughing again. Even still, he sped for the apartment. He flung open the door just in time to collide with Zephyr.

"We're trapped!" Zephyr, shirtless, was wide-eyed and breathing hard.

George grabbed his arm. "This way!"

Immediately, however, he saw that the fire had made progress inside the gift shop, climbing the wall opposite the apartment door and moving into the exhibit halls. The power was now out and the smoke so thick that almost nothing was visible except for hazy flames. Drawing a decent breath had become impossible.

George shifted his hold to Zephyr's hand, which gripped his so tightly that it hurt. Muffled crashing noises came over the sound of the alarms and the fire's increasing roar. Orange tongues licked at the ceiling tiles above them, as if tasting their way forward.

For a moment, raw panic froze George in his tracks. *Then you'll both die*, said a voice in his head. It sounded a lot like his father. *Move it! You know where to go.*

And he did. Because this had always been his home, his cocoon, his prison. He knew every inch of it, even when he couldn't see a thing. He tugged at Zephyr's hand, and Zephyr came along trustingly as George hurried them through the few spots in the gift shop that hadn't already ignited.

He didn't remember closing the door to the courtyard garden, but maybe the fire had done that with an air pressure differential. He struggled to get the door open, and then they were out in the courtyard, where there was little light but at least the air was slightly more breathable.

"Everything's burning," Zephyr gasped.

He was right. There were two other doors—leading from the garden into the workshop and the exhibit hall—but flames were already eating through the roof in those spots. And in lots of other spots too. In another minute or two, the entire structure would light up like an enormous bonfire.

With no other options, George towed Zephyr to the fourth side of the courtyard, edged by a tall, sturdy wooden fence. The left and right ends of the fence were beginning to smolder, and if George and Zephyr didn't act now, they'd be completely trapped.

Getting to the fence was difficult with prickly plants blocking the way. If there had been time, George would have given Zephyr his boots and hoodie to provide some protection, but they didn't have those seconds to spare. They were both hacking and wheezing when they reached the fence. George's eyes stung.

"Can't climb," Zephyr rasped.

"I'll boost you."

And George did. It was like one of those urban legends, mothers lifting SUVs to save their trapped children. For a brief moment, George had the strength of a giant. Of a mammoth. Of a *T. rex*. He lifted Zephyr as if he weighed nothing at all, and Zephyr grabbed the top of the fence and scrambled partway over. George was just beginning to wonder how he was going to scale the barrier when Zephyr draped himself over the top and held his arms down for George to grasp. Scrambling desperately, George made it over as well.

They both fell to the ground on the other side in a painful heap.

It was clear that they still weren't safe. For one thing, the smoke here was bad, perhaps because it was trapped between the Fossil Galaxy property and, only a couple of feet away, a concrete wall. Its height would be impossible to scale and its length limited them to a narrow path. In one direction, a locked privacy gate blocked their escape to the road. The other direction should take them to the Fossil Galaxy parking lot.

"Hurry!" George gasped, taking Zephyr's hand.

Gagging and struggling for breath, they stumbled their way out.

They made it almost to the van before they could draw much oxygen again. There was still plenty of smoke, but better air circulation helped. However, their breath was almost stolen again when they caught sight of the expensive sports car parked in the middle of the lot, its driver's side door gaping open.

"Oh shit," Zephyr moaned.

George was about to agree, but then a figure stepped out from behind the van. Rage distorted his face almost beyond recognition, but the gun in his outstretched hand was perfectly clear.

Zephyr shoved his way in front of George. "Don't!" he shouted, his voice raw.

"You came back to him, you little fucker. You wouldn't come back to me, but you came back to *him*. Why?"

"I was confused. Brandon, put the gun down and we can talk about this."

"Talk?" Brandon's screech barely sounded human. "No more talking!"

"We'll go for a ride, then. We'll go to Vegas, get a suite. Order some food. You can talk and I'll listen. I'll be all yours."

It was hard to pay attention to anything with a gun pointed at the man you loved, but George thought he heard distant sirens, although it certainly couldn't be the fire trucks from Boron already. And... cars. Cars were roaring up the street and screeching to a halt near the entrance to the parking lot. People were appearing too, swarming over from Burger King and the truck stop.

Brandon didn't seem to notice any of this. He—and his gun—were focused entirely on Zephyr.

George had no idea what to do. He was afraid to move, in case that prompted Brandon to shoot. He didn't want to speak, in fear of making the volatile man even angrier.

The heat of the fire baked his back, and at least he had the small comfort of knowing that despite being shirtless and barefoot, Zephyr probably wasn't cold. George was shivering, though, out of fear and uncertainty and other primal emotions that even the beasts in Fossil Galaxy would have recognized. Those beasts were gone for good now, along with everything he and Zephyr owned, everything the Harlows had worked for through three generations. So many millennia turned to nothing. Ashes. All because of one sick, selfish man who now threatened to kill George's beloved.

Zephyr stood in front of George with hands raised, calmly trying to reason with a madman. God, George's fiancé, so strong, so beautiful, even while soot-stained and red-eyed.

Suddenly all of George's feelings fell away except for one: rage. It burned him from inside as fiercely as the flames that were destroying his home.

Roaring, George shouldered Zephyr aside. "How dare you?" he bellowed. "How dare you hurt him again?"

"Shut up!"

Brandon waved the gun wildly, Zephyr tried and failed to get in front of George again, and the smoke roiled, making everything hard to see. There might have been sirens, or that could have been the blood shrieking in George's ears.

"You never owned him, asshole. He never loved you. Nobody loves you." George said this with confidence, knowing that unlike Brandon, he was loved and always had been.

Brandon screeched something, not words, just foaming-at-the-mouth gibberish. George had never hated anyone in his life, but now he did, and that made him hate Brandon even more.

George began to walk toward him with slow, steady steps.

"George, don't!" Zephyr grabbed his arm and pulled hard, but George's superhuman strength had reappeared, and he simply shook him off.

Brandon danced around as if he were on fire. "I'll kill you both!"

"A shitty childhood is no excuse to hurt others. I've had enough of you. I've had enough!"

George rushed forward.

Brandon fired the gun, but the shot went wild. Zephyr was screaming. People in the darkness were screaming. Sirens were screaming. Brandon was screaming. George was screaming too.

Another shot—and this time, a flash of heat grazed George's upper arm. It wasn't important. He could keep running, and he did.

Just as the gun was pointed at him again, someone tackled Brandon from behind, sending both of them crashing to the blacktop. The gun skittered away.

But George was still running, and when he reached the figures wrestling on the ground, he clenched his fists and pulled his foot back to kick Brandon's skull. Zephyr pushed George, hard enough to throw him off balance and keep his boot from connecting. Lots of people converged, some joining the melee on the pavement, some simply shouting, and some yelling something about police.

George couldn't make sense of any of it.

He turned his head and saw Zephyr silhouetted against the orange-red flames that tasted like citrus and asparagus. George sobbed just once. Zephyr wrapped him in an embrace and didn't let go.

CHAPTER THIRTY-FIVE

"IT'S JUST a flesh wound," George said, but Zephyr didn't laugh. Maybe he wasn't a Monty Python fan. But it *was* just a flesh wound, the EMT had said so, and after George insistently refused transport to the Victorville hospital an hour away, she sighed, cleaned and disinfected the bullet scrape on his upper arm, and affixed several butterfly bandages. "Don't let it get infected," she ordered.

"I won't."

"It'll probably scar."

"Don't care."

She looked slightly aggrieved but started putting away her supplies.

Zephyr sat hunched next to him on the ambulance cot, a blanket wrapped around his shoulders. Tears had streaked the soot on his face, but now he was dry-eyed. He and George had been given some oxygen to make up for the smoke they'd inhaled, and the EMTs had treated both of them for a few minor burns, but overall, they were relatively unharmed.

Unlike Fossil Galaxy, which still burned, despite the efforts of the fire crew.

"You could have been killed," Zephyr said. "Just a few inches to the side and you would have been killed."

"But I wasn't."

"Jesus, George, what if—"

"Please." George leaned against him, grateful that Zephyr wasn't sitting next to his wounded arm. "I'm exhausted. So are you. It's been… quite a night." An understatement. He'd gotten engaged. Lost his business and his home. Got shot. Screamed at the cops—"You should have acted way fucking sooner!"—as they were dragging Brandon away.

"Fine," said Zephyr. "But I reserve the right to yell at you later."

"Understood. What should we do now?"

"Triage our issues. Tackle them one at a time."

That seemed less overwhelming than trying to figure out… everything. George had nothing except the clothes on his back; Zephyr didn't even have that much. Neither of them had a phone or wallet.

George wasn't sure if the van had escaped the fire, but even if it had, the keys were somewhere in the burning building. "I don't know—"

"Hang on." Zephyr hopped out of the back of the ambulance and disappeared, but not for long. When he returned, he had a determined air. "We're going to Judith and Benny's house where, I'm told, a hot shower and a guestroom await us. She's going to insist on feeding us something, I think. Santiago will drop some clothing by for both of us. The deputies will wait a couple days to get our complete statements. They already have more than enough to make sure Brandon spends Christmas in jail. Tomorrow we'll start dealing with everything else."

"I have insurance."

"Tomorrow." Zephyr waved him forward. "C'mon, Saint George."

ALTHOUGH GEORGE had intended to get an early start, Judith's guest bed was comfortable and apparently his body and brain needed downtime. It was well after nine when he woke up. He dressed in borrowed clothing and found Zephyr already at the kitchen table with their hosts.

"I have to—" he said, but Zephyr held up a hand.

"You have to eat something. That's first. James should be here in about an hour—he's got your insurance claims up and running, so I guess he'll talk to you about that. We've been working on getting you access to your bank account and scoring a replacement driver's license. Things are slow because of the holiday, but you should have a new credit card and debit card by Friday. Santiago brought us enough clothes to get us through until then, although I'm a little shook by the deviation from my normal look." With a wry smile, Zephyr patted his slightly too-large flannel shirt.

Still standing near the table, George gaped stupidly. "James?" he finally managed to ask.

"Your brother? He's the closest sib, and besides he's familiar with all the insurance shit."

"He's... on vacation." George felt dazed.

"And yet still accessible by phone. Modern technology is a wonder. He sounded like a nice guy, by the way. Now sit down and eat."

Benny made one of his omelets—world-famous, he claimed, and it was in fact very good—and Judith gave him toast with Jessica's homemade jam.

"I can't bring you nopales," George said sadly.

She looked concerned. "Are you all right, honey? Are you in shock?"

He didn't think so, although he'd never been in shock so he couldn't know for sure. Mostly, he felt rather lost. He'd assumed that he'd have at least a little time to prepare for his post-Fossil Galaxy world. Obviously, he'd assumed wrong. So he ate his breakfast and assured Zephyr that his arm felt fine, which was the truth. He'd been in worse pain after childhood tussles with Mary.

After he finished eating, he thanked Benny and Judith and looked at Zephyr. "I need to go see."

"You don't want to wait until your brother gets here?"

"No."

At least Zephyr didn't argue.

Judith had laundered George's hoodie and sewed up the bullet gash in one sleeve. George frowned at the Fossil Galaxy logo but put it on; at least it would keep him warm. He was going to offer it to Zephyr, but then Judith appeared with a faux-leopard-fur trench coat, which she held out to Zephyr. "Too much for you?" she asked.

He took it and gave it a few pats before slipping it on. It fit him well. "Oh my God, not too much. It's amazing."

"I wore it exactly once, on New Year's Eve 1999, for an end-of-the-millennium bash. I don't know why I've held on to it all these years. It looks far better on you than it ever did on me. Wear it in good health."

She was right—it suited Zephyr perfectly. He grinned and spent a few moments posing before they started walking the few blocks to the site of the blaze.

It was odd how bright the sky was, as if it hadn't been filled with smoke the night before. Zephyr held George's hand as they walked along the patched blacktop that had carried thousands of vehicles every day until the bypass arrived.

"You lost everything," George said to him.

"Nothing important. I still have the only thing I need." Zephyr raised their joined hands and kissed George's knuckles.

"But—"

"I've lost my belongings before, George. Lots of times. It's just stuff, and everything can be replaced."

Now that George thought about it, this was one of the things he loved about Zephyr. Although he sometimes enjoyed dressing up, he didn't care much about money, and he never complained when things were tight. He'd certainly never made George feel as if he were less desirable than people like Brandon, even though George was nearly broke.

Except he wasn't broke anymore, was he? Thanks to his father's insistence and James's professional connections, Fossil Galaxy was well-insured. When the payout arrived, George and Zephyr would have enough cash to support them for a long time.

They walked past the Burger King, and from the edge of his property, George got his first look at what was left of his home and business. Which was very little. He stopped in his tracks when he saw the ruined shell of the building. Roofless, windowless, many of the walls collapsed. He could see into the garden, where little remained aside from the charred remnants of orange trees. Even the big Fossil Galaxy sign was blackened.

It was hard to breathe, as if the smoke were still present but invisible.

But then he noticed that about a dozen people were moving slowly amid the rubble. As he watched, they lifted and looked under pieces of debris. Sometimes someone would pick something up, carry it to the far edge of the lot, and add it to a growing pile. He recognized the people, his friends and neighbors. Santiago and his wife, Lucas, Lyle Cohen, Kayla and her mother, Doug from the mini-mart, Debra the mail carrier.

"What are they doing?"

"Salvaging, I think." Zephyr spoke quietly, his voice reflecting the same wonder that George felt. "Isn't that your safe over there?"

Zephyr was right, and the safe appeared intact. If so, the cash had survived, along with George's most important paperwork. The family photo album might even be all right. Of course, Zephyr's sculpture had been destroyed, but George had taken lots of photos, which remained safe in the cloud. For that matter, the sculpture lived on in the hundreds of selfies that visitors had taken in the short time it had been on display.

"You're so beloved," Zephyr said very seriously.

"I'm—"

"You *are*. And I know I've given you a hard time about your stubborn loyalty, but look. You have a crisis and they all hop right in to help without hesitation. Even when there's a fuckhead with a gun involved. You deserve their support, and they deserve yours." He shook his head as if he couldn't quite believe it. "I never believed people could really be this way. But now I know better."

George let go of Zephyr's hand, but only to free up his arm. He wrapped it around Zephyr's shoulders and drew him close. Then he took several deep breaths and looked—really *looked*—at the ruins, steeling himself for the grief.

But it didn't arrive.

In fact, although he felt a tinge of sadness, the main emotion washing through him right now was… relief. When the fire had burned Fossil Galaxy, it had also destroyed the heavy boulder George had carried on his shoulders.

"I'm free." Of debts, of unwanted obligations, of the specter of his father's disapproval, of constant worry. Free of the chains that had bound him, up to this point, to the bitter-flavored desert. And though he was free of all those things, he still possessed everything that was truly important: his friends, his family, his lover.

"I'm the luckiest person on earth," George said, squeezing Zephyr tightly.

"That's funny, because I was just thinking the same thing."

Later today, they could start talking seriously about wedding plans. But now a car honked softly and rolled to a stop a few yards away. Smiling broadly, George took his fiancé over to meet his oldest brother.

Epilogue

Salem, Oregon
October 2022

"It's raining. Again."

Zephyr rolled his eyes and tried, for the second time, to tug his husband out of the kitchen chair. "It's misting. And you won't melt. You have boots and that nice blue rain jacket that brings out the color of your eyes. Come on. Let's go."

But apparently George wasn't going to be swayed by flattery. "We have studying to do."

"It'll wait. If we don't take a break, all the brainpower's going to overwhelm the house and cause an explosion. Or at least scare the cat."

Three students under one roof was… a little overwhelming at times. Al muttered about exceptions to the hearsay rule; George complained that his long-ago math credits from California—why did an ecology major need so much math?—hadn't transferred to Oregon State; and Zephyr sighed over the first of many community college classes he'd need to pass in order to transfer to a BFA program. Getting his GED in the spring had been easy, but learning how to be a good student was proving to be a lot harder.

George remained stubbornly hunched over his laptop. "I need to do well in these classes. I mean, I think I'm doing okay now, but if I start slacking…."

"Saint George doesn't slack. And even if he does, so what? We're going to turn out fine, no matter what."

"But—"

"Georgie."

Maybe it was Zephyr's firm tone, but George finally looked up at him and appeared abashed. "Sorry. Still getting used to not being the sole captain of my ship."

"And you've concluded that now you need to switch from desert and dino metaphors to nautical ones."

As Zephyr had hoped, that brought a smile. "It's all the rain."

"If it's really bugging you that much, we don't have to live here. I'll move anywhere you want."

"You would, wouldn't you?" George smiled but then sighed. "I'm actually fine with the climate, although I hope we can return to the desert when we're done with school."

Zephyr knew that George missed his friends in Conrad Junction, as well as the stark mountains and stubborn spiny plants. His academic advisor had recently told him that one of her former students worked in the resource stewardship division of the Mojave National Preserve. George would have to get some field experience and maybe even a master's degree to be eligible for a position like that, but it was his dream job. And Zephyr had been cheerleading him along ever since George mentioned it.

"I think a temporary change of scenery is really good for me," George said. "I'm just feeling a little stressed, that's all. I'll talk to my therapist about it next week. She was saying something last time about teaching me some calming techniques."

Zephyr leaned down and kissed the top of George's head. "She's good, isn't she?" Al had recommended her, and now both George and Zephyr had sessions, often separately but sometimes together. She was helping Zephyr work through a lot of trauma. He still had quite a ways to go, but as she liked to point out, he'd been accumulating emotional baggage for a quarter of a century. Dumping it all at once was unrealistic.

She had been helping George too, as demonstrated now when he clicked the laptop shut and stood up from the table. "Where are we going?"

"Surprise. Boots and jacket. Mmm, maybe a sweater too. It's chilly out."

George loped upstairs while Zephyr zipped into his new boots. They were the color of grape jelly, but George said they tasted like french toast. And interestingly, they were marketed as unisex, which pleased Zephyr. It was nice to see even a small acknowledgment that people of all genders should be free to choose whatever color and style of clothing they wanted.

Boots on, Zephyr took a hair tie from his pocket and formed a ponytail. He was glad he'd grown out his hair again, but sometimes it got in the way. It also tended to get frizzy in the dampness, and Zephyr was too vain to walk around looking like a skinny Sasquatch. Hell, maybe he should just avoid the issue altogether. He took a knitted beanie off a hook near the door and pulled it on. It was George's favorite shade of yellow.

Which was partly why George grinned when he came downstairs and caught sight of Zephyr, then rushed over to pull him into a kiss. "You could distract me indoors too, you know. Exercise could be involved."

"Nope. It's the great outdoors for us."

Zephyr got behind the steering wheel of his little Honda. They'd bought it used, and even though it was a boring silver, it was the first car he'd ever owned, and he loved it. Thanks to the lawyer he and George had hired before they got married, Zephyr even had all his personal paperwork in order, including a completely valid license. Small accomplishments, maybe, but they made him feel normal in a comforting way, as if he'd finally left the fringes and entered regular society.

As soon as George had buckled in beside him, Zephyr pulled out of the driveway, pausing for a moment as he always did to smile at the house that had become their home. It was a cheery-looking little place. He and George had spent a lot of time discussing where to go after the fire. The insurance money meant they could choose anywhere reasonable, but in the end, they'd accepted Al's invitation to move in with him. It made sense on so many levels. There was a manageable commute to Oregon State for George and a nearby community college for Zephyr. The location was different enough from the Mojave that George enjoyed the adventure, but not so different that he felt uncomfortable. He and Zephyr had insisted on paying all the household bills, which meant that Al was able to quit his job and devote more time to law school.

Also, there was Smiley, who loved Zephyr the best.

Someday they would return to the desert. George missed it and his friends in the Junction. But there was no hurry.

George and Zephyr hummed along with the radio during the drive, George sometimes giving Zephyr's leg a friendly little squeeze as a reminder of his affection. Zephyr could have happily driven all day like that, but they had a destination, which they reached in about half an hour.

George seemed intrigued when Zephyr pulled into the lot. "State park?"

"Don't worry—we're not doing anything hard-core. Just a little walk and some fresh air. Then I thought we could head back to town, clean up a bit, and have dinner out."

"That's a nice plan."

"It's a celebration, actually. Come with and I'll tell you about it."

There were no other people in sight, partly because it was a weekday afternoon and partly because, well, it was wet. Not pouring by any means, but Zephyr was thankful for their waterproof gear. Besides, his jacket had a zebra print that he loved.

The trailhead was just a few steps away, and soon they were walking along the tightly packed earth and gravel. As in the middle of the desert, no sounds of machinery intruded and it was easy to imagine they were the only people on the planet. Massive trees towered on either side, while the ground was covered by a dizzying array of bushes, ferns, and other small plants, none of which Zephyr could identify. Maybe George could, although he was having to learn about a climate very new to him. During the spring, he'd enthusiastically taken over the gardening projects at their house. No orange trees, but they did have blueberries, blackberries, and apples.

"It's beautiful," said George. A droplet of water fell on his nose from an overhead branch, making him scrunch up his face adorably.

"Recommended by Al. He's got good taste."

George squeezed Zephyr's hand. "Runs in the family."

"There are a bunch of waterfalls here, but we'll save them for another time. Today I have something to tell you."

"You could tell me right here."

Zephyr gave him a pointed look, and then they walked along silently, simply enjoying each other's company and stretching their legs amid beautiful scenery.

About half a mile in, the trail gently ascended and then curved, creating an overlook for the river fifteen or twenty feet below. No waterfalls in sight, although Zephyr thought he heard one. In any case, it was a scenic place to stop.

"What you're going to say isn't anything awful, is it?" asked George, possibly only half joking. He still had a hard time accepting that doom wasn't waiting around every corner. Hell, so did Zephyr.

It was weird. The fire had been such a huge fucking disaster, complete with George getting shot, but in the end, everything had turned out remarkably well. George hadn't been seriously injured, and although he lost his family business and home, he'd actually been relieved. He kept saying the same thing to Zephyr: *You. My family. My friends. I still have everything that's important to me.* And George had finally taken steps toward pursuing his dreams, while at the same time helping Zephyr do the same.

For a few months, both of them had been haunted by the specter of Brandon's potential return. After all, he was wealthy, and the justice system never seemed to land heavily on rich guys. And sure enough, Brandon had made bail.

And then, just a few days after being released from jail, he'd driven his Ferrari into a palm tree near Beverly Hills. The tree had survived the collision, but Brandon had not. The coroner said his blood alcohol level was well over the legal limit, and he'd ingested a small pharmacy's worth of drugs. Nothing too surprising there.

Zephyr hadn't rejoiced over Brandon's death. Mostly he'd just been relieved that Brandon hadn't killed anyone else in the process—and that the specter was now gone from Zephyr and George's life. When George had heard the news, he simply sighed, gave a cryptic smile, and informed Zephyr that California fan palms are native to the deserts of the west.

And nowadays, somehow all of the news they shared with each other was pretty damn good.

"No, this is not an awful thing," Zephyr said. "James found out about it yesterday and texted me. He thought I'd like to tell you in person."

"Tell me what?"

"You know how you asked James to deal with the things that survived the fire?"

George made a face. "Yeah."

A surprising number of items had remained more or less intact, including a lot of the mineral collections and quite a few fossils. George and Zephyr had been busy handling a lot of other details related to Brandon and the disaster he'd created, so George's siblings had offered to take care of the artifacts and specimens. George had accepted immediately and hadn't mentioned the stuff since.

Zephyr patted George's arm. "Everything that could be saved was donated to a natural history museum in Lancaster."

"Really?" George looked pleased. "I visited that place a few times when I was a kid. They had good exhibits. Way fancier than Fossil Galaxy."

"Let me show you the letter they sent James." Zephyr had it ready on his phone, which he handed to George.

"Dear Mr. Harlow," George read aloud, "we are delighted to inform you that thanks in part to recent fundraising efforts, arrangements have been finalized for the display of the wonderful items you so generously donated to us. In anticipation of this exhibit, we'd like to request a brief narrative history of your family and Fossil Galaxy. The new exhibit will debut in early March of next year. The exact date has yet to be determined, but we sincerely hope you and your family will be able to join us for a small grand opening ceremony for the Wally and Rick Harlow Collection."

George returned the phone to Zephyr. He might have been sniffling due to the damp, but Zephyr doubted that was the real cause.

"That's… that's amazing," George said.

"Are you okay with it?"

"Okay? I'm…. God. It feels good. Feels right." George took a deep breath and let it out with a smile. "When we move back to the desert, we can visit now and then. It's perfect."

"Your sibs think you're the ideal person to write up something for the museum. Maybe you can even send them scans of a couple of photos from your album."

Looking a little wobbly-chinned, George nodded. They hugged and kissed, and then they simply held each other while water dripped and rushed and whispered all around them. The hope and peace that had taken root in Zephyr's heart as he got to know George had grown a little every day, and now they suffused his entire body, feeling warm and solid and beautiful.

Eventually they separated a bit, but they remained standing, taking in the scenery. Even in the watery light, the deciduous plants shone in scarlets, golds, and creams, while mosses and firs, hemlocks, and cedars provided notes of deep green. Zephyr wished he could taste them all like George did.

"What are the flavors?" he asked.

George grinned. "Complex. Birthday cake. Ranch dressing. Bacon. Earl Gray tea. Olive oil."

"That's quite a feast. What about the greens? Are they bitter?"

"No. Forest green is a delicious oatmeal raisin cookie." George laughed and then hugged Zephyr again, as if the very fact of good-flavored plant life was worth celebrating. And maybe it was. So much of their shared life was worth celebrating that Zephyr had to laugh as well.

"I love you," he whispered into George's ear. "So much."

"I love you too, Zephyr Harlow."

Even the name made Zephyr's soul sing.

But now the rain was coming harder, and curling up naked in bed with George seemed like a much better idea than getting waterlogged in a park. "Ready to go?"

George took his hand and kissed it. "I'll go anywhere as long as you're there. Blow where thou wishest, gentle Zephyr."

Laughing, they hurried together to the car and pointed it toward home.

Keep reading for an excerpt from
Love Can't Conquer
by Kim Fielding

PROLOGUE

JEREMY COX first heard the news about Keith Moore at the Sav-Rite.

Mama had sent Jeremy to fetch some milk and cigarettes, and he took his time along the way, scuffing his tennis shoes over the dusty asphalt and listening to the cicadas shrill. He had his T-shirt balled in his hand, the heat baked him like a biscuit, and the sun turned his hair a shade paler as it birthed another freckle or two on his bare shoulders.

When he was halfway to the store, a car inched up behind him. He stepped onto the dry grass of the shoulder, but the car kept pace until he looked up.

"Hey, Germy!" called a familiar voice from the driver's seat of the beat-up Buick. It was Troy Baker with his usual crew, and Jeremy anticipated the taunts that followed: "Germy Cox, ugly as rocks. Cox-sucker. Pansyass. Faggot!" The last one was accompanied by a tossed can that bounced off Jeremy's shoulder and dribbled its final drops of warm beer onto his arm. Finally Troy sped away, trailing mocking shouts and leaving Jeremy with lungs full of exhaust.

Jeremy had hoped the torture would end when Troy and his friends graduated in May. But they'd all stuck around Bailey Springs, Kansas—Troy working at the gas station and the rest staying on their family farms—and they hadn't yet lost interest in tormenting Jeremy. He realized that the only way out would be graduation and escaping town. *Three more years. Just three more years.* It sounded like forever.

Inside the Sav-Rite, he didn't pay much attention to the little cluster of adults at the checkout. He walked back to the coolers, where he snagged a carton of milk and a glass bottle of Coke, which he'd drink on the way home. But when he went to ask for Mama's Virginia Slims, he overheard the store manager.

"...as if the Moores need any more heartache in their life," Mr. Stoltz was saying.

Mrs. Peasley nodded. "The Lord knows those poor folks have been through so much already." Her purchases lay on the counter in front of her, not yet rung up. Looked as if she was getting ready to make coffee cake for the Wednesday card game at her house. Jeremy's grandmother went every week and always came home complaining that Mildred Peasley couldn't bake worth a darn.

"Are you sure he meant to kill himself?" asked Betty Ostermeyer, reaching for the bag of flour. She'd graduated from Bailey Springs High just a couple of years before. Her husband had run off and left her while she was still pregnant with their little girl, so now Betty kept the toddler home with her mother during the day while she rang up groceries at the Sav-Rite. "Maybe he just wanted to go for a swim. It's been hot."

Mrs. Peasley clucked her tongue. "Not even the Moore boy would be foolish enough to jump from the Memorial Bridge just for a swim. It's too high, too dangerous."

Jeremy's heart was beating so fast he was certain they must hear it, but none of them even glanced his way. The carton and bottle felt heavy in his grip.

"That boy's a delinquent, but he's not stupid," Mr. Stoltz said. "He'd know better than that."

Mrs. Peasley nodded and leaned forward, as if intending to share a secret. But she didn't lower her voice. "And anyway, *I* heard he tied a rope around his neck before he jumped! But the rope broke."

Jeremy must have asked for the cigarettes and paid, although he didn't remember doing so. He was dizzy, his stomach roiling like it had at the county fair when he rode the Fire Ball after eating three corn dogs and a cotton candy. Somewhere between the Sav-Rite and home, Jeremy upchucked into a clump of scraggly weeds. The bile stung his throat, and the hot sun burned the back of his neck.

Eventually he stood, wiped his mouth on his forearm, and continued to his house. He didn't notice the little bungalows as he passed, each with sunflowers and hollyhocks nodding in the yard, some with Big Wheels or chalked hopscotch squares on the walkways.

What he saw was Keith Moore, clothes too baggy on his tall, lean body, dark hair hanging in his face, legs constantly jiggling as he sat. Keith was two grades ahead of him, but they'd shared math and biology classes because Keith had flunked them the previous year and Jeremy had been allowed to skip ahead. Few of their classmates spoke to either of them—Jeremy because he was a freshman and Pansyass Germy Cox, Keith because he was scary. But sometimes Keith would look at Jeremy, and while he never quite smiled, one corner of his mouth would lift a little. If Jeremy blushed, which he usually did, Keith's hazel eyes would sparkle for a moment. He made Jeremy feel funny in a way that both exhilarated and terrified him.

Only now Keith had jumped off the Memorial Bridge.

The rest of the story came to Jeremy in bits and pieces during the following days. His father mentioned it over dinner before Mama glanced significantly at Jeremy and changed the subject. A couple of junior high kids whispered about it loudly in the public library. Jeremy's best friend, Lisa, called to tell him what she'd heard from her older sister. Some of the details were contradictory.

By the time school started two weeks later, Jeremy had the truth, or at least as close as he was going to get. Keith Moore had slipped out of his parents' rambling Victorian one night and walked the mile and a half to the river. He'd crossed to the middle of the bridge, climbed over the concrete railing, and leaped into the dark water far below. He hadn't used a rope; police found one nearby, but it likely had nothing to do with him. Just after dawn, a fisherman had discovered Keith far downstream, caught on a sandbar. Broken and unconscious, but alive.

Nobody in Bailey Springs saw Keith Moore again. Some said he ran away after being released from the hospital, while others insisted that he'd eventually died of his injuries. The most persistent rumor was that he'd been locked up in a loony bin somewhere out of state. Dr. Moore continued to treat his patients, and Mrs. Moore continued to reign over the garden club, the women's club, and the PTA. Neither of them spoke about their son.

Over the next three years, Jeremy thought about him now and then. He wondered if Keith would still be the taller one now that Jeremy had finally had his growth spurt. He remembered the crooked hint of a grin and the way it made Keith look beautiful instead of menacing. And when several make-out sessions—first with Jenny Novak and later with Pam Archer—failed to inspire him, Jeremy grudgingly admitted to himself why Keith's scrutiny had made him blush.

And finally Jeremy was free. He got a scholarship to a small private college in Oregon. Learned to love misty gray skies, the scent of Douglas firs, the sight of a snow-covered mountain on a clear day. He hardly ever thought about Kansas. And almost never remembered a boy named Keith Moore.

KIM FIELDING is pleased every time someone calls her eclectic. Her books span a variety of genres, but all include authentic voices and unconventional heroes. Winner of the 2021 BookLife Prize for Fiction, she is also a Rainbow Award and SARA Emma Merritt winner, a LAMBDA finalist, and a three-time Foreword INDIE finalist. She has migrated back and forth across the western two-thirds of the United States and currently lives in California, where she long ago ran out of bookshelf space. A university professor who dreams of being able to travel and write full-time, she also dreams of having two daughters who occasionally get off their phones, a husband who isn't obsessed with football, and a cat who doesn't wake her up at 4:00 a.m. Some dreams are more easily obtained than others.

Blogs: kfieldingwrites.com and
www.goodreads.com/author/show/4105707.Kim_Fielding/blog
Facebook: www.facebook.com/KFieldingWrites
Email: kim@kfieldingwrites.com
Twitter: @KFieldingWrites

Follow me on BookBub

LOVE CAN'T CONQUER

A LOVE CAN'T NOVEL

KIM FIELDING

A Love Can't Novel

Bullied as a child in small-town Kansas, Jeremy Cox ultimately escaped to Portland, Oregon. Now in his forties, he's an urban park ranger who does his best to rescue runaways and other street people. His ex-boyfriend, Donny—lost to drinking and drugs six years earlier—appears on his doorstep and inadvertently drags Jeremy into danger. As if dealing with Donny's issues doesn't cause enough turmoil, Jeremy meets a fascinating but enigmatic man who carries more than his fair share of problems.

Qayin Hill has almost nothing but skeletons in his closet and demons in his head. A former addict who struggles with anxiety and depression, Qay doesn't know which of his secrets to reveal to Jeremy—or how to react when Jeremy wants to save him from himself.

Despite the pasts that continue to haunt them, Jeremy and Qay find passion, friendship, and a tentative hope for the future. Now they need to decide whether love is truly a powerful thing or if, despite the old adage, love can't conquer all.

www.dreamspinnerpress.com

LOVE
IS
HEARTLESS

A LOVE CAN'T NOVEL

KIM FIELDING

A Love Can't Novel

Small but mighty—that could be Detective Nevin Ng's motto. Now a dedicated member of the Portland Police Bureau, he didn't let a tough start in life stop him from protecting those in need. He doesn't take crap from anyone, and he doesn't do relationships. Until he responds to the severe beating of a senior citizen and meets the victim's wealthy, bow-tied landlord.

Property manager and developer Colin Westwood grew up with all the things Nevin never had, like plenty of money and a supportive, loving family. Too supportive, perhaps, since his childhood illness has left his parents unwilling to admit he's a strong, grown man. Colin does do relationships, but they never work out. Now he's thinking maybe he won't just go with the flow. Maybe it's time to try something more exciting. But being a witness to a terrible crime—or two—was more than he bargained for.

Despite their differences, Colin and Nevin discover that the sparks fly when they're together. But sparks are short-lived, dampened by the advent of brutal crimes, and Colin and Nevin have seemingly little in common. The question is whether they have the heart to build something lasting.

www.dreamspinnerpress.com

LOVE
HAS NO
DIRECTION

A LOVE CAN'T NOVEL

KIM FIELDING

A Love Can't Novel

Yet another series of poor decisions lands Parker Levin back in his mother's house, working at her coffee shop, and feeling like a failure. Then he learns his ex-boyfriend has died by suicide and things go from bad to worse. When he meets a handsome stranger, he doesn't have much left to lose.

Ten years ago Westley Anker made a grave mistake. Since then he's lived in near isolation, supporting himself by making custom furniture and only rarely connecting with other people. When he attempts to make amends, he encounters Parker, a beautiful and colorful young man, and he agrees to Parker's impulsive request to join him.

Together, Parker and Wes find quick friendship and fierce attraction. But Wes's past demons haunt his footsteps, and Parker's struggle to plan a future has him stumbling through life. Then they uncover evidence that suggests Parker's ex's death might not have been a straightforward suicide, and every path seems to lead to dead ends and destruction. Can Parker and Wes find their way to lasting love when the route is hidden?

www.dreamspinnerpress.com

KIM
FIELDING

POTENTIAL ENERGY

Sometimes a hero is
just a scoundrel with his
back against the wall.

When interstellar smuggler Haz Taylor loses his ship, his money, and his tattered reputation, drinking himself to death on a backwater planet seems like his only option. Then the Coalition offers him a contract to return a stolen religious artifact. Sounds simple enough, but politics can be deadly—and the artifact's not enthusiastic about being returned.

Haz didn't sign up to be prisoner transport, but he's caught between a blaster and hard vacuum. Still, that doesn't mean he can't show his captive some kindness. It costs him nothing to give Mot the freedom to move about the ship, to eat when he's hungry… to believe that he's a person. It's only until they reach Mot's planet. Besides, the Coalition would hate it, which is reason enough.

Then he finds out what awaits Mot at home, and suddenly hard vacuum doesn't look so bad. Haz is no hero, but he can't consign Mot to his fate. Somewhere under the space grime, Haz has a sliver of principle. It's probably going to get him killed, but he doesn't have much to live for anyway….

www.dreamspinnerpress.com

KIM FIELDING

BLYD
AND PEARCE

Born into poverty and orphaned young, Daveth Blyd had one chance for success when his fighting prowess earned him a place in the Tangye city guard—a place he lost to false accusations of theft. Now he scrapes out a living searching for wayward spouses and missing children. When a nobleman offers him a small fortune to find an entertainer who's stolen a ring, Daveth takes the case.

While Jory Pearce may or may not be a thief, he certainly can't be trusted. But, enchanted by Jory's beauty and haunting voice, Daveth soon finds himself caught in the middle of a conspiracy. As he searches desperately for answers, he realizes that he's also falling for Jory. The two men face river wraiths, assassins, a necromancer, and a talking head that could be Daveth's salvation on their quest for the truth. But with everyone's integrity in question and Death eager to dance, Daveth will need more than sorcery to survive.

www.dreamspinnerpress.com